Praise for John Ramsey Miller's

Inside Out

"INSIDE OUT is a great read! John Ramsey Miller's tale of big-city mobsters, brilliant killers and a compellingly real U.S. marshal has as many twists and turns as a running serpentine through a field of fire and keeps us turning pages as fast as a Blackhawk helicopter's rotors! Set aside an uninterrupted day for this one; you won't want to put it down."
—Jeffrey Deaver, author of *The Vanished Man*

"John Ramsey Miller's INSIDE OUT needs to come with a warning label. To start the story is to put the rest of your life on hold as you obsessively turn one page after the other. With a story this taut, and characters this vivid, there's no putting the book down before you've consumed the final word. A thrilling read."
—John Gilstrap, author of *Scott Free*

"Full of complications and surprises. . . . Miller gifts his characters with an illuminating idiosyncrasy. This gives us great hope for future books as well as delight in this one."
—*The Drood Review of Mystery*

"Twists and turns on every page keep you in phenomenal suspense until the last page. A superb novel."
—*Rendezvous*

And for John Ramsey Miller's debut thriller

The Last Family

"A relentless thriller."
—*People*

"Fast-paced, original, and utterly terrifying—
true, teeth-grinding tension. I lost sleep reading
the novel, and then lost even more sleep thinking
about it. Martin Fletcher is the most vividly drawn,
most resourceful, most horrifying killer I have
encountered. Hannibal Lecter, eat your heart out."
—Michael Palmer, author of *Silent Treatment*

"The best suspense novel I've read in years!"
—Jack Olsen

"Martin Fletcher is one of the most unspeakably evil
characters in recent fiction . . . A compelling read."
—*Booklist*

"The author writes with a tough authority and
knows how to generate suspense."
—*Kirkus Reviews*

"Suspenseful . . . Keeps the reader guessing
with unexpected twists."
—*Publishers Weekly*

Also by John Ramsey Miller

The Last Family

inside out

John Ramsey Miller

A Dell Book

INSIDE OUT

A Dell Book /June 2005

Published by
Bantam Dell
A Division of Random House, Inc.
New York, New York

ISBN 0-553-58337-9

Manufactured in the United States of America
Published simultaneously in Canada

OPM   10 9 8 7 6 5 4 3 2 1

Dedicated to the memory of

Beverly Lewis

Acknowledgments

For Susan Dedmon Miller, my wife, my best friend and inspiration for the past twenty-six years. To my sons: Christian McCarty, Rush Lane, and Adam Ramsey Miller, and my daughter, Natasha. Also to my Father, Rev. R. Glenn Miller, and my second mother, Joann, for their love and steadfast belief.

This book would have remained desk ballast without the efforts of my agent, Anne "Anniehawk" Hawkins, of John Hawkins & Associates, NYC. There is no better.

Thanks to my remarkable editor at Bantam Dell, Kate Burke Miciak. I have been so lucky in my writing life to have only worked with the best. KBM made me understand both what this book needed to be and how to build a better one next time.

Heartfelt thanks to Irwyn Applebaum and Nita Taublib. They know why.

Everyone at Bantam Dell who has touched *Inside Out* has added something of themselves, and they should know that I value the efforts of each and every one of them.

I hope this book reflects the enormous respect I have for the ability and professionalism of the men and women of the United States Marshals Service. The Federal Bureau of Investigation and the Central Intelligence Agency are often plumbed for villains. I did it in this book, but we should never lose sight of the fine, brave, and dedicated individuals who make up those organizations, all of them dedicated to our continued well being. They, and our armed forces, are all that stand between the devil and the deep blue sea.

The inspiration for Winter Massey came from knowing United States Chief Deputy Marshal David Crews of Oxford, Mississippi, who is now a member of an anti-terrorism task force. Any parallels between Winter's and David's lives are the sincerest flattery I can pay a friend who is a truly amazing professional. Also thanks to my shore patrol pal, Regional Security Director Commander for Navy Region Hawaii, Lieutenant Eugene "Dusty" Rhodes Jr. Any technical inaccuracies were either necessary for the story or because I wasn't paying close enough attention.

I want to thank my readers, Rush Glenn Miller Jr., Judy Dedmon Coyle, Faith Ann Lyon, Mike and Ellen Nash, and Lesley Krause.

My "blood" brothers, Jay McSorley and Kerry Hamilton. My dear friend and confidant, fellow thriller author John Gilstrap. His steadfast friendship over the years has been a special gift indeed.

My close friends, Faith and Kip Lyon; Bill, Ann, Will, and Leslie Cannon; Robert D. and Kelia Raiford. God bless the Wing Nighters who gather weekly to festivate.

Finally, a heartfelt thanks to all of the warm, remarkable people of Concord, North Carolina, who, for the past eight years, have somehow suffered this fool. If there is a better place on earth to live, I have yet to find it.

1

New Orleans, Louisiana

A blanket of angry black clouds passed over the Crescent City, blotting out the moon and suffusing the air with the scent of rain. A paddle-wheeler glided upriver, making for its dock on the edge of the French Quarter. The voices of the revelers on the deck fought a pitched battle with the optimistic strains of the Dixieland band. After the boat passed by, its wash slapped at the pilings under the pier and the warehouse.

A dark Mercedes sedan was parked in the doorway of the warehouse, its trunk open. Dylan Devlin looked up and down the pier, then finished loading the cargo, closed the trunk gently, and removed his gloves.

People usually visited New Orleans because of the fine dining, for the atmosphere of revelry—to stroll up and down Bourbon Street clutching a plastic cup of beer. Tourists flocked to the city to enjoy the architecture, the history, the casinos. But Devlin had no interest in any of that. To him, New Orleans was just another piece of geography to be learned, streets to be navigated, and problems to be solved or avoided. Dylan was a lucky man who had discovered his true passion: He was paid to do something he would have done for free.

A red-haired man of thirty-six with a youthful face, he had light-green eyes, and his smile was as disarming as a baby's. Since he was a child, women had wanted to coddle him and, as he matured, to offer their bodies and hearts, although only the former held any interest for him.

He opened the car door, climbed in, and drove out of the lot, leaving the loading-dock door wide open—like an unblinking yellow eye staring out over the Mississippi River.

The wall of rain moved down the river and closed like a curtain over the departing riverboat. Dylan pressed a button and the window purred up just as the downpour slammed into the pier.

The two boys were seventeen years old. They were in a white Lexus 400, which belonged to the driver's mother, a divorced real-estate attorney.

The teenagers had consumed two six-packs of Heineken and had managed to smoke most of a half an ounce of marijuana in the hours since sundown. It was raining hard and the wipers kept a beat along with the music. The Lexus was doing sixty-six miles an hour as the car approached the intersection of St. Charles and Napoleon Avenues. The driver saw the light change to red, but its meaning didn't penetrate the fog in his brain until it was too late to apply the brakes. A black Mercedes seemed to materialize before him, as if from nowhere.

Far out.

The Lexus sent Dylan Devlin's Mercedes skidding seventy feet into the oncoming lane. It rolled over and disgorged the trunk's contents into the middle of St. Charles Avenue—a spare tire and two limp bodies. The bloody sacks on the corpses' heads and their contorted limbs made them look like a pair of discarded scarecrows.

Devlin shoved aside the physician's case on the passenger seat, which held his tools—the .22 automatic and silencer, the handcuffs. More than enough evidence to send him to death row. He slid from the stolen Mercedes through the shattered side window, dragging himself toward the curb like an injured dog. He gazed across the rain-slick asphalt at the corpses and marveled at how ridiculous they looked. He remembered shooting them, loading the two heavy bodies into the trunk.

Cars were braking and people were running into the street, shouting. When he saw the blue lights converging, he smiled because he knew it was over. He knew, too, that it was only just beginning.

2

Two days after the newspapers and TV news teams in New Orleans first reported that a man had been arrested with the bodies of two warehouse workers he had murdered gangland-style, Florence Pruette started her day without once thinking about it. She'd seen the pictures of the bodies lying in the middle of St. Charles Avenue, but she hadn't paid much attention to the fact that the two dead men had worked for one of her employer's competitors.

At precisely 6:45 that morning, Florence got out of a taxicab in front of Parker Amusement & Vending Company on Magazine Street to open the offices for business. At five that afternoon, the seventy-year-old woman would turn on the answering machine, lock up the office, and go home to her one-bedroom apartment on the eighth floor of the Versailles apartment building. Florence had kept the same routine every weekday all her adult life. The exceptions to the rule were Christmas day, Thanksgiving day, and Fat Tuesday. In 1971, the office had closed for Dominick Manelli's funeral. Manelli had founded and run the company for thirty-nine years before he retired.

There had been four mornings in the fifty-two years when Florence had been too ill to come in, but otherwise she was as punctual as the sunrise. Florence had worked at Parker Amusement first as a receptionist, then secretary, office manager, and finally as private secretary to Dominick. After his death, his son, Sam, kept her on. In all her years with the company, she had never asked either of her employers a non-business-related question. She was paid generously, lived comfortably in an apartment she owned outright, and had good medical insurance. She could eat at any of Sam's restaurants for free as often as she chose. Because she tipped generously, Florence was fussed over by the restaurant staff. The taxi that chauffeured her to and from work was an additional perk. Best of all, Sam had promised her a paycheck for as long as she lived, and, although he had offered to let her retire whenever she wanted, the company was her life.

The offices had not been renovated since the company moved into the building on Magazine Street in 1967. The walls were stained brown from decades of cigarette and cigar smoke issued from employees who, like the non-smoking employees, answered to Florence.

The office workers kept the books, taking orders for vending and gaming machines. The warehouse workers delivered the machines. Collectors picked up the coins and bills and stocked the machines with candy, soft drinks, cigarettes, CDs, and condoms. One warehouse stored the machines and was the site where necessary maintenance was performed, while another held the stock and was a subsidiary—MarThon Distributing Company. All of Manelli's businesses were separate entities, grouped under the master banner of SAMCO Holding Company. SAMCO owned bars, gas stations, adult bookstores, a travel agency, a tobacco shop, a French Quarter art gallery, an antique shop, a tour company, a limousine firm, parking lots, and more. Its entire holdings were worth over 60 million dollars, every dollar of which was squeaky clean. Every morning at seven-thirty Sam Manelli showed up at his Parker office to preside over his kingdom. It was unnecessary because people seldom stole anything from Sam Manelli. The downside of stealing his money was too frightening to contemplate. Sam was the most feared man in Louisiana for good reason. He was a Mafia don, a monster whose sadism was the whole cloth from which nightmares were cut.

Florence was aware of Sam's reputation as a gangster, but she had never seen any evidence of it. She had heard that his illegal companies generated four times what SAMCO Holding was worth in cash, every year. A million dollars a day was the figure she had read in the *Times-Picayune*. It was said that Sam owned everyone he needed to maintain both of his empires. Books had been written about him, documentaries filmed, movies were based on his legend. He was famed as the last of the big-time mobsters, a tyrannosaur that had somehow survived the evolutionary process. Everybody knew what he did, but Sam had never once been convicted of a felony.

Florence came in that morning, like every other, but on that Tuesday something was different. It was so different, it almost gave her a stroke. Minutes after Sam arrived, four FBI agents strolled into the office. They flashed badges, passed by Florence without answering her questions, and handcuffed Sam.

"What's this about?" Sam asked calmly.

"You're under arrest for conspiracy to commit murder. Among other things."

"That's a state rap."

"We're getting the first bite on the federal charges. The state can dine on the crumbs after we've boxed you up for life."

"Whose murder?" Sam demanded.

"You hired one Dylan Devlin to come to Louisiana and kill two of your competitors' employees: Austin Wilson and Wesley Jefferson. You are charged with paying Devlin to murder an additional ten people."

"That's crazy! I don't know no Dylans, period."

Florence trembled as the four men hustled Sam out. Sam, sensing that she was upset, stopped in his tracks, forcing the agents to do likewise. He smiled at Florence and then winked, dropping the lid over a bright-blue eye. Florence Pruette relaxed instantly, certain that everything was going to be just fine.

"Miss Flo, do me a favor and call Bertran Stern. Tell him to get to the Federal Building and straighten these birds out."

3 | JFK Airport, New York City
Two weeks later

Since she had left Buenos Aires she had been holding on to a mental picture. She would be in a throng of people walking down a wide corridor and he would be standing framed in the throat of the hallway, in the waiting area with a hundred other anxious people. He would be wearing an Italian blazer. His red hair slightly damp from the shower, he would have rushed to the airport, parked, and walked in as close to the customs area as he could get. After a year of marriage, he was still romantic. He might be holding flowers behind his back, or he'd have a small gift in his pocket. He would beam at the sight of her. After two weeks apart, he would be more attentive than ever and they would end the evening in bed, making noise. That part of the image made her smile—in fact, blush.

She caught her reflection in a glass panel. The glove-leather jacket, tailored to accentuate her shape, was an Argentine purchase, as were the matching boots. Her shoulder-length dark hair was combed back and the glasses she wore made her feel—and look—like a model. She was young enough to be one, had been told that she had the bone structure, the figure. She was aware that she turned heads, but the only head she was interested in turning was her husband's.

Her customs agent was a woman with stiff bleached hair. The tightly cinched belt around her waist made her look like a wasp. Her fingernails were an inch long and had stars painted on them. She stared at the passport picture and back at Sean.

"Anything to declare?"

"This jacket and the boots," Sean said, handing the agent the American Express receipt.

"That's all?"

"Yes," Sean said.

The agent looked into her eyes, then handed Sean her passport back. She opened Sean's briefcase. "What about this computer?" The woman had Sean lift out the Apple laptop and turn it on.

"It's mine. I took it with me. I don't have the receipt because it was a gift."

Satisfied, the woman nodded. A man wearing a skycap jacket strode up and placed Sean's bags on a dolly. "Mr. Devlin asked me to escort you outside," he said.

There were people waiting in the lobby, staring down the corridor, checking for arriving travelers. Several livery drivers stood in a receiving line, each holding up a sign containing the last name of their fares. Moving rapidly, the porter stayed just ahead of her.

They moved through the length of the terminal, passing empty ticketing counters for commuter airlines. They walked across an expanse without seeing anyone except a janitor polishing the floor. They kept going until they were at the last set of doors at the very end of the terminal. "We're just about there," he told her.

The porter pushed the cart outside. The sidewalk was deserted. She didn't see her husband's black BMW 750 or her prized 1991 Buick Reatta convertible that had belonged to her mother. Sean looked down the covered walk to where, some fifty yards away, vehicles were picking up and letting off passengers.

"You'll be safe if you just do what we say, Mrs. Devlin."

When she turned, the porter was standing beside the cart. His right hand grasped the handle of a machine gun, its barrel concealed under his jacket.

A battered blue van raced up and stopped, its tires screeching in protest. A back door flew open and a young woman wearing a black jacket and jeans jumped out. Sean saw the bulge of a gun inside her jacket. A scruffy man leaped from the front passenger's seat. The woman grabbed Sean's right arm firmly below her shoulder as the man seized her other arm, immobilizing her. They pushed Sean toward the van as the "fake" porter tossed her suitcases in the rear, then leaped into the van's front seat.

Sean's panic diminished sufficiently for her to try to break away.

"*Help!*" she yelled at the top of her lungs. The people down the walk didn't hear her—couldn't hear over the noise of the airport. She started kicking and flailing at her assailants, hoping at least to get someone in a passing car to notice and help—take down the license number, anything.

"Get in now!" the woman snarled as the pair strong-armed her into the van and slammed the door. Sean was trapped between them. The skycap jerked his wig off, leaned back over the seat, and snapped Sean's lap belt.

"Who are you?" she asked. "Let me go!"

"Any tails?" the woman asked the porter.

"Didn't see any inside." The tires screamed again as the vehicle sped away.

"What's going on?" Sean demanded. "What in God's name are you people doing? Where's my husband?"

"You'll find out soon enough," the woman beside her said.

"We're federal agents," the porter said, as he stared over Sean's shoulder to study the traffic behind them. "We're all alone," he told the driver.

Sean Devlin didn't believe for a second that these people were cops.

4
Concord, North Carolina

Winter Massey had visited the tombstone at his feet countless times in the past three years, most often at night. Tonight it was cold for October, and the wind whipped the black raincoat against his legs while icy rain stung his face. He wore a wool baseball cap and clenched a single long-stemmed rose in his gun hand. He had bought the rose, along with eleven others wrapped in tissue paper, from a young couple outside the airport for ten dollars. He suspected the pair were cult members because they wore identical, vacant smiles.

Winter twisted the gold band on his finger. The vow said until death parted them, but he couldn't let her go even now. Maybe, he thought, that's because the time they had lived together, only fourteen years, was so terribly short ... flying by like clouds in a fast-moving thunderstorm.

He should have gone straight home, not driven five miles out of the way to the cemetery. He had spent two months tracking a fugitive, Jerry Tucker, the last two weeks never quitting the trail. After the capture, Winter had spent a full day processing Tucker—working to match the stolen property to descriptions of things known to have been taken from his victims—with homicide detectives from five jurisdictions and three FBI agents. He was tired, irritable, but he was also filled with a sense of accomplishment, knowing he had put a multiple killer on the long march toward the needle.

The fact that a young female deputy marshal had invited him home with her earlier in the evening had spooked him. How could he? Maybe that's what had made visiting this place so important. Or perhaps he held out a faint hope that in coming to this desolate spot he might see his wife one more time, hold her tight against his chest and perhaps fill, if only for an instant, the aching void inside him.

Winter remembered how hard he had prayed in those hours before she stopped breathing. Those prayers had done no more good than a wish tossed with a penny into a fountain. He knew that visiting her grave was tantamount to visiting a pair of her shoes, or a dress she could no longer wear. But he couldn't escape her memory. He would wander from it for a time, but a thought of her, triggered by a scent, a sensation, a sound, or a random feeling, would always slam him back to the past like a rifle shot.

Winter Massey looked five years younger than his age of thirty-seven. He was five-feet-ten, weighed one-sixty-five, and could look forward to twenty more years of doing what he loved before he would have to retire at fifty-seven. He took good care of himself, ate as well as he could, ran, did push-ups, lifted weights, and swam. He had recently taken up boxing, sparring a few times a month.

Before his wife's death, it had never occurred to him that he was powerless to keep harm away from his family. He had spent so many years hunting down the scum of the earth, trying to protect society from evil beings. He hadn't known he was the cobbler whose children go barefoot, the photographer with the empty family album.

Feeling sorry for himself was not his style, and after

three years he had no tears left to shed, just a sense of loss he had steeled himself to. He removed the withered rose from the vase in front of the stone and slipped the fresh one in its place. As he walked away, the heavy pistol in his shoulder holster swung like a pendulum against his ribs, a ticktock reminder of what he was.

Winter had moved his wife and son to North Carolina six years earlier, when he was assigned to the Charlotte office. While they were house-hunting in nearby small towns, looking to get the most bang for their buck, Winter and Eleanor had taken a wrong turn down a side street. After a couple of curves they saw a FOR SALE sign in front of a place on the hill that looked like a Spanish restaurant to Winter. "Look, Eleanor, the Alamo," he said.

"I love it!" she exclaimed. He thought she was joking until she made him pull over and peer in through the windows, both of them circling the house like opportunistic thieves.

The yellow-brick home had been built in 1938 and it had most recently belonged to a writer. It was an example of California Spanish Mission Revival, a style not often seen in North Carolina. It had arches on the front and a red barrel-tile roof, and to Winter's dismay, Eleanor had to have that house. Of the three other couples who had looked at it over that weekend, two had already made offers that were being considered by the owner. Winter figured that the other bidders would try to beat the owner down, demand repairs, dicker on every crack in the mortar, every patch of peeling paint. So he offered the asking price—and the house was theirs. Four bedrooms, four baths, three parlors, three working fireplaces, a breakfast room, a formal dining room, and two porches. Three thousand square feet of solid oak floors under ten-foot-tall ceilings. For three years straight it devoured their weekends, chewed holes in their savings, soaked up electricity in the summer and hogged natural gas in the winter. Eleanor had attacked the house, painting and directing Winter like a drill sergeant. God, he remembered, how she had loved life.

Winter steered his Ford Explorer up the steep driveway and, as the vehicle passed hidden sensors, bright security lights illuminated the front of the house and walkway. As he passed the back corner of the house, another bank of floods lit the backyard and driveway. He parked in the two-car garage beside a dark LeSabre. He took his canvas duffel out of the backseat, picked up the eleven roses from the floorboard, and dropped them into the trash on his way to the door. The remaining roses would only serve to remind him of the one he'd left behind.

His mother had woken when he came up the driveway and had beaten him to the door. Seen through the glass panels, Lydia Massey looked like a wraith bent on haunting his entrance. She snapped the lock and opened the door as if she didn't believe that he could locate the lock without her assistance and would stand there frozen all night with his key poised. She was wearing a wispy robe over her rayon gown, and as he kissed her cheek he was overwhelmed by the lemony scent of her cold cream. She patted his arm absently and said, "I wasn't expecting you back until tomorrow," then set about trying to reshape her hair where the pillow had flattened it. "I'll fix you something to eat. We had hamburgers for supper."

Winter said, "I've already eaten." He hadn't eaten since morning, but food was the furthest thing from his mind. The US Air steward had handed him a rubbery turkey sandwich, but he had given it to the man beside him and substituted it with a Johnny Walker Black.

Lydia studied him. "You look like a gaunt old tomcat that needs a meal and a week under the porch. Your son went to bed early. I don't think he felt well."

Winter's mother was a product of rural Mississippi, the daughter of a Methodist minister, and in her world breakfast was breakfast, but lunch was "dinner" and dinner was "supper." She referred to African Americans as coloreds, sometimes negroes, the way older Southerners occasionally did.

"Did Rush have a fever?" he asked, trying to squelch the panic he felt. Since Eleanor's death he knew that he had become overly protective, but he couldn't help it.

"No fever," Lydia answered. "I double-checked. But he's been dragging around the last few days. Just sits there listening to the television. I think something happened, but he isn't going to admit it to me. Boy's just like his father. Keeps everything inside where it can make ulcers, heart troubles, strokes, and cancer. I haven't seen you smile in a very long time, Winter Massey. You lighten up and so will he, I bet."

"I'm beat, Mama," he said, "but let me give this smile thing a shot." He grinned, showing his mother his large even teeth. She swatted his chest and he hugged her. "I promise I'll smile once a day from now on, whether I want to or not, Mama."

His watch said it was only ten—he hadn't reset it since Memphis. He pulled the stem and spun the hour hand around. "I'll check in on him."

He watched his mother head toward the guest room, her home since his wife's death. He then stuck his head into his son's room, which always seemed to smell like a hamster cage, or how he remembered the cage smelling when the boy had owned one.

"You awake, Rush?"

The three-year-old Rhodesian Ridgeback, Nemo, whined loudly. Nemo licked Winter's hand, delighted to see him again. Rush was sitting upright in bed, staring in the direction his father.

"Nemo heard your car."

Winter took a seat on the bed and hugged the boy, who smelled of shampoo and whose cheek was as soft as satin. At almost twelve, Rush was between the age when he wanted to be hugged and when he would be mortally embarrassed by any sign of affection. Nemo lay back down near the bed, his muzzle pressed into the rug, eyes locked on Rush.

Rush ran his hand over his father's face, the fingertips as light as a butterfly's touch. "You're purely tuckered, Marshal. You get your bad guy this time?"

"Villain's freshly acquainted with the sound of a jail-cell door slamming shut."

"Way to go, man!" The boy raised his palm and Winter slapped it. "Wow, howdy, he never should have gotten himself in your sights, right?"

"Yep, drawing the attention of this deputy marshal was the biggest mistake of that desperado's ill-spent life."

They both laughed.

In the shadows of the bedroom Winter couldn't see the scar on his son's face. In the light it was a line no thicker than a kite string, which ran from the middle of the right temple, to the edge of the left one. It passed over the eyelids, the bridge of his nose. In the dark, Winter could pretend nothing terrible had happened to his boy. Each time he looked at that scar he experienced that hollow feeling he got as a child when the roller-coaster car he was in topped the first hill.

The light that had once radiated from his son's beautiful blue eyes—exact duplicates of Eleanor's—had been replaced by spots of white paint expertly applied to the surface of the acrylic replicas. An artist had painted them using, for reference, a color photograph Winter had taken of Rush only weeks before the accident.

"So, what did you bring me?" Rush asked, his tone businesslike. When he was three, they had started a tradition. Every time Winter was away from home for more than a night he would bring his son a gift. The memento could be a pack of gum or just a seashell. There would always be an entertaining tale about the trinket, the longer the better.

Winter reached into his pocket for the dark hoop, pushed it over his son's left hand, and squeezed it down to fit his wrist.

Rush let his fingers investigate it. Since the accident he had learned to feel, smell, taste, and hear what he couldn't see. What he comprehended using these senses was often remarkable to his father—almost as if the boy had psychic abilities. In his occupation, Winter had to be a reader of eyes, muscle twitches, and body language. But his son seemed to have learned to read those things without being able to see them.

"What is it?" Rush demanded, giggling now with anticipation. God, Winter lived for the sound of his son's happiness.

"It's a bracelet."

"I know that! What's it made of?"

"Guess."

"Aw, man. No fair." But he nodded and played the game, running his fingers over the bracelet, biting down on it, rubbing it against his teeth and his cheek. "Well, it's sort of like braided gold or silver, but it isn't. It's not cotton or wool."

"It's from something powerful, fearless, had a mouth full of teeth and is strong of odor."

Rush laughed, delighted. "Shakka! Shakka the lion?"

"I had it woven for you from hair I clipped from Shakka's mane."

There was a gallery of family pictures in the Masseys' hallway—a conglomeration of old and new, prints of different sizes in mismatched frames, some black-and-white, some color. In one, Eleanor Massey was still Eleanor

Ashe, a skinny little girl with missing front teeth. In another, Winter's parents were still together and Lydia held a baby Winter in her arms. In another, Winter was a Cub Scout, and framed beside that was a photo of Rush as an infant being bathed by his mother. The most recent showed Rush wearing sunglasses with his arms around the neck of a moth-eaten lion. The lion's teeth were worn down so close to the gums they looked like small whitecaps on a dark sea.

The lion had been the property of a Charlotte drug dealer, who kept him in a basement and used him to frighten children and drug runners. The federal judge had ordered Winter and another marshal to put the cat in a U-Haul van and escort it to an animal rehabilitation center in Florida. The lion was so gentle that Winter had taken Rush to the warehouse where Shakka was kept before transit was arranged and had let the boy use his hands to get to know it. The old cat's tongue had made a hivelike abrasion on Rush's cheek. Winter had read a book once that described how a man-eating lion used its tongue like a rasp to remove the skin from human prey before consuming it. He hadn't told Rush that.

"Shakka liked me, didn't he?" Rush said now. "He was really big, wasn't he?"

"Nemo sure didn't like Shakka," Winter reminded him.

Winter had left Nemo at home that day, and when they got back to the house the dog planted his nose against Rush's chest. He growled fiercely for a long time, the fur over his spine standing like quills. Winter had been afraid at first that he was going to bite the boy, and, when he tried to pull his son away, the usually gentle dog had snapped at Winter. His behavior seemed to be a chastisement for allowing Rush so close to something that smelled like an enemy of children. Nemo's breed originated in South Africa. Some ancient warning had obviously risen up within the dog.

"How are you feeling?" Winter asked his son.

"Fine. Why?"

"Gram said you moped around all day, went to bed early."

"Is a bracelet for a man?" Rush asked, avoiding the question.

Winter saw a corner of one of his late wife's bandanas peeking out from under Rush's pillow. They had been one of Eleanor's trademarks; she'd used them to keep her long blond hair under control when she was outdoors or working on the house. Rush had taken to carrying one in his pocket. After three years, he was down from a half dozen to a pair; one red and one blue. When it was absolutely necessary, he washed them by hand and laid them on a towel to dry.

"Sure. I.D. bracelets are for men. Lion-hair bracelets are strictly for men who need some luck. So why the moping?"

"Well, Angus is mowing yards next summer and when I said I would help, he said if I took a tin cup and some pencils downtown, people would buy them."

"That was mean."

"No, Angus didn't mean it like that. We were talking about ways to make money, but it made me think a lot about what I'm going to do someday. It sure as heck won't be selling pencils."

"No, it won't. But you need to get some sleep." Winter kissed his son's cheek, tucked him in, hung Nemo's Seeing-Eye harness on the chair, and walked out. Nemo was supposed to sleep in the harness, but tonight Rush had merely leashed him to the bed, a minor violation of the rules for Seeing-Eye dogs. In the hallway he paused to look at the picture of Eleanor standing under the wing of a Cessna 120 she had soloed in at sixteen. He kept a picture of another Cessna, the one the insurance company sent him, in his file cabinet. He still couldn't look at it without feeling lost, like being pinned under tons of earth and rocks.

He lay down on his bed in the dark. A few weeks after Eleanor's death, he had changed the room, bought a new bed, moved the furniture. He kept her jewelry in his gun safe, thinking he'd give it to his son's wife someday. Eleanor had three gold bracelets, a small strand of cultured pearls, a wedding ring, a Seiko tank watch, her flight chronometer, and a pendant made from Winter's Kappa Alpha Order fraternity pin. Nothing worth putting in a bank vault. Her favorite piece had been a pin that Rush picked out in a Walgreens. It was small, shaped like a soldier's medal, and said MOTHER on the gold-toned bar at the top, with a pink plastic heart hanging by a ribbon. Winter had asked the funeral director to pin it to her gown before the casket was closed, because she would have wanted it close to her.

Winter had not looked at his wife's body after she stopped breathing. He had not left her side from the moment he was ushered into her hospital room until he gave the nod to pull the plug and she ceased to exist. Her face had been so swollen that she hadn't looked like Eleanor, which had allowed him to imagine that some stranger was in her bed, dying or dead. She was breathing, but not on her own, and for no good purpose except to keep her organs alive for someone else. At that point he knew that he was on the edge of exactly how much he could endure.

He had managed to get through his wife's funeral by convincing himself that the casket was empty, that Eleanor was waiting for him at home, that some other woman had crashed the plane. After all, his wife was a master pilot, an instructor. In a glider she was a thing of the air, knew the secret winds, soaring on the thermals with the arrogance of a hawk. He had only once sat in front of her in a glider. He'd been certain the wings would fold up as she performed lazy loops so high above the earth. But he had loved every second of the sensation, sharing her passion.

Rush had stayed in the hospital for a full month after the crash and spent months after that adjusting to his blindness. He seemed resilient and began testing the limits of his handicap almost immediately.

Before Rush was blinded, the dark had been the one thing he was afraid of. Since he was first put into his own bedroom at the age of two, he had slept with the door open a crack, a night-light in the hallway illuminating the way to his parents' bedroom. Since the accident, Rush hadn't cared whether the door was left open or closed. Another small thing that feasted on Winter's heart.

5

New York, New York

It was almost eleven when a gimp-gaited Herman Hoffman walked up from the subway stop at 72nd and Broadway and started making his way toward the meeting. As he turned the corner, he spotted an elegant gray Towncar parked across the narrow street from the small coffeehouse. He ignored it, knowing that the driver was studying him, relaying to the man inside the shop on his mobile phone that Herman was approaching, without backup. A sign on the door said that the small business was closed. As he approached, a large man unlocked the door from the inside. As Herman slipped into the coffeehouse, he caught a reflection in the window—a small, ancient man wearing a tweed jacket, whose body seemed shaped like a question mark—the man he had become.

Herman's limp was his badge of honor, the visible remains of his courage—compliments of an ill-mannered Stasi agent who had used a wood-carver's mallet on his knee in a futile attempt to elicit information. Men like Herman knew that torture rarely led to useful information. He was seventy-eight and his face looked like a ca-daver's. The smell of ointment wafted from him. He looked like a man on the edge of the grave, not someone who held the reins to organized death and destruction.

The New Orleanian he'd come to meet, Johnny Russo, was Sam Manelli's nephew-in-law, operations manager, enforcer, trusted messenger, and heir apparent to Sam's crime empire. Russo sat at a table in the rear, wearing an expensive sports jacket that shone like wet fish scales. With his buzz cut, his high-tech wire rims and patent-leather boots, he might have been mistaken for a forty-something art gallery owner instead of the savage he really was.

Herman sat directly across from Russo, who closed his magazine, laid it aside, and folded his hands together. "Mr. Hoffman," Russo said, concentrating his attention on the old man. "Coffee?"

"Hello, John." Herman allowed his face to communicate a flicker of amusement. "Too late for coffee." He pursed his lips, shrugged his narrow shoulders and placed a small plastic box on the table. The green light set into its surface blinked a steady beat.

"What's that?" Johnny Russo asked.

Herman slipped the apparatus back into his coat pocket. "It's a little bird that chirps in the presence of any electronic devices like transmitters, even recorders."

"Where can I get one of those?"

"They're not available. Is everything in order?"

Russo raised his eyebrows. "Sam said yes to the figure. Who the hell's he going to shop prices with at this late date, right? I mean, it isn't like he has any choice."

"Things are in place."

"Sam wants out of that place like you wouldn't believe. He's hot as a two-dollar pistol over all this. All of the fee up front and he didn't even flinch. I guess three million for a single hit is some kind of a record."

"Nowhere near it." Herman forced himself to smile. "Certainty always costs more than maybe. This is a complicated, expensive operation. Sam will get his freedom. You will get what you want. And I will get the satisfaction of performing the impossible—one last time."

"And three million, tax free." Russo's eyes shifted focus and Herman realized that the mobster was staring at the large flakes of dead skin on the shoulders of his jacket. The disease that ravaged his skin was humiliating, especially considering the man he had once been. When their eyes met, Russo peered over Herman's shoulder at his man near the door and then gave Herman a we-are-going-to-rule-the-world smile. "When is this gonna happen? Sam wants it real soon. Every day he's in that jail is like a year to most people."

"I can't give anybody outside my group the date of an operation, John. My people have not failed once in fifty years. I know where the marshals have Devlin. You can assure Sam that the trial is never going to take place. Dylan won't even make it to testify before the 'secret' congressional committee on organized crime. My people are already staging. That's all you need to know."

Russo's eyes danced with excitement. "That's great! If everybody gets the message that there is no safe place to hide if they betray me ... The feds are gonna be hugely pissed."

"They'll know Sam was behind it, but they will never prove it unless you, Sam, or I talk."

Herman knew Russo well enough to understand that he was no Sam Manelli and when this self-important turd didn't have Sam on his shoulder, the empire was doomed. Of all the alliances Herman had ever formed, this one was singularly unpalatable.

"Where is it?" Herman asked.

"What?"

Herman stared down at his hands again as if he were memorizing the liver spots. "The three-million-dollar fee."

Russo snapped his fingers. "Spiro!" The muscle man by the door strode over carrying an attaché case and placed it on the table. Russo popped the locks and rotated the case to expose a stack of engraved documents.

Herman thumbed the edges of the bearer bonds, not counting to confirm there were sixty of them, just making sure they were real. With so much at stake Johnny Russo wouldn't dare hand Herman bogus paper, but Russo might have been screwed over by someone else. He looked at his watch and stood up. "I have a subway to catch."

"You want me to send Spiro and the car to make sure you get home with that?"

Herman stared down at Russo. "You're kidding, right?" Herman wasn't about to have Russo know where his home was. Personal danger had nothing to do with it.

Herman rode the nearly deserted subway with the stainless-steel briefcase on the floor beside him. He sat patiently with his eyes closed.

He had dealt with some of the country's most infamous gangsters from the late 1940s. No matter what talent each possessed that had elevated them to their positions of leadership, not one in a thousand rose above the level of an expensively dressed ape. Herman had always admired Sam Manelli. He was remarkably intelligent, utterly ruthless, and knew more about human nature than anyone. He was also a man of his word. He would rather be tortured to death than inform on anyone. When Sam was gone, the last of the honorable crime bosses was gone, which was just as well. Even if a code of silence was possible with these new gangsters, modern electronics were making secrets a thing of the past.

At his stop Herman picked up the briefcase, got off the train, and walked slowly up the steps out onto the street. His building was near the Stock Exchange, Battery Park, and Trinity Church, and although the neighborhood was teeming with people during the week, it was fairly deserted after five-thirty and a ghost town on Saturday nights, when all the office buildings were empty.

Herman walked casually, swinging the briefcase containing 3 million dollars' worth of paper—every bit as negotiable as cash. He saw two men seated on a stoop in front of a closed deli a block away. He didn't make any attempt to cross to the other side of the street—he maintained a course that would place him an arm's length from them. He didn't look at the two men until they stood and made it impossible for him to pass without stepping off the curb.

One of the men was large and dark as pitch, with a deep scar that gave his cheek the appearance of buttocks. His clothes smelled like something that had been pulled from a muddy ditch and left wadded up for a few days. "Hey, man. You got the time?"

Herman stopped and looked at his watch. "Twelve-ten."

"Nice watch, old man."

The smaller man moved around and stood slightly behind Herman.

"It's platinum," Herman said. "Do we share an appreciation for fine Swiss timepieces?"

The man behind him was a stocky, bandy-legged Mexican.

"You got a couple dollars?" the Mexican asked. "We han't eat all today."

"Would you gentlemen use my money to buy food or crack rocks?"

The large man laughed. "What do you care? You're a rich man."

"I certainly wouldn't stay that way if I gave it to every periodontally challenged crackhead I encountered."

"Whas een jur shiny little suitcase?" the man behind Herman asked.

"Bearer bonds." Herman took his right hand from his coat pocket. He held it up so both men could see the thick stack of bills in it, fixing their attention to one spot. "I have around two thousand dollars here. How about I let you have this, you forget the briefcase and go get all cracked up for a couple of days, and I'll just go on my way?"

Herman saw the large man's eyes flash a signal and he knew the smaller man behind him was moving to smash his skull or something equally unimaginative. If he hadn't been so tired he would have enjoyed this encounter. In the years he had lived in Paris, London, Washington, and now New York, he had never been robbed, never even been menaced by street thugs. He had anticipated the remote possibility of Russo's greed getting the better of his good sense, perhaps setting up something to steal back his money. But these two were just hungry cats who'd had a mouse walk right up to them.

"How about you give me the cash, the watch so I know what time it is, and the little suitcase for carrying stuff."

"Ralph?" Herman said.

"Yes, sir?" the answer came.

Herman saw the large man's ravenous expression change at the sound of the new voice. Herman turned to see that the smaller of the two was looking to his right, where a man dressed entirely in black had materialized. Ralph had the small man's wrist in his left hand, and the knife in the Mexican's fist was quivering like the hind leg of a dying rabbit. There was a silenced pistol in Ralph's left hand that was aimed at the large man's heart.

"Or how about this?" Herman suggested as he slid the money back into his pocket. "I keep my cash, and Ralph teaches you scions of the alleyway one final lesson."

Herman sidestepped the larger man and walked down Pine Street swinging the metal attaché. He didn't look back. He knew that the cops would soon come upon two very unpleasant, drug-addicted thugs lying on the sidewalk who had squabbled over something and killed each other with a single cheap knife.

Of all his men, there were only two he trusted totally— Ralph and Lewis.

6 | Concord, North Carolina
Sunday

An hour before the sun rose Winter climbed from his bed, dropped to the floor, and did one hundred push-ups. Immediately afterward he locked his ankles under the bed's frame and did as many crunches. Over the course of a day he would try to do another two hundred of each to stay limber and maintain his muscle tone.

He put on shorts, a gray T-shirt, and his running shoes. On the way out, he unleashed Nemo from Rush's bed.

Winter and Nemo ran around to Union Street, picking out an even stride that would take them to the end of Union, to Highway 136, back the five miles to Corban Street, and home.

On his street Winter saw a figure leaning against the grill of a pickup truck. As he approached the man, Nemo started wagging his tail.

"Howdy, old pal," the man said as he bent to stroke the dog's head.

"Hank," Winter said. "What brings you all the way up here?"

"Lydia's coffee."

Chief Deputy U.S. Marshal Hank Trammel was Winter's boss. Trammel was exactly what most people would expect a U.S. marshal to look like. His preretirement paunch protruded over his belt, obscuring the big buckle—a Texas-size silver and turquoise oval. Test samples of paint in the weather-abuse simulators at the Dutch Boy laboratories didn't get the wear and tear Hank's skin had received as a child on a ranch exposed to wind-driven sand and scorching sun. His duty piece was a stag-handle 1911 Colt .45 cradled in an Austin holster designed by Brill and made by the El Paso Saddle Company in 1950 for a new Texas ranger named Trent Trammel, Hank's father. Hank's father and grandfather had both died by the gun.

"I wanted to congratulate you on the Tucker capture. Media's going to be all over it. They'll be after interviews."

"They'll waste their time, because I'm not talking about it." Winter never spoke to the media unless he was ordered to, but normally there was someone else involved who was happy to instead.

"You could have congratulated me tomorrow," Winter said.

"There's this. Faxed to me yesterday morning." Hank reached into his pocket and handed Winter a folded-up sheet of paper.

Winter read it, then offered it back. "I'm not interested."

"I didn't see where it asked if you are interested."

"Aw, come on, Hank. Why me?"

The chief deputy shrugged. "It's got to be a big deal. You see the signature."

"Hank, the twentieth is Rush's birthday. That's next Sunday. It'll be the first one I've been here for in three years. I don't plan to disappoint him again. It means a lot. Why do they need me? I'm not WITSEC."

"Maybe they figure you can give an account of yourself in a tight spot."

Winter grimaced involuntarily.

"I like to believe that every once in a while the big guys

know what they're doing," Hank said. "They issued this, and I expect what they want is more important than what you want."

"Doesn't make sense."

"I couldn't agree more. There's a world of men a lot better qualified than you. Nice, even-tempered fellows who don't get edgy sitting in a cheesy motel room watching some criminal pace the carpet. I got a million other things I'd like to throw your lazy ass at, Massey, but I'm not being paid to run the Justice Department. John Katlin is."

Winter took a shower while Hank sat in the kitchen and talked to Lydia. After he toweled off and slipped on his boxers, he picked up the orders and reread them. It was temporary assignment to Witness Security. He was to report to Spitfire Aviation at the Concord Regional Airport on Sunday at thirteen hundred hours to meet his transportation. The order was signed by John T. Katlin, attorney general of the United States, and countersigned by Richard Shapiro, chief U.S. marshal and director of the United States Marshals Service.

Winter was surprised. The Witness Security program, WITSEC, was a specialty. In his course of duties, he often transported prisoners, often kept them overnight in rooms or houses. If the USMS had been a medical discipline, Winter would have been a general practitioner who could operate in an emergency, whereas the WITSEC deputies were surgeons.

There were just two things left to do: pack his bag and say good-bye.

7 | Charlotte, North Carolina

A twin-engine Cessna was waiting for Winter on the tarmac outside the fixed-base operation at the Concord Regional Airport. Since he wasn't booked on a commercial flight, Winter figured he was going to a remote safe house. The other option was that the destination was so secret, WITSEC wanted no paper or electronic trail left for anyone to follow. He figured he'd know soon enough.

Winter climbed aboard and set his duffel on an empty seat. The plane's cloth upholstery was worn, the carpet stained, and the exterior paintwork dull for a government-owned aircraft.

He settled in and stared out the window, but his mind was on his son's reaction to the news that he was leaving again. Rush had said he didn't mind, but Winter knew how disappointed the child was. He had promised that he would do his best to make it back for Rush's birthday. Lydia had maintained a cheery demeanor, but Winter knew she was upset, too. She had never understood why he wanted to be in law enforcement. She often said she thought he was a wonderful teacher, and she couldn't understand why he had left that field. But he just knew inside that he was made for something else, something that being a deputy offered him. He loved everything about the job, and he was good at it.

The Cessna turboprop maintained an easterly course for nearly an hour before the pilot landed at a military base, where aircraft crowded the tarmac. When the door of the plane opened, he could smell brine in the air.

A Humvee appeared, and a silent marine delivered him to a waiting Blackhawk ready for takeoff.

Winter handed his bag to the flight officer and climbed inside. Two women passengers, both in their midtwenties, were already seated together on a bench directly across from the sliding door. He took a seat next to them and belted himself in.

Due to the noisy engines, Winter merely nodded a greeting. The women nodded back, acknowledging his presence. Once cleared for takeoff, the helicopter lifted off, climbing rapidly.

The well-tanned woman seated closest to the rear of the compartment wore a soft cap with a long curved bill, a microfiber jacket, jeans, and cross-trainers. She looked Latin, and the freckles on her cheeks and nose gave her the aura of a tomboy. She wore her shoulder-length auburn hair tucked behind her ears.

Winter figured the Latina was a deputy marshal. For the time being, he tagged her "Freckles." He glanced at the three suitcases behind the cargo net and matched her with the seriously scuffed, bright-blue hard-shell Samsonite. No doubt she traveled a lot, lived out of that suitcase.

The other woman's two leather suitcases had canvas outer shells to protect their expensive skins. She had money, taste, and a meticulous nature. She wore a wedding band.

"Married Woman's" hair was neatly pinned back. The angular black frames of her sunglasses were too heavy for her features, but the lenses were light enough so that her almond-shaped eyes were visible behind them. She wore slacks, a collared shirt, a glove-leather sports jacket, and matching boots. Nervously, her fingertips tapped the briefcase in her lap. An expensive gold wristwatch peeked out from under her cuff.

In other circumstances she could be an executive, or a curator at a major museum.

The Blackhawk flew a few miles out over the ocean before it banked hard to the north. When the engines changed pitch, Winter stared out between the pilot and copilot, and spotted an island isolated in an expanse of the Atlantic. The helicopter dropped to about three hundred feet over the water as it approached the sliver of land.

A line of pine trees bisected the island like a fence. On its western side there were several corrugated metal buildings with matching tin roofs. The entire installation was perched above a deepwater bay where a sport-fishing boat and a cigarette boat were tied to a floating dock. Twin radio towers loomed over a windowless concrete bunker on the edge of the cliff. Radar dishes were affixed to one of the towers. A basketball court was sandwiched between a barracks and what looked like an equipment shed. Two men, both wearing shorts, stopped their one-on-one and stared up at the approaching chopper. An asphalt switchback was cut into the sheer wall, joining the buildings and the dock below.

On the eastern side of the island, a single-story house with a wraparound porch faced the Atlantic. There was a water tank just south of the house. North of the house, he saw tennis courts and a covered swimming pool.

A hundred feet away, the beach sloped gently to the water line. Two lounge chairs had been arranged to take advantage of the shade cast by a bright-red umbrella. The chopper's descent halted the conversation of two casually dressed men seated on those chairs. Both raised their hands to shield their eyes from the billowing sand. As the helicopter landed, the umbrella lifted off the ground, flipped upside down, and scooted like a sled into the breaking surf.

After the Blackhawk touched down, and while the pilot kept the blades turning, the flight officer slipped back and opened the door. Manners dictated that Winter climb down onto the helipad and help the women. Married carried her briefcase and moved away, bending over as though the blades might dip six feet to hit her. The flight officer handed the bags down one at a time. Freckles took Married's two pieces of expensive luggage. Married held out her hands to take a bag from Freckles, but the cop shook her head, dismissing the offer. Winter took his duffel, slung it over his shoulder, grabbed Freckles's Samsonite case, and carried it to the women, who stood waiting at the walkway. He reached out to take one of the canvas-covered bags from Freckles.

"I can carry them," she called out.

The larger of the two men on the beach had run after the umbrella. Both men wore semiautomatic pistols in high-rise hip holsters, with enough extra magazines in clip holders to produce sustained annihilating fire. The smaller man also had a "room broom" suspended by a shoulder sling. The stockless version of the Heckler & Koch's fully automatic MP5 looked like a pistol on steroids. As the helicopter became airborne, the two men waved at Freckles. "Hey, Martinez, welcome to paradise!" the smaller one yelled, as the Blackhawk lifted away.

"Who you kidding, Beck? Manhattan is paradise!" she yelled back, laughing throatily. She turned back to Winter as the Blackhawk vanished behind the trees.

Married, briefcase in hand, was heading for the house.

Freckles followed. "Thanks for carrying my stuff so I could carry hers. I'm Deputy Marshal Angela Martinez," she told Winter.

"I'm Deputy Marshal Winter Massey. What's her story?"

"She's the package's wife. I've been with her since yesterday. Winter, hey, that name sounds familiar."

"Consequences of loaning your name to a season."

"Come again?"

"Never mind."

Winter entered the foyer of the house just after

Martinez. The sight that greeted him almost bowled him over. Life had given him two friends who were as good as family. One, Hank Trammel, was his boss; the other was standing in the foyer talking to the package's wife.

"You old dog," Winter said.

"Winter Massey." Greg Nations was a light-skinned African-American with a middleweight's build, a million-dollar smile, and intense eyes with irises the color of buckskin. "How's that little nephew of mine?" Greg's laugh was a resonating deep boom. He looked at Martinez and winked. "Winter and me were raised by the same she-wolf. We used to tussle for the hind teat."

"Rush is great. I should have known you were behind this sudden, mysterious journey."

"And how's your mama?"

"Lydia is Lydia."

"You're that Massey?" Martinez exclaimed. "Of course! I knew you and Greg"—she caught herself—"Inspector Nations were friends."

A voice interrupted the gleeful greeting. "Excuse me, might I please see my husband now?"

"I'm sorry, Mrs. Devlin," Greg said, turning his attention back to the other woman. "This man and I go back a lot of years, and our paths don't often cross these days." He reached out and took her briefcase. "I'll have to search this."

Mrs. Devlin removed her glasses and folded them. She lowered her eyes and said in a low voice. "But they've all been searched, X-rayed and sniffed by two different dogs. And that was *after* I cleared customs. I just came back into the country yesterday. I haven't lost sight of them since."

"Rule number one," Greg told her. "Everything coming in is hand-searched. Martinez, assume the position."

Martinez turned and put her hands up, and Greg ran his hands over her body and pinched the material of her clothes. He searched her thoroughly, making no apology for checking the contours of her breasts and pressing his fingers against her genitals.

Mrs. Devlin bit her bottom lip like a child accused of something she was innocent of.

Greg pointed to a door. "Martinez, take Mrs. Devlin into the bathroom there and search her, please."

After the women left, Greg searched Winter, giving them a chance to catch up.

"We'll bring your bags to you," Greg told Mrs. Devlin when she returned.

"I'd appreciate that."

"Go right down the hallway, Mrs. Devlin. Your husband is behind the second door on the left. Martinez will be staying across the hall from you. If you need anything, just ask. You don't leave the house without an escort. You will be served meals in the dining room or in your room. Snacks, drinks anytime. We can go over the house rules later. Questions?"

Wordlessly, Mrs. Devlin turned. She hesitated at the door Greg had indicated, perhaps to compose herself before she entered the room.

The marshals walked through the arch and into an open living room.

"Who owns this place?" Martinez asked, looking around. The majority of the paintings were nautical in nature, depicting sailing ships firing cannons or caught in fierce storms. The furnishings looked expensive. The house had the feeling of being someone's home.

Greg said, "Welcome to Rook Island. Four hundred yards at its widest, a mite over a quarter mile long. House is eight thousand square feet of hand-built space, engineered to withstand a hurricane. The Navy maintains it as a vacation retreat for admirals, commanders, congressmen, and senators who have some impact on military appropriations. I'd doubt the whole shooting match cost much more than a Tomahawk missile."

"What's the story on the package?" Winter asked as Greg led them through to the formal dining room. Greg set the suitcases on a gleaming table beneath a brass chandelier.

"He's a very big deal. Dylan Devlin is the latest mobster to turn state's evidence. His testimony can hang Sam Manelli."

Winter whistled, impressed. "I heard Manelli was arrested on conspiracy to commit murder. But they've had that old razorback by the ear before and he's pulled away. I lived in New Orleans years ago. Manelli's an icon. He doesn't get physically close to anything illegal, never writes anything down, never makes a comment where it can be heard. He owns judges, senators, congressmen, local politicos, and cops. The newspaper did a poll years ago, and the majority of the population thought Manelli kept street crime down. His philanthropic gestures are continuously played up by the politicians who take his money. Only in a place as unconventional as New Orleans would Sam Manelli be a pop hero."

Greg nodded, his face serious. "He's never spent a day in jail, because no witness has ever testified against him. Our Mr. Devlin flipped on Manelli after he performed a dozen hits for him. So Devlin's a much bigger deal to the Justice Department than Sammy the Bull ever was. He's a bit bruised up from a car crash."

Something clicked in Winter's mind. "Wait, was he the guy who got rammed and had the two stiffs shoot out of his trunk in New Orleans a couple weeks back?"

"That's him," Greg said.

"I missed the connection to Manelli," Winter said.

"Because nobody made one. That connection is a well-guarded secret. I was told in no uncertain terms that we do not discuss Mr. Devlin's career as Sam Manelli's hired killer or ask him about anything he's done."

"Ours is not to question why," Martinez said.

Greg was searching Martinez's suitcase. Martinez opened Mrs. Devlin's luggage and carefully ran her hands through it, feeling for any hidden contraband.

"Anything interesting?" Greg asked her.

Martinez twisted the suitcase so the open top obstructed Greg's view. "That's none of your business, Inspector Nations, sir."

"In my time I've seen it all. Feminine hygiene products, vibrators of every configuration and power level, diaphragms, *Hot Rod Mama In Leather* magazines. I could tell you stories that would curl your toes, Martinez."

"Save it," Martinez said. "You don't want to get me all excited when none of the men around here are my type."

"What type is that?"

"Sane."

Greg unzipped Winter's duffel, then pulled out a picture of Rush and Nemo. "I can't get over how much he has grown in a year."

Martinez looked over at the picture. "That a Seeing-Eye harness on his dog?"

"Yes," Winter said.

Greg put the picture back in the duffel. "Martinez, take everything out of her bags and inspect the linings. Make sure every stitch is factory and feel for any differences under the lining anyway."

He opened Mrs. Devlin's briefcase and lifted out her Apple laptop computer. "What have we here?" He turned it on and waited until it had booted up. He selected a document, opened it, and started to read. "Little woman writes poems. Proves my point. Poetry's a fantasy thing, right, Winter? Bet Mrs. Devlin's a real firebrand."

"Is the poem any good?" Martinez asked.

"Poetry is personal. Like a diary," Winter said.

"Here I was assuming that all a stone killer's wife thought about was if her detergent will get those stubborn bloodstains out of his white shirts," Greg said.

"You think she knew?" Martinez wondered. "You think he told her? She doesn't seem like a killer's-wife type."

"They never tell their wives," Greg replied. "I never knew a criminal's wife who knew shit. Like getting fur coats delivered at two in the morning from the trunk of a car is just the way people shop. 'Aw, babe, do you gotta hang that dead guy upside down in the shower? Can't you take him outside and drain him in the backyard?'"

Greg shut down the computer, removed the battery and peered inside the cavity. Satisfied, he put the laptop aside and searched the other articles in the briefcase. He opened each of the pens and pressed his fingertips over every inch of the case's interior lining. Then he went through Martinez's Samsonite suitcase equally as carefully. "Aw, Angela, what a boring suitcase. Not so much as a vibrator."

"Not on a deputy marshal's salary. Batteries are expensive," she said flatly.

8 | **Rook Island, North Carolina**

Sean left the bathroom feeling violated. She couldn't look the young deputy who had strip searched her in the eyes. She had persisted in trying to find out what the hell was going on—where Dylan was and why she was being held against her will. If she heard: *Ma'am, your husband is fine. You'll be seeing him very soon. I wish I could tell you more. He will explain everything when you see him* one more time, she'd lose her mind.

After Inspector Nations directed her to Dylan's room, she had to fight the urge to run weeping to him.

Now she was close to seeing Dylan, to understanding

what this was all about. She paused at the door and took a deep breath to compose herself before she tapped at it.

Her heart leaped when she heard his voice call out, "If you ain't my young, brilliant, beautiful wife, don't you dare come through that door!"

Sean smiled and opened the door. Dylan was propped up against a stack of pillows on the bed, wearing a blue robe. She saw crutches leaning against the wall, bandages around his chest where the robe fell open. She rushed to his open arms and hugged him, careful not to hurt him by squeezing too hard.

Their kiss was wonderful; she drank in the scent of him, the familiar touch, which erased the memory of being humiliated by the search two minutes earlier. Dylan broke the kiss and held her face in his hands as he studied her, his million-dollar smile warming her heart.

He drew her in and kissed her again and now she felt the familiar hunger in his kiss. She knew where this was leading.

"Close the door," he whispered urgently. "Lock it."

"Dylan, first tell me what the hell is going on. I was grabbed at the airport and nobody will tell me anything. What in God's name has happened? What do they think you did? Why are *we* here?"

He held her close and kissed her gently. "It's very simple, kitten. We are together again. You go over there and throw that lock and come back here and I'm going to let you—"

"Tell me first."

He kissed her cheeks, her nose, and gently nibbled her lips. "And come get into this bed and . . ."

God, after spending a day surrounded by grim-faced marshals, it was comforting being with him. "Please, Dylan." Her pent-up fear and resolve to know what had happened was dissipating. "Dylan." She felt herself sliding into a warm place as his familiar hands moved over her body. "You don't understand what I've been . . ."

He pressed a fingertip to her lips. "Please, Sean. Let's not spoil this with words."

"But I . . ."

He put his lips to her ear and whispered, "Lock that door and come back here and I will tell you absolutely everything. Word of honor . . . after we say hello."

9

Leaving Mrs. Devlin's things in the dining room, the marshals passed the security room and the closed door to the Devlins' room. Greg showed Martinez the front suite of three rooms, their windows facing the ocean. The Devlins' room, he explained, had windows on the north wall, but there were locked hurricane shutters on them.

The overstuffed couch was large enough for a man to sleep on comfortably. A solid door opened into the large bedroom, which contained a king-size bed, chest of drawers, writing table and chair, and two closets. Another door opened into the bathroom. Martinez approved, adding that the suite was larger than her apartment.

The team was bunking in the servants' quarters, four rooms located down a hallway behind the kitchen. The largest one belonged to the cook. The second was where Greg and Winter would be staying. The other four deputies were split up between the third and fourth rooms.

The servants' rooms might have been a Motel 6 in Kansas. Each bathroom was located directly to the right of the entry; the closet hangers were locked to the rod, as though the military's servants, like transients, needed coat hangers badly enough to steal them. Each twin headboard was attached to the wall, and the mattresses looked like sushi plates.

Winter unpacked, placing his things in the bottom two drawers as Greg sat watching him from the edge of the nearest bed.

"Sure good to see you, Win. Brings to mind better times."

"So why don't you tell me what I'm doing here?" Winter replied.

"I was given carte blanche in putting this team together and I wanted the best group in the history of WITSEC. I got a sniper can shoot a fly off a can at a quarter mile: Robert Forsythe."

"I saw him shoot in competition a few years ago."

"I got Bear Dixon, the strongest son of a bitch I know. He could throw Devlin over his shoulders and run ten miles. Dave Beck and Bill Cross would eat cobras from the tail forward with their hands tied behind their backs to keep a witness safe. And Martinez ain't here because I needed someone to hand Mrs. Devlin tampons. She earned a black belt in tae kwon do before she was ten. Nobody's as good with a handgun, or reacts faster, or sniffs out trouble like you. Dylan Devlin is a huge package, Win. And the payoff at the end can be massive."

"Payoff?"

"It'll look great on our sheets, and when we cash out it'll bring in clients who won't spare any expense to have a piece of us. We'll keep Devlin safe when every professional hitter and connected lowlife with a gun or a bomb is after his hide. Word from the Justice Department is that the contract for Devlin is for millions. Know what that means?"

"World-class talent."

"If we handle this one without a hitch, we're set for life,

Winter. We'll be able to open the doors of Massey and Nations Security International and fill the place immediately. I can get plenty of investment money. Tell me you wouldn't dig thousand-dollar suits, a checkbook you don't have to balance. Don't you want to live some, Win? I sure as hell do. The idea of surviving on a pension in a trailer holds no appeal for me. I plan to be stupid rich, and I am taking you with me even if it kills you."

"We'll see." *The company again*—Greg's dream. He had grown up poor and thought material possessions were more than the temporary distractions Winter believed them to be. Winter preferred his own life simple.

Winter took the SIG from the shoulder rig and slid a high-rise holster onto his belt, pushed the handgun into it, and snapped the thumb release. He clipped on the dual magazine holder that added twenty-four shots. "I appreciate your confidence and I value your friendship, but your timing sucks rocks," he said. "I need one big favor."

"Anything in my power."

"I need to be home Sunday, even if it's just for the day."

"Why?"

"I promised Rush I wouldn't miss his birthday this year. Your *request* forced me to break it."

"You're serious?"

"When it comes to that boy, I'm always serious."

"I'll do what I can."

"Way I see it, Greg, is you brought me here, I expect you can get me back home. You want me back on Monday, I'm all yours for as long as you need me, but I need to be home on Sunday."

The kitchen seemed scaled to accommodate the woman who ran it. The space had commercial appliances, and the table easily fit eight chairs. There were doors on three of the four walls. Just through an open butler's pantry was a swinging one that led into the formal dining room; a second opened to the main hallway, and the third out onto the porch.

"Jet Washington, greatest cook on the face of the earth, I want to introduce to you the number-one greatest deputy marshal, Winter James Massey."

"Don't get in my way, now," the cook said, without turning from the huge stove. "I'm at the crossroads with this gumbo." She was dressed in a starched white uniform, an eye-popping contrast to her skin, which was the color of damp mink. "Okay, here comes the other side of it." She held a spoon to her lips, sampled the liquid, and murmured gratefully, "Thank you, Jesus! Okay, it's safe now."

Only then did she turn and eye Winter with some degree of suspicion. The skin on her face was stretched so tight that he couldn't judge her age within a fifteen-year span. She had an amazingly warm smile and her eyes were so bright that they seemed illuminated, like dials in a dashboard. The rich scent of the food was making his stomach growl.

"Glad you finally got here," she told him. "Mr. Gregory been driving everybody crazy with all this talk 'bout Winter this and Winter that and jus' y'all wait till Winter Massey gets here. From the way that man's been going on, I figured you'd be ten feet tall, with a halo made of lightning bolts."

"He exaggerates a little," Winter replied, grinning.

She wagged a finger at him. "I got three rules nobody breaks, unless *they* want to be broken. One is, keep your nose out my fridge and your hands off my cookin' utensils. Two is, nobody ever goes hungry in this house. And three is, you want something to eat, you tell me and I'll fix you something filling. Don't matter what time day or night. I'm not in here, just tap on my door. You got all that, Deputy Winter Massey?"

"Yes, ma'am."

Placing her hands on her hips, she countered, "Uh-huh. Then tell it back to me."

10 | **New York, New York**

Herman Hoffman sat in the communications room of his six-story building studying a pile of satellite pictures, one by one, on the counter in front of him. The shots were so critical to intelligence that the entire operation had hinged on getting them. From here on in, this was all going to be as simple as connecting numbered dots.

He held a magnifying glass above the first print to examine the detail. He could barely contain his excitement, as he could clearly see two men standing between the surf and the house. He lifted that one from the stack and carefully laid it facedown on the pile to his right.

He set the magnifying glass down on the print and rubbed his eyes. "We have a lot to do, Ralph," Herman said. "They have selected one hell of a safe house—one hell of a safe house, indeed."

"Cherry Point is twenty-six miles away. It's a Marine air rework base, but they've added active air power." Ralph slipped a picture of the base from the left stack: The tarmac was replete with war birds. "There are SEALs training near there. Since that isn't a SEAL training area, I think they're there to add cover for the WITSEC operation."

Herman was elated. "The more secure they imagine they are, the more complacent they will be, Ralph. That will work to our advantage. Whether they sit tight or leave, this is checkmate. They will stay on that island until Thursday or a little bird will let us know of any changes. I can't count the times I've had far less time to mount far more complicated operations, with far less intelligence to go on."

Herman opened a notebook and studied the equipment inventory carefully. Everything was in hand. The signature of his quartermaster assured him that everything would be waiting at the staging area. He had to be certain he didn't miss anything—one missing object, no matter how small, and the consequences could be catastrophic. This operation would be his masterpiece, even though he would never get the recognition for it. When ops went right, someone else always got the credit.

"How do you feel?" Herman asked Ralph.

"Sir?"

"In your gut. How do you feel?"

"Fine."

"Are you nervous? Any unease? Premonitions?"

"Nothing at all."

"And the others? Focused? Eager? Chomping at the bit?"

"Sure."

Herman closed the notebook and stood up. He felt like a hunter at wood's edge, ready to release his dogs.

11 | Rook Island, North Carolina

"This is Winter Massey," Greg told the other five members of the WITSEC team. "Starting with Cross, I want each of you to introduce yourselves."

"I'm Bill Cross. Welcome aboard." Cross had an auburn crew cut and gunmetal-gray eyes. He was about Winter's size, in his midtwenties.

"Dave Beck." Beck had obviously been awakened for

the meeting. He was in his early thirties, no taller than five-six, and in need of a shave. The ball cap he wore splayed his mousy hair out over the tops of his ears. "We're all looking forward to working with you, Massey."

"I'm Ed Dixon."

"We all call him Bear," Greg said.

"Ed," Winter said, extending his hand.

Dixon shrugged shyly as he shook Winter's hand. "Bear's cool. Been my name since I was in diapers."

"Bear" was a nickname that fit the man perfectly. Dixon was six-four and weighed at least two hundred and fifty pounds. His deep-set eyes seemed too small for his head, and his voice was pitched so low it vibrated.

"Bob Forsythe," Greg said.

"Robert," Forsythe corrected.

Forsythe was in his late thirties, and his features were acute. He wore his slick, jet-black hair combed straight back against his skull like a gangster in an old B movie. Winter's instant impression was of a thrifty man who didn't waste expressions or words. His eyes were as alert as a falcon's. He looked at Winter as though he were sizing him up as competition.

"I saw you shoot a few years back," Winter told him.

Forsythe formed what might have been a grin if his lips hadn't been so tight. "How'd I do?"

"You came in second on account of that sudden gust of wind."

"I took first the next year—ninety-eight," he replied, too quickly.

"I know," Winter said. "Then you quit competing."

"What's the point in repeating yourself?" Forsythe said.

"We've all seen *you* shoot!" Bear blurted out. Then he blushed. "Sorry. It's just that you're a phenom. Like Forsythe. Naturally the rest of us wish—we just get by."

"Get by?" Greg said incredulously. "Bear here can hold

a Jeep off the ground while you change the tire and not even break a sweat."

Winter nodded. He knew that for the past seven years every recruit entering Glynco had viewed the court security tapes of Winter's Tampa shootout. The tapes, taken as a record for the Justice Department of the trial of a drug lord, were included in the training as an example of a deputy putting himself between a threat and innocent people. That was the official excuse for showing the tapes, but it was strictly a prurient exercise of "Watch the marshal get shot at and somehow not die. Now watch him even the score. Man, that was some shooting, but don't try and trick-shoot like that, rookie, or you'll be dead." He had been invited to speak to the first class that viewed the tapes, but he had declined in such a way that the invitation had never been offered again. Winter had never seen the tapes and didn't want to.

"And you know Angela Martinez. Okay, sailors, back in the barrel," Greg told them. "I need to show Winter and Martinez around the island."

Winter and Martinez accompanied Greg on a tour of the island. Starting in front of the safe house, Greg pointed at the water tower forty yards to the south. "That doubles as a shooting platform for Forsythe. It gives him a good view of our side of this island." He pointed to the north side of the house. "The tennis courts and pool are closed for the season."

"Hard to believe they pay us for this," Martinez said.

"This isn't a vacation," Greg reminded her sharply. "The Devlins are never to leave the house unescorted. Anything feels wrong, use whatever force you need to get on top of things. Neutralize the situation, ask questions later. We are authorized to use any lethal force we deem necessary, which is why this crew is made up of the people it is. Shifts are listed on the board in the security room."

"Cherry Point is supplying heavy protection. They've moved in some combat-equipped attack helicopters and even have some SEALs bivouacked just down the coast. We sound an alarm and cavalry arrives in minutes. I'll show you the other side the island."

After taking the path behind the house that led through the trees to the west side of the island, the marshals stood overlooking the naval facility. "Radar station is manned by six sailors," Greg informed them. "They're under orders to stay on this side of the tree line while we're here. Cover story is that there's an admiral vacationing with his wife. As far as anybody knows we're Navy security.

"That big building is the barracks and the one just behind it is an equipment shed. The radio room is the building with the dish tower on top of it. The ramp beside it leads down to the pier. Store boat normally delivers supplies on Thursdays and ferries sailors as necessary. The cigarette racer and the sport-fishing boat are for the brass."

"How long we here for?" Martinez asked.

"Devlin is set to testify before a congressional committee on organized crime early next week. I doubt we'll be returning here after that. With this guy, if the Justice Department gets nervous, we could be asked to make a move onto a military base without warning."

"How do you get orders?"

Greg smiled and reached into his pocket. "This is a Palm organizer bought by some civil servant's wife—it can communicate wirelessly through an account in her name. I send encrypted e-mails, our people reply. It's about as immediate as a phone call and absolutely secure. There's not a working phone on our side of the island."

Martinez said, "Great food, sun, surf, hazardous-duty

pay, and an army over my shoulder. They'll have to drag me out of here kicking and screaming."

Greg chuckled. "Please don't throw me in de briar patch!"

Back at the safe house, the trio of marshals found Dave Beck sitting at a console watching the monitors hooked to cameras covering the entire western side of the island.

The security room was carpeted, windowless, and large enough for two chairs and a couch. Three of the monitors showed views of the house's exterior doors and porch, the beach, pool, and tennis courts. Three other monitors showed interior views: the hallway outside the security room, and other halls and rooms in the house. The view on each screen changed every five seconds.

"This is a restricted zone we're in. The sailors report any craft in the sky or on the water," Greg said. He pointed to the panel. "Whenever an outside door is opened, that light flashes. You can zoom and pan the cameras. After dinner, Beck will show you how everything here works."

"In an emergency, hit this red button and we get help."

"Once it's triggered, they come to investigate," Greg said. "A helicopter gunship arrives first, followed by a Blackhawk packed with our SEAL friends. Time to introduce you to our Mr. Devlin," he added. "If he's receiving."

Greg tapped on the door to the Devlins' bedroom. "Mr. Devlin, it's Greg," he called out. "Got some people to introduce."

"Enter, Inspector," a male voice replied.

The Devlins were sitting on the bed holding hands. Dylan was wearing boxer shorts and a T-shirt; his left ankle was bandaged.

As soon as Winter got a close look at the killer, he was sure that Dylan's smile, carrot-colored hair, and pale green eyes made him seem harmless to his victims until it was way too late. Dylan Devlin looked about as dangerous as a week-old puppy. Mrs. Devlin had changed into something casual. She didn't look directly at the deputies, keeping her eyes fixed on the bedspread. She didn't seem exactly displeased that the marshals had interrupted them, but their presence seemingly held no interest for her.

"This is the first face-to-face we've had in eighteen days. Lots to catch up on," Devlin told them.

"I can imagine," Greg replied. "I wanted to take a second to introduce you to the new additions to the detail, Deputies Massey and Martinez."

"Pleased to meet you both," Dylan said, "and welcome aboard."

He focused on each deputy in turn.

"We'll let you and Mrs. Devlin get back to your discussion," Greg said.

"Call her Sean. My wife is far too young and lovely to be referred to as *Mrs.* And, please, call me Dylan. I insist."

Sean Devlin nodded absently. She turned her gaze for the first time and met Winter's eyes for a fleeting moment, her honey-colored eyes communicating nothing at all.

Party's over, lady, Winter thought. *And here's the bill.*

After they left the Devlins' bedroom and were back in the living room Greg turned once more to Winter and Martinez. "Always keep in mind that Dylan Devlin is a professional—a psychopath who can listen to Mozart while dismembering a body in a bathtub and eating potato chips. A badly sprained ankle and some busted ribs have slowed him down, but he'll be mobile soon enough. There's always a possibility he might decide that life on the run is preferable to showing up in court and exposing himself to the possibility that another stone killer like himself will take him out."

"So Mrs. Devlin is here as an anchor," Winter said.

Greg shrugged. "The A.G. wants him to be content."

"Ain't domestic bliss wonderful," Martinez said.

Winter realized suddenly what being in Devlin's room reminded him of. The reptile house at the Audubon Zoo.

12

There was very little talk during dinner, because the food was too good. Jet ladled rich, dark gumbo into deep bowls half-filled with steamed rice. There were loaves of broiled-to-a-crunch French bread, the center wet with garlic butter, and a salad that had a distinctive citrus twang. Compliments flew from the deputies.

A large black cat rubbed against Winter's leg. It peered up at him with fluid golden eyes and tilted his head, requesting a crumb from the table.

"Midnight!" Jet roared as she swooped up the animal in a well-practiced motion. "Let these people eat in peace."

She crossed the room and thrust the feline out the back door. The cat stood on the porch and stared in through the screen. "That cat's always messin' with something. Midnight's not much company, but some's better than none. I could say the same thing about my last husband," Jet added.

After the meal was over, Greg helped Jet clear the plates. Then he sat back down and got serious. "What we do here is about prevention, about keeping someone safe from being a target. That's WITSEC. Winter here is accustomed to staying in motion, handing out summonses, escorting prisoners hither and yon, and hunting down fugitives. Two different worlds."

"I hope you don't get bored, Winter," Forsythe said, a sharpness to his voice.

"I'm sure I won't find this boring."

"Tampa." Dixon shook his head. "Most thrilling fifteen seconds ever filmed. Three methed-up hit men firing Uzis. And—"

"Look," Winter interrupted. "Tampa was a long time ago. I'd really rather—"

"Want to know all there is to know about Winter?" Greg cut in. "No better friend and no worse enemy. What more does any of us here need to know?"

Jet passed them, carrying a bowl through the swinging door into the dining room. Winter caught a glimpse of the table as the door closed. The Devlins sat facing each other across the polished walnut, again holding hands. Jet opened the door by pushing it with her hip, turned and reentered the kitchen carrying an empty pitcher. Winter glimpsed the hands again, joined in the center of the table.

"Winter is a scholar. Got a master's degree from Sewanee. Taught at private high schools. What was it you taught? Poetry?"

There was a muffled burst of laughter from the dining room. Winter wondered what the Devlins found so funny.

"Literature," Winter told the marshals.

Martinez pushed her chair back and stood. "I'm going to catch a nap before my shift."

Yet another happy burst of laughter from the dining room. Winter wondered what sort of jokes a killer told his wife to entertain her. In his experience, a woman who could be in love with someone who had forfeited his soul probably had denial down to a religion.

13

Winter's dream might have been complex and rambling, but all he remembered of it when he awoke was how it ended. He was in a house, in a bed with Eleanor. They were very young. Rush, who technically shouldn't have been there at all, was sitting on the bed staring angelically at Winter and his mother. He talked about how wonderful it was to be able to see again and how great it was having his mother back, due to a time machine's reversing everything bad that happened the day their plane crashed. When something touched his shoulder, Winter jerked awake to find that Greg, lit by the yellow light bleeding in from the bathroom, was staring down at him. Winter sat bolt upright, and Greg jumped back reflexively, putting his hands up as if to protect himself.

"Your turn on deck," Greg said as he dropped down on his own bed, yawning.

Winter swung his legs off the bed and planted his feet on the carpet.

The roar of the surf drowned out every sound past the railing, ten feet beyond the wicker chair that Winter had backed up against the house, in the shadows. He had set the 9-mm Heckler & Koch MP5 machine pistol on the table beside the chair. *Constant motion,* he thought, watching the froth as the water gobbled up the shoreline. Sharks moving from birth to death, octopuses slithering from rock to rock—monsters galore, always moving in search of food. He remembered how Rush had always worn tennis shoes in the surf after he had once stepped barefoot on a crab.

The creak of the front door opening had the impact of a sudden slap. Winter sat upright, reached for the H&K, and placed the gun in his lap. Martinez stepped out, nodded at Winter, then opened the door to let Mrs. Devlin come outside.

Sean Devlin carried a cup of coffee in both hands as she moved to the porch rail. She stared out at the ocean, set her cup on the railing, zipped up her canvas jacket, and flipped up the collar. Then she lifted the cup and took a sip. Martinez crossed her arms against the chill.

"You can go back inside," Sean Devlin told her. "You're cold."

"No can do," Martinez replied cheerfully.

"He's right there," Sean said. She tilted her head toward Winter. "How many guards do I need? Does one always have to be a woman?"

"Not necessarily," Martinez said.

"Go back inside," Winter told Martinez.

Martinez looked uncertain. "Okay, Winter, I'll be in the security room."

Winter held up his walkie-talkie, then clipped it back on his belt. "If I need anything, I'll call," he promised.

Martinez went back inside, leaving Winter to watch over Sean.

She seemed somehow sad standing at the banister for a silent five minutes as she stared out at the waves, sipping coffee like she was the only soul for miles. When the cook's cat leaped up onto the rail beside her she gasped, knocking her cup over the rail, where it landed soundlessly in the sand. She laughed, reached out tentatively, and touched the cat's head with her fingertips. The cat nuzzled against her and she rubbed it behind the ears. "Well, you like that? What's your name?" she asked the animal.

"Midnight," Winter volunteered.

"Male or female?" She didn't turn her head a fraction of an inch toward Winter.

"I think Mrs. Washington called Midnight a him."

"I didn't know her last name. She told me to call her Jet." As she stroked the cat's head, it purred audibly and pressed against her hand. "You are a sweet boy, aren't you, Midnight?"

Winter scanned the beach in both directions.

"My mother thought dogs were unruly." Sean Devlin spoke as if to herself. "She let me have a cat, thought they were less likely to be disruptive. I called her Punkin. She ran away and never came back. What do you suppose cats think about?"

Winter felt less like carrying on the cat conversation than having a tooth pulled. "Probably think about where to get nine more lives," he replied.

She laughed. "You suppose?"

Eleanor had been allergic to cats. Winter saw them as sneaky and untrustworthy, letting you pet them, then suddenly turning their claws and teeth on you. With dogs you knew what was up most of the time.

Midnight promptly jumped down and trotted away. "You ever have a cat?"

"I don't recall any."

She turned and leaned against the railing. "Do you have children, Deputy Massey?"

He twisted his wedding band and wished he had left it at home. She was staring at it. "One, a son."

"How old is he?"

"Twelve on Sunday."

"Being a deputy, doing this, I suppose you are away for long stretches."

"Sometimes."

"I guess you're a federal agent, not technically a policeman?"

"More cop than agent," he replied.

"It must be hard on your wife."

Winter didn't want the conversation to go any farther down the personal path. Maybe she was a nice enough woman, but being the wife of a criminal put her squarely on the other side of the wall. "I don't imagine anyone enjoys being separated from those they care for."

Sean turned abruptly and started down the steps.

Winter stood. "Hey, where are you going?"

She bent down, held up the cup she had dropped and placed it on the floor beneath the railing. He relaxed, fractionally.

"I'd like a walk on the beach, get my feet wet in the surf. Is that possible?"

"If I accompany you." He lifted the MP5 and slipped the strap over his shoulder.

The radio was a two-way, low-frequency system very much like the walkie-talkies that mothers bought to remain in contact with their children in a mall. It had been selected because the frequency was likely to be overlooked by any eavesdropper searching for professional bands. He pressed the microphone button. "S-one, W.M. and P-two proceeding south on the sand."

"What's all that mean?" Sean asked.

"S-one is control in the security room, W.M. is me, Winter Massey, and you are P-two. Cross is out here, too, and now he knows to expect us."

"Why P and not D for Devlin?"

"Package. That is anyone we are watching. It's—"

"SCJ?"

"Sorry?"

"Standard cop jargon?"

"*Want company, W.M.?*" Martinez called out over the radio.

"Negative that. Visibility's a solid ten. I'll stay in sight."

Winter walked on the shore side of her, slightly higher

up the slope. As they walked, his eyes darted constantly, scanning the ocean, the beach, the tops of the dunes.

Sean stopped, lifted each foot, removed her sandals, and held them by their back straps. "God, I hate the feeling of sand in my shoes," she said.

He didn't respond.

"You ever been to South America?" she asked out of the blue.

"Fugitive recovery in Colombia and Costa Rica. Never been for pleasure. Don't speak Spanish very well."

"I was just in Argentina looking at ranch land. I liked South America okay. Dylan loves the idea of living in Argentina, but I'm not so sure. Land is cheap, but it's so volatile economically and politically."

Winter visualized the scenario. Devlin commits a few murders for money, gets caught, and turns on his employers. Then, after the trial is over and everybody is in prison, he and his princess relocate to Argentina. Historically speaking, Argentines didn't make moral judgments on things like multiple murder. "I'm sure you'll love living there." *Maybe Adolph Eichmann's house is vacant. Or you could try the old Mengele place in Paraguay, or was it Bolivia?*

"Your son. What's his name?"

"Rush."

"Winter and Rush are both unusual names."

"I suppose." Winter could have explained the origins of his and Rush's names, but he wasn't being paid to socialize. She said something else but Winter didn't hear it— something had caught his attention. The texture of the beach ahead had been physically altered, slightly churned.

Winter grabbed Sean's shoulder, planning to press her to the ground where she would be a slimmer target as he flipped off the H&K's safety and put his finger inside the guard. The second he gripped her shoulder, however, she

shifted her weight, grabbed his hand off her shoulder, pivoted, and forced her narrow knee straight up into Winter's
testicles with perfect accuracy and surprising force.

His vision filled with brilliant yellow light and fireworks; three distinct booming reports echoed inside his
skull. The explosions were real enough. When her knee
had struck home, his finger was on the trigger. The gun in
his hand had fired a three-shot burst into the air. Without
thinking, Winter used his body weight to pin her down.
"Freeze!" he snarled as he aimed the barrel at the place
where the tracks went up over the dune.

"Get off me!" Sean yelled.

"*Shots fired!*" Cross's voice called over the radio.

"*What was that?*" Martinez's voice crackled over the radio. "*Winter!*"

Winter keyed the microphone and managed to say,
"We've got company."

"*You under fire, Win?*" Greg's voice demanded.

"Negative, accidental discharge. But at least two sets of
footprints coming in from the ocean. I'm a hundred yards
north."

Sean stopped trying to wriggle free. Winter growled,
"Lie still!" He couldn't regulate his breathing, the pain between his legs was overwhelming. His stomach seemed
intent on giving up Jet's gumbo.

Two figures bolted, sprinting over the dune away from
Winter and his charge. He aimed at them, following their
flight with the barrel. Both looked like divers in skintight
wet suits, carrying bundles in their arms as they fled.

The security lights mounted in the trees sprang to life,
making it high noon on the beach all the way from the
house.

Sean Devlin froze under him like something dead.

Winter called for the pair to halt, but either they
couldn't hear him or didn't plan to stop. He fired a warn-

ing burst wide of the running figures, spraying sand. They fell forward, into the shadow of the dunes.

Martinez was first out the door as three deputies rushed from the house. Cross fell in behind her; Beck bringing up the rear. In the headset Winter heard Greg shout orders for Forsythe and Dixon to stay with the package. As they closed, Winter kept the subjects covered while watching the dunes to his left for a possible third man.

"Cross, secure my left flank!" Winter shouted into his radio. In the excitement, the initialisms were forgotten.

Cross turned instantly and went up over the dunes with his M16 before him; his rifle's barrel leading the way. As Martinez approached, Winter signaled her to stop. She dropped to her knees beside him. "You all right?" Her eyes were wide with excitement.

It was painful to stand.

Cross's voice came through Winter's ear piece, *"The dunes are clear, Massey. Hold your fire, I'm coming in."*

"Martinez, get the package home," Winter told her.

"I'm really sorry—" Sean began.

"Get her out of here, now!" Winter snapped as Greg ran toward them from the house. "Greg, can you cover Martinez and P-two—coming your way now?"

"Affirmative," Greg's voice came over the radio.

Cross came over the dunes dragging a wool blanket behind him.

The two women hurried toward the house, looking back frequently over their shoulders. Martinez had the look of a dog that had been pulled away from killed game.

Greg, carrying a shotgun, came running up wearing a T-shirt, khakis, and no shoes. He had a bandolier of twelve-gauge shells strung across his chest like a Wild West bandit. "You two, up on your knees, hands where we can see them!" he yelled out.

As the deputies advanced on the sprawled figures, it

became obvious that instead of two scuba-diving assassins, they had captured a naked couple. The woman had dropped her clothes in the sand when Winter fired. The man clutched what appeared to be wadded-up fatigues.

Winter thought about curling up in the sand like a fetus and staying there motionless for a while. A low hollow roar of pain seemed to run from the base of his spine through his testes and up to his lungs.

Cross held up a ripped-open condom package. "This was on the blanket."

"Damn," Greg said, laughing. "Winter, you shot at these people for *screwing*?"

"I didn't know what they were doing," Winter managed to say.

"Better safe than sorry, Inspector," Cross said. "Maybe he was planning to knock Massey over the head with his weapon after he finished using it on her. Maybe the condom was so he wouldn't leave a prick print."

The tension was dissipating rapidly. Winter almost laughed himself. He was never going to hear the end of this one.

"You two, stand up! Empty hands on your heads, and turn around slowly!" Greg bellowed. They scrambled to their feet and turned.

"Aw, that's mean," Cross said, trying not to snicker.

"Gotta do this by the book," Greg said.

"*The Joy of Sex?*" Cross shot back.

An Apache gunship, probably flying night maneuvers nearby when the alarm was sounded, thundered in from out of the darkness, stopped on a dime, and hung above the beach fifty yards south of them. Greg signaled the pilot that he had things under control. The chopper tilted, pivoted, and slid out over the water, shining its blinding spotlight on the scene below as it passed by. Satisfied the situation was under control, the pilot banked the chopper and flew off west.

Greg said, "Looks like a pair of swabbies from the other side. Let's keep a straight face, make sure we make an impression."

He lifted the man's dog tags and glared at him. Winter and Cross relaxed, lowering the muzzles of their weapons.

"What the hell are you two doing here?" Nations growled.

"Navy, sir! Ensign Signalman Lawrence Tacket, sir!"

"Ensign—" the woman started.

"I don't give a damn what your names are! What I asked was what the hell you are doing over here." He scooped the clothes up and searched the pockets. He dropped a sealed condom on the sand, along with some change and a pocketknife. He opened a wallet and checked its contents.

"We were just out for a walk," Ensign Tacket offered.

"And the wind tore your uniforms off?"

Tacket was a muscular young man and he stayed at full attention, his eyes ahead as if a drill sergeant was on a parade ground inspecting him. The young woman was shivering in the evening chill, her teeth chattering violently. Neither could have been more than eighteen or nineteen years old. The naked woman suddenly giggled nervously. "Can I cover up, please?" she pleaded.

Greg allowed his eyes to drop down below Tacket's waist, then shook his head. "Remove that condom, Ensign. And don't drop it on my beach."

"Please," she repeated.

"Cross, give the lady her clothes."

Cross scooped up the woman's shirt and pants, checked them, and tossed them to her. She turned to one side and slipped them on.

The ensign reached down, peeled off the condom, and hid it in his large fist.

"Okay, you two. You're damned lucky my man didn't kill you both. The admiral's wife got an eyeful, and you'll be fortunate indeed if she doesn't ask her husband to skin you two alive. Next time, if you want to play 'punch the monkey,' do it on your side of the island," Greg said.

The woman giggled again.

"Don't ever let me catch you on this side of this island again. Go! Run!" They started to go up over the dunes but Greg thundered, "All the way around! Stay the hell out of my trees!"

Winter turned and walked toward the house like a man with a broken foot. It was sobering to realize that if the two ensigns had come straight over the hill in the dark at a dead run, he might have killed them. Winter doubted Greg would make an official complaint. It was a good story that would be spoiled if Nations had to end it with the fact that he caused two kids to be busted out of the service, probably their only tickets out of otherwise bleak futures.

Greg fell into step beside him. "What happened to you?"

"What do you mean?"

"You're walking like somebody pounded sand up your butt."

"Strained a groin muscle, I guess."

The security lights died and it was night again.

Martinez stood waiting on the porch with one hand on the doorknob. "Winter, Mrs. Devlin is really sorry about kneeing you in your noogies. She thought you were making an advance . . . of a sexual nature."

"Guess there's more than one way to pull a groin muscle," Greg said, grinning.

"Forget it," Winter muttered. He was certain he would never again produce another ounce of semen with anything swimming in it.

Martinez rolled her eyes and went inside, laughing. Greg followed, and Cross strolled off down the beach, still snickering.

Winter slumped in the rocking chair. Midnight bumped

against his leg. A few minutes later, Jet came out and handed Winter an ice pack.

"Mr. Greg said you might want this for your pulled muscle."

When Jet went back into the house, Winter clearly heard several people whooping with laughter.

He decided that for the remaining time on the island, whenever the deputies thought about him, the Tampa incident would no longer be the first thing that sprang to mind. He put the bag between his legs. It helped.

14 | Atlanta, Georgia
Monday

The guard stared out through the bulletproof glass at the attorney as though the latter were a thief come to steal the gold out of his mouth. The man before him wore a bedraggled hairpiece. Bertran Stern had a nose like a parrot's beak and sad eyes. He was stoop-shouldered and his suit coat hung on his lanky frame like a drape. Liver spots dotted the hand with which he pressed his driver's license through the slot.

"Here to see Sam Manelli," Bertran said.

"You his attorney?"

"I am."

"Bertran Stern?" the guard read. He looked back up and again at the license, comparing the picture against the real thing.

Stern nodded once.

"From New Orleans?" the guard said as he inspected the Louisiana license.

"Yes."

"Manelli had another attorney here yesterday."

"Mr. Manelli has several legal representatives. I am his

private counsel." Stern exhaled heavily. The guards always asked the same questions. He supposed it was some form of harassment, but he didn't care. He was already thinking about the trip back home, knowing he would be resummoned as soon as he settled in. He had never liked traveling and was terrified of airplanes. But he had been flying back and forth from New Orleans, ferrying messages between Johnny Russo and Sam, since the mobster's arrest two weeks earlier. Johnny had been running Sam's crime empire for five years and doing a pretty good job as far as Bertran could tell. Sam seemed pleased with what Johnny was telling the attorney and Johnny liked the messages he got back.

After a few long minutes the solid steel door slid open. A female guard led Bertran to the exercise yard reserved for maximum security prisoners.

Sam was in his early seventies but looked a decade younger. The gangster was a swarthy man, five-six, one hundred and ninety pounds, with jowls like a bulldog. His full head of gray hair was slicked neatly back, which accentuated his square skull. His meaty hands had untanned places where he usually wore his rings, and his nails were still shiny from his last manicure. He was dressed in an orange jumpsuit and plastic flip-flops and had a thirty-dollar cigar clenched between his teeth. He came at Bertran Stern like he was going to stick a shiv into his heart, his intense blue eyes ablaze.

"Follow me!" he growled. Bertran followed.

Sam headed for a concrete picnic table under a small metal shelter, but before they arrived Sam grabbed the attorney's elbow and propelled him to an exposed table standing alone in the yard.

Sam told Bertran to sit on the bench seat and planted himself on the tabletop so he could look down on him, for the psychological edge. In Bert's mind, Sam was ten feet tall.

"Music would be good," Sam said.

"Oh, right." Stern took a small radio out of his briefcase and turned it on to a classical station. "I guess I have jet lag. I'm getting a little old for this running back and forth."

"You want to swap complaints?" Sam said. "I got a list long as a Jew's nose."

"No, of course not." Bertran was Jewish.

"You don't want to come here no more, is that it?"

"I like coming here, Sam." Bertran's fingers were trembling. "To see you."

Manelli clenched the cigar in the side of his mouth and spoke around it so no one could read his lips, even with binoculars, which the feds would do.

"How's my boy doing?"

"He says business is normal—nothing down at all. He has some concerns if you remain here long, but he says he'll worry about that when he has to."

"You think he's doing good—on the level?"

"He wouldn't say something unless it was on the square."

"And he ain't dumb."

"I haven't seen any evidence of it." *There are far worse things than being dumb.*

"Okay. What about the other thing?" Sam asked, pleased at Bert's take on Johnny.

"The guy? Johnny says it's just a matter of time until it's handled. Things are moving."

"And as soon as it's done, I'm outta here?"

"No one to talk, no evidence but the guy's word. Yes, it's certain."

"What about her?" Manelli said.

Stern didn't want to give Manelli bad news, but he had no choice. "She was supposed to be back in the country Saturday," the attorney said carefully. "Johnny was at the airport personally and he said she didn't come out of the terminal and never showed up at her house. He's got someone checking there periodically, but Johnny thinks she got intercepted by the cops and might be with *him* someplace."

Manelli growled, "I want her waiting for me when I get out of here. Tell Johnny I said that better be the way it is."

The mobster's eyes grew hard, his lips rigid with fury. "I got three million reasons why they better get it done. If it don't get done, heads will boil. Make sure the old man knows that if the rat squeaks, history or not, I ain't gonna like it a lot. I want that Mick bastard in pieces so small a skinny crab would have to eat a dozen to keep his stomach from growling."

Stern nodded solemnly.

"You just remember you said I'd be out in a few days, and here I sit two weeks later."

"When I said that, I didn't know what they had behind the charges, Sam." Bertran's palms felt clammy.

"By the way, how's your grandbabies doing?" Sam asked.

Bertran smiled nervously and told Sam they were all fine. Over the forty years they had been doing business, Sam had threatened his family so many times he'd lost count. But no matter how many times he had heard the question, its impact had never lessened. Bertran Stern knew that Sam would not hesitate before having Johnny Russo take a hammer to a child, nor did he doubt that Russo would welcome doing it for him.

15 | **Rook Island, North Carolina**

Twenty minutes before the helicopter landed, Greg told the deputies on duty that it was on its way, bringing a physician to the island. Forsythe was up on the water tank. The waist-high safety rail around the tank was made of steel plate. His weapon was a tricked-out .308-caliber assault rifle with a thicker-than-normal barrel, a thirty-shot magazine, and a scope. The mirrored sunglasses he wore gave him a decidedly sinister appearance.

The helicopter landed, and a casually dressed man climbed down and strode toward the house carrying a black leather bag. Winter led the doctor inside, where he and his bag were searched. Greg asked Winter to escort the doctor to Dylan's room and remain with him.

Though it was open, Winter knocked at the door. Sean Devlin was seated in an armchair, reading. Winter had not seen her since their encounter the night before. She looked up at him with amusement in her eyes.

"Ah," Dylan said, seeing them. "Here to make me whole again."

The doctor was all business. He moved straight to the bed and placed his bag on the mattress.

"You put weight on this yet?" He nodded at Devlin's ankle.

"Some," Dylan said.

The doctor removed the bandage, moved the foot around. "That hurt?"

"No."

"That?"

"No."

"Lose the shirt."

"What, no foreplay?" Dylan said. "You know what foreplay is where I come from?"

The doctor said, "A six-pack?"

"'Get in the truck, bitch.'" Dylan laughed. "But 'a six-pack' works for me."

Sean frowned at the joke.

The doctor cut the tape and bandages away from Dylan's ribs, exposing a yellow bruise the size of a dinner plate. He asked Dylan to stand and walk around the room.

Sean closed her book and watched.

"No pain?" the doctor asked.

Dylan slapped his rib cage hard, then hopped up and down on his unwrapped foot. "Good as new," he bragged.

"You have an impressive threshold for pain. Those ribs need more time before you go slapping them, so take a few days. Use the crutches if you need to. Any pain medication?"

"I have some, but I can control pain without medication."

Dylan looked at Winter and winked. "I can start taking walks on the beach now to protect you from my wife."

Sean opened her book and looked down, perhaps embarrassed.

Winter stared flatly at Dylan, ignoring the killer's mocking grin.

While Winter and Greg were watching the helicopter carry the doctor away and Winter was wishing he was a passenger on it heading home, the Devlins appeared on the porch. Martinez came around the side of the building and stopped in the sand. Dylan reached up, stretched, and inhaled noisily.

"Gentlemen, my wife and I wish to take a leisurely stroll on the beach," he announced. "Perhaps Deputy Massey would like to accompany us. If he feels up to walking, that is."

Greg lifted his radio and asked Forsythe for an all-clear. From the water tower, Forsythe leaned the rifle against the rail before him and scanned the water, the sand, and the tree line with his binoculars, then radioed back that the turf was secure.

"Okay, Mr. and Mrs. Devlin, the beach is all yours. Winter, grab a Colt and tag along."

Winter went into the house and got an AR-15 carbine

from the locker in the security room. As he returned, Dylan was saying, "My wife is getting as dark as a Spic. Pretty soon she'll be chattering Spanish at her." He indicated Martinez.

Martinez raised an eyebrow but otherwise didn't react.

"Perhaps it *is* too bright for a walk," Sean said. Her cheeks were flushed pink. "Maybe later would be better. When the sun isn't so strong."

Dylan agreed easily. "An evening walk, then. I, on the other hand, need some rays."

Winter figured Sean didn't want to displease Dylan. It looked to Winter that the latter exercised control by undermining his wife's confidence. Wouldn't be the first husband who operated that way. His own father had done the same to his mother.

Winter and Dylan started down the beach side by side. "Where was it my wife racked you? On the beach, I mean."

Winter pointed at the spot at the dune's edge where the sand was still churned up. "About there. Maybe she'll reenact it with you."

"I know who you are, Massey. I overheard Cross and Dixon talking about a little square dance in Florida a few years back with three Latino gun boys. They seem to think you're some sort of a handgun god."

"I never cared for dancing," he said laconically.

"Must have been exciting. Facing those machine guns, and you with only a little pistol. The marshal and the outlaws in a real old-fashioned shoot-out. I bet your blood was up—facing death, looking it in the eyes, and walking out alive. Nothing like it. No one who hasn't been there can understand being tested in the crucible and coming out in one piece."

"A man would really have to be wired wrong to enjoy a thing like that," Winter said dismissively.

"The elation after the kill. The adrenaline rush. Don't

shit me, Massey, you felt that euphoria. We have that in common, you and I. But where I never felt the slightest pang of guilt, I bet it nearly ate you alive."

Winter had indeed felt that euphoria. But the shoot-out in Tampa had been followed by nausea, cold sweats, and nightmares. "I sure as hell didn't kill because some-one was writing me a check for it," he said, betraying his emotions.

"Don't be so sanctimonious. They pay you, Deputy. I just get fatter checks."

"Different *theys*. And my they doesn't want me to kill anybody."

"Do you think about your own death, Massey?"

"Some."

"Are you afraid to die?"

"Not looking forward to it." Winter could feel his blood rising and wished Devlin would get off the subject.

"How would you go, given a choice? Heart attack in bed? Bullet in the brain? Swan-diving into an active vol-cano?"

"I doubt I'll get to choose. Can we change the subject?"

"Man like you could be anything, and yet this is what you chose." Dylan persisted, savoring Winter's obvious discomfort. "All the things you could have had, and you're walking down the beach, putting your life on the line for what, sixty thousand a year? I have a beautiful, rich wife who thinks I hung the moon, but I never touched a penny of hers because I make a lot of money. A *lot* of money."

"I don't go hungry. I can drive only one car at a time, and I have a good medical plan with dental."

"You're a fucking *security guard*, Massey," Dylan snarled. "You know what my favorite thing is?"

"I don't care."

Devlin stared down at the AR-15 in Winter's hand. "It's taking a target's weapon away and giving him the business end of it. Gun, knife, once it was a baseball bat. The expression on their faces is always worth the extra effort. It's the ultimate humiliation, like pissing on them—a caveman high."

"Can I be totally honest with you, Devlin?"

"I'd welcome it."

"I like chasing down bad guys. The sense of satisfaction I get when I put human garbage—like, say, a cold-blooded murderer—in chains is priceless. Hell, I'd do it for free if they didn't pay me to."

"That so? So tell me one thing."

"Yeah?"

"What's it feel like to have your balls bashed in by a woman?"

"About half as painful as talking to you."

Dylan threw his head back and laughed. "That's a good one! You're a piece of work, Massey." He turned back toward the house, shaking his head. "And I had hoped we could be pals."

"Now, *that's* a good one," Winter said flatly.

When they returned, Sean was in a rocking chair on the porch with the cat in her lap, rubbing its head. Winter stopped beside Martinez at the railing. When Dylan reached down to rub it, Midnight hissed, clawed his hand, and ran off.

Sean took Dylan's hand and inspected the scratches. "He seemed so friendly," she said softly.

"Things aren't always as they seem," her husband snapped. He sat in the chair beside her, rubbing the bloodied hand against his pants. "Nine lives. Living out here with no cars, no other cats or dogs, that little black shitter could die of old age with eight of those still tucked away in a celestial savings account." He stroked his wife's hand, looked up at Winter, and smiled. "Unless he does something dumb."

16

Winter watched as Angela Martinez concentrated on the puzzle in front of her, working as methodically as a jeweler checking a consignment of diamonds. She rubbed each piece of the anodized steel with a Teflon-saturated cloth and then set it on the newspaper. When she was finished putting it back together, the puzzle revealed itself as a Glock pistol. Forty-caliber shells were lined up at attention like soldiers. One by one she inserted the rounds into the mouth of the magazine, then slapped the back of it against her palm to seat the bullets. She jacked the receiver, fed the chamber, removed the magazine to add a round, and slammed the magazine home. Satisfied, she put the gun into her hip holster and snapped the thumb-release strap.

"Think it'll shoot now?" Cross asked.

"Better than yours."

"In a million years you couldn't outshoot me."

"Give me a break, Cross. There's nothing you can do that I can't do faster and better."

"Sexual discrimination suits filed by crybaby dykes and bleeding-heart judges have screwed up everything by trying to make all of us equal. Well, that's just paper equality, it can't make women physically equal to men. Strength and stamina can't be altered by court rulings."

"You think you're stronger than me?" Martinez said, snickering. "Twenty dollars says I can take you arm wrestling," she told Cross calmly.

"You have twenty dollars, Cross?"

Beck reached into his wallet and tossed a twenty onto

the center of the table. "Arm-wrestling contest? I'm in. Even odds?"

"Whatever you can stand to lose," Martinez told him.

"Who's covering your losses?" Cross asked.

"There won't be any," she said with total confidence.

Five minutes later the kitchen was crowded and there was a heap of money in the center of the table. When Cross and Martinez squared off, all the money was on Cross.

Jet laid a ten down and pressed it flat. "On him to win."

"Traitor," Martinez said.

"Sorry. I'm a woman, but I've never been called a stupid one."

The cat fled the room and Dylan was suddenly standing in the doorway.

"Winter, you want in?" Greg asked, ignoring Devlin.

"I don't gamble," Winter said. He figured Martinez was going to get creamed and he didn't want to waste money, or take any of hers.

Dylan walked over to the table and thumped a hundred dollar bill down. "On Deputy Cross," he said. "Can you cover this, *señorita?*" He winked. "Or maybe we can just work out some kind of a trade."

Martinez stared down at the bill and then at Winter. He could see her confidence faltering.

"On Martinez to win, okay?" he said, taking his wallet out. He took out five twenties and tossed them near the pile.

"Sean, honey," Devlin called out cheerfully. "Come watch your deputy get his noogies kicked in again."

Sean came into the room and stood near the stove. Cross put his elbow on the table. Martinez slipped off her jacket.

"You can take off your shirt, too," Cross told her. "Might distract me."

Martinez planted her elbow on the table and straightened her forearm.

"What little hands you have, my dear," Cross crooned, as he took her hand in his. "You want to stand up and lean in to get some leverage?"

Greg covered their hands with his. "When I let go, it begins." He looked at Martinez. "Anybody wants to back out, do it now. There's a lot of money on the table."

Greg counted down from three, then let go, and for a second Martinez's arm sank slowly back toward the table. Her face contorted. Cross seemed to be enjoying himself. When Martinez's arm was almost touching the surface of the table, Cross tilted his head and looked at her quizzically. Martinez smiled and started moving her opponent's arm back up to center.

Cross started to sweat. He clenched his teeth, and the veins in his temples began to bulge.

"I know how you're feeling, Cross," Martinez said. "It's like the heavens are all out of balance and your little Super Boy world is about to collapse around you. Welcome to Club Humiliation, you smug male bastard." She smiled as she inched Cross's hand back toward the surface. He was giving it everything he had.

"You want to stand up, for leverage?" she mocked. Cross's hand hit the table hard. He sat there, bewildered.

"Again, double or nothing?" she asked. "Left hands?"

The room was silent.

Martinez stacked the bills tidily and picked them up. She took Devlin's C-note and Winter's twenties and handed them to Winter.

"How the hell did you do that?" Dylan asked Martinez, incredulous.

"Black beans," she shot back.

Winter pocketed the cash and repeated something to Dylan that the killer himself had said earlier. "Things aren't always as they seem . . . darling."

"I thought you didn't gamble, Massey?" Devlin snapped back, his eyes smoldering.

Winter shrugged. "I don't."

Devlin pivoted on his heel and left the room. His wife stared into Winter's eyes for a long second, then smiled and followed Devlin out.

17 | **Tuesday**

Winter awoke to Greg tapping his shoulder.

"Time to get up and run. Mind some company this morning?"

"Of course not. You feeling a sudden urge to exercise?" Winter asked.

"Nah. You mind running armed this morning?"

Winter's mind snapped to full alert. "Aw, not Devlin."

"Not Devlin," Greg replied, smiling. "The Devlins."

"Tell you what I'll do. I'll jog with the Devlins if you'll get me home for Rush's birthday. Just one day. It means a lot to me, Greg."

"I'll consider how best to handle your request. See, I'd need someone to take your place for just a day or two and—"

Winter sat up. "Damn, my foot hurts. Maybe I shouldn't run this morning. You jog with the happy couple."

"Okay, okay I'll do it. Somehow I'll get you home."

When Winter arrived on the porch, Greg was leaning against a post, watching the sunrise. The Devlins were already on the sand, stretching. Winter had done his push-ups, crunches, and stretches before he left his room.

Since Monday, Winter had been running a course that took him from one tip of the island to the other. He ran south against the tree line, followed the bow of the beach north, then back. Ten laps was a nice run.

Winter stepped down onto the sand.

"I hear you're quite a runner," Dylan commented.

Winter didn't respond.

"Inspector Nations, didn't I hear you say something the other day about Winter competing in the Ironman? That the illustrious deputy finished in the top twenty twice. That's biking, swimming and running. Man's a triple threat."

"Y'all better get going," Greg told him curtly.

"What hasn't our deputy accomplished?" Dylan mocked. "I wouldn't be surprised if his turds came out shrink-wrapped in cellophane."

"Dylan!" Sean scolded. "That's crude."

Dylan's eyes registered the reprimand, but he didn't shift his gaze from Winter. "I'm sorry, dear. I get *crass* and *crude* mixed up. If I called the inspector there a jigaboo— would that be *crude* or *crass?* Sambo, *crude* or *cute?* Nigger, *crude* or *factual?*"

"Dylan?" she murmured placatingly. The color had drained from her cheeks.

"Darling, didn't anyone ever tell you that you shouldn't correct family in front of the help," Dylan told her, his voice icy. She looked away, embarrassed, perhaps angry.

Greg smiled. Winter knew that, under other circumstances, Devlin would have been sifting through the sand for his teeth. Winter swallowed his anger at Dylan's remarks.

"Best go on your run now, Win," Greg said. "Before the sun rises and sets Mr. Devlin there on fire."

It appeared to Winter that Devlin was trying to see how far he could push before someone took him on. The killer knew how valuable he was to the attorney general, and he knew he could push pretty hard before anyone would dare push back. Winter had seen it before, a criminal who had to admit to himself that he had turned into the one thing all criminals hated—a rat—then needed to take his self-loathing out on others.

They started running north along the surf.

Dylan was quiet for the first hundred yards. Then he said, "Your boy sure was touchy this morning. Probably not getting enough sleep. You keeping that buck awake?"

"You here to run or talk, Devlin?" Winter said.

"Here to run, ironman." Dylan sprinted ahead, showing off.

Winter stayed even with Sean. Her stride looked effortless; her arms and legs showed muscle definition from a pattern of exercise.

"We have a gym in the house," she said, as if reading Winter's mind. "Weights and Nautilus machines. Dylan works out and runs every day. He says staying in shape is the single most important thing there is. You get lazy, let the workouts slide, and everything slows down: stamina, strength, eye–hand coordination. Even your mental ability."

Winter managed a grunt.

"Winter—may I call you Winter?"

"Sure."

"I want to apologize for my husband's remarks. He's never been remotely like this before. He's on edge, and who can blame him, really?" She sounded as if she was almost trying to convince herself.

"You don't need to make excuses to me."

She stared ahead. "Dylan really isn't racist. He just—"

Winter had had enough. "No disrespect intended, ma'am, but I don't care what he was like before all this. We refer to the people we protect as packages, footballs, or units. The package's prejudices don't mean anything to us. An apology to Martinez or Greg won't make any difference, because they don't give a damn what Mr. Devlin thinks or says—just what he does. But as far as I can see, the idea that any of the deputies on this crew might get hurt trying to protect his life is an absurdity of biblical proportions."

The effect of Winter's words was immediate. Her lips tightened, and she lengthened her stride, pulled ahead of him, and caught up with her husband.

Winter watched her body as she ran. It was a thing to admire. He would have liked to leave them, but he had to make sure nobody appeared from out of the water or behind the dunes and blew Dylan's brains out.

Something like that, while erasing an impurity from the surface of the planet, wouldn't look good on Winter's record.

18

"Assistant U.S. Attorney Avery Whitehead from the New Orleans District is visiting us today, kids," Greg Nations announced at breakfast. "Let's look sharp."

When Jet came through the kitchen door, Winter caught sight of the Devlins at the dining room table. Sean Devlin's expression was unreadable, but she was not holding hands with her husband—nor was there any laughter. That seemed like a healthy development. He couldn't help but wonder if Sean might be taking a fresh look at the wisdom of her spousal choice.

An hour after breakfast, a Navy-version Hughes 500 landed and deposited Avery Whitehead and his assistant.

Whitehead struck Winter as being one more arrogant prick in an expensive suit who felt condescension was a God-given right.

Greg led them into the dining room, where he searched them and their briefcases. Afterward, Whitehead set up at the table like a grand inquisitor, his assistant at his right elbow. When Dylan Devlin entered the room, he sat across the table from the prosecutor. Winter and Dixon followed Greg out, leaving the three men alone.

Forty minutes after Whitehead's arrival, Sean came outside, sat down in a chair four feet from Winter's, and opened her laptop. Within a few seconds she was totally immersed in what she was doing. With her hands on the keyboard and her eyes closed, she seemed to contemplate, then type. Then she read what she'd typed and repeated the process. Winter watched her fingers, thinking how beautiful her hands were. There wasn't anything about Sean's appearance that wasn't pleasing to the eye.

When Jet's cat sauntered around the corner of the house and rubbed against Sean's ankle, she set the computer on the side table and lifted Midnight onto her lap. She reached into her pocket for a small plastic bag, took out a piece of bacon, and offered it to the cat, who sniffed it before turning his head away.

Winter could see enough of the computer screen to make out the form of what was there. Sean caught him staring and turned it toward her.

"I like poetry," he said.

"Do they teach poetry at police school?"

"You know the shortest poem in the history of literature?"

"No." Her eyebrows rose.

"Fleas. Adam had 'em."

She struggled not to smile. "You memorized all that? It's hardly 'The Rhyme of the Ancient Mariner.'"

Winter was fully twenty lines into that poem before she interrupted him. "You learned Coleridge in high school? That's like Frost—hardly Ginsberg."

Winter began reciting "Howl."

"Okay, now I feel foolish." She cocked her head. "And

you have me convinced that you aren't entirely one-dimensional. Tell me how you got interested in poetry."

"Before I went to police school I got a degree in American lit. I taught high school for four years before I decided police work was safer."

She studied him for a moment, then turned the laptop toward him so he could read it. "Okay, critique this."

Winter was sorry he had asked, figuring he would have to lie politely—until he started to read it. The lines contained powerful images. Winter wasn't easily impressed, but with amazing clarity, Sean had captured a child's relationship with a distant father. It struck a chord with Winter, and not just because of his own experience.

"It's very good," he told her after he had read it through a second time.

"That an honest assessment?" she asked suspiciously.

"Yes, it is. I'd like to read more. I really would. You have a gift."

She smiled. "Maybe I can print them out for you when I get to a printer."

"Maybe you can publish under your new name," he said.

She looked at him quizzically. "You mean under a pseudonym?"

"You'll get new identities after Dylan testifies and has served whatever time he ends up getting."

She turned off the computer and closed the top with a snap. "That may be what they told you, but it isn't like that. Why would we need new names?"

It was his turn to be confused. "He wouldn't live long using Devlin."

"What are you talking about?" she asked angrily.

He had never before seen her eyes filled with fire, and he had no idea why she was getting so upset with him for stating the obvious.

"A standard requirement in witness security dictates

that you can't have any contact with anyone you knew before you joined the program. You'll get new identities and move to a new place to start over. That's just how it works," he told her.

She smiled as though Winter was some poor, addled idiot who had just declared that candy bars had souls.

"You're quite mistaken, we'll be perfectly fine after he testifies."

"Mrs. Devlin, when a man commits twelve murders for profit and testifies against the man who hired him to do them, a name change *and* a rural Argentine address wouldn't hurt. The world is getting to be a smaller place every day."

"Murder? You said twelve murders?" Her hands trembled as she moved the cat to the floor gently, then picked up her laptop. She walked inside, letting the screen door slam behind her.

Winter followed as she strode into the dining room and pulled the door shut behind her. Was it possible that Sean imagined that her husband could testify against Sam Manelli and then go back to their previous lives as though nothing had happened? He took a seat in the living room and picked up a golf magazine.

Voices filtered through the closed dining room door—rising and falling—building in intensity. Winter couldn't make out what they were saying.

No more than a minute from the time she went in, Sean stormed out and strode down the hall to her bedroom. Thirty seconds later, Dylan followed her, shooting Winter a nasty look.

Winter stood. He could see Whitehead and his assistant in the dining room with their heads close together, talking in low tones, like conspirators. He could hear the Devlins' angry voices coming from their bedroom.

Greg hurried into the dining room. When he came

back out, he said to Winter, "Tell the pilot to start his engine. They're done."

Five minutes later, the helicopter rose and disappeared over the trees, taking Whitehead and his assistant with it.

Winter walked back into the house. Dylan was now yelling at Sean, and she was giving it right back to him. Greg stood listening in the hallway, hands on his hips.

"What started it?" Winter asked him.

"Whitehead told me you did," Greg answered.

"I made a comment to her about their getting new names after the trial, and I think it was the first Mrs. Devlin had heard of it. It was like she didn't know why they're here. That's not possible, is it? Think maybe she thought this was summer camp for psychopathic husbands?"

Greg shook his head. "The prosecutor is not pleased that she's upset. If she's upset, Dylan's upset, and he wants Devlin as calm as possible. Whitehead said that I obviously didn't make it clear enough to the team that there were to be no conversations about the behavior that put Devlin here."

"I didn't with *him*. You didn't say not to discuss that with his wife. You don't mean to tell me that nobody told her what he did?"

"Maybe we should start thinking about that security business real soon. Whitehead strongly hinted that he might mention his displeasure with both of us to the A.G."

The cat broke from the kitchen and made a run for the front of the house, territory Jet had banished him from entering.

The animal sat beside Winter, stared down the hall, and seemed to be listening to the Devlins' argument.

"Just be glad you're a cat," Winter said, wishing he hadn't spoken to Sean Devlin at all.

19

In the late afternoon, Winter took a longer than normal run, showered, and then napped until dinner. Beck, Martinez, Forsythe, Dixon, and Greg were gathered around the kitchen table. Martinez frowned at Winter when he joined them.

"Thanks a lot," she said sourly.

"You're welcome," Winter replied. "What was it I did for you?"

"While you slept," Greg said, "the safe-house politic changed dramatically, as did the living arrangements."

"I lost my bed," Martinez said sullenly.

"You can share mine," Beck offered.

"Screw you, Beck," she snapped. "And I don't mean that in a good way."

"Mr. D. failed in an all-out attempt to bring his rebellious wife back under his control using his extensive persuasive powers. Mrs. D. packed up and moved into the suite with Martinez, taking the bedroom," Greg told Winter.

"Exactly," Martinez said. "And that bed was heavenly."

"Into every cow pasture some rain must fall," Winter mused.

"Does anyone aside from Mr. D. give a damn if Mrs. D. moved out? I think it shows that there is hope for her yet," Dixon said.

"Bear, nobody has any desire to see Sean reunited with her creepy racist bastard husband," Martinez said. Jet entered from the dining room carrying a tray of food. "She's not hungry," the cook informed the deputies. "She's mad as hell. I don't know what all that man said to her, but it must have been a lulu."

Winter's shift had him walking the house's perimeter. He stood and watched Sean Devlin's figure as she moved back and forth behind the panes of her window. He thought about the poem she had shared with him and felt sorry that he had stirred up so much trouble—that he was responsible for bringing more unhappiness to this woman who seemed so refined and gentle for a psychopath's wife.

She didn't seem like just another criminal's wife who had made her bed for a large fee.

If she didn't want to stay with Devlin, that was good. The Devlins wouldn't be the first couple split by the reality of WITSEC. A lot of witnesses' wives, accustomed to living the high life, failed to see the allure of working in small-town Arizona, forever cut off from friends and family. Life in a trailer, driving a rusted-out station wagon, could put a real damper on marital bliss. In this case, he didn't think a loss of status was what troubled Sean Devlin.

Winter believed that the marshals service had owed Sean the real story before they deposited her on the island to pacify Dylan. Winter didn't give a tap-dancing damn who was pissed off because she had learned the truth.

The only problem was the potential negative impact on Greg's WITSEC career, maybe a black mark in Winter's file. It wasn't like he cared if he ever joined another WITSEC detail. He wanted nothing more than to go back home to his family and his nice, comfortable USMS satellite office.

20

The King Air 300 sat in the center of the cavernous hangar illuminated by a bank of quartz lights. Herman Hoffman surveyed the work in progress while the six members of his assault team stood nearby watching him. Even though he was worn out from the flight to the staging area, Herman took several minutes to study the craft's modifications, inspecting how the tubes and wires had been expertly rerouted. This was the level of craftsmanship he expected from his people, but he admired how rapidly they could accomplish their tasks and maintain the quality. When the trapdoor was closed, the belly of the plane would appear to be normal, but it would have a lot in common with military bombers.

"Perfection," he declared, clapping his hands together. The compliment was met with smiles. It was the first thing he had said since he walked into the hangar twenty minutes earlier. "As always."

He moved over to a line of folding tables and reviewed the hardware. As he passed the assembled articles, he touched and straightened here and there—a fastidious shopkeeper inspecting his merchandise in preparation for opening the doors to customers.

He ran his finger along a kilo block of Semtex. Moving to the next table, he hoisted up one of the sleek MP5-SD machine guns, admiring the balance, the noise suppressor. He selected a magazine from a stack of forty and pressed it into the opening, drew the bolt back, and released it. He flipped the safety off and set the selector switch to automatic. Using the laser-aiming device, he pointed the weapon at a fifty-gallon barrel, positioning the red dot on the target someone had taped to it. When he squeezed the trigger there was a sound very much like quails taking wing, accompanied by the tinkling of the empty brass shell casings as they landed on the concrete floor. Sand poured to the floor from the holes in the drum.

Herman handed the weapon to Ralph as though he was his caddy. "Please, carry on," Herman said, cheerfully.

Within seconds the hangar was filled with the sound of his men at work, which to Herman's ears was as comforting as classical music.

21 | Atlanta, Georgia

Sam Manelli had the patience of a python coiled in the shade. He sat on the edge of his mattress with his feet on the floor of his cell. It was cool enough that he had been tempted to drape the wool blanket over his shoulders, but he couldn't let anyone think of him as weak.

Sam had no regrets. Everything he had ever done was necessary to build and maintain his business interests. He had successfully defended his world from any and all comers, and he hadn't done it by showing compassion.

So much for his golden years of rest and relaxation. He had never been as focused on anything as he was on erasing Dylan Devlin from the face of the earth. The 3 million dollars Herman Hoffman had requested for taking Devlin out was chump change considering what was at stake. Sam would have given far more, and gladly. Devlin could steal from him the one thing Sam Manelli valued more than anything—his freedom.

Sam heard the sound of approaching footsteps and braced himself. A young guard with a blond crew cut stopped at the door and peered inside at him. Sam stared back, keeping his expression neutral. The guard took his hand out of his pocket and held out a small black object. Sam slipped from the bed, crossed to the bars, and took it.

"This is yours from midnight until two A.M.," the guard said in a whisper, even though the cells on either side of Sam were unoccupied. "It's totally safe to use."

Sam nodded. The guard walked away.

He sat on the cot, punched in the numbers, and pushed SEND. After two rings a familiar voice answered.

"It's me," Sam said in a low voice. "You sure this thing's clean?"

"Squeaky," Russo said. Sam didn't believe any electronic conversation was safe. He'd been speaking face-to-face and in code for so long he didn't know how to say anything incriminating.

"So, how's things?"

"I had a red thing leak dye in the washer ruined the gowns," said Johnny.

Sam's heart sped up. Someone was stealing. "Red thing leaking dye" was the code for red ink—someone skimming. Gown was high-dollar prostitution.

"I'm gonna bleach it out tonight."

"Is the old man cleaning the pool?" He was referring to Herman Hoffman.

"His boys are handling it. Soon as I know how it looks I'll let you know."

"Good."

"Can't wait to see you back home."

"You and me both," Sam replied grimly. He pressed the END button.

Johnny Russo was family by his marriage to Sam's niece, but Sam had known Johnny for all of the young man's thirty-nine years. He had stood as Johnny's godfather, and even though he wasn't a religious man, had taken that responsibility to heart. Johnny's father, Richie Russo, had been Sam's chief enforcer, a man he had been close to since his childhood. Richie had died in a warehouse fire when Johnny was ten. From that day on, Sam had sent Richie Russo's wife a nice monthly check and called it a pension. It was just a necessary business expense. He had genuinely cared about Richie, but Johnny had not made it into the son-he-never-had category.

When Johnny was fourteen, Sam had hired him to work at one of his amusement companies, beginning with odd jobs and granting him more responsibility as he grew older. Johnny had been a polite kid, a hard worker who never made the same mistake twice. Always smiling, always ready to show Sam that he wanted to learn more. Sam's father had trusted only Italians, but Sam had discovered that limited business. Sam had ways of determining who was trustworthy, who would keep the necessary secrets and remain loyal. "Family" was a relative term, and ethnic lineage didn't ensure omerta. Sam had a system of rewards and punishment, both of which had to remain certainties in an uncertain world.

Johnny ran the rackets effectively, but Sam had stayed on top of the business, making sure things ran smoothly under Johnny's care. The trust Sam had in the young man hadn't come easy. He had set a hundred traps over the years, hoping he wouldn't catch Johnny taking advantage of him, and, to his amazement and delight, he never had. Sam had rewarded Johnny by degrees, turning over more and more of his crime enterprise to his protégé, until he was competent enough to handle the day-to-day demands. From the start, Johnny had handled Sam's business and dealt with Sam's enemies like they were his own. Sometimes Johnny could get carried away with the violence, but a man's reputation was what kept people in line.

Sam paid millions each year to the people who would otherwise arrest him and to those who knew when there was an imminent threat from law enforcement. The feds had never found enough evidence on Sam to secure an in-

dictment, and the locals feared losing his largess. The authorities had snagged members of his upper-level management over the years, but between lawyers, friendly judges,
missing evidence, witnesses with failing memories, and
bribed or frightened jurors, most walked away relatively
unscathed. Those who went to jail did easy time, and Sam
saw to it that their families never went hungry.

Two years back, Sam had completely turned over the
day-to-day operations to Russo, advising him when things
started to slip. He knew that, regardless of who was in
charge, the business would never be what it had been in
his day. But there would be plenty to go around if Johnny
could hold off the ethnic gangs and freelance criminals.
As long as Sam was the gold backing Johnny's promises,
Russo was relatively safe. But alliances like the one with
Herman Hoffman that Sam, and his father before him,
had forged would end with Sam's passing, and it would be
up to Johnny to cut new deals and make his own allies in
order to hold on to the rackets.

What nobody except Sam and Johnny knew was that
two years before, a doctor had discovered that Sam had
cancer in a place nobody should get cancer. It had been
growing for a while, and taking it out was impossible. The
doctor, a man Sam owned, had explained it in simple
terms. The cancer was growing slowly, but with insidious
intent. He told Sam that he might live longer with radia-
tion, but he would be bald and feel awful. That was impossible because as soon as Sam's enemies saw him
deteriorating, they'd run in and gobble up his empire
faster than Johnny could deal with them. Such was the
way of nature. Survival would be Johnny's problem alone
and he would have to sink or swim. Sam wasn't afraid to
die, but the old gangster drew a line at dying in a cage like
a rat somebody forgot to feed.

Sam hoped there was a heaven. If there was a heaven,
there was a hell. If hell existed, a lot of people he knew

would be there. The first thing Sam was going to do when he got down there was hunt down that bastard Dylan Devlin and show those demons running the joint what real torture looked like.

22 | Saint Jean, Louisiana

Johnny Russo had one more thing to do before he could call it a night and be in bed to get his normal five hours of sleep. His driver, Spiro, steered the speeding Lincoln Towncar out of River Road while Johnny stared at the passing white tanks, fifty feet tall and twice as wide. The International Liquid Storage tank terminal operation was completely legitimate and belonged not to Sam but to a consortium of foreign investors. At any given time, there was everything from food-grade vegetable oil to gasoline stored in the tanks. The product was pumped directly from, and into, vessels moored at ILS's dock on the Mississippi River, just over the levee. Their clients paid for storage and, if they somehow failed to pay, the company held the product as collateral against storage costs, and then sold the liquid for a nice profit. Sam Manelli was a consultant. If there was a problem requiring a political or unorthodox solution, Sam saw that it was handled. As compensation for his help, the corporation gave Sam the duck-hunting lease on sixteen hundred acres of swampland behind the tank farm. Sam had built a lodge and boat shed on the property, where Spiro and Johnny were now headed.

Spiro pulled up in front of the shed, where two of his enforcers waited inside beside a naked man whose hands and ankles were lashed together. The man sat in a chair on a sheet of plastic, beside a table whose wood surface had also been covered with the same material. When Russo jerked the duct tape from the bound man's mouth, it took a good deal of his goatee with it. The man took several gasping breaths and his eyes blinked anxiously.

Russo stood over the shivering man and studied him silently. Spiro covered a yawn with his open palm.

"How much did you skim, Albert?" Russo said, finally.

"I di-di-di-didn't ... short Sam!"

"Didn't short me, you mean? Do you see Sam in here?"

"I wouldn't du-du-do that, Johnny!" The panicked words tumbled from Albert's mouth, tears streaming down his cheeks.

"Sheri said different, not four hours ago in this very room. She said you took at least ten large from the girls this year that you didn't pass along. She said she begged you not to do it."

"No, I never!"

"She's your main girl, Albert—mother to your children. Why would she make something like that up?"

"She's l-l-l-lying!" Albert's eyes were fevered circles, futilely blinking back tears.

"That's a problem, because I believe her."

"Let me talk to her! She's l-lying. Lying. Lying. She'll cu-cu-cu-come clean!"

"Okay, I'll let you talk to her."

Johnny Russo walked over to the fridge directly opposite the man and lifted out, by its thick black hair, a woman's head. The dry brown eyes were unblinking, the mouth frozen wide open as if in midscream.

Albert's expression changed until it mirrored that of his late girlfriend's.

"How much of my money did Albert skim, Sheri?" Russo asked the severed head. He took Sheri's jaw in his free hand and worked it up and down. "Lots and lots," Johnny said in a high voice. "If I'm l-l-lying, may I g-g-give head."

The men in the shed burst into laughter.

Russo returned the head to the fridge. "What you are going to do, Albert, is go back to work and pay me back everything you stole."

"But, I never—"

Russo slapped him so hard the chair Albert sat in fell over on its side. "Stop lying, or you can join Sheri and fatten the crabs. You will make me an additional fifty grand over last year's numbers or you'll wish you were dead a long time before you will be. Do you understand me? You'll pay me back the ten large at reasonable interest of two points a week."

Russo took a wad of money out of his pocket and peeled off a fifty. He bent over, pressed the bill into Albert's mouth, pushing it between the man's teeth with his fingertip.

"Albert, you take that and buy your kids a little something and tell them it's from their uncle Johnny. What do you say?"

"Thank you," Albert said weakly.

"You're welcome. Boys, get Albert dressed and take him home."

23 | Rook Island, North Carolina
Wednesday

The sun's rays tinted the clouds a luscious orange. As bacon sizzled, Jet stood at the stove muttering to herself. Cross sat beside Winter, rubbing his eyes sleepily. Greg wandered in, poured himself a cup of coffee, and sat across from Winter. The deputies ate in silence.

After breakfast, Winter and Jet were left alone.

"Miss Sean has bruises on her arm where that man squeezed on her," she said in a low voice.

"That so?" Winter said, trying to keep his voice even.

"She's been under his spell, but it sure is broken now. A woman can be blinded by a buttery-talking man. Now she's gotten her first good look at him."

"If you say so."

"I do say so. She has seen his true side, and that man is gonna kill her if he gets half a chance."

"I'll keep my eyes open," Winter said, almost paralyzed by the inexplicable rage rising in him.

Jet looked at him skeptically.

"I promise, Jet," he said sincerely.

After breakfast, dressed for his morning run, Winter passed through the living room.

"I have a bone to pick with you, Massey."

Winter drew up short. He turned to face Dylan, who sat on the couch, twenty feet away.

"That so?"

"This is all your fault. Soon as Whitehead gets to the attorney general, you're history here."

"I'll start packing," he replied, desperately wanting to pound this cretin into oblivion.

"You shouldn't have been talking to my wife. Just what the hell did you think you were doing?"

"Devlin," Winter said, "I didn't realize the fact that your entering the witness protection program was going to be a surprise to her. The truth will always come out."

"I could kill you, right here, right now."

"You want me to give you my gun and kneel so you can shoot me in the back of the head?"

"You get between my wife and me again and you're going to wish you had never set foot on this island."

"I've wished that since I got here, Devlin," Winter said. "What got between you and your wife wasn't me. It was her good sense." He walked out the door.

24 | Ward Field, Virginia

The afternoon sun lengthened the shadows of the two boys who were pedaling their bikes down an isolated asphalt road as fast as their young legs could pump. The road had been constructed before World War II by the Army Air Corps, cut through rolling wilderness of an inhospitable nature. In order to avoid any misunderstanding about who owned the road and access thereto, warning signs were posted for a mile before the riders reached the first barricade. That initial barricade was comprised of foot-tall concrete stumps that looked like worn-down teeth. The ground on either side of the road allowed vehicles with a reason to proceed, to skirt the structures. The boys quickly guided their BMX bicycles between the bumps.

Over the next hill, a large faded sign read:

U.S. Government

Restricted Area

No Trespassing

For all of the attention the two young bikers paid it, the warning might as well have been written on the surface of the moon.

George Williams and Matthew Barnwell were both twelve years old, although George was six days older. They were, by mutual pact, best friends forever. George was skinny and his hair spiked out from his head like porcupine quills. A cup of rust-colored freckles seemed to have been poured over his face, scattered ear to ear and from his chin to his forehead, with more spilling down his neck. His small canvas backpack had his initials hand-lettered on the flap.

Matthew was shorter than George by a head, thirty pounds heavier, and had skin the color of a buckeye.

George pumped along, but Matthew had to get off his bike and walk it to top the final rise in the road. He stared down at Ward Field. The main gate was located a hundred feet below them. Several miles of chain-link fence topped with barbed wire enclosed the entire air-training facility. The gate was closed, wrapped with heavy chains and padlocks. The signs on either side of the gate were ill-tempered: ARMED RESPONSE! The gatehouse door and window were nailed shut. The boys coasted down the hill outside the fence, their tires cutting narrow tracks in the tangled weeds.

George and Matthew didn't know anyone who had been inside the fence, but for years kids had passed down tales of people who had gone missing after last being seen heading toward the old base. The red and white water tower, an attractive object to young men with climbing ambitions, had been partially disassembled, and the door to the wire safety cage surrounding the first twenty feet of ladder was padlocked.

Plywood covered every window of the barracks, and the roof of one had collapsed. Quonset huts were scattered around the facility: all of the structures were joined by a system of footpaths and narrow paved roads. Weeds proliferated through the concrete runway and parallel taxiway. There were three hangars; the most recent, far larger than the other two, had been built in the Vietnam era so C-130 cargo planes with tall, wide wings and tails that rose up behind them like scorpion stings could taxi straight inside.

The first time the boys scouted the fence, at the beginning of the summer, they had discovered their entrance—a depression where runoff had carved a shallow channel under the fence. George slid under easily, but Matt needed him to pull the fence up while he squirmed under.

They started across the field of knee-high weeds toward the control tower, which was barely more than a square room built on wooden telephone poles marinated in creosote. Its narrow steps were mostly rotted away and the windows were coated black with grime. Inside, a plywood table was anchored to the wall facing the runway, and a thin mattress provided a place for the boys to sit. They had a supply of old nudie magazines, candles, matches, playing cards, and a few cigarettes. The two boys didn't visit more than every other week or so, because it was so far from home. In the weeks since they had first come out, they had never seen a living soul.

As they passed close to the large hangar, they suddenly heard the unmistakable sound of a power saw. Both dropped hastily to the ground and were hidden by the tall weeds. The racket was coming from inside the building. "Somebody's here," George told Matthew. His heart felt hot in his chest, and his mouth had gone dry with excitement. The sounds of raised voices filtered out of the structure.

"No shit, Sherlock," Matt said.

"Think they're going to fix this place up again?"

"Naw, it's way too fucked up. Maybe they got a UFO in there. Shit, what if those men are aliens and we're gonna be invaded unless we can stop them and be heroes and get millions of dollars and be on television?"

George said, "We better get out before they catch us."

"Split?" Matt exclaimed. "You nuts? We can sneak into the little part of the big building and see what they're up to."

"If they're in that part, too..."

"Don't be chicken. If they do have a UFO, they can move it later and we couldn't prove it was here," Matt said. "I'm going to spy on them."

George was terrified, but he wasn't about to back out.

They approached a familiar entry point and knelt beside the sheet of weathered plywood covering a window. George gripped the corner of the thin board and held it up while Matt propped a cinder block under the bottom so they could climb inside.

What had once been offices now served as crowded storage rooms for the equipment not worth taking when the base had closed. The boys moved as quietly as possible through narrow aisles formed by dozens of dust-covered desks, adding machines, light fixtures, typewriters, file cabinets, and boxes stacked to the ceiling.

They made their way cautiously through the maze created by the stored equipment, using the weak light that entered the room through a grime-encrusted transom window.

Because he was the heavier of the pair, Matt boosted George up onto a file cabinet. George then planted one foot on the cabinet and the other on Matt's shoulder. From this position, he could peer through the narrow wedge at the side of the transom window.

"See any aliens?" Matt asked hopefully.

"Shhhhh. Just a bunch of guys working on airplanes and stuff." George opened his backpack and removed the binoculars they had found in the tower. The lens on the left side was shattered, but the other side made a perfectly good telescope.

Even without uniforms, the men inside the hangar looked like soldiers to George. He knew that adults usually joked around when they worked, smiled some. But it was almost like these men had never learned how to smile, each concentrating hard on what he was doing.

"There's two airplanes and an army helicopter," he reported. "There's a guy up on a ladder painting numbers on the big plane."

"What else?"

"Aw, man, there's some tables full of really, really neat stuff."

"Like what?" Matt demanded.

"Some machine guns. Bombs . . . or diver's tanks."

"You're lying. I wanna see."

"And all kinds of boxes. There's this real old man that must be the boss, because he's just looking at a computer and writing stuff down. These guys are so cool."

"I want to see!" Matt whispered.

The old man closed the laptop and called out, "All over here!" The seven men in the hangar walked over and sat like students in chairs that had been set up.

"There's seven Army men plus the wrinkly guy," George reported.

"Hurry up, my shoulder's gonna fall off."

"Just a minute, he's going to talk. Be real still, and quiet." George was so excited he almost spoke above a whisper. This was way better than a new video game. He strained to hear, hoping the discussion would be about UFOs or something just as exciting.

The old man spoke loudly and then more softly. It was hard for George to get most of it.

"What's he saying?" Matt asked, impatiently.

"Talking about . . . the teams and . . . two possible points of insertings. He doesn't know yet which one they will do. Marshals and devils. Whipstick has never been . . . breached." The old man went on talking, but the words became harder to decipher.

Matt sneezed and George almost fell, but he grabbed the edge of the transom just in time, and regained his balance by shifting his weight onto the file cabinet.

"Damn it! I almost fell."

"Sue me, I sneezed from the dirt mite poop in here."

When George raised the binoculars back to his eye, he was struck dumb by what he saw, or didn't see. The eight men were gone—vanished. George scanned the space frantically, but to his horror, he saw nothing.

"I heard something," Matt insisted.

"Shut up!" George hissed. "They're not . . ." His binocular lens went dark. He opened his left eye, which he had clenched shut while peering through the single lens, and found himself staring straight into incredibly deep-blue eyes, inches from his own. Before George could scream, Matt suddenly twisted under him and George fell to the floor, landing hard on his side. When George opened his eyes again and looked up, a large man with a crew cut was looming over him, holding Matt by the arm. The man was also holding the scariest knife George had ever seen.

"What's clickin', chickens?" the knife man asked. Matt started blubbering, a high-pitched squeal that quickly became a cry. His whole plump body was trembling.

Like ghosts materializing from shadows, men suddenly filled the room. The sight of them, the knife, the sour smell of their sweat, made George feel very weak. As one of the men bent down toward him, the boy was aware of a warm wet spreading underneath him.

Five minutes later, now seated in one of the metal folding chairs in the hangar, George Williams was embarrassed, frightened, and physically uncomfortable. His clammy jeans clung wetly to his legs and bottom, and the stench of his urine was embarrassingly obvious to all. The old man and the seven others standing behind him looked fierce and evil. Matt sat on a similar folding chair inches from his.

The old man was really angry. "You boys are trespassing on a restricted military complex. That's a federal crime. Prison. Government can take away your parents' houses, cars, anything of value. You two hooligans will be in a youth facility with hard-core, butt-boogering, rap-talking, gold-toothed niggers who'd as soon cut your throat as look at you."

George was certain this was the worst moment of his life. *Why did I come through the fence? Why did I peek into the hangar? Why, why, why?*

Matt snickered. "What's a hoolican?"

The old man's face abruptly reddened and became so contorted with rage that George was sure he would simply explode. "You little twit! Do you think this is a fucking joke? Do these men look like comedians?"

Terrified, the boys fell silent, stunned and trembling. George wasn't thinking about the men or their weapons. He was thinking about two years earlier, when he had been caught shoplifting and the store's manager called the cops, who called his father, who took him home and thrashed him with a belt.

The old man pulled a chair in front of the boys, then took a folding knife from one pocket and an apple from another. He sliced the apple down the center and handed each of them half. They stared down at the fruit in their hands, confused. George's father often went from ranting to silence in the blink of an eye. Maybe the old man was tired of yelling.

"What are your names? Please don't lie to me or you will be very, very sorry."

"George Williams."

"Matthew Barnwell."

"How old are you?"

"Twelve," George said.

Matt nodded. "Me . . . too."

"Did anyone come here with you?"

Both shook their heads.

"No one at all?"

"Nope," Matt said.

"Does anyone know you're here?"

"No, sir," George said.

"Where do you boys live? How far from here?"

George said, "Three miles. Green Meadows subdivision."

"How did you get here?"

"On our bikes."

"You've been in here before?"

"No," Matt said.

"Don't lie to me," he snarled.

"Lots of times," George said quickly, not wanting to piss him off again.

"Alone? Just the two of you?"

"Yeah. The tower out there . . . it's our secret clubhouse. Was before, I mean. We never bothered nothing."

"We don't ever hurt anything," Matt added soulfully.

George thought Matt sounded pathetic.

"Where did you get these?" The old man picked up the binoculars.

"They were in the tower. They were already broken."

"Theft of government property," the old man said with a sigh. He looked as fragile as ash.

He stood behind them and placed one wrinkled fist on each boy's shoulder. George eyed the pocketknife in the old man's right hand, the blade inches from his cheek. "Aren't you scared to come here alone to this dangerous place?" the old man asked softly.

"It's not dangerous," George said, grasping for straws. "If you're careful on the broken stairs, it isn't."

"Signs say 'armed response.' Did you know you could be shot for sneaking in here?"

"We thought it was a bluff," Matt protested, eyeing the solemn-faced men watching them. "Nobody ever came before."

George looked at the guns on the table. The stacks of loaded magazines. The large pistols. The table was filled with fascinating equipment.

"Nobody till you," Matt added. "Are you Army men?"

"We're Special Forces," the old man answered. His eyes flickered to take in his men, standing nearby, watching silently. "I am a general. My men and I are not going to be here long. But it's vital that nobody bothers us while we're working. This is a top-secret mission. I'm not entirely sure I should let you go. You might tell people, and then it could get back to the other side and we could lose a very important and extremely expensive war game."

"We wouldn't ever tell, no matter what," Matt vowed. "We're real good at secrets. We never, ever told anybody about this place. It's our secret and if we told, other kids would take it away."

"If you don't tell my dad, I won't tell anybody about you guys fixing up your stuff here. He'll kill me, honest," George heard himself say.

The old man was silent for a long time. Then he said tenderly, "Eat your apple. I'm not going to put you in jail this time...or even call your parents. But, George and Matthew—if you ever mention our presence, you and your parents will be in serious trouble. Just so you understand this is not a joke. Do I have your word of honor you will never speak of this? Both of you?"

Both boys nodded enthusiastically. "Well," Matt said, "we thought it was a UFO you had in here."

"Wouldn't that be something," the old man murmured. "If you two can keep the secret and not tell anybody, you can come here anytime you like after we're gone and play all you want."

"I bet riding in a helicopter is real fun," Matt said. "When I grow up I'm going to be a helicopter pilot in the Army and fight with missiles and machine guns like yours."

"I'm sure you will. You keep my secret and I'll make certain you get in the Army."

"You sure got a lot of guns and stuff," George said, relaxing, his excitement growing. "Are they real?"

"When you were spying on us, did you learn anything?" the general suddenly asked George.

"I heard you talking about devils and marshals. And how you are going to do something nobody's ever done before."

"What did you hear?"

"Break into whipsticks."

The general's face froze; his smile became a grimace.

"I have an idea," the general said. "Boys, this is Ralph. He's a helicopter pilot. He will take you both for a nice helicopter ride."

"Yes!" Matt exclaimed, not believing their good fortune.

"I have to be home by five-thirty," George told him, hoping that wouldn't make the general cancel their ride.

"Oh, you'll be down well before five," the old man assured him. "Don't want you two out after dark. Nobody knows better than I do how dangerous a place the world is." The old man looked at Ralph. "Take special care of these boys."

25 | Rook Island, North Carolina

Martinez followed Sean out onto the porch, where Winter sat in a wicker chair with Midnight on his lap. Sean took a seat in a rocking chair near Winter. Midnight hopped down, sprang up into her lap, and looked up into her eyes. She stroked the animal, seemingly comforted by its soft fur, its purring, as she seemed to noticeably relax.

"Traitor," Winter said to Midnight.

"I want to thank you for telling me the truth," Sean told Winter, without looking at him. "I'm sorry if I got you in hot water." It was the truth. She felt terrible despite the fact that her reaction to what he had told her wasn't her fault.

"It's not a problem," Winter replied.

"Somebody should have told you the truth," Martinez said. Sean liked Angela Martinez. The woman had shown her nothing but kindness.

"That would have been nice," Sean said quietly.

When the front door swung open, Midnight leaped from her lap and raced off around the corner. Sean looked up to see Dylan step out onto the porch with Cross following behind him.

Dylan walked over and stood directly in front of her chair. Instead of turning her eyes away from him, she met his stare with a new kind of determination in her eyes.

"We *are* going to talk," he told her.

Sean felt a sudden rush of anger. "I've said everything I am going to say to you, and I am not interested in anything else you have to say. Ever."

She was aware that Winter, Cross, and Martinez were exchanging concerned glances, but she didn't care. After what she had just discovered, she would never care what anyone thought of her again.

Dylan smiled, but his smile, once so comforting, made her feel sick.

"You have time for a cat but not your husband? Where's your capacity for forgiveness?"

"The cat has integrity," she snapped, wanting to get up, get away from him, but he blocked her by leaning in and gripping the armrests.

"Move!" Sean ordered.

"Not until you agree to talk to me."

"There's nothing to discuss." Nothing he had said to her or could say mattered in the least. Sean had never suffered from indecisiveness. Once she made a decision, that was it.

Winter stood. "Back off, Devlin. Cross, escort Mr. Devlin to his room."

Thank you, Winter, Sean thought, wishing she could confide in him how grateful she truly was.

"You don't have the authority to interfere between a man and his wife. You can't tell me to do anything, Mr. Ironman," Dylan replied without taking his hands off Sean's chair or shifting his eyes from hers.

"Cross," Winter said, "escort Mr. Devlin inside—now!"

"Fuck you, Massey," Dylan told him.

Winter keyed the microphone. "Inspector, you might want to come out front. We have a situation."

"You haven't seen a situation yet, Deputy," Dylan said in a calm voice. "Sambo isn't going to change anything."

Sean was relieved when Greg suddenly appeared, carrying a gun-shaped device Sean was unfamiliar with.

"Ms. Devlin, would you like to get up from the chair?"

Sean shook her head. "I would prefer *he* leave me alone." Sean wasn't inclined to allow Dylan to control her at all, ever again. She would never again play the role of submissive, dutiful wife, blinded by passion.

"Mr. Devlin, step back," Greg ordered.

"No," Dylan said evenly. "Stay out of our business. My wife and I are going to have a talk—*boy.*"

"You see the stun gun I have in my hand?" Greg motioned menacingly. "If you don't back off, I am going to put you on the floorboards and restrain you for the duration. Choice is yours, Devlin. Back up or ride the lightning." The Taser fired barbs that delivered 50,000 volts of electricity through wires connected to the weapon.

Sean wondered if Greg would really use the thing on Dylan, wondered if it would hurt him. She dearly hoped it would, with a newfound vengeance that would have shocked her the previous day.

"Touch me and Whitehead'll have your ass."

"I don't take orders from Whitehead," Greg told him. "I

go by our protocols concerning whatever means are necessary to keep you safe, which are also designed to keep you from harming others. Our choices range from a takedown, like this Taser I am about to use on you, to cutting you in half with a shotgun."

"I am not *just* another witness," Dylan said, his eyes still locked on Sean's.

"No, you're a multiple murderer. The bottom line is that you will do what I say, when I say to do it, or I will fry you. End of discussion."

"Mr. Devlin," Martinez interposed. "Nobody can win here. We won't allow you to force Mrs. Devlin to do anything against her will. Inspector Nations won't back off and he isn't bluffing. Your call."

Dylan finally turned his head to look at the marshals on the porch and at Beck, Bear, and Forsythe, who had appeared out on the sand behind them, armed. Dylan shook his head slowly, lifted his hands, and stepped back.

"You're a bright girl, *Mar-tee-nez,*" Devlin said. "Calmer heads should always prevail. I'll just say good afternoon."

Sean stared at her husband's back as he walked inside. A burst of wind hit and brought with it the scent of rain.

"He won't bother you again," Greg told her.

"If he comes near me again I will be forced to hold the USMS responsible," she carped more out of pride at having been shown up as a victim in front of men. She knew this wasn't the fault of the deputy marshals on the detail. Keeping her in the dark was someone else's doing. "I want to leave now—tonight," she said, meaning it, unable to back down now.

"I'll advise Control of the situation immediately. We're all leaving the island tomorrow. I have no idea where we'll be staying after we go. Under the circumstances, we'll make arrangements for separate quarters."

"I will not spend another day near my husband. I absolutely refuse to travel anywhere with him."

"Let me work on that," Greg said evenly, trying to calm her down. "He won't bother you again. You just stay in your room as much as possible. Martinez will remain with you from now on. I wish I could do better."

"So do I," Sean replied curtly. "I won't stay locked up in my room like a criminal because of him. He is the one who should be locked up."

Greg handed Martinez the Taser—a stun gun—and went inside. "Don't hesitate to use this. We have more."

26 | Wednesday night

What had happened with Dylan on the porch had nearly been a disaster. It was obvious that the dynamics of the safe house were rapidly deteriorating. Greg had to make some changes to stay on top of Dylan, who was obviously desperate to trigger a confrontation. Perhaps he was just playing games to entertain himself, but the consequences of a game designed by a psychopathic mind could be both unpredictable and deadly.

Winter had been scheduled for a shift in the security room, but he wanted to be outside. Just before the shift started, Bear agreed to swap places with him. As Winter and Beck were about to leave the house, Greg appeared and took Winter aside. He waited for Beck to close the door before he spoke.

"We're taking Dylan out tomorrow evening because a night move is safer. I've got permission to leave Beck and Martinez behind with Ms. Devlin. They'll escort her out on Saturday and you'll be home for Sunday."

Winter spent from midnight until three walking the perimeter of the house. He liked the solitude, the soft roar of the surf, the pelting of the rain on his hood. He found himself unable to stop thinking about Sean Devlin. He admired her intelligence and tenacity but was perplexed at how a woman like her could have married a man like Dylan. Even so, there was something very special about Sean: hidden depths that had gradually begun to reveal themselves. Despite her strength—the fact that she was perfectly capable of taking care of herself—he found himself wanting to shelter and protect her. Something in her he couldn't define had gotten to him. He hardly knew anything at all about her and he knew he shouldn't waste his time thinking about her. In less than eighteen hours he would be gone and would never see her again. But still . . .

Beck waved Winter up onto the porch.

"This is miserable," Beck grumbled. "Who in their fucking right mind would come out here in this shit to pop that bastard?"

"Maybe killers in raincoats."

"This island isn't even on a map." Beck lifted an empty thermos. "Jet could protect Dylan out here."

Winter didn't respond.

"You think she's pretty?" Beck asked.

"Too bossy for me. Good cook, though."

"Not Jet. Martinez. She's fine. You've noticed, right?"

"She's good at her job," Winter said noncommittally.

"I think she's hot. But she's never so much as . . . I don't know, it's weird. It's really something to see her laugh."

"You ever asked her out?"

Beck shook his head. "I wanted to a bunch of times. I mean, sure, I hint around and sometimes she . . . I mean, I think she likes me okay. Hard to tell. I've been meaning to ask you something. You weren't betting for her, but against Dylan, right? You didn't think she would win over Cross?

Hell, that was cool, the way she showed everybody her stuff. And you pissed off Devlin big-time."

"I need coffee," Winter said, uncomfortable discussing someone he respected behind her back.

"I'll go in and get us some," Beck offered.

"No, I'll do it," Winter said, eager to get out of the wet. "S-one," Winter said into his mouthpiece, "W.M. coming in for coffee."

There was no response.

"Maybe Bear's in the crapper?" Beck said. "Or hibernating."

Winter instinctively slung the AR over his shoulder and drew his SIG.

"We go to the security room together. Cover my back," he said quietly yet determinedly.

Entering into the foyer, Winter slipped to the arch ahead of Beck and aimed his gun down the hall. He nodded that it was clear and moved with stealth toward the security room door, which was open a crack. No light showed under either Dylan's or Sean's door. Winter stood in front of the security room door, pushed it open, and lunged inside, aiming his gun at the dark figure bent over Dixon. "Freeze!" Winter ordered.

Beck moved in swiftly behind Winter, aiming his rifle at the figure dressed in pajamas, bent over Dixon.

"Greg?" Winter lowered his gun and moved farther into the room. Dixon was as fully reclined as the swivel chair allowed. His eyes were closed and his face was so pale it looked like it had been bleached white.

"He's out cold." Greg turned his attention back to Dixon and slapped his cheeks. "Wake up, Bear," he coaxed angrily.

Winter saw that the coffeepot had started to smoke, so he turned it off before leaning his AR against the wall. He slipped his coat off and dropped it beside the rifle.

"Help me with him, then go and get me some water,"

Greg told Beck as he and Winter lifted the big man from the chair and lowered him to the floor. Panicked at the unexpected turn of events, Beck left his Colt carbine propped beside Winter's and stepped into the bathroom, filling a glass.

"I was having trouble sleeping, went to the kitchen. I smelled the coffee burning," Greg said.

"Heart attack?" Winter asked.

Greg shook his head. He lifted Dixon's eyelid. "I don't think so. He's breathing fine."

When Greg poured the glass of water over Dixon's face the reaction was immediate.

"What thafuckeryoudoing?" he growled, flailing at them. "Jesus H. Christ," he groaned, gripping his head.

"What's wrong, Bear?"

"My head!" Dixon moaned in agony.

"Stroke?" Beck asked Greg.

"He's been drugged," Winter said.

"Bear, did you take anything?" Greg asked.

"Nothing. Had coffee with Martinez and she left and . . . I was just sitting there. And . . ."

Winter picked up Dixon's cup of coffee from the console, dipped his finger in just enough so he could get a drop on his tongue. "Maybe there's something in it, but with the sugar and milk, I can't tell."

Greg removed Bear's pistol from his holster. Dixon tried to sit up, then gave up. Winter pulled his flashlight, turned it on, and locked it against the receiver of his SIG. "Dylan," Winter said.

The three marshals left Dixon on the floor and rushed into the hallway, their guns poised. Greg kicked open Dylan's door and Winter, seeing the killer sit up in bed, moved swiftly to Sean Devlin's suite with Beck. He opened the door to the sitting room and flipped the light switch on.

Martinez sat slumped on the couch. A cup of cold coffee was on the table beside her. Winter put his hand on the pulse in her neck, then left her for Beck to rouse. Sean's bedroom door was slightly ajar.

Using his foot so he could maintain his aim, Winter pushed the door open. Sean was lying facedown across the bed, wearing only panties. Winter pressed his fingertips to her neck to check for a pulse and got more than he expected. She yelled out, scrambled upright, and pressed her back against the headboard. Realizing that Winter and Greg were staring at her, she jerked a pillow up to cover her breasts. "What!" she screamed.

After Greg moved into the room, Dylan came up behind him.

When she saw Dylan, Sean jumped up, jerked the sheet off the bed, and wrapped it around her. "All of you, get out of my room!" she yelled. "What are you doing?"

"I'm sorry," Winter said. "Dixon and Martinez were drugged."

"I don't understand."

"Ask him." Winter indicated Dylan.

"Ask me what?" Dylan said.

"He thought it would be me," Winter told Sean.

"Thought what would be you?" Greg asked.

"I was listed on the board to be in the security room, but I traded with Dixon. Devlin planned to take me when I was knocked out."

"You're a paranoid fool," Dylan said, smiling. "I could take you if *I* was knocked out."

Martinez was awake when they returned to the den but looked like hell.

"What happened?" Greg asked.

"I don't know. I was just sitting here."

"You got coffee from the security room?"

"Yeah. Then I came in here thinking I would read."

"You didn't lock the door?"

"Of course I locked it."

"It was open," Winter said.

"You don't suppose the wind blew it open?" Dylan asked.

"Sean's wasn't locked, either," Winter said.

"I locked my door," Sean insisted.

"Goodness," Dylan mocked. "This is frightening. Someone could have harmed me."

Without a word, Winter went straight to the security room. "What's up?" Bear asked, staring at him blearily.

"Devlin drugged you."

"How?"

"Was he in here at all earlier?"

"For a minute, around eleven, talking to Cross."

Crouching low and close to the coffee table, Winter spotted white residue on the surface. He pressed his finger to the powder and touched his tongue. Hurriedly, he left for Devlin's room.

Greg followed him and watched grimly as Winter started pulling open the drawers and rifling through their contents.

"Can I help you?" Dylan asked from the doorway. Winter reached into the table beside the bed, lifted out a bottle, and tossed it to Greg.

"Here you go."

"Prescribed for pain," Dylan needled. "You think they might be too strong for me?"

"You put them in the coffee, you son of a bitch," Winter told him.

"That's crazy talk, Deputy. Why would I?"

Greg had poured the capsules out into his palm. "Bottle says there should be twelve. They're all here."

"I didn't take any. You can become an addict taking narcotics."

"Maybe you figured if you knocked us out you could talk reason to your wife," Winter said.

"Unnecessary," Dylan replied, smiling confidently. "She's

my wife. While she might be a bit miffed, she still loves me as much as ever, probably more. Sean's a good Catholic, loves and obeys the Pope. Doesn't believe in divorce."

Winter took one of the pills from Greg. He pulled it apart and poured the contents into his palm and looked at the granules. "It's sugar."

"They're *all* sugar," Greg said after he had emptied two more, tasting to make sure.

"Someone stole my drugs? What if I had been in pain? You can't even trust United States marshals anymore! I demand an investigation." Devlin crossed to the bed and climbed in, snickering at them. "Cut out the light and close the door after you, boys."

Greg suggested they account for all of the weapons in the house, even the kitchen knives. They found that every gun was where it was supposed to be—all loaded, all firing pins in place.

"Dylan didn't drug the coffee to gain access to the guns," Winter said. "The only other reason for him to do it would be to get to Sean. He was in her room."

"Unless Martinez was zonked, opened the door herself, and then didn't lock it," Greg said.

"And Sean unlocked her bedroom door and forgot? No, he picked the locks."

"Maybe he *was* planning to get to you," Greg told Winter.

"There's no love lost, but I can't see Dylan risking his deal with the government to punish me."

"Unless he could make it look like an accident." Greg yawned. "One more thing I need to know, pal, and I want the absolute truth."

"Yeah?"

"In all of your life, have you ever seen two more perfect breasts than Sean Devlin's?"

27 | **Thursday morning**

Just after Martinez had left her bedroom, Sean saw the first light flares, which would be followed by nausea and blinding, incapacitating pain. She had immediately taken two of her migraine pills, then lay in the darkness waiting for them to work. She had suffered from the headaches since she was a teenager, but as long as she managed her diet and stress, they were infrequent. Since her miracle pills effectively stopped the headaches as they formed, she was never without them.

Sean propped herself up against a stack of pillows, wearing only her robe. She had never felt more angry with herself. If only her mother had still been alive when Dylan came along. Olivia Marks would have sniffed him out for what he was. She had always warned her about making friends too fast with strangers. The rule had always been that they didn't trust anybody but each other. There were things you just didn't share, and she had held to that, even with Dylan. Was it because she never fully trusted him? She wanted to believe it had been that she had sensed she couldn't trust him fully. She hadn't asked enough questions, pushed him for answers to the mystery that was his life before they'd met. He'd been guarded and so had she. She didn't think for a moment that was how normal married people behaved. If she was honest with herself now, she had suffered misgivings from the start.

He had absolutely and completely betrayed her. It was as though the disarming and handsome man she married had been kidnapped while she was in Argentina and switched with his evil twin brother. She despised and feared this alien creature who had murdered twelve people. She wanted to get as far away from him as fast as she could.

She had been in bed for three hours since the marshals left—ransacking her memory for clues she had missed about Dylan's secret life—but there were none to be found. Angela had done her best to comfort her, but Sean had wanted to be alone. Besides, what could she have told Angela that didn't make her look like an idiot, a complete fool?

It was true the marshals hadn't told her anything from the time she was seized from the airport, except that things would be explained to her as soon as she saw her husband and that he was perfectly fine. *Perfectly fine how?* She had taken as gospel everything Dylan told her after she'd arrived because she had wanted and needed to believe him. And that bastard had known she would.

They had never fought. In fact, she now realized, they had never talked about anything that mattered. He had listened to her opinions without disagreeing. He had always liked what she had, shared her dislikes.

She thought back to the day Dylan had walked into her life—a chance meeting in a South Hampton coffee shop. She had turned from the counter straight into him and doused his expensive suit with her coffee. He had been such a gentleman and was so charming that she had sat and had her coffee with him. That small entrée was all he'd needed. In the space of two months, Dylan had gone from being a total stranger to caring sensitive friend to tender lover, and finally to perfect husband. *Way too perfect.* Dylan Devlin had been everything she had ever wanted in a man, but she was sure now that he had become so by design. He was a consummate actor, a shell filled with lies.

In hindsight, her feelings for him had somehow become diluted during their marriage. While she had been in Argentina looking at the properties Dylan had made a list of, she had felt guilty for not thinking of him more—for not wishing that he had come with her. In fact, she had felt relieved that he wasn't with her. She had relished her privacy. Had she started to question even then, that perhaps there was someone else lurking behind her husband's bright green eyes? She knew she would not miss him, was glad to be rid of him. When Sean was done with a thing, she could walk away without looking back. It was part of her training—her nature.

After all was said and done, the most troubling part of all this was why a sociopath had chosen her out of all of the millions of women out there who were far richer, more beautiful, and more vulnerable than she. Although it was possible, she didn't want to believe he had picked her at random the way a hawk selects a single mouse from the many he watches. She had been vulnerable because she was lonely—because her mother hadn't been there to offer advice.

He's insane, she thought, and shuddered.

She had never been afraid of him before. Now Dylan had drugged marshals and crept into her room while she slept. Had he intended to harm her tonight? Had something interrupted him before he could do anything to her? What did he stand to gain?

Through the shutters she could see the sun rising. She would feel better after she showered and dressed. Getting out of bed, she slid a drawer open to select underwear and a top.

She picked out a sky-blue T-shirt, then opened another drawer for a pair of jeans and was startled to see a towel laid carefully on top of her clothes. *Odd.*

Puzzled, Sean lifted the towel away.

The thing she saw there, a nightmare lying between the stack of folded pants, made her scream in horror.

28

Winter was in the security room watching the monitors when he heard Sean. Drawing his handgun, he ran out into her bedroom just behind Martinez. Sean, her face as white as porcelain, stood pointing at the open drawer. Except for the fact that its severed head had been placed inches from its body, the cat looked as if he had climbed into the drawer and curled up to nap.

"Midnight," Sean murmured.

"Jesus wept," Greg muttered over Winter's shoulder.

"Hee-yere kitty, kitty, kitty," Dylan sang out cheerfully from his bedroom.

Sean sat on the edge of her bed and sobbed. Martinez sat beside her and put her arm around her.

Winter lifted Midnight from the drawer, wrapped him in the towel, and carried the animal past Dylan's open door without looking in.

"Whut has happened to mah pussy?" Dylan called out as Winter passed. His laughter filled the house like acrid smoke.

"He killed Midnight," Winter said gently, when Jet saw the bundle.

Tears of grief and anger rolled down her cheeks. "That man's the devil. He drugged me, too. Came into my bedroom and took Midnight."

Winter wrapped the towel containing Midnight in old newspaper and secured the bundle using twine. Greg sat beside Jet and placed his hands on hers, speaking in a voice so low that it was impossible to hear what he was saying.

"Winter," Greg said, his voice choked with anger, "Jet

will be leaving on the store boat as soon as it gets here for the Thursday delivery."

"I'm sorry, you'll have to get another cook. I can't stay here now."

She stood slowly, as if her bones were brittle, and put on her raincoat. Gently, she took the bundle from Winter and went out the back door.

Greg went to the doorway and gestured for Dixon.

"You feeling all right, Bear?" he asked. When Dixon nodded, he said, "Then go out back and help Jet bury her pet."

"Sick son of a bitch!" Winter's temper was blazing. "He did all that just so he could kill the cat and plant it so Sean would find it. That miserable, sick bastard."

"This is a Taser," Winter explained to Sean. "It's nonlethal, but it will knock Dylan on his ass for several minutes, which will give you time to get away from him."

Sean weighed the plastic handgun-shaped object in her hand.

"It's instinctive, like aiming a gun. Point it like you're pointing your finger and squeeze the trigger. Don't jerk it." Winter instructed her. "Fires tiny darts that pull wire leads out, darts stick into the target, completing a circuit from a nine-volt battery in the handle."

"Isn't that much electricity dangerous?" she asked, hoping he'd say yes.

"No amps, just voltage."

"It makes the muscles seize up. If you ever have to use it, yell for help while you're running away," Martinez added.

"So, do I just carry it around in my hand?"

"When we're close, you won't need it," Martinez told her. "Tell you what. Take my jacket. There's a pocket inside for my duty piece. That okay, you think, Winter?"

"If it makes her feel safer," Winter said.

Sean was comforted by the control over Dylan the strange weapon could offer her.

An hour later in the living room, when she looked up from her book and saw Dylan coming, it was too late to reach inside the jacket for the Taser. As he loomed over her, his expression was one of amusement. Martinez was coming back and Beck appeared at the door to the dining room, then started across the room. "I see your escort isn't any better than mine."

"Back off, Mr. Devlin," Martinez ordered, crossing the room.

"Stay where you are, Deputy," Dylan said, his voice icy calm. "Still don't want to talk, Sean?"

Sean knew that Dylan could hurt her, perhaps kill her, before Martinez could stop him.

"What's the matter, darling? Cat got your tongue?"

Sean was frightened until he said that, but after the words registered, she felt white-hot rage. Before she knew she was going to do anything, she had lashed out, striking Dylan's cheek with her open hand hard enough to rock his head.

Beck and Martinez rushed to intervene, but Dylan's response was instantaneous. Sean saw stars and had a numb realization that she had been punched square in her mouth. Martinez tried to grab him, but Dylan pushed her away. Sean reached into her jacket and drew out the Taser, but before she could fire it, he grabbed her hand and twisted it. Sean wasn't sure whether she triggered the weapon or Dylan did, but when the apparatus popped loudly, Beck fell heavily to the floor, convulsing.

When Dylan drew back his fist to hit her again, Winter seemed to materialize out of thin air. He caught Dylan's wrist, spun him around, and punched him hard on the nose.

In a blur of motion the two men fell backward. Dylan now had Winter's wrist, and he used Winter's weight to pull him off-balance. When Winter landed on the floor, Dylan was straddling his chest, pressing the muzzle of Winter's pistol, which he had managed to grab in the struggle, against the supine deputy's forehead.

Blood ran in dual streams from Dylan's nose, dripped from his chin onto Winter's shirt.

"With your own gun, you meddling piece of shit," Dylan told him calmly.

Sean was afraid, but Winter merely looked defiant. His arms were stretched out, his hands resting on the rug, palms open.

Suddenly Greg had his gun inches from the back of Dylan's skull. Martinez aimed at Dylan's temple and Cross at the rear quarter of Dylan's head.

Greg barked, "Think, Devlin. You pull the trigger, you'll be all over this room."

Sean didn't care if the deputies shot Dylan. Of the two men with guns aimed at them, she cared only about Winter.

"Maybe I won't kill this faggot, if he begs."

"Dylan," Sean said in a steely voice, "you're making a complete fool of yourself."

"I'm not bluffing," Greg said calmly.

Dylan placed the gun flat on Winter's chest and stood. "Next time, son," he said to Winter.

"Cross, see that Mr. Devlin gets packed immediately. We're leaving here at six to meet the plane," Greg announced. "Devlin, that was your last stunt. You are going to be in handcuffs until we get you to D.C."

"What about my wife?" Dylan asked.

Sean's heart was pounding. She held her breath, waiting.

"She's staying here," Greg told him.

A wave of relief surged through her, and when she

smiled, the pain caused her eyes to tear up. Sean put her fingertips to her lower lip and they came away smeared with blood.

29

Sean's lip was split open and bloody. Winter took a tissue from a box on the coffee table and handed it to her.

"Should get some ice on that," he said.

"I thought he was going to kill you," Sean said.

"It crossed my mind," Winter admitted.

"Thank you for stopping him. He would have killed *me*," she said.

"Did you see Dylan move?" Greg said incredulously.

"He's faster than he looks," Winter said.

"You okay?" Greg asked him.

Winter straightened and Sean saw him wince. "I'm fine."

Martinez knelt to help Beck sit up. "I think I can get up," Beck said, dismissing her assistance.

Winter caught his eye and shook his head. *Don't be an idiot!*

"Maybe I *could* use a hand," Beck capitulated. "That Taser hurt like hell."

"Come to the kitchen," Winter told Sean, taking her arm until she was seated at the table.

She watched as Winter filled a sandwich bag with crushed ice. When he placed it against her numb lip, tears flooded her eyes—tears of anger, not pain.

She held the bag against her lip. "He is utterly and totally insane."

"What's his military training?" Winter asked.

Sean looked baffled. "He was in marketing and public

relations. He never said anything about being in the military."

"He didn't learn those moves at an ad agency."

"I think he ran track in high school," she said.

"That would explain it."

"Was that sarcasm, Deputy Massey?" she asked, trying to smile.

"Absolutely."

Greg entered the room, pocketing his Palm organizer.

"The boat is here. I want you to walk Jet over to the dock."

"Sure."

"I've just reported what happened between you and Devlin. I'm not taking you out with us. You and Martinez'll stay here with Ms. Devlin. After what happened between you and him, I can't risk an incident in transit. You'll make Rush's birthday. Word of honor."

"If I were you, I'd take him out of here in a straitjacket."

"I only wish I could," Greg said.

Sean could see from his expression he was telling the truth.

30

Holding aloft an enormous red and white golf umbrella, Jet mumbled to herself as she plodded over the wet pine needles that covered the sandy trail through the trees. The rain beat down on Winter's coat as he walked a few feet behind her carrying her heavy suitcases.

"I wish Miss Sean was leaving with me. She's been through hell in a red wagon," Jet said.

When they passed the barracks, they could see the

sailors' faces clustered behind two of the rain-streaked windows, reminding Winter of villagers in the old monster movies who know better than to leave the protection of their residence. A sailor with a shaved head was standing inside the doorway of the radio shack; he acknowledged Jet as she and Winter passed by.

The boat, a steel-hull diesel, had an enclosed, all-weather cabin. The stern door allowed Jet and Winter to step down onto the boat, where he handed Jet's suitcases to a crewman. Jet surprised Winter by hugging him. He hugged her back. She left Winter, walked through the cabin door, and took a seat on the bench along the farthest wall. She nodded once to Winter, then turned to look out the window. The deckhand unhooked the lines, fore and aft, and the boat pulled away slowly. Winter watched until a curtain of rain enveloped it.

As he walked up the dock, Winter noticed the sport-fishing boat moored opposite the cigarette racer. The cockpit was open and there was room on either side to walk to the bow. Except for a Plexiglas windshield and roll-up walls of clear plastic, the aft deck and lower bridge were open to the elements. A ladder led up to the flying bridge above the cockpit and the keys hung from the ignition. The Navy obviously didn't think anyone was going to steal it from under their noses.

Winter also noticed that the cigarette racer's engine compartment was propped open and the motor was partially disassembled.

"Jet's gone," Winter told Greg in the foyer.

"I agreed to deliver an olive branch from Devlin," he said, holding up Sean's laptop, "to express his remorse. He said he wouldn't try and talk to her again if she would read one last letter he typed into the thing."

"They're always real sorry after they beat up their wives," Winter said contemptuously.

"Sean reluctantly agreed to let him write the note, but she doesn't want him anywhere near her. She made me stand there while he typed it to make sure he didn't damage her laptop."

"You should read it first," Winter suggested.

Greg nodded, set the thing on the table, and opened the lid. It said:

After six tonight, my darling, I suppose we will be going our separate ways for good. As I fly away, I will imagine you still here with your Spic deputy pal and that faggot, Winter Massey. It is my fondest wish that you all three eat shit and die screaming.

"Sticks and stones," Winter mused, a bitter taste in his mouth.

By five-thirty, when Greg and Winter had collected the deputies' cases and placed them out on the porch, the rain had thinned to a sprinkle. Greg went alone to Dylan's room and dropped off a bulletproof vest for him to wear. The deputies armed themselves with heavy ordnance, and each put on their ballistic vest. Shortly before six, a Blackhawk landed noisily and Winter went out to the porch to see the crew off.

All of the people leaving, including Devlin, wore matching black raincoats and plain ball caps, so that it would be difficult for anyone to single out the package.

Greg came out first. "You have Mrs. Devlin ready for transport at ten hundred hours tomorrow. There's plenty in the fridge you can heat up." He stared at Winter solemnly. "A word of warning, Win. Whatever happens, and I do mean *whatever* happens, don't let Martinez cook anything. If she does, for the love of God, don't put it anywhere near your mouth. Hug the kid for me when you get home, Win."

Greg offered his hand to Winter and for ten seconds they squeezed, trying to get the other to release first. The door opening behind them ended the contest prematurely.

Dylan wore his coat like a cape, his cuffed hands visible. "Until we meet again," he told Winter, menacingly.

Winter didn't reply. He turned his attention to Beck, who came out next, grinning like a schoolboy.

"I did it, Winter," he said, oblivious to the tension crackling in the air.

"Did what?"

"I asked Martinez out . . . on a date."

"And she said?" he prompted teasingly.

" 'What doesn't kill me makes me stronger.' "

"That's great," Winter told him, slapping him on the back.

Forsythe came out carrying his aluminum sniper-rifle case, the Colt 9-mm automatic carbine over his shoulder.

"Take care, Forsythe," Winter said.

"You too, Massey," he said abruptly. They hadn't exactly become the best of friends.

Two minutes later the helicopter lifted off and was swallowed up by a hungry gray sky. Winter's assignment was all but over. He smiled at the thought of his son waiting for his return, just a couple hundred miles in the direction Devlin and Greg's detail were already traveling. As he stood there, Sean came outside and joined him.

"Can I do this?" she asked.

"Do what?"

"Walk unescorted on the beach."

"Sure, but . . ."

"But what?"

"You'll get wet."

She laughed. "I don't want to, Deputy. Just wondering if I could."

"From here on out, Mrs. Devlin, you can do whatever suits you. Within reason."

"I feel like dancing and breaking into song."

It was nice to see his package smiling again.

31

Avery Whitehead preferred to move through life with men in suits encircling him the way sharks ring their prey, whenever possible. He felt vulnerable alone. The federal prosecutor stood out of the rain in an open maintenance hangar, watching the window-rattling takeoffs and landings on the runway a hundred yards away.

Whitehead stared out at a line of faintly illuminated A-10 Warthogs and the Falcon 900B he had arrived aboard. Coming down from D.C. he'd removed his jacket and flown in his shirtsleeves so his coat wouldn't be wrinkled when he saw Devlin. His gray Zegna suit was impeccably tailored, his tie a loud red splash against a crisp white wedge of shirt.

He had come alone because there wasn't room in the jet for his assistant, the marshals, a witness, his wife, and their luggage and other equipment. His short meeting with Devlin on Tuesday had left him rattled and worried that the killer might be self-destructing and about to destroy the government's case. Just before Avery boarded the airplane at Andrews, Attorney General Katlin had called to tell him that things at the safe house had seriously deteriorated. Avery caught the implicit threat in his boss's tone: *Fix it or else.*

It was imperative that Whitehead gain control of his witness before Devlin lost him his case and killed his stellar career.

Whitehead was wondering how long it would take the

two-man flight crew to empty their bladders, when he saw the pair sprinting through the rain toward the Falcon Jet. He had told them that he wanted to take off as soon as the deputies showed up, so they needed to preflight the thing before.

They waved at him and he returned the gesture out of habit. "Yeah, you bastards get my plane ready. Christ, if all I had to do was fly around for a living like a taxi driver . . ."

He checked his watch, a plain gold Patek Philippe with an alligator band. The helicopter was due any second.

He heard the Blackhawk before he saw it. It materialized from the sky as though it was being lowered by cables, and came to rest near the jet. Whitehead buttoned up his Burberry trench coat, snapped open his umbrella, and strode out into the rain as soon as the blades had slowed enough. He was between the Blackhawk and the passenger jet when the marshals stepped down out of the chopper. The black inspector came first, immediately followed by the others, who formed a protective circle for Devlin to step down into. Whitehead was relieved to see that Dylan wasn't wearing leg irons. He relaxed slightly. "Where is Mrs. Devlin?" he asked in a voice low enough so that only the inspector would hear it.

"Due to an incident between the Devlins, I left Mrs. Devlin behind in the company of two deputies. They will be leaving tomorrow."

"The A.G. told me there was some sort of problem at the safe house."

"This morning, Mr. Devlin drugged two deputies, decapitated a cat, punched his wife, assaulted two of my men, and put a gun to one of my people's head. He spent the day in handcuffs."

Avery's knees felt rubbery. "God damn it! In all of my years—Nations, I have never seen such an out-of-control sideshow as your safe house. You are the most incompetent marshal I have ever come across. As soon as I get to

Katlin, I'm making sure Devlin gets a new crew. As far as I can tell, you have not yet been in control of the security situation."

"Your star witness is a complete psycho," Greg said evenly.

"I need a quick word with Mr. Devlin," Avery told him, loudly enough for Devlin to hear. *"Alone."*

Inspector Nations shook his head. "I have to get him out of the open, into the craft."

"There's no danger here, damn it! We're in the middle of a fucking air base—"

"Sorry, sir," the inspector insisted, looking at his watch. "We have a schedule to hold to. We're on a communications blackout and due at Andrews in—"

"Sorry, *suh,*" Dylan Devlin mocked, speaking for the first time since they had arrived. "We is, uhhh, all blacked out."

Whitehead shot Devlin a warning glare over Nations' shoulder. Dylan held up his hands to show the cuffs.

"Dylan and me inside the plane, you and your crew outside. Give me two minutes with him. The pilot can make up that loss."

Reluctantly, Nations agreed. Whitehead knew that what happened while Devlin was under WITSEC's protection was all up to the inspector in charge. Whitehead was hoping that this Inspector Nations felt like he owed Avery something after the trouble at the safe house. Avery intended to see that Nations took a career hit for it. Examples had to be made.

"Beck," Nations called. "Check the plane."

After the deputy marshal searched the jet, Devlin and Whitehead entered. Whitehead positioned him out of the crew's hearing range.

"What the hell happened on the island?" Whitehead demanded of Devlin. As he spoke, despite his best efforts, his voice rose with each accusation. "Dead cat...drugging officers, punching your wife, and, for Christ's sake, pulling a gun on a deputy marshal?"

"A small misunderstanding. Two deputies took drugs and wanted a scapegoat. I think the cook's cat must have climbed into a drawer and my wife accidentally slammed it shut. The rest is—"

"I'm talking about you pulling a gun on a United States deputy marshal! Where the hell did you get a gun?" Avery hissed, cutting him off.

"He gave it to me. Easy, I was getting to that. The man is a loose cannon. Power-drunk and, Avery, he's been diddling my wife."

"Your deal will be history if you don't make sure this goes off without a hitch. Blow this and you'll wish you were in a cell with Sam Manelli and a blowtorch. When we get to D.C., we are going to have a come-to-Jesus meeting. The next time you make the slightest wave you are going to find yourself up shit creek. We don't get Manelli, we still have you. Is that perfectly clear?"

"Absolutely, but I've got a request about changing these guards, Avery. This detail is so fucked, I'd be safer if I was being guarded by Manelli's thugs. I have everything under control. When I testify I will be believed." He winked. "Trust me."

What choice do I have? Whitehead tapped on the window to signal the marshals that it was time to go.

As the plane filled with people, Avery Whitehead closed his eyes and prayed.

"By the way, guys," the pilot called back over his shoulder, "no hot chambers in my plane. I have this morbid fear of one of you guys sneezing and blowing a hole in my airplane and me getting sucked out right along with you."

"No problem," Greg answered. "Guys, clear your long guns."

There was a series of clicks and slapping metal as magazines were withdrawn, the round in the chambers removed, and the magazines returned with a sharp rap of their palms.

"Our copilot will be passing through to the rear, and if anyone wants to stow a coat or anything, he will handle that. We will be without a stewardess tonight because we lack room for one. This is a smoke-free flight. After we are upstairs, and I have turned off the seat-belt sign, you are free to help yourselves to a drink out of the fridge."

The copilot slipped from his seat and made his way to the rear.

"Kinda cramped, ain't it?" Bear said.

"But fast," Beck said.

Dylan yawned and closed his eyes. "Wake me when we get there."

The pilot turned in his seat and looked back into the cabin. "I would appreciate it if you'd close the shades until we are at altitude."

Whitehead closed the shade beside him and, as he turned back, saw the pilot on his feet, holding a silenced pistol in his hand, a tattoo of barbed wire on his right wrist. Whitehead felt like ice water had been thrown in his face. He hadn't been paying attention to the things around him. This pilot was not the same man as the one who'd flown him down. This man was younger, taller. As Whitehead was about to call out, the pilot in front of him and copilot at his back opened fire.

Avery Whitehead's last thought was not that the marshals were dying around him. His last thought, which was interrupted by a Glaser round through his brain, was whether, earlier in the day, he had locked his car door at the airport.

32

The radio shack on Rook Island was Signalman Lane Nash's duty station for another three hours and twelve minutes. It was a concrete bunker with a steeply pitched roof covered in sheets of terra-cotta-colored aluminum. The wires and cables ran up the wall like bright vines, secured to the girders and then routed out to the tower through a weatherproof nipple. The copper and fiber-optic material connected the console's monitoring instruments to the sensory devices. Those sensors, located on the tower above the shack, gathered information about things in the atmosphere or on the water and conversed with the satellites that circled the planet in swarms.

There were no windows in the bunker. The console table was ten feet long and had metal cabinet doors at both sides of the operator's seat. There were storage cabinets for parts and equipment, two swivel chairs, and a bathroom that held only a toilet and sink. A single door that opened out from the room was protected from the weather by an awning.

Lane concentrated on the radar screen. The young radio operator had set his paperback aside on the console and was using his shoulder to hold the red receiver against his ear as he spoke to the air-traffic controller at Cherry Point.

"I got the first return just after that King Air passed four miles to the east of here."

"He was having radio problems and was warned off to the east," the controller said. *"He stayed clear of your position by a half mile."*

"I got returns after it passed."

"Returns looked like what? I didn't show anything on our end."

"Soft returns. One sweep showed a spot at four miles, altitude unknown, four sweeps later there was one a half mile from me, then a few later almost onshore."

"Birds come to shore, right? Go out and shoot a goose." The controller laughed. *"Nothing substantial fell off that King Air. I have it sixty-nine miles south of your position at twenty-five thousand feet, two hundred and thirty-nine knots true."*

"Probably. Just birds," Lane agreed. He took one last look at the screen and signed off with his controller. He ran his hand through the stubble on his head and picked up his book.

The operator was at a particularly good part when the lights over his console flickered, then went out. It had been storming, but the electricity was almost never interrupted, because it was fed by underground cable to the island. The backup generator was supposed to cut in if the main failed, so the operator waited. It didn't come on.

"God damn it," he muttered.

He flipped on his flashlight, walked to the switch, and flipped it up and down. He went to the breaker panel. Nothing. Planning to check the generators, he opened the door.

A gloved hand seized his wrist, and a man dressed completely in black, his features hidden behind a black nylon mask, pushed a remarkably large knife under the place where Lane's ribs met, three inches above his belt buckle. Lane looked down and saw the knife go in, but it didn't hurt. The sensation was like the first twinge of a bout of indigestion. He wanted to push the man away, but he couldn't. He felt so weak, so sleepy.

His vision started closing down like a camera aperture being twisted, the image darkening from the outside in. He just wanted to lie down and close his eyes.

33

Winter flipped his final card, an ace of spades, facedown onto the stack of discards. "Gin."

"You dog!" Martinez complained. "I'm not even going to count up my hand. What's another few hundred points among friends." She turned to Sean, who had started playing with them then decided to read. Despite the relaxed atmosphere, Winter and Martinez kept her constantly in sight, their weapons close.

"Anybody besides me want coffee?" Sean asked.

As soon as Sean was out of the room, Martinez said, "God, I wish she would settle somewhere."

"You want to arm wrestle?" Winter asked her, joking.

"Fine by me. I'd have a chance at *that.*"

"Almost certainly."

"Sean's the first package I've truly liked since I started this four years ago. I might ask for a transfer—leave this baby-sitting for some fugitive recovery, like you. Maybe I'll come work in that office of yours," Martinez said.

"For every fugitive I chase, I serve twenty warrants, escort a hundred prisoners, and fill out fifty reports. Devlin wasn't far off when he called me a security guard."

"A security guard?" Martinez said, laughing.

They joined Sean in the kitchen. She poured a cup of coffee, took a sip, then dumped the contents into the sink. "It's stale." She sighed loudly. "This weather. God, I'm glad I'm not flying in this soup. I hate flying when I can't see the ground."

"As long as they skirt thunderstorms, they'll be all right," Winter said.

"You know a lot about flying weather?" she asked Winter.

"Winter's wife was a pilot," Martinez interceded. "An instructor."

"What does she do now?" Sean asked.

Martinez said nothing.

"She was killed three years ago in a midair collision," Winter told her.

Sean looked genuinely upset. "But when I asked the other night if your wife minded you being away you said something like, 'We all hate being away from people we love.'"

"Sorry, it was purposefully misleading. It's not something I like to talk about."

"I'm sorry," she said. "I was prying. I assumed since you wear a wedding ring . . ."

"Just never got around to taking it off."

Sean blushed and stepped out on the porch, letting the screen door bang behind her.

"I'm sorry if I spoke out of turn," Martinez said.

"Three years is a long time to still wear the ring," Winter admitted.

"So, what do you think of Beck?" Martinez asked, keen to change the subject. "Besides the fact that he needs a haircut."

"That comes from being a bachelor with nobody to make sure you get it clipped regularly."

Sean came back inside more composed. "The rain smells so wonderful mixed with the salt air."

"I like the quiet," Martinez told her. "You grow up in a three-bedroom apartment with six brothers, one grandmother, and two parents, and see if you mind the quiet. Me, I can't ever get enough of it. You think we should hold to keeping watch like before?"

"Fine with me," Winter replied.

"We do two hours on and two off while Sean is sleeping."

"Why?" Sean wondered.

"It's what we have to do until someone in authority says, 'Angela and Winter, don't do it anymore,'" Martinez replied, laughing.

Sean laughed, too.

"You have any brothers or sisters, Sean?" Martinez asked.

"Only child. My mother passed away almost two years ago."

"Father?"

"My parents were separated before I was born."

"You didn't know him?"

"I spent Christmas and summers with him growing up, but I can't say I really know him." She seemed to close up again at this line of questioning, her surface calm interrupted.

"What's he like?" Martinez continued, oblivious to the effect her questions were having.

"He's hard to describe. He's a workaholic, not in the least artistic. My mother was a painter and not in the least ambitious. He and my mother were such total opposites, I don't know how they ever got together long enough to make a baby. He was like an uncle who didn't know how to relate to a young girl. He was always caring but never flexible. He's judgmental as hell and has no sense of humor to speak of. I suspect he'd rather have had a son, but he never said so. For instance, he taught me to shoot because he liked to hunt, not because I wanted to do it. He wanted me to be tough, but I always got the feeling that he thought women were lesser beings, somehow." Sean stopped suddenly, surprised at how she had opened up so quickly.

"He remarried?"

"He's had girlfriends, but no, he never remarried."

"Do you still see him?"

"I haven't spent any time with him since college," Sean said matter-of-factly. "I called him when my mother died and he sent flowers. I know he loved her, but I had this feeling that if I had called a wrong number, anyone who answered could have offered me the same amount of comfort as he did. And we last spoke just before I got married. He sent me a big set of sterling silver cutlery without a note. He sends the same Christmas card every year. I'm waiting to see if after twelve years he will buy another box, or just stop doing it altogether."

"Your parents still alive?" Martinez asked, turning to Winter.

"My mother is still alive. She moved in with us after Eleanor died. My father died when I was seventeen."

"Lydia," Sean said. "Greg mentioned her the day we arrived."

Winter nodded.

"My parents are still around. My father has a temper you wouldn't believe," Martinez said. "But we're close. He treated me exactly like he treated my brothers, until boys came to pick me up. He was like an inquisitor then, and few ever showed for a follow-up. My father was a detective, and he thought every kid who was interested in me was a delinquent. Maybe they were."

"Where'd you go to college?" Winter asked Sean, hoping to change the subject. Not only did this conversation seem to make her melancholy, he himself didn't want to discuss fathers.

"Loyola, in Chicago. Took drama, some art courses." She smiled at him. "Even took some literature courses. Ended up getting a master's in business because I wasn't the artist my mother was. I've been thinking I might open an art gallery because I love being around paintings." Winter had never seen her so talkative.

"What do you think of Beck?" Martinez asked her. "Besides the hair."

"Same thing I told you the last seven times you asked me." She and Martinez both laughed. "I like him. *Except* for the hair."

Martinez laughed. "Before there's even a dinner date, the boy's hair definitely gets a professional shaping," she said.

"Seriously, Angela, he's a nice guy and nice guys are hard to come by. Take my word for it," Sean said.

"It's winding down toward dinnertime," Winter said.

"I can whip up something," Martinez said. "Something with peppers, pasta, and ground beef."

"Tell you guys what," Winter said, recalling Greg's warning. "Why don't you both go sit on the porch and I'll make us some dinner? Roast beef sandwiches sound good?"

"But I love to cook!" Martinez protested.

"Let's all make the food and then sit out there together," Sean suggested.

Winter collected the sliced roast, mayonnaise, pickles, and mustard from the refrigerator for the sandwiches. Martinez poured iced tea into three glasses and got out the plates. Sean sliced the bread from one of the loaves Jet had baked and left in the warmer. Once the sandwiches were ready, they walked to the round section of the porch at the north corner, which had a peaked roof over it. For lack of a better term, they referred to it as the gazebo. As they were starting to sit down, the lights went out; only the house windows were illuminated, from the battery-powered emergency lights inside the hallways.

"Great," Martinez said.

"The sailors will get the power back on," Winter said. "I expect there's a backup system."

"I could go get a lantern," Martinez volunteered.

They ate in the dark, their conversation accompanied by the sound of rain and the surf.

"I'm going to get a jacket. It's cool out here," Sean said, when they'd finished.

"We can go inside," Winter offered.

"No, I like it out here."

Martinez stood. "I need to powder my nose anyway. I'll take the plates back inside and get you a jacket."

Martinez went back through the kitchen, closing the door behind her. Winter and Sean sat in silence listening to the rain.

Winter looked up when he heard the front door open. Over Sean's shoulder he saw Martinez step out onto the porch holding a windbreaker. She took a step in their direction, stumbled like she'd broken a heel, then fell against the wall, dropping the coat. Winter was wondering what she'd stepped on, when she straightened and the wall where she had leaned was stained dark—blood.

"Shhhhhhh," he hissed. He drew his SIG, squatted beside the table, and tugged Sean from her chair to the floor. This time she didn't resist.

Sean's back was to the front door so she hadn't seen Martinez stumble, or the blood. Only when she knelt beside Winter did she see that Martinez was leaning against the wall, her right hand gripping her gun, unable to get it out of the holster. A pair of red aim dots, like annoying flies, buzzed Martinez's face and her head snapped violently back, horribly staining the clapboards behind her. A fury welled up within Winter, but no target immediately presented itself.

Beside him, Sean made a small involuntary squeak as she inhaled sharply.

Winter's mind closed out the anger as it shifted into survival mode. Martinez didn't exist now. Instead, what lay before his eyes, on its side now was a used target that belonged to someone who intended to make him one, too.

He existed and unless he kept it that way, Sean would cease to exist with him. There were at least two assassins armed with laser aiming devices attached to silenced weapons.

A shadowy figure carrying a machine gun sprang up onto the porch, Winter raised the SIG and let his instincts aim for him. Winter fired three .40-caliber rounds. The reports were deafening. The man's head jerked back and he was dead.

Grabbing Sean's hand, Winter led her along the side of the house at a run, passing the kitchen door. "Stay with me," he ordered. "You'll die here unless you do *exactly* what I say."

"I know that!" she snapped back.

Bullets slammed into the wall like fists as the pair ran down the porch in the darkness, but they were moving too fast for another assailant to get a clear shot.

They vaulted over the railing and hit the sand, stumbled, regained their footing, and sprinted for the tree line. The rain was unexpectedly cold. Their clothes were soaked in moments. For a split second, Winter thought about the alarm and the weapons he was leaving behind, knowing that doubling back was not an option.

"How many?" Sean asked.

"Three I know of."

"Who are they?" She stumbled but remained on her feet. "Just tell them Dylan is gone."

"We make the radar station, we should be okay." Winter was thinking about the weapons, radios, a boat, and six shooters to lay down covering fire that were just beyond the tree line.

"Think the sailors heard you shooting?" she asked, her breathing labored from fear and exertion.

"No." Winter knew that the sailors couldn't possibly hear the reports.

They ran the trail full out, breaking out on the other

side of the trees. The buildings were dark—no exterior lights, not so much as a glow in any window.

Thinking he should load in a fresh magazine, Winter reached back and felt his now-empty magazine holder. The two magazines had probably fallen out when he'd jumped off the porch and landed soundlessly into the sand. All he had was the eight remaining .40-caliber rounds. Without help from the sailors, and more firepower, they were screwed. The handgun was no match for MP5s in capable hands, but he didn't plan to face them toe to toe. He had to pray for the ability to surprise the remaining men, whom he knew he couldn't evade for long.

Winter opened the door to the barracks and they went inside.

"Maybe we should just get on a boat," Sean suggested. "I saw boats from the helicopter, right?"

"I need a gun," Winter told her. "We'd be sitting ducks out in the open."

"Damn it, Massey, you have a gun!"

"A bigger gun with more than eight bullets. They might have someone covering the boat, or they may have already disabled it. There might be three of them or ten. Greg said there is an ordnance room here. That means M16s. First I need light to find it." A small amber light illuminated the hand lantern holder. Winter pressed the rubber nipple and it came on, casting a brilliant stain against the wall.

They passed by doors to the sleeping quarters. An OFF-LIMITS sign hung on the bathroom door. Winter heard water running and edged the door open. "Anybody in here?" he called. There was no answer. He stepped inside while Sean held the door open. He played the flashlight over a woman's naked body, prone on the tiles. The water streaming away from her was clear—all the blood that was going to leak out of the two wounds he could see had long since gone down the drain.

"That woman from the beach is in there—dead."

"The others?"

He didn't reply. Winter knew that if they had killed an unarmed woman taking a shower, they had killed the others. Inside the rec room the floor was littered with hollow brass shell casings. He didn't use the flashlight. He didn't want the killers to see the glow and know exactly where they were. He could make out the shapes of corpses near the overturned card table, like sleeping seals. The air was lousy with the smell of cordite and spilled blood.

"Dear lord," Sean gasped.

Once inside the windowless ordnance room, he turned on the flashlight. His heart sank as he looked at the solid steel doors of the weapons locker. A half dozen M16s and six Beretta M9s were inside the heavy steel mesh, along with stacks of loaded magazines. Opening the doors required a combination. He opened a standing cabinet, which was filled with coats and specialized items the sailors might need in an emergency. He jerked down a pair of raincoats. "This will fit you" he said.

"I'm already wet," she said.

He handed her a ballistic vest. "Put this vest on first— under the coat."

Winter cut the flashlight off before they left the room. In the rec room, his ears picked up the chirp of a wet rubber sole against floor tile—someone was coming up the hallway.

He nudged Sean to a steel-frame window on the bay side and swung it open. He whispered, "When I fire, you go out this window. Don't wait. If I'm not right behind you, find a place to hide. Help should be here soon." Since he had no idea if the sailors had sent out an alarm, he had no reason to believe help would come soon enough to make any difference to them.

He moved to a table and set the lamp on its surface, holding it at arm's length with his left hand while he aimed his gun at the door. When the rec room door swung in, Winter braced, but sensing a feint, remained still. After the door swung back into place, it opened again and a figure entered. If their luck held, this man, too, would be wearing night-vision lenses: a double-edged sword. While it allowed him to see in darkness like an owl, it also made him sensitive to bright light.

When Winter triggered the flashlight, the figure against the door was illuminated like a performer on a stage. The man raised his left arm to shield his blinded eyes and fired a burst at the light. Winter fired as he ran for the window, where Sean was scrambling through ahead of him. The .40-caliber bullets knocked the killer backward through the door. Due to the armor, Winter doubted he had done more than slow the man down.

They ran up the side of the barracks toward the radio shack and the switchback beyond it. Winter had only four shots left and at least two other assailants to split them between. As they rounded the radio shack, a lightning bolt streaked overhead and Winter saw a silhouette among the weeds to the left of the path. A man was waiting there on the switchback in case they managed to get past the one who'd come inside—a man who'd soon be on their heels. Winter thrust Sean through the radio shack's doorway, just as the crouching man opened up with his MP5. The bullets struck the bunker like hammer blows.

Sean fell over something and yelped.

Winter couldn't close the door without exposing himself to the man's corrected fire. When lightning flared across the sky again, Winter saw that Sean had tripped over a uniformed corpse. They had seconds before someone came in after them. There was no way out—only the way they'd come in.

Winter knew that if he allowed himself to think this over, he was dead. He grabbed Sean by her arm, almost tripping over an overturned chair.

"What are we going to do?" she demanded.

"Hide," Winter said.

"Great plan," she muttered. "They'll never find us in here."

"Was that sarcasm?" he quipped as he looked around.

"Absolutely," she replied, squeezing his hand.

He put Sean inside a narrow steel cabinet and closed its door. He doubted both killers would enter: One would come in, or both would take this opportunity to make an escape. The assailants had to know their time was running out. Why risk their lives for second-tier targets when the Navy might be coming to the island anytime?

Rain rattled on the awning as he prepared to greet the killer. Something thrown in from outside rolled across the floor. He didn't have to see it to know it was a grenade. Winter closed his eyes, pressed his hands over his ears, and opened his mouth. If it was a CS grenade they could survive the gas. If it was a fragmentary grenade, he would likely die with his mouth open and his hands over his ears. His preference was for it to be a third type—a flash-bang.

He only had time for one last thought: *I did the best I could.*

34

The assailant guarding the switchback fired too late to hit the running couple. The man readied his weapon and watched his partner slip inside the radio shack. Smoke from the flash-bang grenade poured over him through the rain and was sucked off by the wind. If his partner didn't come out pretty quick, he'd kill whoever did. The WIT-SEC deputy they had been pursuing was a lot better than they'd imagined. This cakewalk had cost them their team leader, a man they had all considered the best in their cell.

Within two minutes, his partner backed out of the building, dragging the woman out into the downpour by her ankle. He closed the distance between them just as his partner aimed his weapon down at the woman's head and fired a three-shot burst. The impact of the bullets splattered dark muck against the side of the building.

Curious, the killer joined his partner and kneeled beside her, gripped her drenched hair, and turned her face toward him to confirm the kill. "What about the deputy?" he asked his partner, who stood over him. The woman blinked.

"Live, or die," an unfamiliar voice said. The killer didn't have to look up to know that he was on his knees below the deputy marshal who was wearing his partner's outfit.

The killer pivoted the MP5 in his hand intending to take out the woman, before he was shot himself, but . . .

Winter helped Sean to her feet. Using the rain and his palm, he wiped away the chunks of mud his bullets had splashed. Winter scanned the landscape through the night-vision goggles he had taken from the dead assailant inside the shack and saw nothing that was a danger to them. He didn't look down at the killer's ruined skull. He removed the goggles and tore off the rubber hood.

"I felt the heat from your gun when you shot. Did you have to shoot it so close to my head?" Unbelievably, Sean was angry.

"He wouldn't have fallen for it otherwise. Let's find a radio."

"Where?"

"Should be one on the boat." He reached into Sean's coat pocket, took out his SIG, and put it in her hand. He checked the magazine of the MP5 in his hand and, finding it too light, discarded it for a full one he robbed from the dead man at his feet.

He had expected to find the assassins' boat waiting at the dock for them, but there were only the two he had seen there earlier that day. Running down the switchback, he and Sean approached the dock through the freezing rain. Winter scanned the surrounding area all the way down to the sport-fishing boat. When he looked back up at the tree line he saw, off to the right, the shape of a Little Bird, a four-place military helicopter. He hoped there had been only the three assassins he had killed—one being the pilot.

Winter stepped over the transom after Sean.

"Watch the path," he told her. He climbed into the cockpit of the boat. The windshield was smeared with water, obscuring his view of the dock, the switchback, and the radio tower. Sean stood in the rain with her hood up, aiming Winter's gun at the switchback,

Just as he discovered that the key was missing, Winter heard something hit the deck behind him and turned to see the styrene key fob on the floor at Sean's feet. She stood, staring up at the flying bridge above Winter, her face a frozen mask. A red dot danced in the center of her Navy-issue raincoat.

"Lady, throw that pistol over the side." The Southern accent was thick.

Winter nodded at her to do so. She hesitated, then tossed the handgun out, the rain swallowing the splash. "Now, Deputy Massey, five seconds to toss out that chatterbox or I'll light the bitch up. You can't hit me without me doing her."

He studied the crimson spot that moved from Sean's jacket to her face and back to her heart. He studied Sean's gaze to see exactly where her eyes were aimed. The only question was how close this fourth killer was standing to the edge. Winter switched the rate-of-fire selector to full automatic and raised the barrel.

"Five . . . four," the killer mocked.

Winter concentrated on the red dot playing on Sean's face, now her neck, and down onto the coat.

Winter fired on three—the bullets ripping the fiberglass ceiling to shreds. As he fired, he was aware of Sean being knocked backward off the transom and into the water by a single shot from the man's weapon.

A black-clad body fell sprawling onto the deck. Where the man's legs were chewed up, arterial blood spewed. His pistol was stopped by the transom.

Winter ran to the stern and pulled Sean up into the boat. She began coughing immediately, fighting to breathe.

"It's okay," he said. He checked her face and neck, and she opened her eyes. "Just knocked the breath out of you." He tore open her coat and saw the .45 round deformed against the ballistic vest under her coat.

"You let him shoot me." Her voice was raspy.

"You're fine."

"You let him shoot me!" She slapped him, hard.

He lifted the assailant's pistol, a SOCOM .45-caliber H&K fitted with a noise suppressor. Leaving Sean, he moved to the supine killer, who stared up into the rain, blinking slowly. The bubbles of blood between his lips told Winter that one or more of the bullets had entered his chest after going under the vest—his shattered lungs were filled with blood.

"How did you know my name?" he asked the killer.

The man smiled, smearing dark blood over his teeth. His eyes were losing their focus. He grabbed Winter's ankle, coughing up blood. He said something but the sound was gobbled by the thundering rotors of the attack helicopter that seemed to be suspended over the dock like a wasp, blasting the boat with wind, drumming rain and blinding light. The Cobra's .30-caliber minigun seemed to be aimed at his chest, about to blast him into confetti. He was dressed exactly like the dead man on the deck.

"You, on the deck—hands on your heads, do not move!"

Winter waited for a second, then stood, locking his hands over his head.

The switchback swarmed with running men dressed in black.

"Sean!" Winter called out. "No matter what anyone asks, don't discuss anything that happened before Martinez went down. Understand?"

The men in black slammed Winter and Sean facedown onto the deck.

35 | Ward Field, Virginia

Herman Hoffman stood waiting outside the cavernous hangar in the dark. Since Ralph was flying the Justice Department's plane, the first part of the operation was a success. He knew the boys on the island side had to have done as well, since their degree of difficulty was far lower.

He watched as the jet turned onto the final approach and came in hot and flaring just above the asphalt. Ralph taxied the jet past the helicopter and, cutting the engines, rolled directly into the hangar.

Herman watched as the clamshell door came down and Ralph descended the steps. He picked up the Polaroid camera from the table and returned to the cabin to take the proof-of-death pictures. Two other men came out of the plane a few seconds after the fourth flash.

The first man down was wiping matter and blood from his face with a towel. He saw Herman's proffered hand. "Sorry, sir," he said, laughing. "I'm afraid the government's nice plane is totally ruined."

"Nice to have you back home, Lewis," Herman said, smiling. "Ralph, get the fireworks set and let's get in the sky."

36 | Rook Island, North Carolina

Rain splattered noisily against the blue tarpaulin and the water that ran under it came out dyed pink. The SEALs had covered the corpse to protect evidence. Winter and Sean sat in the boat's cockpit, where rain dripped through the ragged fiberglass. One of the divers handed up Winter's SIG Sauer to a young SEAL, who removed the magazine, cleared the breech, then set the pistol and its magazine on a seat cushion.

Sean had been quiet since the SEALs arrived ninety minutes earlier. She sat huddled in a wool blanket, not meeting Winter's eyes. Winter had identified himself and explained that four unknown men, all dressed like SEALs, had killed the six radar-station crew and another US marshal, before he had killed them.

The SEAL commander approached Winter, clipping his radio onto his belt.

"Lieutenant Commander Reed is on his way here. He's shore patrol."

"Has anybody contacted my people?" Winter asked.

"I'm not sure," the young man said.

Drained of adrenaline, fatigue had caught up with Winter. He felt bone-weary.

"Poor Angela," Sean said softly. "How could anybody do something like that?"

Winter didn't know what to say. He felt grief for Martinez—it was so totally senseless for her to die like she had and, worse still, after the package had left.

"What if he'd shot me in the head?" Sean asked suddenly.

"I'd never hand my gun over to a killer. I did the only thing I could."

"Who was the guy who shot me?" Sean asked.

"No idea."

"He seemed to know you."

She had a point. He had no idea how the man he had shot through the boat's roof could have known his name.

Winter felt the boat rock slightly. He turned to see two men in shore patrol coats climb onto the vessel. The older of the pair squatted, lifted the edge of the tarpaulin, and studied the corpse.

The SEAL commander said, "Sir, this is United States Deputy—"

"I know who he is," the older man interrupted, looking directly at Winter, ignoring Sean Devlin. "Deputy, I'm Lieutenant Commander Fletcher Reed. I'm going to handle this until the NCIS investigators get here."

Fletcher Reed was in his early forties, built like a gymnast twenty years past his last medal but ready and willing to go out and compete again even if his heart exploded doing it. His head was a perfect rectangle topped with hair that would have made a bristle brush jealous. He had small ears and a neck that flared from his sharp jaw out to his wide shoulders. His eyes were so dark there was no difference between the irises and pupils. If he had ever owned a sense of humor it was not apparent from his grim countenance.

"Do you have any questions before I ask a few?"

"Have you contacted the USMS?"

"That has been done. Now, what the hell is this, Massey?" he demanded.

"A corpse," Winter said.

"Does the corpse have a name?"

"We weren't formally introduced."

Reed stared hard at Winter, the two men studying each other across the wet tarpaulin. "In my experience, having a bunch of heavily armed individuals come onto a radar station in peacetime and wipe out six sailors and your partner in such a senseless and brutal manner is hardly a normal event. I'm sure as hell not going to stand here and listen to you making flip remarks."

The man's words made Winter feel like an ass. Sean sat staring down at her lap.

"I understand the seriousness of this," Winter said evenly. "They were doing their damnedest to add us to their tally."

"Can you tell me why this man and three of his pals killed six unarmed sailors and that female deputy over at the house?"

"Angela Martinez," Sean said abruptly. "Her name was Angela Martinez."

Reed kept his eyes locked on Winter.

"No, sir," Winter said.

"You mean to tell me you don't know?"

"I *can't* tell you what their motive was."

Reed laughed disdainfully in total disbelief.

"This is an official United States Justice Department operation. Only the attorney general of the United States can release me to give you that information."

"What about Ms. Devlin?" Reed countered.

Winter gritted his teeth. They had obviously searched the house and found Sean's identification.

"Classified."

"And what exactly *can* you share with me, Marshal?"

"I'll be happy to tell you what happened after they killed Deputy Martinez."

Fletcher Reed seemed to be chewing that over. Reaching a decision, he nodded. "Barnett, take notes."

As Winter went through the story detail by detail, the young ensign scribbled notes. Although Winter had just been trying to keep Sean alive, he had wanted nothing worse than to escape the killers. Killing the men in black had been necessary. He didn't tell Reed this. Instead, he told him how he had hidden Sean in the storage cabinet, climbed up onto the girders in the radio shack from the ruined console, dropped down and broken the assailant's neck, then taken his clothes. He didn't mention the fact that the man under the tarp had called him by name. Neither of those facts was relevant to Reed's investigation.

Reed turned to his assistant. "You get all that?"

"Yes, sir." The SP closed the notebook and slipped it into his breast pocket.

"Best get you two back over to the house," Reed said, smiling for the first time. "Sounds to me like you've earned yourself a rest, Massey."

Winter knew that Reed's smile, which looked genuine, was designed to make Winter confident that Reed was giving up on pumping him further, which was crap. The officer was going to keep right on trying to slip around the classified wall Winter was standing behind. For Reed, and men like him, the ability to classify information was the sole providence of the armed forces.

Winter figured the contest between them, as long as it was allowed to continue, would be an entertaining one. And anything that took his mind off the gruesome event was welcome.

"One more thing," Reed said, like it was an afterthought. "I'd like for you to take a good look at your attackers without their masks. In case you do know who they are."

"I'd be happy to," Winter replied.

"You, too," Reed added, nodding at Sean.

The two killers' corpses, along with the radio operator's, were laid out under the awning of the radio shack, covered by opaque plastic sheets. Sean stood beside Reed, across the three bodies from Winter, shivering under the blanket.

When Reed motioned, the sheet was pulled off the first one. Sean looked away. The body belonged to the man whose neck Winter had broken in the radio shack. He was naked—how Winter had left him—and his hands were at his sides. His head was cocked so that it appeared he was looking at something high over his left shoulder. "No," Winter said.

"Have you ever seen this man before, Ms. Devlin? Could you look at his face?"

Sean glanced down momentarily and shook her head.

The technician replaced the sheet, moved to the second corpse, and lifted the covering away.

Sean shut her eyes, took a deep breath, and shook her head. "No."

Winter studied the man he had shot point-blank with the MP5 as Sean had lain on the ground beneath him. The muzzle blast had scored and burned the skin around the entrance wounds in the upper rear quadrant of his skull. The hydrostatic pressure had caused the eye to bulge from its socket. Where the three-shot burst of 9-mm bullets had exited, the now one-eyed head looked like a poorly scraped out jack-o'-lantern. The missing brain matter and bone fragments had been placed inside a plastic bag, which rested beside the corpse's neck.

"Him?" Reed asked, staring at Winter.

"No."

Winter felt for Sean. For most, violence was something that happened to unlucky people in some place made fictional by being on their television screens. Winter had never envied that virginal ignorance more than now.

"According to where your empty brass was, you shot the one at the house from a good thirty feet away," Reed told Winter.

"About that," Winter agreed.

"All three in the head. Quite a shot, considering you just saw your partner go down."

"Your point being?" Winter asked.

"Under those conditions, most people would have been lucky to have hit the guy with a shotgun, that's all. You went for the head, not the torso."

"He was wearing armor." Winter could not explain how he was able to put his bullets exactly where he wanted them to go. It was an ability that he had discovered while training at Glynco. He didn't know how he did it, he was just glad he could.

"The men have no identification on them. Their weapons aren't available outside our Special Forces."

"Maybe they got them from wherever they got that Navy chopper they flew here in. They look like soldiers to me."

"This stinks," Reed said. "You outwit and kill four men with superior weapons, obviously professionals, without breaking a sweat—"

"Hey!" Sean yelled, startling the men, who turned to her. Color rose in her cheeks. "I have nothing to add to what Deputy Massey has already said, and I am getting sick of watching you men bump chests." She pointed a finger at Reed. "Unless you have some new torture to subject me to, I am going to walk back to the house, take a hot shower, and change into some dry clothes."

And with that she whirled and strode off toward the trees.

"She's not accustomed to this," Winter said, watching her go.

"Neither am I," Reed said sourly.

Winter followed Sean.

"Marshal!" Reed called out. "I need that suit you're wearing. It's evidence."

Winter caught up with Sean. "God in heaven," she muttered.

Winter couldn't think of anything to say, so they walked to the safe house together in silence.

37

Winter stood for ten minutes in the shower and let the hot water pound him. Then he cut the heat and stood in a chilled stream. Reed and his partner had already opened Winter's drawers and searched everything before he and Sean had reentered the house. The only thing he had come to the assignment with that he cared about taking out again was his life.

He dressed and went to the kitchen, where Reed was seated at the table reading what appeared to be the preliminary report of the SEAL commander. The younger shore patrolman was standing at the counter reading through his notebook.

"Feel better?" Reed asked, without looking up.

"Much," Winter said, pouring himself a cup of coffee.

"The men didn't come in on that helicopter. Appears it was for their escape."

"Sorry?"

"We found three chutes near the radio shack, so three of them parachuted in. According to a trace I ran, that chopper was turned into a spare-parts donor due to questionable airworthiness."

"Obviously the record is wrong."

"A King Air passed by at twenty-five thousand feet," Reed told him. "The trio jumped from it and sailed four miles using membranes, wings stretched between their ankles and wrists."

"HALO jumpers."

"The helicopter probably came in below radar after the radio shack was knocked out. The drop plane is in the

Caribbean at the moment, on auto pilot. F14s are flying alongside waiting for it to run dry.

"Massey, we both know those assailants were here because of whatever you people were doing here. You and Martinez, Ms. Devlin, or maybe one of the people who left earlier was their main target."

Winter sipped the coffee and grimaced remembering it was stale. "In your place, I would contact Attorney General Katlin to get the information I can't give you without his authorization. You have the guys' fingerprints. The NCIS can find out who they were in a few hours. I can't tell you anything that would be of any help."

"*Won't* tell me."

"Won't because I can't. I can't tell the NCIS, either, without the AG's permission."

"This was a WITSEC operation."

"If you say so."

"There's six dead kids whose families are going to ask who killed them, why, and what we're doing about it."

"I understand."

"Why did Jet Washington leave this morning?"

"Her cat died," Sean said from the doorway.

Sean's eyes met Winter's, and he tried to communicate that she had said the wrong thing. It was a small thing, a throwaway piece of information, but it was from before Martinez was shot and opened a line of questioning.

"Her cat died? From what?"

Sean sat down, crossed her legs at the ankles, and shrugged. "I'm not a veterinarian."

Winter watched Sean tell that fib. She had a face so beautiful and innocent that it would be impossible to imagine her being untruthful. She lied so effectively that Reed didn't even pursue it.

As a civilian, Sean could say whatever she liked, but Winter needed her to keep quiet, to speak only to the right people when the time came.

"This is my job," Reed reminded them silkily.

"Never said otherwise," Winter replied. They both knew that the Naval Criminal Investigative Service would look into the incident, as they did all military homicides. Reed, despite his understandable desire to collect the information, was just a traffic cop, a military flatfoot who busted drunk sailors, escorted prisoners from one brig to another, and filed reports on petty crime.

A strange buzz filled the air in the kitchen. Reed pulled a cell phone from his coat pocket.

"Reed."

He listened with a bored expression that was quickly displaced by one of intense interest and concentration.

"Yes, sir. No, sir. Yes, sir. Yes, sir. At once, sir."

Reed dropped the phone back into his pocket. He went to the counter, opened a briefcase, and removed Winter's gun and magazine—both in clear plastic bags. He placed them on the table before Winter. His face had turned red, his lips pressed tightly together.

"You can hand your weapon over to the FBI for comparison purposes, Deputy." Reed turned to his partner. "We are to turn over all evidence gathered so far to the FBI."

"What's going on?" Winter asked.

"Classified," Reed snapped triumphantly. He left the kitchen through the screen door, letting it slam shut behind him.

Winter followed him.

Quartz halogen lights on telescoping stands made it daytime on the front porch. Reed stood in the gazebo area at the railing like a ship's captain watching the lifeboats being lowered. He slipped a set of fingerprint cards into his shirt pocket as Winter approached.

Martinez's body and that of the first man Winter had shot were covered by sheets and enclosed in a rectangle of crime scene tape.

"I've seen the admiral who called me on only one previous occasion. He was at Norfolk to attend the dedication of a new building named for him. He called me to tell me to stop what I was doing—the FBI is handling this investigation."

"The Bureau taking over the investigation isn't unusual," Winter replied evenly.

"The FBI comes in after NCIS has investigated and requested their help. The point is that it didn't take an admiral to give me the command. It's like sending the president of a power company to read an electrical meter. I don't have a problem handing this over to the FBI, but this one is queer. Maybe because of you," he said, looking him straight in the eye.

"This had nothing whatsoever to do with me."

"Before I joined the Navy, I was a rookie on a small police force in Georgia. One night I pulled over a car. The kid driving was so drunk he couldn't tell me his name. He blew two point eight. There was a loaded .357 magnum under the seat. A pillowcase packed with marijuana and a bag with over a pound of cocaine and a hundred and thirty grand and change were in his trunk. I arrested the kid as a John Doe, wrote up a report, impounded the car, put the drugs, gun, and money in the evidence vault."

Fletcher Reed took a small cigar from his pocket and placed it in his mouth. "The chief was tickled pink. I was a hero. Two months on the job and I had this kid by the balls. I mean it was the biggest drug bust that town had ever seen. I sent the prints off. Next morning I come in and the other cops wouldn't look me in the eye. I ask the chief what's going on, and he calls me into his office and closes the door, says there was no kid, no speeding car, drugs, money, or gun.

"I had made two sets of fingerprint cards because the first one wasn't perfect. I ran that second set of prints. Turns out the kid was the governor's stepson. Rich man with businesses that were vital to the economy. Half the county worked for him in some capacity. I left the department and joined the Navy so I could be a cop, thinking it would be cleaner. Less political."

"Which do you think is the case here?"

"Nothing new about bunk buddies swapping hand jobs under the blanket. Only a problem when it's justice that gets kicked out of the bed."

"Reed, the oath I took was to uphold the laws of the United States, and I've done that to the best of my ability. Part of my job is to make sure that if men like those four UNSUBs who ended up here ever come along, I make sure they fail. That's all I did—no more, no less."

"It seems like armed assassins don't live long when you're around," Reed commented laconically. "Four here." He lit the cigar with a kitchen match. "Three in Florida. I found out about your fracas in Tampa seven years back. Wasn't for that report, I'd have thought you were CIA or NSA guarding a defector, not a deputy marshal guarding a killer."

Winter was surprised that Reed knew they had been watching a killer but suspected he was still fishing.

"Sean Devlin drew a blank with NCIS, but there was a hit from New Orleans Homicide on a Dylan Devlin who was caught with two dead bodies three weeks back. And I know about a certain Mafia dinosaur who got himself arrested two days later, which I assumed was connected. I figure Dylan Devlin left Cherry Point earlier this evening and those men you killed came here looking for him. What bothers me is why you stayed here with his wife, or sister, when you should have been where the action would most likely be."

Winter was very impressed by this man he thought was just another flatfoot.

Reed surprised Winter by extending his hand, which Winter tentatively shook. "I'm glad you killed those assholes, Massey. It was justice handed out the only way men like that understand it. Do me one favor?"

"Keep away from wherever you are?"

Now Reed did smile. "You are definitely one of those individuals best admired from a distance. After the smoke clears on this mess, look me up and I'll buy the drinks while you tell me what the real deal was."

A roar signaled twin Blackhawks that thundered in and alighted on the beach. As soon as the side doors slid open, figures carrying equipment cases swarmed out and swept toward the house like an invading army.

"FBI," Reed muttered.

The man leading the caravan stomped up the steps to them. "Fred Archer, supervising FBI special agent. I'm the case officer," he said. "You must be Lieutenant Commander Reed."

Reed nodded.

"You're Massey?" Archer asked.

"I am," Winter replied.

"We'll take over now, Lieutenant Commander," Archer said. "Deputy Massey, accompany me inside."

38

Winter sat beside Sean on the living room couch while Archer talked with Reed. They watched as FBI technicians wearing white coveralls and blue surgical gloves went over the inside of the Rook Island house as if it were a crime scene, using vacuums and dusting every imaginable surface for prints. Unlike at most crime scenes, they were wiping the surfaces clean afterward.

"Angela never knew what hit her, did she?" Sean asked him.

"No," Winter lied. "I don't believe she did." He remembered how she was trying to get her gun out of the holster but couldn't. A few seconds had passed from the time she was hit until the second shots ended her life. He didn't want to imagine what thoughts had gone through her mind in those final seconds.

"I was thinking about her family—how close she was to them. It'll be hard on them."

"Yes, it will."

His conversation at an end, Fred Archer sat in a wing chair across from the pair. He looked like a forty-something high school football coach straight from 1962 who went through life with a Bible in one hand and a playbook in the other—and often confused them. His hair was perfectly combed and his alert gray eyes would have seemed at home set below an eagle's brow. He wore an FBI windbreaker over his suit coat and tie. Sand filled the ornamental holes in his shiny black wing tips.

Special Agent Finch, Archer's partner, was a small-framed, pinch-faced man with narrow shoulders and an oddly distended stomach. He had a weak chin, wispy blond hair, and a small pug nose. Archer opened the conversation by clasping his meaty hands in front of him. "Okay, Deputy Massey, tell me everything that happened."

Sean protested, "He already told Officer Reed."

Archer kept his eyes on Winter. "Mrs. Devlin, let me do my job," he said condescendingly.

"I'd like to speak to Director Shapiro," Winter said before Sean could blow up again. "Mrs. Devlin is right. I went through it with Reed, and his partner wrote it down in copious detail, which I assume he shared with you."

"Well, answer this one thing, then. Wasn't there some way you could have captured just one of them?"

"Absolutely not."

"The one you fired on point-blank, from slightly above?"

"He—" Sean started.

"Mrs. Devlin. You can stay here, but only if you can refrain from butting in," Archer interrupted coldly.

"I was there, too," she said angrily. "Winter told him to surrender and he didn't. He tried to shoot me and Winter fired only to stop him."

"Deputy Massey was in charge, was he not? You were just being dragged around, weren't you?"

Sean raised an eyebrow but didn't answer.

"Ms. Devlin wasn't being dragged anywhere," Winter told Archer. "She was extremely helpful and, despite terrifying circumstances, she kept a very cool head."

"Is that so? And that man?"

"I assumed that the UNSUB's decision to bring the muzzle of his machine gun around despite my warning meant he wasn't contemplating surrender. Regretfully, he presented the only opportunity I had to dialogue meaningfully with the UNSUBs. Perhaps if you had been here, you could have ordered them all to surrender."

Archer stared into Winter's eyes. "Deputy, I represent the attorney general of the United States. I take exception to your disrespectful manner, which under the circumstances, I find particularly offensive."

"I'd like to speak to Director Shapiro," Winter said again, dismissing him.

"The chief marshal's got his hands full at the moment. You told Reed that everything that happened before the lady deputy was killed is classified. Let me clarify something, Deputy. This WITSEC detail was never a secret to the attorney general, and he has ordered me here to find out what happened, which I intend to do. You will cooperate fully with me, or there will be serious consequences."

Winter nodded reluctantly. He knew that Archer was right.

"What I hope you can help me figure out is how the four deceased UNSUBs knew where Devlin was. Who do you think furnished them with that information?"

"How could I know that?"

"You have never been assigned to witness security before—is that right?"

"Inspector Greg Nations asked for me."

"I know Nations requested you. Tell me how you came to strike the witness."

"Winter . . ." Sean began. Archer's lifted brow made her pause. Then, resolutely, she continued, "Deputy Massey was protecting me from my husband. You can ask Inspector Nations about it."

Winter saw something change in Archer's eyes—a softening perhaps. "I'd like to."

Winter wondered why he hadn't said, "I fully intend to, or I will."

"Devlin drugged Dixon and Martinez. Then he killed the cook's cat and left it in his wife's drawer," Winter said. "We assumed initially that he did it to gain access to guns, but he was simply trying to torture his wife."

"Wasn't the altercation between you and Mr. Devlin why you remained here with Mrs. Devlin?"

"Yes. After Devlin killed the cat, Mrs. Devlin was upset. He had been warned not to approach her, but he confronted her and she struck him."

"She struck him first?"

"I sure did!" Sean cried. "He *wanted* me to. He knew I was about to explode over Midnight."

"Midnight?"

"The cat was black," Winter explained.

"Did you ever strike him before?" Archer asked Sean.

"Do I seem like someone who would physically confront another person?" She scowled. "Don't answer that."

"May, I?" Winter interposed. He explained how the altercation had started, what he did, and why he did it. Archer didn't interrupt, but his expression was one of dissatisfaction.

"Mrs. Devlin, is there anything you'd care to add?"

"First of all," she told Archer, "I am not easily provoked and I have never struck my husband, or anyone else, before. I didn't know my husband was a violent person. If I had I would never have married him. Deputy Massey saved me from being hurt, and last night he saved my life."

"You didn't know your husband was violent?" Archer asked, incredulous.

"I believed he was a marketing consultant," she replied. "He told me that his boss in Washington had dealings with Russian mobsters and that he was cooperating with the government in the prosecution of the Russian Mafia—certain politicians and lawyers. I learned differently only when Mr. Whitehead confirmed that my husband had been killing people."

Archer sat in silence, contemplating what she'd said.

"If that's all?" Winter asked. "Ms. Devlin needs some rest."

"The bedrooms are all being processed," Archer said curtly. "*Mrs.* Devlin can use this couch." Archer stood. "We'll need your prints for comparison purposes, Mrs. Devlin."

Sean said, "Aren't you wasting time dusting for prints? The killers wore gloves and you have their bodies. So what's the point?"

"That's our business," Archer shot back.

Winter was accustomed to long periods awake punctuated by catnaps, but Sean was obviously getting punchy. After giving her prints and washing her hands, she rejoined Winter in the living room.

"I thought Dylan was being protected from the bad guys," she said under her breath. "Not because he had been killing people *for* the bad guys. I can't blame Archer for not believing that. It must be hard to imagine anyone being so ignorant about somebody they were married to."

"If all you heard was his lies, they probably made sense—especially if you wanted to believe them."

"If it had been you bringing the coat out, instead of Angela, all three of us would be dead now and nobody would know who did it."

"Maybe not, but they'd have known his boss ordered it."

"I know it made you furious that he killed a dozen people and because he testifies, he gets off without a scratch. Now more innocent people are dead because of Dylan."

"Hopefully when he testifies it'll end up saving more lives because it will stop the man who paid him to do it. All I can hope is that there's a net gain on some tally sheet somewhere. If I spent my time worrying about what the courts do or don't do, or how disgusting and unfair the deals the prosecutors cut are, I'd be in a mental hospital on a Thorazine drip. Like the serenity prayer says: Don't waste your life worrying about crap you can't fix."

She began to cry softly and, uncertain how he should respond, Winter put a tentative hand on her shoulder. It had been three years since any woman had been this close to him. He felt for her, an innocent who through no fault of her own had been in the company of ravenous wolves, having to fight for her life.

She regained control, wiping her eyes with her hands.

"Thanks," she said. Her voice was stronger. "For everything, Winter. I mean, even if you did let that man shoot me."

"If it would make you feel better, you can let somebody shoot me sometime," he teased.

She scooted away from Winter, but to his surprise, she lay down, placing her head on his leg like it was a pillow.

Eleanor used to sleep with her head on his leg just as Sean was doing. Sometimes Rush still did. He was glad that she felt secure enough with him to fall asleep. But once the initial impact of the life-and-death struggle they had experienced together wore away, she would probably associate him with an unpleasant experience and do her dead-level best to forget him.

Winter looked down and studied her delicate features. He found himself drinking in the scent of her, daring to imagine what being in bed with her would be like. He realized that this woman sleeping against his leg was a mystery to him. With a sense of unease, he remembered how easily she'd lied to Reed about the cat.

He closed his eyes. Her lie didn't matter. Tomorrow she would be gone and he would go to Washington for debriefing and then home. Later he and Greg would meet somewhere, open some bottles, and dissect the entire operation. Maybe by then—with Greg—he would be able to laugh at the funny parts and not cry at the sad.

 39 | **Friday morning**

The sound of Archer's voice roused Winter abruptly from his nap.

"Deputy Massey, I need to talk to both of you."

Light from outside filled the room. Sean Devlin was curled up, her head still on his leg, sound asleep.

Opening her eyes, she sat up and stretched, running her fingers through her hair, sweeping it back.

"I'm just going to say this outright," Archer said. "The plane carrying Inspector Nations and his team vanished below radar four minutes after takeoff. The assumption was that the jet had gone down in the Atlantic. After the search started, we got word of what happened here."

"You knew that when you got here," Winter said. Anger flooded his mind.

"The Coast Guard and Navy started a search, and I

came to see what had happened here. We assumed both events were connected. When we found the plane, we were certain of it. It was discovered at an abandoned military base in Virginia, a hundred miles inland from where it dropped off the radar screen."

"Emergency landing?" Winter wondered aloud. Despite Archer's unemotional delivery of the information, Winter knew this was going to be very bad news.

"The plane was hijacked, flown to the old base, then blown up."

"Hijacked?" Winter repeated incredulously. "How do you know that?"

"The two Justice Department pilots who flew Avery Whitehead to Cherry Point to meet your detail were found there murdered and stripped of their uniforms. Someone took their places. There is sufficient physical evidence at the Virginia base to conclude there were multiple fatalities. Based on the way these people operated here and at Cherry Point, I think we can assume that the seven people on that jet were murdered and the hijackers escaped."

The idea that Greg was dead would not fit into Winter's brain. Archer was saying something about transportation, but Winter was incapable of listening. He turned his attention to Sean, who sat expressionless. He expected her to ask questions, to at least be curious about her husband, but she merely sat there, numbly silent, as though she was listening to a mechanic explain what was wrong with her car.

"Killing Mr. Devlin," Archer continued, "was the whole purpose of both operations. Looks like there were two independent teams to ensure success even if there were last-minute changes."

"Maybe they aren't *all* dead." Winter felt as though he had been drugged.

"I am going to the scene, Deputy Massey," Archer told him. "Your director is there. I am taking you with me."

"What about me?" Sean asked.

"You will be going on to D.C., Mrs. Devlin."

"I'd prefer to stay with Deputy Massey."

"We'll make whatever arrangements we feel are appropriate. You'll be informed as those decisions are formalized."

"You just said that you're in charge," Sean said coldly. "As next of kin, I should be able to visit the place where my husband died. If you can't okay that, please ask for permission. I'd like a chance to speak to the head of the marshals. Perhaps I have no choice but to be passed around between marshals and the FBI, but I will not be led about by a ring in my nose without protest."

"We wouldn't dream of having you think of us as bullies, Mrs. Devlin," Archer responded, perhaps not wanting to look like a tyrant in front of such a beautiful woman. "I'd be happy to allow you to accompany the deputy here to Virginia and hand you over to the marshals. You have thirty minutes, if you'd like to freshen up. We've moved your things to the cook's quarters."

As he packed, Winter could hear Sean running water in Jet's bathroom. As he exited his bedroom he saw that Jet's door was standing open. Sean didn't see him when she placed Martinez's suitcase outside and closed the door. Bureau technicians had used yellow evidence tape to seal the battered Samsonite case, making it look like a gift.

40

Due to their tight cylindrical cabins, Lear jets were often referred to as executive mailing tubes. Winter and Sean belted themselves into the bench seat in the rear. Archer and Finch were in the foremost seats, across the narrow aisle from each other. Sean's briefcase fit edgewise in the space between her and Winter on the sofalike, forward-facing bench. Winter had stowed their bags in the cargo section behind them.

Winter didn't want to think about Greg. He wanted his mind to stop replaying the images of the night before—Martinez, the flight across the island, the UNSUBs—but he had no choice. He listed in his head what he knew about the UNSUBs. They were as cold-blooded as men get. They'd been trained by the military, probably Special Forces. People didn't learn high-altitude, low-opening jumps from watching television. They had access to the latest weaponry. Two operations, like the simultaneous assaults at Cherry Point and Rook Island, didn't just happen. The killers didn't fly by the seats of their pants, improvising, and they didn't luck into anything. They had known Devlin was being kept on Rook Island. The killers had to have had an inside source for the intelligence their mission required. Winter thought Archer's assessment, that the assassins who landed on Rook were there as insurance in case Dylan's travel plans were changed at the last minute, was probably correct.

Winter stared out the window at the ground passing below, unseeing. His inner theater replayed the last few seconds he and Greg had been together like it was on a video loop.

41

Ward Field, Virginia

As the Lear embarked on its descent, Winter peered out and saw the derelict red-and-white-checkerboard-painted water tank that signified a military airfield. He stared down expecting to see the skeletal remains of a jet, but what he saw was the twisted steel of what had been a massive hangar and an enormous amount of activity on the ground below.

The grassy tarmac on the side of the runway was choked with small jets, a cargo plane, and two helicopters. Police cruisers, trucks, emergency vehicles, and cars were scattered around the blackened hangar ruins. Long black water hoses snaked from a trio of fire trucks.

Their pilot parked near a Gulfstream and cut the engines, and the copilot opened the clamshell door so Archer and Finch could exit. Winter spotted a group of men striding toward the Lear wearing jackets that identified them as either US marshals or FBI agents. One of them was United States Chief Marshal Richard Shapiro.

Archer spoke to Shapiro for a few seconds, then led Finch and the other FBI agents toward two canopy tents. Folding tables, with laptop computers and radios, had been arranged in a horseshoe to define the command post. In the adjacent tent, evidence bags covered several tables. Technicians were photographing the contents of each bag before handing it over to other techs for labeling and cataloging. A mobile chiller unit to handle human remains was located behind the evidence tent.

Winter stepped down and stood in the grass outside the door. Shapiro looked fatigued and concerned. He shook Winter's hand briskly. "Outstanding job on the island, Winter. This is all so . . ."

Shapiro's silence was as heavy with grief as a wail. He cleared his throat and looked past Winter. "Please, Mrs. Devlin. If you'll stay inside the plane for a few minutes. We have a lot to discuss and we will talk soon, you and I. First I need to have a few words in private with Deputy Marshal Massey."

"Sure," Sean said noncommittally. She disappeared back into the cabin.

Two deputies took up positions on either side of the door as though she might try to escape.

"Terrible about Deputy Martinez," Shapiro said. "And this."

"What happened?"

Shapiro took a deep breath. "The jet was inside the hangar when it blew up. There's very little left in the way of evidence."

"Do you know how they were killed?"

"They found a skull fragment with an entry wound, probably .45 caliber. The hijackers murdered the pilots at Cherry Point using manual strangulation. Wearing the pilots' uniforms, they overcame our team after they were inside the plane. Ground personnel saw the men get into the craft but they didn't notice anything unusual. The jet taxied and took off normally. As it climbed out, it rose to ten thousand feet, then plunged below radar and obviously turned west."

Winter was staring at the evidence tent while Shapiro spoke. He saw Archer and Finch inside the tent where technicians were pointing out evidence bags. Archer had clearly taken charge.

"I can only imagine how difficult this has to be for you." Shapiro paused. "I know how close you were to Inspector Nations."

Winter nodded, too full of emotion to speak.

"The FBI suspects someone in WITSEC provided inside intelligence. This is an FBI investigation, and we're
here at their pleasure and are being excluded from participation. Tell me what happened last night," Shapiro said.
"The broad strokes."

Winter told Shapiro the story, ending with the UNSUB
who knew his name. Shapiro listened without interrupting, then shifted so his back was to the FBI's tents.

"I've ordered the WITSEC director to open an internal
investigation to examine everything, including the various
methods of communication we utilized and whether any
of the transmissions could have been intercepted. I don't
believe there is a leak from within WITSEC. We assumed
that there are so many flags, triggers, and hidden traps
that it's impossible. For decades we've tried to imagine
every way a thing like this could be accomplished and we
constantly design, refine, and implement counter mea-
sures. Only a handful of men had access to enough of the
information to furnish the necessary intelligence, and, believe me, we monitor all of them closely. The fact that one
of the assailants knew your name means, either he somehow recognized you, or somebody within the service sold
us out."

Winter nodded slowly. He hoped it was the latter, because the former was too terrible to contemplate.

Later, while Shapiro was in the Lear with Sean, Winter
wandered over to the evidence tent. He listened to the
sound of the refrigeration compressor atop the chiller unit
as he stood outside the tent and studied the bags littering
one of the tables.

He found himself staring at an open case, which held a badge and a scorched ID picture of Dixon beside it. Archer's voice interrupted his thoughts. "Deputy Massey, can you match some of this with individuals for us?"

"Sorry . . . sure."

Inside the tent, he let his eyes wander over the articles, and he pointed to an Astros baseball cap that had been burned away to the brim. "That was Beck's." He lifted a bag containing a watch. "This was Greg Nation's." The watch's crystal was shattered, the stainless-steel band broken at the clasp.

"What about this?" Archer pointed to another bag, containing a foil wrapper and a Spectra film box. "They found this outside the hangar."

"There are no cameras allowed in a WITSEC operation."

"Thoughts?" Archer probed.

Winter inspected the box and foil through the plastic. "Opened recently, because it doesn't look weathered. Was it discarded by one of the firemen or sheriff deputies?"

"Already checked that. No fingerprints on the package or the foil."

"Then I imagine the killers dropped it. Maybe they took pictures of Devlin for proof to the client that they'd succeeded. Easier than lugging a corpse around."

"Good guess."

A technician set an old Boy Scout backpack on the "incoming" evidence table. The initials G.W. were on the flap.

"Just a minute," Archer asked. "What's that?"

"It was out in the debris field," the tech answered. "There are some unusual objects inside."

"Did that belong to any of your team?" Archer asked Winter.

"No," Winter said.

"Put it down," Archer told the tech, pointing to a clean space on the table. The supervising agent in charge tugged his right glove on tighter, then opened the backpack. Winter watched as Archer took the contents out one at a time, placing each on the table.

"A pair of eight-by-forty binoculars with a broken lens, a slightly used votive candle, a partially filled box of cigarettes, *Penthouse* magazine dated August of this year, a book of matches, and a pocket knife."

"Probably belonged to a kid," Winter commented. "When was this place closed?"

Archer called out to a rotund sheriff's deputy rinsing his hands under a flowing faucet. "Hey, Deputy, when was this place closed down?"

"It was in full swing until after Vietnam." He took Archer's question as a summons and approached, shaking his hands to dry them. "It was used some, here and there, until the mid-'80s. It's been locked up tight ever since."

"Maybe a kid of a caretaker, worker's kid?"

"No caretaker that I know of," the deputy replied. His chrome nameplate said SLOOP.

"Well, some kid was in here at some point since the August *Penthouse* hit the racks," Winter said laconically.

The deputy nodded slowly and studied the backpack. "G.W. We got a pair of boys—George Williams and Matthew Barnwell—both twelve-year-olds, reported missing by their parents last night."

Archer turned to Finch, who stood in the nearby command tent ten feet away, watching Archer like a student. "I want a copy of that missing-persons report."

"Where exactly was this pack found?" Archer asked.

"It was outside the debris field," the evidence tech replied. He pointed to several acres defined by a fluttering line of yellow crime-scene tape that ran between metal stakes pushed into the ground. The field was being searched by at least fifty FBI and ATF technicians dressed in white jumpsuits and wearing surgical gloves. Hundreds of small plastic flags on wire rods marked the debris.

Winter knew that red ones indicated where body parts had been located. Other colors stood for personal belongings, parts of the aircraft, or suspected bomb parts.

"I can show you exactly where it was."

Archer called out. "I want a K-nine unit over there."

Several of the men inside the tent filed out into the field like swarming bees, flowing toward the place the tech had pointed out. Winter didn't accompany them. Instead, he looked again at the shattered wristwatch.

The Omega's rear plate, he knew, commemorated the first manned landing on the moon. He remembered Greg saying once that as an orphaned child, he had stood barefoot in his grandmother's hard-dirt yard and stared up at the moon, desperately trying to see the astronauts she had told him were up there. His grandmother had told him it was a mighty long way to go to put up a little flag nobody could see. He knew then that he was standing between two worlds. One world was the only one he had ever known—poverty and hopelessness. The other was a magical place where a man could stand on the moon's surface. Greg told Winter that, at that moment, he didn't know how it would be possible, but he was certain which world he was going to live in. From that night on, he did everything he could to jump into that other world, like it was some passing train, and get a seat inside it. He had purchased the "Astronaut" watch when he was in the military so he would never forget that night—or the vow he'd made—a world away.

Sean and Shapiro stood outside the Lear's door, still talking. As Shapiro began walking toward the tent, Sean used her hand as a visor and scanned the landscape before climbing back up into the airplane.

When Shapiro saw Archer and the others, now a hundred yards distant, he asked, "What's happening?"

Winter set the bag containing the watch back on the table. "Found evidence a couple of missing boys might have been here. They're going to have a dog try and find them."

"God, if the boys ran across *those* people..." Shapiro said, then broke off.

A sheriff's-department Explorer pulled off the road. The driver stopped, climbed out, and opened the back door. A German shepherd bounded out, straining the lead the driver was holding. After the animal sniffed the backpack, he tugged his handler toward the fence on the far side of the field. The officers and emergency personnel followed along like a lynch mob.

"Fred Archer is the case officer," Shapiro said abruptly.

"That so?"

"He broke the Morrow spy ring three years back, foiled a terrorist plot to smuggle six tons of Semtex into San Francisco last year, and recovered sixty of the sixty-two million that was taken from the New York State retirement fund six months ago. That's why he's here, why he has command of the investigation. He's the director's golden boy."

Winter didn't reply, just stared out at the activity.

"Mrs. Devlin's been through an ordeal."

"She sure has," Winter agreed.

"She seems sort of numbed out. I told her I wanted her to take a few days to unwind. Talk to a therapist—weigh her options. I want to make sure she isn't in shock. Beneath that facade, she's got to be a basket case."

Winter found a pair of binoculars in the command tent and raised them to his eyes. The dog had led the crowd across the field. A uniformed deputy slipped under the fence, disappeared into a gully, and came out with a bicycle, which he propped against the fence. He went down again to bring up a second.

"Pair of bicycles," Winter said.

Winter's body tensed with anticipation as he watched for any sign that the two boys had been located. Archer pointed back toward the spot where the dog had started tracking. Winter knew that the dog had retraced its steps from where the backpack had been located to the place where the boys entered the base. The handler would go back now and see if his dog could find and follow the scent in the direction the boys had traveled. Sure enough, the dog took off, leading his handler across the debris field and toward the derelict control tower. The dog stopped below it, sniffed around the riser, and started to bark frantically.

An FBI agent scrambled up on the rotted steps, balancing like a tightrope walker. Once on the deck, he pulled his gun out and moved around the building, out of Winter's view.

"What is it?" Shapiro asked.

Winter focused on the deck. There was movement as the agent came around the corner. And then, like apparitions materializing, two small figures walked unsteadily into view. "They're alive!" Winter murmured. "Thank God," he said. "Finally, something."

The boys stood there above an ocean of armed adults, blinking like owls, covered with black smut like coal miners.

Cheers mixed with the spatter of applause carried across the field. Winter thought of Rush, and the birthday he hoped he could still get home for.

43

Archer led the two boys back to the command tent, where emergency medical technicians cleaned them up, checking them over for injuries, treating their scratches, and finally pronouncing them sound.

The Cole County deputies, emergency workers, and

firemen began to cluster, talking among themselves, some smoking cigarettes. Finch ordered them to disperse. In the debris field, stooped technicians remained on task, oblivious to anything beyond the tape barrier.

While an FBI agent lowered the canvas walls of the tent, Winter saw the sheriff approach Archer and whisper something in his ear. He heard Archer reply that absolutely no members of the press would be allowed on the base under any conditions, due to national security. The sheriff left in his cruiser. Then they went to the tent.

Director Shapiro stood behind Archer. Winter stood alone near the side wall, to Archer's left. Across the table from Archer, the two boys sat side by side.

A technician placed a cassette recorder on the table in front of the boys. Archer pressed the record button. He said, "FBI Supervising Case Agent Fred Archer conducting a field interview of two minor subjects found at Ward Field, Virginia." He added the date and glanced down at a slip of paper. "The subjects being interviewed are Matthew Barnwell and George Williams, both twelve years of age and residents of Raiford, Virginia. The subjects are aware I am recording this interview."

Archer folded his hands on the table and smiled at the boys. "Man," he said expansively, "we sure are glad you two are all right. You gave us all quite a scare, I can tell you. The agent who found you said you fellows had a clubhouse all set up in the tower. You come here a lot?"

The heavier boy watched Archer. The other boy stared down at his lap. He hadn't looked up since the agents and marshals entered.

"Okay, so, George and Matt, which one of you boys is Matt?"

The plump boy held up his hand.

From behind the boys, Finch said, "Speak up and answer either yes or no when Agent Archer asks you a question for the recorder. Is that clear?"

Both boys nodded.

"Affirmative nods," Finch announced, for the benefit of the tape. "Again, please answer the questions yes or no."

"I just need to ask you a few questions," Archer said. Over his insincere smile, his eyes were decidedly predatory. To Winter he looked like a union official at the negotiating table with a Louisville Slugger concealed in his lap in case his sugary words failed.

"Okay," Matt said. "Yeah."

"Last night there was a big explosion here."

Matt showed Archer a look of surprised disbelief. "Huh?" George merely shrugged.

"You saw it?" Archer asked.

Matt shook his head. "Uh-uh."

"Yes or no," Finch insisted.

"Nah," Matt said emphatically. "We weren't here."

The scene took Winter back to his years as a teacher. He studied the boys carefully.

"I suspect you're not telling me the truth," Archer said softly. "You're both blackened from the blast."

"We were," George said to his lap. "We . . ."

Winter clearly saw Matt kick George's ankle under the table.

"We were just walking in and it knocked us down. We were scared and we hid," Matt explained. "We didn't want to get in trouble for being here."

"Boys," Archer said sternly. "Think about this very, very carefully before you answer. Before the explosion, did you see anything? Any people coming or going? Any vehicles leaving the area?"

"Nah." Matt crossed his arms across his chest. "We didn't see nothing but that explosion, then police cars and fire trucks."

George put his finger in his right ear and shook it, glaring at Matt. Winter knew Matt was lying. Why couldn't Archer see that, he thought.

"So you hid in the tower because?"

"We didn't want to get blamed for it," Matt blurted out. "We didn't see nothing, did we, George?" Matt pressed the sole of his sneaker against George's ankle. George shook his head. Winter looked around and realized that he alone had a view of what was going on under the table.

"No," George agreed after a few long seconds.

"Are you both absolutely sure?" Archer asked.

Now, Winter thought. *This is where Archer starts poking and prodding.*

Archer's pager went off, interrupting. He read the number and frowned.

Archer looked back at the boys, smiling at them.

"And, I think we all know the rest," Archer said, putting his notebook away, turning off the recorder and standing.

"Great. If you two young men remember anything later, you get your parents to call the FBI, okay? Do that for us? Let's get their parents out here and reunite them." Archer's interview completed, he walked out.

Winter couldn't believe what he'd just seen. The interrogation was done? What the hell was wrong with Archer?

Finch cut the recorder off and told Matt, "Your days of trespassing here are over. They'll fix that fence, bulldoze the tower."

"We have permission," George said softly. Winter didn't hear it, he read the boy's lips.

Winter left the hut and went after Archer.

"That's it?" Winter demanded.

Archer snapped his cell phone open and, looking at his pager's display for the number, began punching it into the keypad. "Is what *it,* Deputy Massey?"

"The interview . . . it's over? Those kids are hiding something. They're lying to you."

"I doubt it," Archer said. "If you'll excuse me, I—"

Winter snatched Archer's phone away and closed it. The agent's expression was one of shock and outrage.

Shapiro appeared beside them. "What in heaven's name is going on?" he demanded.

Handing back Archer's cell phone, Winter spoke softly but forcefully, "The special agent in charge of this investigation just turned his back on what could very well be key evidence!"

"That's enough, Deputy," Archer demanded, turning his eyes on the people crowding behind Shapiro. "Doesn't everyone have something to do?" he called out. The agents began moving slowly away, with the reluctance of kids forced to abandon a school-yard fistfight.

"What evidence?" Shapiro asked Winter.

"Archer—"

"Special Agent in Charge Archer," Shapiro snapped at Winter.

"Those boys lied. They know something. They saw something. They were here all night after the explosion. Maybe they were here earlier and saw the plane land. Maybe they are afraid."

"We put them at ease," Archer said.

"Look, maybe they were threatened by someone."

"Nonsense," Archer said. "Finch, do you agree with Deputy Massey?"

"Totally absurd. They're just children who obviously didn't see anything useful."

"So this evidence would be what, Massey?" Archer asked sarcastically.

"Whenever George tried to expand an answer or volunteer anything other than what Matt said, Matt kicked him under the table. Just after you left, when Finch said they would never be allowed back, George said, 'We *have* permission.' Present tense. From whom? Their parents reported them missing so who gave them permission to stay? Finch, you were standing close enough to George that you *must* have heard it."

"I didn't hear any such thing," Finch protested.

"But you heard it?" Shapiro asked Winter.

"I read his lips. They were here when the plane exploded. Maybe they were here before that. I know they saw a lot more than they've admitted to."

"You read lips? You see underneath tables?" Archer asked.

"You have a crystal ball, too?" Finch mocked.

"Did you see the boys kicking each other?" Archer asked Shapiro.

"No," Shapiro said. "But if Deputy Massey says he did, I believe him."

"You'll excuse me if I say that I hardly see Massey as impartial here. Understandably, he is in shock, if not *temporarily* mentally unbalanced by grief and the deadly combat he went through. So, I'll let it go . . . this time."

"Perhaps," Shapiro insisted, "this is something we could discuss privately."

"I've got work to do," Archer said,

Shapiro added. "If the interview with those boys was a little more superficial than it could have been, there's no good reason it can't continue—"

"I disagree," Archer interrupted. "And let me remind you that I'm calling the shots. If Deputy Massey can't control himself, if he ever lays a hand on me again or creates a scene, I'll have him in a psychiatric facility undergoing evaluation."

"Agent Archer," Winter said, with a calm he didn't feel, "I'm sorry. I'm not myself. People I cared about have been murdered. My best friend is scattered across the landscape. Last night I killed four men. What you said about my state of mind is true. Even so, I taught boys that age. I have a son that age. I know how boys that age act and think when they're hiding something."

Archer glared at Winter. "That about it?"

"Just separate the boys. Talk to them individually. Don't

close the door because of your ego, or what you already believe is true. If they saw anyone—"

"Listen to me, you—" Archer hissed.

Shapiro interrupted. "Let's drop this for now, Deputy Massey."

"Massey," Archer said hotly. "I want those murdering bastards caught every bit as badly as you do. I don't believe those kids saw anything, because if they had, there's no reason on earth for them not to tell us."

Winter fought to keep the desperation he felt from showing through. "Sir, just let me talk to George Williams. He's the weak link. If I'm right and he knows anything, I'm sure he'll tell me."

"You are?"

"What do you have to lose?"

Archer frowned as he weighed the request. "I don't want it said later that I wasn't open to all possible avenues. And, seeing his background, I suppose it's possible that Deputy Massey may know ways to elicit information from children."

Shapiro nodded solemnly.

"Intuition is a valuable tool."

"Nobody can say that you weren't ready to explore every possible angle, sir," Finch agreed.

"Very well, Massey. But I won't stand for any rough stuff. You got that?"

A female FBI agent took Matt Barnwell to the ambulance under the pretext of a hearing examination. George Williams stood out beside the command tent gazing at the airplanes. Winter walked over to him. If they were going to find the bastards who were responsible for murdering Greg and the others, he had to make a start there and then.

"You like airplanes, George?"

The boy looked up at Winter. "Sure. I guess."

"Which is your favorite?"

George shrugged. "Fighters."

"You hungry?"

"I guess so."

"Let's get a sandwich and I'll show you around the planes."

George wolfed down the sandwich as though he'd been starved for days.

"Let's go look at those planes," Winter said when he'd finished.

"You FBI?" George asked as they walked.

"U.S. marshal."

"Are you a whipstick marshal?"

Winter felt his heartbeat quicken. "You mean WITSEC, George?"

"Yeah, what's that mean?"

"WITSEC stands for witness security. WITSEC deputies protect men who are testifying against bad men in court. They make sure the witnesses get safely to court. Where did you hear about WITSEC?" he asked.

George stopped and seemed to be studying a King Air. "TV, maybe."

"Must have been some explosion," Winter said easily. "I bet it was loud and bright. George, earlier you said that you have permission to be here."

George stared at him silently.

"We're not here because of the explosion," Winter continued. "That would require only the ATF bomb squad people out there and a few FBI agents. We're all here because some bad men hijacked an airplane with seven

people in it, including a man WITSEC was protecting.
Those men flew it here last night and they blew it up with
you watching. The reason there are so many cops and FBI
agents here is because those seven people were still inside
that jet when it exploded."

"For real?"

"Word of honor."

George seemed to be thinking it over, so Winter gave
him a nudge.

"I don't know who you guys saw, or what those people
said to you, but they are murderers, and we need to find
them and make sure they don't kill anybody else. And the
truth is that you are the only one who can help us catch
these people. I know it's hard for you to tell me about it,
but it's really important that you do and I think you want
to tell the truth. If anyone threatened to hurt you or your
families, we'll make absolutely sure that nobody does."

"He said it was just a war game," George blurted out,
his eyes alive with fear and excitement.

"Who said that?"

"I thought he was too old to be a real general."

George sat silently until Winter started the recorder.
Archer and Shapiro were nearby to monitor.

"First time me and Matt saw the men here was day before yesterday," the boy started.

George told Winter how he and Matt were caught by
the men and about their leader, who told them he was a
general and that the boys had stumbled on a secret war
game the general said the men were playing with the
WITSEC marshals. He told Winter about the weapons
and described the activity in the hangar. The general had
promised the boys that if they didn't tell about the activity
at the base, the pair could come anytime they liked. He
even promised to give them a pass and keys to the gate,

and he said a man named Ralph would give them helicopter rides anytime they wanted. George said he didn't like the general or his men—they scared him. The general had made wonderful promises, but he made threats, too, about what *could* happen if he and Matt betrayed his men, since the boys had been trespassing and *would* go to jail and their parents *would* lose their houses and possessions to the government.

He and Matt had come out again late the previous afternoon to see if the men were still there. He said the general seemed to have been there alone, moving in and out of the hangar. George said the runway lights came on, then a jet landed and taxied into the hangar. The general and some men left in an airplane. After they were sure the plane wasn't coming back, the boys had come onto the base to see if the general's men had left anything worth taking.

"How many people did you see leave here last night?" Winter asked.

"Four."

"Three and the old general?"

"Yes."

"Who were the others?"

"I think one was Ralph, the helicopter pilot. They had an army helicopter, the big plane with two propellers and a smaller one they left in.

"We were watching from outside the fence and it was dark then. We came in here after they were gone. The big explosion knocked us down. My ears didn't work. The fire went way up in the sky and it was so hot you couldn't believe it. I couldn't hear and Matt kept yelling and jumping up and down, then a police helicopter came and we hid up in the tower."

"What does the general look like?"

"He's really old, and his hair is white and dandruff falls out of it on his clothes. He has about a million wrinkles.

Oh, and big brown freckles on his hands. And he has a weird blue eye where the little black hole part of it goes down in the blue part so it's like those old door holes you can look in."

"What about Ralph?"

George thought for a moment before replying. "He has muscles like a wrestler, and sunglasses that's got purple glass in them and stuck-up hair that's white and a tattoo of a barbed wire on his wrist. That's all I can think of."

"The other men?"

The boy shrugged. "I didn't really look at them much."

"How many were there? Beside Ralph and the general?"

"A whole lot. Maybe seven or eight. I'm not sure. I know they all had muscles and short hair, too. We didn't talk to them, just to Ralph and the general." George placed his palms on the table. "I guess that's all I know."

"George, could you help an artist draw some pictures of the general and Ralph?" Archer asked.

"Sure," he said, then seemed to clam up again. "You don't think he meant what he said—about our parents' houses and jail. Do you?"

"No. You're safe. You won't be seeing him again, George," Winter said, patting the boy's shoulder before he left the tent.

Archer joined him outside. This time his smile looked genuine. "Deputy, I owe you an apology. You read those kids right."

"Agent Archer," Winter said, "we're on the same side. Just find those bastards."

"I intend to," Archer said.

Winter was relieved that Archer sounded sincere.

45

Inside the Gulfstream II, Chief Marshal Richard Shapiro stood up from a gray leather couch, opened a cabinet, and removed a bottle of Oban. He handed Winter a glass with an ounce of the golden liquid in it. Shapiro poured one for himself and reached over to touch his glass to Winter's.

"You're off duty," Shapiro said. "Drink up."

The scotch ignited a velvet fire that burned the length of Winter's throat.

"Another?" Shapiro offered.

"No, thank you, sir." *If I start drinking now, maybe I won't ever stop.*

"The FBI has a good start, thanks to you," Shapiro said. "The Citation will take you home as soon as you're ready. I want you to take some time off."

Winter was relieved—he desperately wanted to go home and resume his life. He looked through the window at the water tank and his mind painted Forsythe standing at the rail, on the island.

"That's odd," Winter said.

"What?" Shapiro's eyes narrowed.

"That professional killers felt secure enough to stage this operation from here. They were smart. Their planning was perfect. They modified a King Air. Flew in and out. They stole a helicopter from the Navy. They killed maybe sixteen people like it was nothing. They blew up the jet in the hangar to destroy any evidence they might have left behind to lead to them. But those same killers let two kids who could identify them walk away. Why would they do such an obviously stupid thing?"

"The boy said they threatened and bribed them," Shapiro

reminded him. "Perhaps they didn't want to harm kids. Maybe they were afraid if they killed the boys there would be a search, they'd be discovered."

"There's something wrong," Winter insisted. "Like they believed it wouldn't matter if the kids told."

Shapiro shook his head and got to his feet.

"What about Mrs. Devlin?" Winter asked him.

"No reason they'd bother her. She's just an ex-witness's widow now. We'll take care of her, watch her just in case."

"I'll get my things," Winter said and started down the steps.

"By the way," Shapiro called from inside the plane, "the A.G. wants this all to stay classified for the time being. So, you weren't here, or on Rook, either. Media blackout is in force. The A.G. wants us to sit on everything. We don't want those bastards to know the FBI's right behind them."

Winter intended just to grab his bag and leave. Sean sat in the rear of the Justice Department's Lear 31 and fixed him in her gaze as he entered. She closed the computer in her lap and set it aside. Her face looked like porcelain, white and as hard, the bruise under her bottom lip like a water stain. Winter reached into the cargo hold and retrieved his duffel. "Guess this is good-bye."

"I suppose so," she replied. "I'm so sorry about your friends."

"They were doing their jobs, and we all accepted the risks knowing something like this could happen. Someone paid those men to kill your husband and they figured out a way to do it."

"You're an interesting man, Winter Massey. Don't guess I'll be seeing you again," she said softly, smiling faintly.

"Not likely. I'm going back to Charlotte, where it's quieter." God, he hated to leave this fascinating woman he longed to learn more about.

"What's next?"

"FBI will take all the evidence they have, identify the unidentified dead subjects, and go out and catch the others."

"What about the man behind this? Does he win?"

"It depends on whether or not the government can convict him without Dylan's testimony. The A.G. will most likely have to drop those charges associated with Dylan's killings, maybe try and go for something else. They might have to let the old gangster out of jail unless they can prove conspiracy to commit murder. They'll probably dangle death sentences over the weakest of the killers, and probably one will turn over Manelli to get off with a slapped hand and join WITSEC."

"Manelli?"

"Sam Manelli." Winter realized, too late, he shouldn't have revealed his name. Dylan obviously hadn't told her, either.

"From New Orleans?"

"The Justice Department has been trying to get him in jail for forty years," he said, privately cursing his stupidity.

Winter saw something in Sean's brown eyes that he hadn't seen before, not even during the life-or-death battle of the previous evening. Anger? Bewilderment?

"Sean, what is it?"

"Its nothing." Her smile seemed uncertain. "It's just that I know who Manelli is—who doesn't, but it never crossed my mind that Dylan worked for him. Now, this all makes more sense . . . sort of."

He offered his hand and Sean gripped it like a child being left at a nursery the first time. "Thanks for protecting me from Dylan, for saving my life and for making me feel safe. And, for being my friend, I suppose."

"You are safe. Talk to the USMS psychiatrist. His specialty is these kinds of emotional roller coasters. I've talked to him a couple of times myself. He'll make you feel better. I promise." He smiled, studying her features one last time to lock them into his memory.

Her eyes turned up into his. "Maybe someday I'll come to Charlotte, buy you dinner, and you can tell me how all of this turned out."

He remembered that Fletcher Reed had said pretty much the same thing on Rook Island, the night before. "It would be my pleasure," he said meaning it.

When he lifted his bag from the seat, she stood up, put her arms around him, pressed her cheek against his, and hugged him. "Good-bye, Deputy," she told him. "God bless you and keep you safe."

Winter turned at the door and looked back at Sean, who waved tentatively. Maybe it was his imagination, but it looked as though her bottom lip quivered. He nodded one final time, stepped down from the plane and walked toward the waiting Citation. The sensation of her cheek against his stayed with him for a long time.

Sean waited five minutes, then descended from the Lear-jet to watch the Citation carrying Winter Massey lift off. She kept the plane in sight until it was a speck in the Virginia sky. She had met very few men of Winter Massey's equal. Now he was out of the equation, and she felt both sorry and relieved.

She realized her hands were shaking. She had never been more surprised than when Winter said that Dylan had been involved with—had crossed—Sam Manelli. No wonder Dylan had wanted to keep her in the dark. No wonder the killers found them. If only she had known, she would never have joined Dylan on Rook Island. Dylan was lucky—he obviously had died fast.

She scanned the base as if memorizing the positions of the vehicles, the men and women who dotted the landscape. She spotted Archer in the command tent and stiffened. Manelli's name meant everything was different now and everybody had to be evaluated anew. She knew better than anyone that when it came to his influence, his money, anybody could be an enemy.

A female deputy strode from the Gulfstream toward the Lear. Her boxy body looked hard and her face, beneath the USMS cap's visor, rigid. "I'd like you to get inside the plane, Mrs. Devlin, and remain there until further notice," she ordered.

"I just came out."

"It's a security matter."

"If you can explain how I might be in danger here, I'll consider your *request*."

"If you do what I say, we'll get along just fine."

Not a chance. "Could you please tell your boss, Director Shapiro, I want to have a word with him?"

"The chief marshal is busy. Tell me what you want and I'll relay the message." It seemed to be an effort for the deputy to keep her voice even and pleasant.

"Tell Chief Marshal Shapiro that I will be leaving now. I'd like my things removed from the jet and I want someone to drive me to the closest airport or bus station."

Sean went back inside the Lear. Through the window she could see the woman speaking with two male deputies, one of whom went into the Gulfstream. A few seconds later, Shapiro left the G-II and headed her way, just as she had expected.

"You want to leave?" he asked her.

"I intend to," she corrected.

"We'll need to work some things out first. We need to consider what's best for you. We're going to request some psychological help so you can deal with what you have been through. We certainly owe you that."

"First, I never asked to be involved, but now that my husband is dead I assume I am no longer needed to keep him occupied. I haven't committed any crime and I don't have any information to give anybody. I have no intention of remaining here in this horrible place while people pick through that pile of rubble. And I won't spend another instant in the company of 'our lady of the perpetual sneer' out there. If you will call me a cab, or have one of those policemen drive me out, I can take charge of my own life from now on."

"You don't even know where you are," he protested.

"I assume wherever we are is connected somehow to roads which lead to towns and eventually to a commercial airport. At this point I'd hitchhike before I'd stay here in this cracker box another ten minutes."

"I'll take you back to Washington within the hour. And if Deputy Munsen isn't to your liking, I'll replace her."

I doubt your deputy is to anyone's liking, except the man who sells her steroids, she thought.

"Mrs. Devlin, you are our guest. We feel a responsibility for you and we will do everything we can to make you comfortable. I'll have your bags moved to my plane," he said solicitously, hoping to appease her.

"Sir," she replied, "I have not yet been comfortable being your guest. I just want my life back. And a stiff drink."

Shapiro lifted her briefcase. "If you will follow me," he said, "the United States Marshals Service will make every effort to oblige you."

Two minutes later Sean was seated in the Gulfstream holding a scotch on the rocks. She swiveled the chair, looked out, and caught Deputy Munsen staring up at her sourly from the tarmac. Sean touched her glass to the window and smiled.

47 | New York, New York

The ebony Lincoln pulled up in front of a six-story building in lower Manhattan. The driver got out, walked around to the passenger's side, and opened the door. Herman Hoffman and four other men climbed out of the vehicle. Herman moved with the confidence of a man who was certain his brittle legs would snap if he dared go any faster.

The driver, a blond with a tattoo of barbed wire wrapping his wrist, used a key to open the building's door. "Thank you, Ralph," Herman said.

The four men followed Herman inside and stepped into the elevator with him, affording the elderly man more than his share of space.

"I'm bushed," Herman said. "Could sleep for a week."

"Yes, sir," Ralph said. "I expect we all could."

"First, Ralph, find out why my other team hasn't reported in. If they were captured, we have to get to them immediately. If there were casualties, we need to get them collected. If they didn't get the target—if by some miracle she made it through—we'll have to deal with that immediately. Get me all the intelligence you can compile ASAP."

Herman looked at the man in the corner wearing a black all-weather coat and matching baseball cap and smiled weakly. "I doubt even the hand of God could have saved the inhabitants of that house if the men made it there. If they didn't make it to the island, we'll deal with fixing that. I can't assess the situation until I have all the information."

The elevator stopped at the fifth floor and the four

other men got out, leaving Herman and Ralph alone in the car.

"You men get some rest and we'll meet later and see what we have left to do, or if we are done." Herman raised his head slowly and stared at the man in the ball cap until the doors closed.

"Sir?"

Herman opened his eyes to find Ralph kneeling beside the chair where he had dozed off after lunch.

"Sir, sorry, but we have word on the island team. All four were erased and their equipment was captured."

"I was afraid the sailors would somehow get an alarm out to the Marine base. Damn."

"That deputy, Massey, killed them."

"What?" Herman sat up, fully awake now. He had taken a risk, knowing the marines could respond before the team was done, but... "A deputy marshal killed four of my boys? That's impossible. The intelligence is wrong. The SEALs must have caught them in the open."

"The Devlin woman and the marshal are definitely alive, sir. Our four are confirmed dead."

"You're absolutely certain?"

"Their fingerprints have already been put through the system. Control picked them up and Fifteen is on the phone, wanting to talk to you."

"What else?"

"The radar staff was neutralized. The female marshal was, too. They got that far without a problem. But Massey turned it. He took them one by one."

Herman felt like a great weight was sitting on his chest. "Send the snapshots to the client as planned. We have to find Sean Devlin."

Herman lifted up the encrypted telephone on the table beside the chair and put it to his ear.

"What the hell is going on?" Herman wasn't surprised that the demanding voice on the other end was icy. Herman had known Fifteen since he'd recruited him twenty-four years earlier. For the past six years his protégé controlled all of the dark cells except Herman's. After Herman's death, he would have them all. But until that happened, Herman didn't answer to Fifteen or anyone else.

"Fifteen, how thoughtful of you to call. I need assistance with some light sweeping."

"I know that," Fifteen replied. "When were you going to mention this to me?"

"When you had a need to know," Herman said.

"I presume I have, now that all hell has broken loose. We have to discuss this matter, Herman."

"I'd be happy to talk with you anytime, Fifteen. Perhaps in a few days."

"So, *this* thing—whatever it was—is over, right? You don't plan any more surprises, do you?"

"Very close to being done. I have a couple of loose ends. Nothing for you to worry about. Everything is hunky-dory." Herman hung up the phone.

"Ralph, we'll need to put some effort into finishing Mrs. Devlin before our client finds out and reacts stupidly."

48 | Atlanta, Georgia

Sam Manelli took his meals alone in his cell. The Justice Department wanted to make sure he didn't have any contact with other inmates, or anyone except his lawyers, who they couldn't bar from the prison. They needn't have worried. No one in the population would have dared approach him without Sam's first instigating that contact. If he had been sentenced to life without parole, perhaps he might have been in real danger. Even Al Capone, once he was in prison, became just a middle-aged mop-pusher who was physically assaulted by more powerful inmates. Only if Manelli was cut off completely from his organization, his money, and his political influence would he be in danger, and everyone knew it.

Occasionally, when Sam was being escorted to the day-room or the yard to meet one of his high-dollar lawyers, a mob-connected inmate in the prison hallway would meet Sam's eye and nod. Sam might, depending on his mood and who made the gesture, acknowledge this with a low-ered chin. Or he might ignore it. Word in the facility was that the feds were inclined to turn their backs and allow Manelli to fall victim to foul play. Inmates knew better: No reward outweighed the hell awaiting the man who lifted a hand against Sam Manelli.

The young guard carrying the tray containing Sam's dinner arrived on the other side of the bars. His appear-ance distracted Sam from his thoughts, which, these days, centered solely on the murder of Dylan Devlin. Sam was wondering when Dylan would be dead, how he would die, what he would think in his dying moments when he knew Sam had gotten to him. The gangster would have paid any amount to have the rat bastard handed over to him. He daydreamed constantly about the most painful way for Devlin to die. The challenge for Sam was to keep from al-lowing his temper to cause him to kill what he could keep alive but in amazing pain for days, weeks, even years.

"Hello," Sam said. He even managed a smile for the guard. He didn't have to be nice to the kid, but what the hell did being friendly hurt?

The guard returned the greeting cordially and slid the tray halfway through the slot in the bars. He was set to re-ceive the second half of twenty-five thousand dollars in cash the day Sam was released. Johnny Russo had, at Sam's instruction, been generous with Sam's money. It was easy to make sure that the men Johnny passed it to were in positions to help.

Sam's father had taught him well, rules Sam had never broken, rules that had always before kept him out of jail. Make the right friends. Buy people who can help you. Information is life, ignorance is death. Never write anything you don't want some D.A. showing a jury. Don't be stingy. Never waste money. Use threats only as a last resort. Never go back on your word. Never apologize, never cry or show any sign of weakness. If you say you'll do a thing, do it, no matter the cost. Never trust anyone but yourself. Assume everybody steals. Know when to make an example of a thief, when to overlook theft. Pay your people right, but not too much, because that is weakness. People who owe you hate you. A friend will kill you faster than an enemy will. Mercy breeds contempt, so never show any.

Sam knew all of the Manelli Rules. Hundreds of them—all passed down from mouth to ear. The one that made the deepest impression on him was when his father said, "Sammy, I love you more than anything I ever loved. Way more than I can say. But if someone thinks they can make me do something by threatening you or your mama, I tell you this for true. I gonna tell them, Go on and kill my wife, kill my sweet baby. 'Cause you are gonna be dead after a long time in pain you ain't gonna believe."

"What if they give us back?" young Sam had asked. "You just forget what they did?"

"Of course, I'd take you back, but I'd still do to them what I said. The most important rule, Sammy, is never let love make you break any rule you have to live by."

Then, in his old office on Magazine Street, Dominick Manelli had placed his massive hands on Sam's ten-year-old cheeks and kissed him full on his mouth. All those decades later, sitting in a cell in Atlanta, Sam could still close his eyes and feel his father's stiff afternoon whiskers. Sam could also remember the look on his father's face when, years later, just before he died, Dominick had summoned him close and whispered through his last gasps, "Sammy, listen. I want you to give the archdiocese two hundred and fifty thousand dollars. In my name. Tell the priests they can pray me into heaven for it."

Sam had replied, "You crazy, Papa? Nothing the priests can pray will keep you out of hell." Sam thought he'd seen a smile flicker in his dying father's eyes. Dominick had waited until the last seconds of his life to offer God money that he knew was now his son's. Dominick could have made the contribution himself when he was in control. The old man could tell Saint Peter that he had asked Sam to donate to charity in his name, so if he didn't, it sure wasn't Dominick's fault. Even in death, Dominick Manelli had an angle to work.

Sam took his tray from the guard and set it on the table. He opened the stainless-steel lid and admired the meal. The plate held a filet medium rare, scrambled eggs, baked garlic, and a slice of toasted French bread lathered with butter before it was broiled. There was a glass of fresh-squeezed orange juice and a thermos of very strong coffee.

Sam bowed his head and said a brief prayer. He ate slowly, saving the filet for last, chewing every small piece he placed into his mouth exactly thirty-seven times.

The last thing Sam Manelli wanted to do was to choke to death.

49 | Concord, North Carolina

Winter had almost fallen asleep lying in a lukewarm bath, a wet washcloth covering his eyes. The loudest sound in the world right then was the rhythm of the drops from the faucet as each hit the surface of the soapy water. A tapping at the door brought him around.

"Winter?"

"What, Mama?"

"Don't fall asleep in the tub."

"I won't," he said, smiling to himself.

"Hank is stopping by the school to pick up Rush on his way here."

Winter smiled. "So Hank is coming up."

"Well, that's what I said."

He heard her close the bedroom door, then reopen it.

"You forget something?" Winter called, his eyes still shut behind the washcloth.

"Wash behind your ears."

Winter let the water drain before he stood and took a hot shower. He was dressing when he heard a car pull into the driveway. Seconds later the back door opened and Lydia called out a welcome. Winter listened to Nemo's barks, Hank's booming voice, and his son's words, filtering through it all like notes from a flute. He slipped into loafers and hurried to the kitchen.

"Is it cool for twelve-year-olds to give their father a hug?"

Rush immediately put a clench hold around Winter's middle, while Nemo stood on his hind legs, put his forepaws on Winter's back, and licked any skin within reach of his long tongue. "I'm not twelve *yet*," he squealed.

"Nemo, get down!" Lydia said.

"This is some homecoming." Winter turned his gaze to Hank.

"Chief marshal called me to say you were heading home."

Lydia's face reflected an insatiable curiosity, but she didn't ask any questions. "Dinner will be ready in an hour. Y'all get out of my way. Go on out to the living room."

"I knew you'd make it home for my birthday," Rush told Winter. "Gram said you probably couldn't, but I knew you wouldn't go back on your word."

It took all of Winter's resolve not to burst into tears.

After dinner they sat out on the front porch. Winter and Rush were on the swing, Hank Trammel and Lydia sat in rocking chairs.

"Where were you, Daddy?" Rush asked.

"Not sure, exactly."

"Doing what?"

"I did some sitting around on a porch sort of like this. I ate, I slept, I ran, did push-ups and sit-ups. Ate more. Slept some more. Sat, talked. Listened." He battled back memories of the dead WITSEC crew and the treacherous flight across Rook Island.

"Didn't hunt down any bad guys and arrest 'em?"

"Didn't make a single arrest the whole time I was gone. I'll have to make two arrests next trip out."

"Bet you will, too!" Rush exclaimed.

Winter usually told the boy what he had been up to, sparing him the hard-core details. He liked for Rush to believe that being a deputy marshal was no more dangerous than strolling through Walt Disney World, which was mostly the case.

"Rush," Lydia said, stretching. "Let's get you to bed. Let the old men jabber." After only a mild protest, Rush kissed Winter and went inside, Nemo trailing behind.

"Not all night, y'all," Lydia cautioned the two men.

As soon as Lydia was safely inside, Trammel pulled a flask from his coat pocket and poured a couple of ounces into his glass. "Chill in the air," he offered as an explanation. There was a silence while Trammel savored the golden liquid. "Whiskey's a lot like pussy."

"I know, Hank. The worst you ever had was wonderful. Sort of like comparing apples to house slippers."

"You think? They're both sure as hell a great comfort. You want a sip?"

"No thank you."

"Shapiro told me what happened."

"He did?" That was a surprise.

"Yeah, he thought you ought to have somebody to talk to, if you were of a mind to."

"Not much to say about it. Nothing I can change by talking. I'm fine."

"You did your job. You got nothing to regret."

"My luck is going to run out one of these days, and where'll that leave Rush? We both know I could end up like Greg. I think I should consider a career change."

"I 'spect Miss Eleanor would pitch a fit if you show up in heaven too soon."

"She'd kick my ass," Winter agreed.

"It's getting ready to rain," he said, screwing the lid on the flask. "Maybe you should get some sleep."

"I know."

"I'm real sorry about Greg. Wish I'd known him better. Any people?"

"No family. His mother abandoned him. He was raised by his grandmother. She's dead. Nobody closer than me, far as I know."

"You going to tell Rush?"

"I shouldn't until they release the names." Winter knew that he wasn't up to that yet. It just didn't seem right for someone so young to have been through so much suffering, to have lost so much.

"I doubt it'll be a secret for long, media being the way it is."

Winter walked Hank out to his car and stood in the driveway watching him drive away.

After he locked the back door, Winter went to his room and lay in bed, tired but unable to sleep. The rain started to fall in torrents. Thunder crashed and the sky lit as though artillery shells were being lobbed. Winter's door opened slowly and he turned and stared at the shapes framed in the doorway.

"What's up, Rush?"

"Aw, Nemo's scared. You can't reason with him when he's like this."

"I imagine I can bunk down a good deputy and his side-kick."

Winter knew the dog could sleep on an operating rifle range. Rush wasn't going to admit his fear of lightning. From the time he was an infant he had never stayed in a room alone during a storm. Not being able to see the flashes made it worse because there was no warning of any kind for him before the crashing booms.

Winter threw the covers back for Rush. Nemo curled up on the floor. Father and son lay shoulder to shoulder listening to the storm rage outside.

 50 | **USMS headquarters
Arlington, Virginia**

It was dark outside. Sean tried not to yawn, but she did anyway. Richard Shapiro's office was one enormous space divided into three areas. In the five hours she had been there, she had read through a stack of magazines, eaten a ham sandwich, and drank more coffee than she usually did in a month.

The chief marshal's conference room was enclosed by a wall of soundproof glass. Through it, Sean could see Shapiro railing at his men like a basketball coach. She'd seen and heard enough to know that the marshals had been shut out of the investigation into the murders. And nobody at 600 Army Navy Drive was at all pleased about having to wait for the FBI to share the information it was compiling. Sean had seen Shapiro on the phone, his face so red she was sure he would blow an artery. For the past hour his staff had been in the glass room and she had watched them like fish in an aquarium.

Bored, she went into her briefcase, took out her computer, and turned it on. She opened the nasty note Dylan had sent her. She closed the document and, dragging it into the garbage deleted it. If only she could only erase memories as easily as she had Dylan's final message to her.

She was beyond ready to leave. She looked up and waved at the marshals behind the glass wall. One saw her and spoke to Shapiro, who looked wearily out at her. She waved good-bye to him.

He said something to his men and they all seemed to relax.

Richard Shapiro came out and sat near her on the couch. "I'm sorry," he said.

"I'm tired," she said, thinking how stress might trigger a migraine.

"Listen, Mrs. Devlin. We want to do everything we can to help you through this. I have a few thoughts."

"Can we discuss it later? As I said, I'm quite tired."

"Sure. You don't have to make any decisions right away. I think we can give you the equity in your house."

Sean made her voice firm. "I'm not your witness. I am not changing my name, and I want my belongings put back in *my* house, which did not belong to my late husband."

"Let's discuss all of that tomorrow, okay? We'll get you a death certificate so you can get to your husband's bank accounts, which as his widow, you are entitled to."

"Do you seriously think I would take money he made murdering people?"

"I assumed you could use it."

"I don't need it and I'd sweep streets before I accept one cent of that blood money."

"We intend to compensate you for what you went through."

"Do that. Figure out what keeping my husband's killings a secret from me, and what I have been through in the past few days is worth. In the meantime, I want to go to a hotel and sleep."

"I'll have a couple of deputies—"

"No! No more deputies, no guns, no protection. If you want my cooperation, I demand some consideration. I am not testifying against anyone. I will not agree to be watched over or followed. I do not want the United States Marshals Service knowing where I am. If no one here knows where I am or what I'm doing, nobody can tell anybody anything." Sean was reaching the absolute limit she could take. She had to get away.

"I'm sorry you feel that way."

"Tell me the truth. Do I have to accept your protection?"

"No, I can't force you to. You can decline it, but I can't emphasize strongly enough how dangerous that might be. Mrs. Devlin, please—"

"I am officially declining protection of any kind. Do I need to sign anything for that?" she said briskly.

Shapiro's eyes hardened. "We can't force our protection, but the FBI can decide that you are crucial to the investigation, declare you a material witness, and take you into custody. Obviously, I'd hate to see that happen, even if it was for your own safety."

"I suppose if the FBI decides to do that, there's nothing I can do to prevent it," she replied. "I'd be happy to relive that night over and over, if you'll treat me like a friend and not a prisoner. You can start by calling me a cab. I will return first thing tomorrow if you like."

"Very well. I accept that you have declined our protection and I will see you first thing in the morning. Fact is, we have a hotel suite reserved for you."

"I'll stay in the suite if you'll give me your word you won't have deputies hanging around. I've had it with being spied on."

Shapiro stood and nodded decisively. "I'll call you a cab."

Shapiro strode into the conference room and conferred with his assistant. He went to his desk, pulled open a drawer, then returned with a cell phone, which he handed to her.

"If you need anything at all, just press star eighty-one to reach me. I can have people outside your room in minutes."

Sean nodded and slipped the phone into her coat pocket. She knew that, despite giving his word, Shapiro wasn't about to let her leave his office without having her followed and watched over. Now, that was something she couldn't allow.

At the hotel, the cabdriver popped the trunk and set her suitcases on the carpeted stoop. She tipped him, as well as the doorman who carried her suitcases into the hotel lobby and placed them before the counter.

"Sean Devlin," she told the clerk.

The clerk typed in her name into the computer and watched the screen. "You'll be in..." She penned the room number—1299—inside the little folder.

Sean slipped her Visa card onto the desk.

"That's not necessary," the woman said. "It's been taken care of."

Sean left the credit card where it was. "I'd like another room for my mother, who is arriving later this evening."

"Your suite has two bedrooms with private baths."

"A single on a lower floor. My mother has a fear of fire, so nothing higher than an extension ladder can reach," Sean said firmly.

The clerk typed again, then ran Sean's card. She placed an electronic room key into a folder and wrote *321* inside it.

Sean turned and saw that the cab that had delivered her was now parked across the street. *Those bastards!* She was angry that Shapiro had lied to her but also relieved that his action had released her from her word.

A bellboy pulled the cart holding Sean's suitcases into the elevator and pressed twelve. Sean reached into her coat pocket, took out Shapiro's cell phone, and slid it between her suitcases on the cart. She pressed three and the elevator stopped there.

Using her foot to keep the elevator door open, she handed the bellboy the key card for 1299 and fished a ten dollar bill from her purse. Taking her briefcase from the cart, Sean handed the bill to the bellboy and smiled. "Take my bags on up, please. I'm going to check out my other room first."

"Yes, ma'am."

She waited for the elevator door to close before she made her way quickly to the stairs, carrying her briefcase and her purse. She found the back entrance to the hotel and exited close behind an elderly couple so she would appear to be with them. She saw two men sitting in a Crown Victoria parked near the driveway, but neither looked at her as she passed, still sticking close to the old couple. As the couple stopped at a Lexus, Sean kept walk-

ing. Two blocks farther she saw a cab approaching and
hailed it.

The driver was obese. His face showed his disappoint-
ing effort to grow a beard, and he studied her with dull,
lazy eyes. She climbed in and was instantly repulsed by
the interior, which smelled as though someone had recently boiled cabbage in it.

"I want a cheap hotel. One that rents rooms by the
hour. Water beds and X-rated films are fine."

She saw his now curious eyes appraise her in the mirror.
She glanced at his identification card. "And, Warren—one
suggestive proposition out of you, you'll lose a nice tip."

"Lady, I know just the place," he said. "You'll love it."

51 | Atlanta, Georgia

Sam Manelli had an hour before the guard came to pick
up the cell phone he smuggled into Sam each night after
midnight. Sam slipped it from under his pillow and dialed
Johnny Russo, who would be waiting for the call. If the
numbers on the bill were traced someday, who could
prove who was at the pay phone, who had made the call?
Sam smiled at the thought of Johnny standing by a pay
phone outside a rural grocery store in Fantee, Louisiana,
in his fancy suit, fighting off hungry mosquitoes.

"It's me," Sam grunted. "What did the dentist say?"

"He pulled the tooth," Russo answered, promptly.
"X-ray pictures be at your guy's office in the morning so he
can check them. You want the guy to bring the X-rays so
you can see, too?"

"Of course not."

"You be leaving there soon, I believe," Johnny said.

"So, if I'm still here, I'll call same time tomorrow."

Sam ended the call and pondered the information.

He was delighted that Devlin was dead and that the proof, by way of pictures of the corpses, was going to put his mind at ease. It had been expensive, but money well spent. He just couldn't believe that Johnny would even suggest that Bertran bring the pictures of a corpse to him in jail—he knew that Bertran would have refused. As much as he would have loved to see them, it was a stupid suggestion.

Sometimes he wondered about Johnny. In order for him to make it, he was going to have to think clearer and let his emotional side take a backseat to his business mind.

The simple fact was that times had changed, making crime on the scale Sam had known it almost impossible.

Sam had done his best to pass his understanding of business on to Johnny, he couldn't help but wonder sometimes if he had put his money on the wrong horse. Perhaps his fondness for Johnny's father, and now Johnny, had clouded his own judgment.

He was resolved to the fact that he had done his best and ultimately couldn't control what Johnny did or didn't do. All he had wanted to do was finish this one bit of business with Devlin and live the rest of his days running his legitimate businesses.

Sam lay back on the cot, closed his eyes, and thought about better times.

Fred Archer rubbed his eyes, afraid he might fall asleep at the wheel. He hadn't had more than a catnap in the last forty hours, and now it was closing on midnight. He figured he could sleep at least five hours.

Upon arriving back in D.C. from Ward Field that afternoon, he had met with his director and the attorney general. The director had told the A.G. that he had every confidence Archer would get the Rook-Ward murders solved in a matter of days—that Archer was the only man who could get the evidence to charge Sam Manelli with new counts of conspiracy to commit murder. The attorney general had stressed the importance of putting it to bed immediately and insuring that Manelli's impending release was a very short one. Although neither his director nor the A.G. had said so, the meeting's purpose was to let Archer know that either he would accomplish their goal with all due haste or he would find himself in some dismal place like the Fargo office, wearing heated socks to discourage frostbite.

The long absences from his family, which Fred's job demanded, had taken the standard toll on his personal life. His wife, his three children, and even his dog had become strangers a long time before Fred's wife finally filed for divorce. In the first months after the divorce Fred had made an effort to visit his children, but they seemed to like it better when he didn't. Fred had stopped visiting altogether, which allowed him to work even longer hours than before—without the guilt his wife had always heaped on him.

He parked his Bucar, a silver Crown Victoria, a block from the brownstone where he rented a shabby studio apartment in the rear of the main house over a narrow garage. He parked in a loading zone—not caring if he got a citation this time.

He unlocked the gate and walked along the side of the house, his soles scratching the cement driveway. As he slid the key into the door to his apartment he heard the click of a cigarette lighter behind him. He had his hand on his duty weapon before he recognized the man whose face was illuminated by the flame. "Jesus, Fifteen!"

Half of the man's face was deeply burned. The man he knew only as Fifteen was a shadowy member of the espionage community. Fifteen was in his late forties and always dressed in loose-fitting outfits, which Archer figured covered a badly scarred body. He wore cotton gloves, an obvious wig, had a single eyebrow, and his nose looked as though it had been created by unskilled surgeons.

"Jumpy from the long hours?" Only half of his mouth moved when he spoke.

"Come in," Archer said, cheerily.

Archer had first met Fifteen only after a dozen phone calls over a three-year span. He had given Archer golden evidence, which had allowed Fred to break eight high-profile cases, making him look like a brilliant investigator. It was after they had established a relationship that Archer had finally met the burned man. The fruits of their relationship had taken Archer from being an obscure agent in Seattle to a position on his director's speed dial and a coveted office in the Hoover Building. Archer carried a blue ID, which held a top secret access number, the same one as those given to deputy directors.

Fred was excited that Fifteen was carrying a nine-by-twelve manila envelope and suppressed an urge to snatch it away. For the sake of ceremony, Fred went straight to his kitchenette and poured two fingers of Glenlivet in two glasses, added ice, and, after putting in a drinking straw, set that glass of scotch on the coffee table before his guest. The good half of Fifteen's face smiled. "Thank you, Fred."

Fred sat down in the chair opposite and tried his best to ignore the envelope in Fifteen's lap.

"Fred," Fifteen said after he had taken a pensive sip of his scotch, "I have in my possession something I believe will be of great interest to you." When he tapped the envelope in his lap, ash from his cigarette fell onto it.

"Anything you have is always of interest to me."

"This concerns the incident on Rook Island."

For a second, even though he knew Fifteen was hot-wired into the CIA, NSA, and other covert intelligence sources Fred could only imagine, he was stunned at the speed with which Fifteen had acquired information on a fresh investigation.

Fifteen handed the envelope to Archer. "It contains the identifications related to the four sets of fingerprints you sent out to all branches of the military, Interpol, and CIA."

The four deceased UNSUBs' fingerprints had been run against millions of prints in the FBI's computer and had all come back unknown, baffling Archer. He was certain the four were ex-Special Forces—everything indicated it.

Archer's hands trembled as he opened the envelope, which contained a typed document and eight photographs. Archer hastily thumbed through them. The first four showed sharp-featured, hard-eyed skinhead soldiers wearing what had to be Soviet military uniforms. The other four were surveillance pictures, one taken of each of the same four men while they were in public. He recognized the men as being the corpses.

Fifteen crushed out his cigarette and placed the butt into a tin he kept in his pocket. "Those four men are absolutely your Rook Island killers. They were Russian ex-soldiers who have been under surveillance since they came into the country ten days ago. They slipped the CIA watchers and resurfaced on Rook Island. We figured that they were up to something. Now we know what that something was."

Archer knew that if the CIA conducted surveillance on subjects inside the United States, they were obliged by law to involve the appropriate federal agency and step back, since CIA operations on American soil were illegal. The CIA, being the creature it was, didn't always comply. Like most intelligence agencies, the CIA lived to collect information but was reluctant to share it unless it would result in a net gain. If the agency had been tracking four men they suspected were up to no good, then hadn't alerted the FBI, that would be bad enough. But the fact that the same men had slipped their watchers to murder six sailors, six United States marshals, two Justice Department pilots, a federal attorney, and a protected witness made such an admission impossible at this point. He figured that it was sensible for the CIA to have Fifteen now make the information available to the FBI so they didn't have to admit their involvement. It was a win-win deal for the CIA because they could still take credit for identifying the Russians without getting a black mark for their failure to bring in the FBI.

Fifteen took a sip from the straw. "You could compare the prints yourself, but for the unfortunate fact that their bodies were somehow misidentified and misplaced. Chunks and ash by now."

Archer knew Fifteen well enough to believe that the "accidental" cremations would prove to be true, but he didn't see the reasoning behind it.

"What about the others?"

"Others?"

"There were more than the four. There were at least eight, maybe more. I have a sketch of an old man with a malformed pupil who was their leader."

"The sketch is worthless. This old man is merely a figment of a young boy's imagination." Fifteen straightened in the chair. "I'll give you the other four because I know how important it is to *your* investigation. The Russian Mafia is a problem that concerns us all, and of course the remaining troops have to be accounted for, which they will."

Archer couldn't afford to press his benefactor for details. What Fifteen said was how it was, period. Archer knew that asking questions was pointless. Fifteen told Fred only what he wanted to, when *he* decided the time was right.

"Let me see what I can do. You have there Sam Manelli's connection to the killers—picture-perfect proof that he hired them to do what they did. His Russian pals made them available to him and that evidence will be forthcoming"

"The A.G. expects me to close this yesterday," Archer said, belaboring the irony of the statement.

"No problem." Fifteen reached into his jacket and handed Archer a folded search warrant. "Judge Paul Horn issued this. Have a team of FBI agents in New Orleans serve it. It will yield proof that the killers were working for Manelli."

"Enough to convict him?"

"Enough proof for the world, if not enough to actually convict him. That, you and I will take care of shortly."

"I don't know what to say," Archer replied, as he read the warrant.

"One hand washes the other, Fred. Is there anything else?"

"Just one more thing. We have to figure out how Manelli's hitters found out where Devlin was. I'm sure there was someone on the inside of WITSEC, probably inside the detail."

"Obviously, there was an inside person," Fifteen told Archer. "Someone in WITSEC got the intelligence out.

You'll need proof of that. So, of all the likely candidates, whom do you most suspect?"

"The supervising deputy, WITSEC inspector Gregory Nations, is the most logical."

"Let me see what I can scrounge up. If he was linked to Sam Manelli, I will get you evidence of it, financial records of payoffs for motive—he had ample opportunity. Is Sunday night soon enough?"

"Of course," Fred said, his excitement barely under control.

"In return for assisting you in putting this disaster to bed, I may need a few small favors from you . . . when the time is right."

"What sort of favors?"

"Nothing at all, really. In order to help you effectively, I need to stay involved."

"Involved?"

"You'll need to keep me in your loop."

Archer was taken aback. Fifteen had never requested such a thing and if Archer was caught at it, he would be dead in the water. This changed the face of their relationship to what was technically espionage. "Well," Archer said, swallowing hard. "I don't know how I can do that."

Fifteen reached down and picked up the envelope and its contents. "If you can't, I'll understand, Fred. But of course, someone else might end up with the case who does know. I'm sure you can function just as well in the future without my help. It's your decision."

It was a decision Fred Archer had no trouble making.

Sean awoke at eight A.M. without receiving the wake-up call she had requested for seven-thirty. Based on what she had seen of the place, she had no trouble believing that the management hoped she would sleep past the ten A.M. checkout time so they could charge her for a second night. The room stank of stale smoke, the carpeting was stained and the curtains frayed. As far as she could tell, the sheets were clean.

She showered under a weak stream of lukewarm water with a minuscule bar of soap and dried herself with a thin towel hardly larger than the washcloth. She rinsed her mouth with tap water and used her fingertip to clean her teeth. She studied the dark bruise on her lip as she ran her fingers through her wet hair.

Now able to think with a clear head, she felt relieved her life was back under her control. She started a mental list of the things she needed to accomplish in the next few hours.

She slipped into her stale clothes, opened the telephone book, and looked for the places most likely to help her with her next step. She found a likely candidate, memorized the address, pulled on her leather coat, slipped her purse into her briefcase, and left. She had eluded the marshals and, at least for the moment, she had what mattered most—her life. Now all she had to do was keep it. She asked the desk clerk to call her a cab.

The sign on the building read, URBAN WARFARE. Below those words, smaller print added, FASHIONS FOR THE

BATTLE OF LIFE. Sean studied the mannequins in the windows and decided that they looked as though they had been brought in off an active battlefield. She felt exhilarated as she contemplated the leather and the T-shirts brandishing insults intended to pass for social statements. Satisfied she would find what she was looking for, she walked inside.

The saleswoman peered at her from behind a glass counter. She had luminous white skin, jet-black clothes to match her hair and lipstick, and an extremely large hoop that seemed to run through her septum. Her hair looked like it belonged on a doll found in a landfill. She was wearing dark-framed reading glasses.

"Yeah?" When the woman spoke, a stud in her tongue sparkled.

"I need a new wardrobe."

"No offense, but you're more the Junior League type. My stuff is a bit more cutting-edge, don't you think?" The clerk's raspy voice sounded like it had been tuned by twenty years of cigarette smoke and liquor.

"I need a change."

"You think I don't know who you are?"

Sean was stunned. She had assumed it was too soon for Manelli's network to be looking for her.

The woman came from around the counter. "Judging by the lip, you gotta change your look and then run like hell."

The clerk had her pegged for a battered wife on the run. *Perfect.*

"What appeals to you?"

Sean looked at the tag on a pair of jeans. "You take Visa, MasterCard?"

"I have to take plastic, but I hate the shit. Costs me three points. I always prefer cash."

"These clothes are sort of expensive."

"Quality costs. Some of these are originals. I get famous people in here, you know. Johnny Depp shops here—anyway, he did once. I got an autographed picture he sent me around here somewhere. People are funny. Something's cheap, they stick up their noses, if it's real expensive they'll stick up a bank to get it. My name's Hoover. I own the place." She glanced at Sean's wrist. "Nice watch. Could I see it?"

Sean promptly removed the watch and handed it over.

Hoover studied the watch. "Real?"

"A gift from my husband."

"Fakes are so good now. This one's real, it goes for what, four grand?"

"Twelve," Sean said coolly.

"How do you know it's not a copy? Guy who hits you, sweet pea, could be a liar, too."

"I had the band shortened myself at Cartier and it's been on my wrist ever since. If it was a fake, they'd have told me."

Hoover raised her brows. "Tell you what. Let's get you outfitted up and we'll discuss payment options."

Sean fixed her eyes on Hoover's. "Here's the deal. I need a few changes of clothes, the trimmings, something to carry them in, hair and makeup to fit."

"Sergio next door is a great hairdresser." Hoover extended her arms out, cocked her hip in a pose that reminded Sean of a model on a revolving stage posing in front of a new automobile. "He does mine."

"Perfect."

Hoover studied Sean carefully, then she nodded. "Let's get started, angel. We'll stick to basic black. You got a great body for my clothes."

Sean had no problem with black. She was, after all, a widow.

Sean only knew that she was the person staring back at her from the mirror because she had been in on the transformation process. Two hours had passed since she entered the store. Now Hoover and Sergio stood at the counter evaluating their creation.

"You look eighteen!" Sergio cried. "Could be my best work."

"Yep, a true work of art, sweetie. Now, get the hell out." Hoover waved a hand in the air, dismissing him. "We'll settle later."

Sergio blew them a kiss from the front door and was gone.

Hoover folded the clothes they had chosen into a new nylon duffel bag. Sean put her computer and her purse into a small backpack and set her empty leather briefcase on the counter. "My financial situation is this: What cash I have, I'll need for my relocation."

"The clothes, the hair, and makeup, glasses, boots, socks . . . Normally that'd run twenty-five, twenty-six hundred, plus tax."

Sean rested her hands on the briefcase. "This was eleven hundred new."

"It's used and, anyhow, do I look like I'd carry a case like that? Tell you what, just use your credit card, and, for you, I'll eat the three points."

If Sean used her plastic, Hoover would get her money, but, it would lead people straight to the store. When Hoover described how Sean now looked, she'd be easier to find than ever. Sean slipped off the Cartier and set it on the briefcase. "This will cover what I owe you and then some."

"I can't take it."

"Eighteen-karat. Look at the hands. The second hand sweeps. That means self-winding Swiss movement, not quartz. Listen to it. Look at it. Feel the weight."

"I believe it's real. Problem is, I can't make change on that. You said twelve grand? What would I do with it? This is no pawnshop."

Sean thought about it. The watch was worth ten used. It was a magnificent piece of engineering, precious metal, and art. Besides, Dylan had given it to her, which made it worthless. She had another thought.

"Hoover, you wouldn't happen to know where I can get a gun, would you?"

Hoover's right eyebrow rose. After a moment, she reached under the counter near her knees and lifted up a very large revolver. "Forty-four. Storekeeper's best friend. I get some tough customers."

"I was thinking something smaller."

Hoover promptly reached into a drawer behind her and took out a small dark revolver with checkered hickory grips. "Smith and Wesson .38 Chiefs. It conceals like a champ, holds five shots, and has plenty of punch. And it's not hot."

Sean studied the gun. "The Cartier for everything, the Smith and extra bullets if you have them. We both know a jeweler who thought my watch was stolen would pay three grand, which gives you a nice profit on the clothes, which probably cost you twenty-five percent of what the tags say. Gun's value is maybe three hundred on a good day."

Hoover slid the gun across the counter to Sean, then lifted the watch and slipped it onto her wrist. "Done."

Sean lifted the revolver, broke it open, and pressed the ejector to empty the shells into her palm. She looked into the empty ports, eyed the inside of the barrel for dirt. She reloaded it and closed it with a snap. "And keep the change."

Hoover reached into the drawer behind her again and placed a box of shells on the counter. Then she offered her hand. Sean set the gun down and the two women shook on it.

———

Sean bought a newspaper before she boarded the train. The front page of *USA Today* carried two seemingly unrelated stories. A jet carrying United States marshals had crashed while trying to make an emergency landing at an abandoned airfield in rural Virginia. The names of the dead marshals were being withheld until notification of next of kin. In the second article, six sailors at a radar facility on Rook Island, just off the coast of North Carolina, were dead. Neither the Navy nor the FBI would confirm reports that the incident was a shooting rampage perpetrated by one of the six sailors, who subsequently took his own life. An FBI spokesman said only that the details of the tragedy would be forthcoming as soon as their investigation was completed. The names of the six dead sailors were also being withheld. Sean closed her eyes and bit her lip.

 Richmond, Virginia

Sean carried her bag out of the railway terminal on her shoulder. She was about to hail a taxi when one made a tire-squealing U-turn and pulled up to the curb in front of her. It happened with a suddenness that froze her in her tracks. Other taxi drivers, already in line, honked in protest.

The driver's voice carried out over the blaring horns. "Get in quick before one of those old fuckers starts shooting!"

Sean leaned down and instantly understood why the driver had done what he had. He was a kindred spirit of the girl Sean had become. He was wearing a T-shirt that advertised German beer, and his jeans were two washings away from becoming shop rags. Tattoos covered both arms to the wrists and most of his neck. His hair was blazing orange with bright-blue tips, and he had stainless-steel hoops through his earlobes, studs in his nose, and a ball under his lower lip. A pair of enormous blue eyes were set in an enthusiastic face that looked like a clean page waiting for experience to line it.

Sean climbed in the front door—the one the driver threw open. She rested her duffel between them and placed the backpack in her lap.

"Where to?" he asked as he pulled out into traffic.

"What I need is a hotel room where I can get some work done. Where it's quiet and not too expensive."

"What kind of work?"

"I'm working on a novel."

"No shit? I know a place that's perfect. My aunt used to stay there, paid by the month. It's a great old place. Classy, but it's in a funky part of town."

"Sounds good," Sean said.

He reached into an ashtray overflowing with receipts and gum wrappers and found a business card. It had a lightning bolt hand-painted on it, WIRE DOG was hand-printed over the bolt, and a phone number written below it. "They call me Wire Dog."

"Wire Dog?"

"I'm a soundman. Electronic wires. Dig?"

"I dig, Dog."

"Cab belongs to my old man. He's down with bottle flu at the moment. I pick up a few coins this way. You got a name?"

"Sally," Sean lied. "Sally McSorley."

"Anytime you need a ride, Sally, call Wire Dog. Best ride in town and reasonable. Hotel Grand it is."

The neighborhood had seen better days. A few of the buildings were boarded up. The structures which had businesses in them—a thrift shop, a beauty supplies store, and a used office furniture store—seemed to be holding their collective breath so they wouldn't be noticed by wrecking crews. The cab passed a church where a half-dozen disinterested people were perched on the steps taking in the sunshine. Wire Dog pulled up in front of a hotel skinned in stained brick with carved sandstone accents and air-conditioning units plugging a majority of the windows from the second floor up. He carried Sean's duffel into the lobby. The Grand had once been an elegant establishment, but age had added a subtle patina that made the interior resemble a photograph taken in another century.

The front desk was directly across, forty feet from the front door, at one end of a cathedral-like lobby at least sixty feet long. The floor and counter were covered in marble. Two twenty-foot-tall columns, located just inside the front door, stopped at a ceiling laced with detailed plaster molding. A chandelier loomed over the lounge, which consisted of two facing leather couches and four armchairs all set on a massive oriental carpet. The elevator was at the far end of the lobby, positioned between a pair of columns identical to the ones framing the front door.

Wire Dog dropped Sean's bag at the desk and palmed the bell.

An elderly man dressed in a sports coat and green tie shuffled from the office.

"Hello, Skippy," he said to Wire Dog in a surprisingly deep voice like a Shakespearean actor's. He lowered his bald head and stared at the boy over his reading glasses. "New earring? Is that a ball bearing under your lip?"

"You aren't moving forward, you're sitting still, Max."

"And more tattoos. Aren't you afraid of ink poisoning?"

"They're vegetable-based."

"Imagine how much that's going to cost to remove when you grow up." Max peered at Sean. "Room?"

"Yes, please."

"How long?"

"Three or four days."

"Forty-five dollars per night. How will you be taking care of this?" Max asked.

"Cash." She pulled folded bills from her jacket pocket.

Wire Dog sighed out loud. "Aw, Max, give her a price break. She's a friend of mine. If she had a lot of money, why the hell would she stay here?"

"Oh, a friend of *yours*, Skippy! In that case it should be double. No telling what manner of sand a friend of yours might kick up. For old time's sake, I'll call it thirty-five a night, payable each day before two in the afternoon. Skippy's aunt Grace," the old man explained to Sean, "was with us for almost thirteen years, which makes the boy family once removed."

"I'll be out for a while if anyone is looking for me, Max," an elderly woman's voice chirped.

Sean pulled the guest card toward her and started filling it in with lies.

"I'm just going to the coffee shop," the old woman continued. She was frail and bright-eyed like a bird. "If my niece calls, tell her I'll call her back. Do I have any mail? I'm expecting a note from my great-nephew Peter."

"I'll be right here, Betty," Max promised. "No mail delivered yet today." He took the card from Sean. "Phone calls are extra. No loud music, no overnight guests."

"No getting drunk and setting fires, no bothering the resident spooks, and no cloning sheep in the rooms," Wire Dog added.

Max scowled at Wire Dog. "No cloning of anything."

Sean said, "I'm a writer looking for a quiet place to edit something I've been working on. You won't even know I'm here."

"She's a novel author," Wire Dog boasted.

"A novelist." Max winked at Sean and held up a finger. "Room four-sixteen will be perfect. Tom Wolfe stayed in that room once. Native son, you know. If you need anything, just let me know." He looked down at the card Sean had filled out. "Miss McSorley."

Sean handed over the cash and took the receipt.

The brass fence on the ancient elevator gleamed. The operator looked as if he had come with the equipment. He was a stooped man in a crisply starched white shirt with cuff links and a belt cinched tight just below his chest. He called out the floors as the numbers crept by outside the cage. "Two. Three. Your floor, ma'am. Four."

Four-sixteen was unexpectedly large, with high ceilings and tall narrow windows, which, when she opened the drapes, let in plenty of daylight. She could get onto the fire escape platform by unlocking the window without the A.C. unit. The push-button telephone and the TV set were the only contemporary evidence in an otherwise perfectly preserved '40s room. There was a small brass plaque on the front of the table which read: AUTHOR TOM WOLFE SAT AT THIS DESK ON 10–13–1969.

The tiled bathroom had a deep, claw-footed tub, a pedestal sink, and a toilet with its porcelain tank set up high on the wall. Sean wouldn't have been surprised to have found a TOM WOLFE SAT HERE sign on the seat.

55 | New Orleans, Louisiana

Bertran Stern was waiting for the Saturday morning FedEx delivery. Four decades as Sam Manelli's personal attorney had given him something of a cast-iron constitution. Bertran didn't worry about anything, didn't fear anyone but his own best client—and only then what his client was capable of doing to those few people Bertran loved. The lawyer had willingly traded his morals, ethics, and very soul to the devil for a seven-figure income and substantial perks.

Bertran had once believed he was better than Sam Manelli. His superiority complex had been a shield he had hidden behind—a lie worn so thin it was transparent as window glass. He now knew he was infinitely worse than the mobster he worked for because he had entered his world with his eyes open, even if he'd been blinded by pure greed. He'd lunged at the opportunity to skip the hard work of building a practice. He had known from the beginning what Sam Manelli was, who he was getting involved with.

Out in the open, Stern's firm handled Sam Manelli's legitimate businesses. Stern & Associates prepared contracts, filed incorporation papers, foreclosed on collateral, collected debts, and filed lawsuits for Sam's companies.

Bertran rarely had to defend Manelli's companies from lawsuits because there had only been one that made it to a courtroom. The injured parties either dropped the suit as soon as they discovered who owned the company, or they gladly accepted the first offer Bertran made them. On the only occasion someone had insisted on taking their grievance to court, the judge demanded it be settled. The judge was a man who had an appetite for high-dollar male prostitutes. In New Orleans, all prostitutes worked, however indirectly, for Sam.

Stern hand-delivered cash to judges, cops, and politicians. He carried the money in a briefcase that was designed so that when he pressed a button on the handle, an envelope filled with cash dropped on the floor or desk, depending on the recipient's paranoia level. Bertran had specific knowledge of thousands of crimes. In fact, he had lost track of how many felonies he had been the conduit for. He received his orders from Sam's mouth only, usually at Sam's favorite meeting place—his sauna room in the basement of his house. Even naked in this sauna, deep in the bowels of his home, Sam spoke in code. Luckily Bertran dealt with Johnny Russo only when neither could avoid it.

Bertran had daydreamed about pulling a gun and killing Sam a million times. But Bertran, for all his complacency, was not a killer.

The receptionist buzzed in the FedEx delivery guy who deposited three overnight letters on her desk. Bertran took the envelopes from her and his heart almost stopped when he read the return address he'd been expecting on one of them. FARNEY, JAMES & COMPANY, 221 STONE STREET, NEW YORK, NY 10016. The letter had been sent out from some drop-box service, paid for in cash.

The lawyer strode straight back to his office and slammed the door shut.

Johnny Russo sat behind Bertran's desk, his hand already out for the envelope. Russo opened it, and three pictures spilled out on the blotter. Bertran didn't care to inspect the images. In the split second before he closed his eyes and turned away, he saw what he needed to see. The instant and sickening impression was of blood and heads with features rearranged into perspectives that a cubist painter might have imagined.

"Mission accomplished!" Johnny Russo's enthusiasm for violence repulsed Bertran. "Smart cops. You can tell by the fucking *brains.*" He snickered. "Herman's guys are *something.* Christ, will you look at this!"

"I'm glad Sam got his money's worth," Bertran murmured.

"You got a problem with this?" Johnny gloated over the pictures. "It was necessary."

"Necessary or not, it's grotesque."

"Then get out," Johnny snarled. "You don't need to look, you fucking hook-nose, liver-lip, sack-a-shit-kike fuck!"

"You just make sure you turn those pictures into confetti," Bertran reminded him calmly. "You get caught with those and you'll get buried so far under the jailhouse you'll be hearing Chinese through the walls."

He stepped out, softly closing the door behind him.

Johnny Russo stared down at the photos, each showing another view of the carnage inside the cabin of an airplane. This was too good. He was elated, he wanted to laugh out loud, to yell and destroy things. It had seemed impossible, but here was the evidence. Here was something wonderful, something rare and beautiful. The whole thing was coming together more perfectly than he had hoped. He stared at each of the pictures as long as he dared. Then he fed all but one into the shredder beside the chair, turning them into tiny squares of confetti.

In the remaining photograph, Dylan Devlin's eyes were open and the front of his shirt was covered with blood and gobs of brain tissue. The entrance wound looked like a dot applied with a Magic Marker. Another man's shattered head was resting on Dylan Devlin's shoulder. In the background, there was what had once been Avery Whitehead, a man Johnny Russo was familiar with. "Now, this shit is art."

Johnny lifted a pencil and pushed the photo under some papers on Bertran's desk. "You'll get a close look now, you prick." Johnny loved screwing with the stuffy lawyer's head. If it weren't for Sam, Johnny would have made the guy vanish years earlier. But Sam needed the lawyer and knew Bertran loved money and his family too much to rat Sam out. Besides, a lawyer couldn't testify against a client. But Johnny believed the old attorney knew too much about too many things. The second Sam was gone, Johnny would take him out. There were lots of greedy attorneys to replace him with.

Johnny fed the FedEx's address sheet into the shredder,

stood, and opened the seemingly solid bookcase by twisting the ornamental column on it. He exited into a secret hallway that led into the next building, which was used as a storage facility for retired amusement games. Sam had a business that refurbished the bell-ringers and other vintage arcade games, then sold them to dealers across the country, who in turn sold them to rich people who liked to put them in their fancy houses.

Johnny's driver, Spiro Feretti, was waiting in the Lincoln. Johnny slid in beside him and lifted the magazine Spiro had laid down before he started the car.

"You been reading this rag for a solid week, Spiro," Johnny told him.

"I like to take my time. It only comes out every other month."

Johnny thumbed through the pages. "You know, I gotta wonder about this bodybuilding shit. I mean this staring at greased-up men and bodies of those she-he muscle chicks is sort of..." He stared down at a fold-out of a well-oiled man on a stage, posing. "Spiro, it's *queer.*"

Spiro was pressing a remote door opener. "You mean odd, right?" he said, staring ahead at the opening garage doors. "Not *fagola.*"

"This muscle shit is dick-sucking queer. There's nothing normal about looking at this shit."

"I work out hard to maintain this—"

"Hey, don't sulk on me," Johnny cut in. "You got a build scares the shit outta people. You are one strong-looking bull. Enough already. Maybe I have to get a new guy who don't look like some fucking sausage filled with marbles, like he's gonna explode."

"Sure, Johnny. I got the cuts, the definition I like. I ain't going to compete or nothing. I mean, that takes pumping eight hours a day."

"Just remember, Spiro. You start looking at me like you want me to screw you, you're a dead man."

Spiro turned and looked at Johnny with wounded eyes. "I ain't ever had no such a thought," he declared solemnly.

Johnny laughed and popped Spiro in the shoulder. "Of course not! I'm just messing with you. I know you ain't no sissy. You'd look like shit in a dress. Chill—those steroids are supposed to shrink just your dick, not your sense of humor!"

Spiro drove out into the street and waited for the garage door to close before proceeding. As they neared the intersection, three vehicles crossed in front of them and pulled up at the curb. Men and women, all wearing jackets with FBI emblazoned on them, streamed out of the cars and ran up to Bertran Stern's front door.

"What they doing?" Spiro asked. "Can they go into a lawyer's office like that?"

Johnny slunk down in his seat. "Get the hell outta here!"

Spiro steered the car away from the attorney's office and drove in the other direction. Johnny stared out the back window.

"He knows a lot of shit, Johnny," Spiro said.

"He can't tell—it's client privilege. And he has a big family that can't hide out with him. Anyway, we can always pay to have some guys we know whack him. It would be real expensive, but doable."

"Like an investment in the future."

"You know, Spiro, it's too fucking bad we can't write hits off as a business-related expense."

Spiro laughed.

"See," Johnny said, "you still got your sense of humor."

Bertran was in the kitchen making a mug of English breakfast tea. He planned to wait until Johnny was gone before returning to his office. He would spray Lysol to kill the eye-tearing cologne odor Johnny always left lingering in the air.

He was sitting there sipping his tea when he heard his receptionist squeal, "They, they're . . . the FBI!"

"What?" he said. "What the devil?" He felt his heart race, then the icy grip of real fear. He thought about the photographs that had been delivered to his office. Did the feds know about them? Was it possible they had already seen them? He heard fists pounding at the door.

"What should I do, Mr. Stern?" the receptionist shrieked from her desk, in full view of the people demanding to come inside.

"Give me a few seconds."

Bertran bolted into his office and slammed the door. Johnny was gone. He grabbed up the shredder and looked in at the confetti before he opened the bookcase and set the machine in the secret passageway. He pushed the bookcase closed until it clicked into place, then sat at his desk. Sweat poured from every pore in his body. He mopped his brow with his handkerchief and gulped down a glass of water.

The agents didn't bother to knock. The door flew open and the room filled up with blue jackets and hard eyes set in determined faces.

"You people have a legal emergency?" Bertran Stern joked.

One of them handed him a search warrant. He made a show of looking for his glasses, then read the warrant, summoning whatever courage he could pull together into a wall of bluff to hide behind. *There is no evidence. It doesn't exist. Even the scraps are not on my property. I never touched those pictures. No evidence equals no arrest. How did the FBI know about the pictures?*

The warrant, issued by a federal judge named Horn, sought evidence of conspiracy between Sam Manelli and other unidentified parties to commit murder. The warrant didn't specify which murders had taken place, but Bertran knew good and well from the images what murders the warrant referred to. The smug expressions on the feds' faces said they knew that he knew. A "John Doe" informant was credited with furnishing the information.

"This warrant seems a bit vague," Bertran pointed out. "A fishing expedition. But there is nothing here that could possibly help you."

"That right?" an FBI agent said.

"Search away, ladies and gentlemen," he said graciously. "If you have no objections, I have paperwork to catch up on."

"Would you open your safe?" The man in command was short and not particularly threatening in either his speech or manner.

Bertran pointed his finger at the safe. "It isn't locked. I never keep much of anything in it. I don't deal with cash or dark secrets."

He didn't keep any records of anything incriminating in his office. There was nothing like that within miles. Russo certainly had books on what came and went on the dark side of Manelli's empire, but Bertran had never even seen the "dirty" books. He envisioned thick leather-bound volumes, but they could be computer diskettes or images carved into wax tablets, for that matter.

The agents opened the safe door and started removing the items and laying them on the coffee table.

"Just put it all back in when you are done," Bertan said.

"We'll be taking them," the agent in charge told him.

Bertran felt their eyes on him, felt the hate, the anger. But he knew the agents were going to be a lot madder when they left. He lifted a stack of papers from beside his blotter and placed it tidily before him.

The agent in charge stared down at something that had been under the papers Bertran had moved and was now exposed.

When the lawyer realized what he had just unwittingly uncovered, a vise tightened on his left arm near the shoulder and his eyes felt like they were being vacuumed out of his skull. Something took his heart in its jaws and crunched it.

The rectangular image of three obliterated heads stayed with him until he was swallowed up by absolute darkness.

56 | Richmond, Virginia

Sean left the hotel Saturday afternoon to walk around the neighborhood. She had located a coffee shop where Max had told her that most of the residents and guests ate. The restaurant was closed on Sunday, so Sean went to the convenience store and stocked up on bottled water and enough food so she wouldn't have to go out until Monday, when business demanded she must.

She also replaced some of the things she had abandoned in Washington—undergarments and necessary toiletries.

She wasn't sure yet where she would go when she left Richmond. She needed to decide on somewhere she could lay low and let the search cool down without attracting any attention.

She was aware of Sam Manelli's reach and what he was capable of doing to anyone he felt had betrayed him. She knew he was single-minded when he perceived a threat to what was his, and the lengths he would go to in order to make sure everybody knew there was no such thing as a safe place for an *enemy* to hide. Her best chance was to hide and wait and hope that his desire for revenge would ebb to the point where other things occupied his atten-

tion. It was possible that Sam could be arrested for sending the killers after Dylan and decide that she was no
longer worth pursuing.

She thought about Winter Massey. Of all the people
who could and would protect her, he was the only one she
could trust, but she couldn't bring herself to drag him
back into danger. He didn't owe her anything. Their relationship had ended when he left Ward Field. She was on
her own, and it had to remain that way.

She found herself fantasizing about the deputy, wondering whether, if she had met him under other circumstances, things might have been different. She told herself
that her attraction to him was probably due more to their
circumstances than anything else. Maybe someday she
would see him. But for the time being, she decided, it was
best for both of them if she forgot all about him.

When she went to sleep Saturday night, it was after a
long, heartfelt prayer and with the loaded .38 under her
pillow.

57 | Concord, North Carolina
Sunday

Winter sat at the table, watching his son fight to contain
his growing excitement. Winter had stayed busy around
the house all weekend. There were plenty of minor repairs
to take care of. While he worked, Rush stayed close and
they talked and laughed. It helped to keep his mind off
Greg and the other thoughts that stalked him. He and
Lydia decided to celebrate Rush's birthday on Sunday afternoon. Winter didn't know what Monday would bring
his way.

The handicap had taken its social toll on Rush. Most of

the friends he had made before the accident hadn't remained close for long. After the novelty wore off, most sighted children found it difficult to maintain a relationship with someone so radically different. Friendship with Rush meant the loss of things that were important to children that age: video games, basketball, baseball, movies, bicycles. Since the accident, Rush had become more and more comfortable with children like him. Angus McGill, a neighbor Rush's age, was the only one of Rush's old pals who still visited, but he was out of town with his parents.

"Well," Winter said. "What should we do now?"

"We could sit on the porch," Lydia said.

"Aren't you guys forgetting something?" Rush asked, fighting back a smile.

"I don't think so," Winter said, trying to sound sincerely confused. "Mama, what's that?" Winter got up, lifted a package from the sideboard and placed it on the table in front of his son. "A present?"

Rush placed his hands on the package.

"I don't know," Lydia said.

Rush felt the edges of the box. "What is it?" he asked.

"Open it and see."

Rush removed the ribbon, peeled off the paper, and pried open the box. He reached in.

"It's something plastic."

"Could be," Winter said.

Rush lifted the object by the edges and placed it down on the table, flat-side down.

"Sculpture art?" Rush had been to museums where there had been sculpture and other tactile work he could appreciate with his fingers. In art classes, he had made three-dimensional objects in clay, wood, cloth, and paper.

"Sort of art. That guy Moses Mink who brought his statues to your school made it for me. You tell me what it is," Winter said.

As Rush's fingers moved over the surface of the piece,

the contours started to make sense. What he was feeling suddenly appeared as an image in his mind, and his heart leaped with sheer joy. "It's . . . you!" He started laughing and ran his fingers over the cast impression of his father's face. "It's a picture of you!"

"It's a mask, so you won't forget me. How cool is that?"

"That's way, way far-out cool! That's the number-one best present ever." He laughed again. "I can't believe it."

Rush made a big deal over the other gifts: a stack of audiobooks from the Trammels, two sweaters and two pairs of jeans from Lydia, and a check from Eleanor's father, who had moved to Nova Scotia with his third wife. When Rush left the table, he was carrying the mask.

58 | Charlotte, North Carolina
Monday

From his Explorer, Winter watched Rush and Nemo join other students to walk up the stairs to his school. His cell phone buzzed.

"Yeah?"

"Where are you?" Hank Trammel asked.

"Dropping Rush off."

"Can you come see me?"

"What's up?"

"I'd rather tell you when you get here."

It was impossible to read Hank's voice.

His phone rang again almost immediately after he'd set it aside.

"Yeah?"

"Say hello first, Winter," Lydia scolded.

"I thought it was Hank."

"I wondered if you would mind stopping by the grocery store on your way home."

"Something's come up. An important meeting at headquarters. It may take a while."

"I don't know why one tells you to rest a few days and then another tells you to come to work," his mother complained. "It's like they don't care what you go through. I know that news story about the plane crashing upset you. I know you didn't want Rush to think about all that, but you can tell me."

"Tell you what?"

"Did you know any of those people?"

"I knew most of them."

"Did it—"

"Mama, if I could discuss it with you, I already would have. When I can, you'll be the first to know."

Hank Trammel's stiffly formal manner and his stern face set off warning bells in Winter's mind as he sat across the uncharacteristically ordered desk. Hank flipped open a file folder and studied the first page. "Chief Marshal Shapiro got preliminary findings from the FBI this morning and faxed this to me, asking that I share it with you."

Winter felt his anticipation growing at the possibility that the case had already been broken.

"Were you aware that Greg Nations had an offshore bank account?"

"No," Winter replied. The question surprised him. He couldn't think of one reason he should have one. "But people have bank accounts all over. I doubt it's illegal to have an offshore account."

Hank pushed the photocopy toward Winter, spinning it around so he could read it. He pointed to the balance.

"Four hundred thousand dollars was deposited by wire before Nations arrived on Rook," Hank said. "His cell phone records show that he called the bank the day that transfer was made. He's had this account for two years.

He opened it with a ten-dollar deposit and, over its life, the amount of wire transfer deposits has ranged from twenty thousand to fifty thousand dollars. Eleven days ago, four hundred thousand was wired into it from a Swiss bank."

"Come on, Hank. What proof do they have that this is Greg's account, that he had any knowledge of it?" The notion that Greg had that kind of money was ludicrous.

Hank pushed over the second sheet from the folder—the paperwork to open the account. Winter recognized the scribbled signature as Greg's, unless it was a superb forgery. He felt nauseous.

"Anybody can put anybody's signature on a document. This is a photocopy."

"The FBI found the originals hidden in his house when they searched it over the weekend."

"So they say."

"They say Greg knew Sam Manelli."

Hank showed Winter a grainy picture of Greg talking to Sam Manelli. It looked like a surveillance shot taken from a distance.

"We meet criminals all the time," Winter said. "Besides, pictures can be faked."

"I'm not saying it's true," Hank told Winter. "But Greg specifically asked for you to be attached to this operation."

"Yes, he did."

"How often before this had he asked for you on a WIT-SEC operation?"

Hank already knew the answer.

"Shapiro has to consider that maybe Greg didn't expect any of his men to be killed. Maybe he was double-crossed. Maybe they were supposed to shoot Devlin from a distance."

Even though Winter realized Hank was just passing the information along, he felt like he was being tortured. "If Greg was dirty, he would never have brought me into it."

"Did Greg tell you about his military experience?"

"He trained Special Forces."

"Winter, according to the FBI, Greg trained people in special weapons, effective and unorthodox killing, and interrogation techniques. He tell you that? Did he tell you he started with military intelligence, worked directly with the CIA? He guarded defectors."

"No, he didn't. What about the dead UNSUBs on Rook?" Winter offered. "They were obviously soldiers. The armed forces fingerprint and take blood for DNA. Those dead men won't lead to Greg."

"Those four killers were soldiers. The FBI matched their prints."

"I knew it."

"Winter, according to the Bureau they were Russians—ex-shock troops. You know what happened after the wall fell—Russia couldn't even afford to fix their equipment or feed their soldiers. A lot of them hired themselves out to the Russian mob as freelance killers out of necessity. The four you killed on Rook Island arrived in this country after Manelli was arrested."

"They weren't Russian soldiers, Hank. One of them had a distinctly Southern accent. I'll tell you what this is. The FBI is lying, or being fooled. And you can tell Shapiro to tell the Bureau that no matter what they come up with, they can't convince me that Greg sold out a witness."

"Have you thought about . . ." Hank started, then reconsidered. "Winter, what if it's true? What if they're right? What if Greg did take money from someone like Manelli for doing a small favor? Someone could use that to blackmail him and make him do something much worse."

"Not Greg," Winter said, resolute in his conviction that Greg was being made a patsy in this investigation.

"Nearly a half million dollars . . ."

"Hank, once when we were in Georgia leaving Glynco,

he turned around and drove back ten miles because he found out a clerk had given him change for a twenty instead of the ten he had given her. We were looking at missing a flight because of it. That's the kind of man Greg was."

"We're not talking about ten dollars. It isn't like you to ignore evidence because it doesn't fit what you think is true."

"What I think is that somebody is framing him. Maybe it's the FBI."

"Why?"

"Because they have to explain how this all happened. They have to make people think they're on top of everything, which is as far from the truth as it gets. Think what solving this is worth to careers, what not solving it will cost them. It wouldn't be the first time they put a spin on something to suit their purposes."

"This is more than public relations. You just got through saying that Greg didn't tell you the truth about his military service."

Winter was dumbfounded. "I never asked, and it doesn't matter."

"You know, it isn't smart to be behind a bull when you know he's gonna sit down. There are bound to be some complicated politics in all of this."

"What are you saying, Hank?"

"Greg didn't have a family to get hurt. You do. If you're right, this is a done deal. You don't understand the politics at work here well enough to know when to get out of the way. Fight the Bureau and the A.G. on this and they might make room for you in the same fire they're looking to roast Nations' reputation over."

Winter wasn't so naive he doubted that could come to pass.

Hank said, "Sometimes a situation comes along where somebody gets sacrificed. Maybe holding up one bad apple would be a way to save the USMS and maintain the credibility of the entire witness security side. You can see what's a stake for the USMS, Justice, and the FBI." .

"If Greg didn't do it, then somebody else did. If they stop looking at Greg, then whoever's responsible might do the same thing again," Winter said.

Hank scowled and placed his hands on the file. "Winter, all I know is what Shapiro wanted you to know."

"Does he believe what the FBI told him?"

"He told me that he thinks the speed at which everything was put to rest is unusual. The Russian military cooperated immediately here; even though identifying those men as theirs makes them look bad and has the potential to create an embarrassing incident when our relationship is delicate. There's a chance they wanted to cooperate with us, since it means clamping down on their Mafia."

Winter shook his head. "Bull."

"I'm your friend, Winter. The truth is that there's nothing you can do."

"What, we all just let this run its course?"

Hank shrugged and put the pages back inside the folder. "The only reason I know about what happened on Rook and Ward Field is because Shapiro thought I needed to know. There's one other thing he asked me to tell you. Sean Devlin slipped away from the marshals who were watching her."

"I'm sure she had a reason," his calm tone belying the stab of terror he experienced on hearing the news.

"He didn't say."

"Is he sure she wasn't grabbed by Manelli's people?" Winter tried to keep his voice even, despite his mounting sense that Sean was in grave danger.

"She slipped surveillance on purpose. She pulled some kind of a ruse with two rooms."

"Is he going to search for her?"

"I think he's looking for her. I'm sorry about all of this, Winter. You know that."

"So am I, Hank," Winter said, standing. "So am I."

When Winter climbed into his Explorer and slammed the door, two men in a Chrysler sedan three blocks away knew it because a light on the computer screen between them began blinking. The driver waited beside the curb and didn't move into traffic until the Explorer exited the garage and the driver saw it coming toward them.

"You got audio?" the driver asked the second man.

The man with the earphone in place nodded and held a thumb up. "He's growling."

"Growling, as in like a dog?"

"Yep."

59

Rush Massey was at the computer with his fingers on the keyboard. As he typed, a pleasant electronic voice spoke the words.

DEAR SIRS COMMA IT HAS BEEN BROUGHT TO MY ATTENTION THAT
YOUR BREAKFAST FRUIT BARS CAN CAUSE FIRES IN TOASTERS PERIOD
AS AN UNSIGHTED PERSON I BELIEVE I HAVE ENOUGH TO WORRY
ABOUT WITHOUT FLAMING DEATH RESULTING FROM MY DEEP
AFFECTION FOR YOUR TASTY BREAKFAST PASTRIES PERIOD I HAVE
SOME IDEAS FOR FIRE-RETARDANT FOODS PERIOD

Rush heard a snort from behind him. He hadn't smelled Mrs. Holland's perfume and was unaware that the principal had snuck up behind him.

"Rush, you could be a comedy writer."

"I'm going to be a federal judge so I can sentence the men my daddy catches. And when you're a judge, the blinder the better. Like when you're an umpire."

Mrs. Holland chuckled and placed her hand on Rush's shoulder affectionately. "Your father is out in the hall waiting to see you."

Winter led Rush into the auditorium and took seats close to the entrance. "I have something to tell you."

"Okay." His son's face remained emotionless. Rush was preparing himself mentally for virtually anything.

"What I am going to tell you is a classified secret, so I have to ask you to keep it between the two of us."

Rush crossed his heart.

"You know the USMS airplane that crashed Thursday night?"

"Yes."

"Right." *God give me the strength to do this.* "Those WITSEC marshals were taking a witness to Washington to testify."

"WITSEC like Uncle Greg?"

"Greg was . . ." Winter's voice broke. He hadn't felt the emotion coming. "On that flight."

Rush was silent as he absorbed the information.

"He's in heaven, right?"

"I'm sure he is."

"Then Mama will have somebody for company that's her friend." Rush smiled. "So we should be glad about that."

"Greg loved you. He was so proud of how grown-up you are. He said so the other day. Here's the thing," Winter said. "The plane didn't accidentally crash. It was hijacked and blown up by some men who didn't want the witness to testify. The men who did it got away. That's the biggest secret."

Rush contemplated the direction the conversation was taking. "Are you going to go catch them?"

"The FBI is supposed to do that. They are trying to blame Greg to explain how the bad men found the witness."

"It's not fair, to blame someone who can't defend himself. And Uncle Greg wouldn't do anything wrong on purpose."

"I agree. The FBI has some evidence they say proves Greg did what they say he did. I know it's a lie, but it looks like they might make it stick."

"You can't stop them?"

"There's nothing I can do. Sometimes, no matter how bad we want to, we just can't set things right."

"Why don't you try—tell the FBI that Greg was good? Go get some evidence." Rush seemed confused.

"I'm not an investigator. I just wanted to tell you that even if people say it's true, we know it isn't. We know Greg was a good guy."

"Yeah, sure. What else?"

"That's all I had to tell you. And that I love you more than anything on earth."

Winter hugged his son to him.

"I'm sorry you feel so sad, Daddy."

Rush reached into his pocket and handed Winter a folded red bandana, one of Eleanor's cotton handkerchiefs. "I want you to take this one."

"That's yours."

"It'll make you feel less sad, like it does me."

Wire Dog found a space and parked his cab a block from the Second National Bank of Eastern Virginia. Sean walked to the bank's entrance and strolled inside. When it was her turn, she handed the young teller a one hundred–dollar bill.

"Could I have that in tens and fives?"

The teller reached into her drawer and swiftly counted out ten fives and five tens.

Sean asked, "Is Paul Gillman still with the bank?"

"Mr. Gillman's our president."

"Is he in today?"

"I think so." The teller looked up and across the lobby. "There he is."

Sean turned. She saw Paul Gillman standing in an office door holding some papers. Paul had gained a few pounds in the five years since she had seen him, the blond hair was thinner on top, and he looked as though he didn't smile as much as he once had. Tucking her money into her purse, she started across the lobby, and her old friend from college looked straight at her, or through her, then turned and went back to his desk. She stopped at a kiosk, scribbled a note on a deposit slip, and crossed to Gillman's secretary.

"Excuse me. I'm an old friend of Paul's. I know he's busy, but could you give this to him?"

The secretary stared at Sean with a look teetering between hostility and curiosity. Sean suddenly realized how alien she must look to the middle-aged woman who spent her days focusing on numbers. It amused and excited Sean to see how people responded to superficial differences between themselves and others. Had Sean Devlin, instead of Sally McSorley, appeared in the bank, the secretary would have been tripping over herself to accommodate her.

The secretary took the note reluctantly and went into his office.

Paul Gillman beat his secretary out of the room. Looking right past Sean, he scanned the lobby with a hopeful look on his face.

"Paul," Sean said. "Here."

The banker turned and stared at her. "Sean?" he stared in disbelief.

"Who else?"

He grinned with delight. "God, you look like Billy Idol!" He hugged her and actually lifted her off the floor.

The secretary stared down at her desk and shuffled some papers.

"What brings you to Richmond?" Paul remarked, finally setting Sean back down.

"Business."

"How's Olivia?"

"Mother passed away."

"Sorry. I really liked her."

Sean smiled. "She liked you, too."

"How long will you be in town?"

"I'm on the ground for three hours and I thought I'd say hello, take care of a loose end."

"Come into the office."

"The *presidential* office."

"What's with you and the getup?" he demanded as she settled into a leather chair. "What happened to Sean Marks, the little debutante?"

"I married this guy a while back. I was crazy about him. He's a federal agent whose temper is legendary." She touched her bruised lip and grimaced.

"Son of a bitch. Aw, Sean, I'm sorry. What can I do?"

"I need to get something from my lockbox."

"Of course." He reached into his desk and sifted through the contents until he found an envelope with SEAN MARKS typed on it and an address over a year out of date. "I labeled it so you'd get it back if the sky fell on me or something. You never know."

"The address is no good," she admitted. "Guess I haven't been much of a friend, not staying in touch."

"You always were mysterious, Sean. But this punk thing is quite a departure from your old look."

He handed her the envelope, which she opened and removed the key. "You and Ally still happily married?" she asked.

"Well, I am as happy as a man with three little boys running amok all over the house can be. Everything is great. But I'd throw it all away and do something insane if you only crooked your little finger."

Sean smiled warmly at her old friend. "I envy you."

Before they entered the vault, Paul asked Sean to sign her name on an index card. She had signed it once before, five years earlier, so the signature could be verified. The signature above was looser, from a less stressful time. He located the box, inserted his and then her key, opened the door, pulled out the box, and carried it to a cubicle. "Take as long as you want. I'll be right outside."

She opened the box, which she had in case of an emergency. At the time it had seemed silly, but her mother had insisted. Olivia Marks had subscribed to the belief that everyone should have mad money, a secret stash in a safe place to draw on. Olivia Marks had been a woman who had lived her entire adult life in quiet terror.

No one but Paul knew Sean had the lockbox, and she alone knew what was inside it. Paul had never asked about its contents. She had made few very close friends—had rarely let anyone get close emotionally. She listened carefully, patiently, but she rarely volunteered information.

She evaded. If pressed, she lied. And she lied with an ease that prevented her friends from being certain they ever really knew her. Sean had been raised to be a survivor. There had been a price and she had paid it. For the first time in her life she was glad she had.

There were only two objects inside the box. She lifted out the stack of fifty hundred-dollar bills held together with a rubber band. The second object was a passport in the name of Sally McSorley. She reached into the bottom of her jacket pocket and took out the wedding band Dylan had given her fourteen months before, whose design matched the one Dylan had worn. She felt a surge of relief as she dropped it into the box and closed the lid.

While she had been inside the cubicle, Paul had straightened his tie and carefully combed his hair. She felt a pang of guilt. As she handed him the box, she caught the scent of breath spray. All of her life, she had been an actor. Affecting and manipulating men had been an effortless exercise, but she had never before consciously manipulated people who cared about her.

"Can't you lay over and have dinner with us tonight? Ally would sure love to see you. You could meet our children: the Grub, Splashy-cat and Goop-slinger."

Sean laughed. "I wish I could, Paul, but I have an appointment with an attorney in California," she lied. "Next trip through, we can all get together and I can finally meet those boys of yours, whose given names, I am sure, aren't what you said."

"Jacob, Stephen, and Murray. They'd like you a lot, Sean. You know, if there's ever anything you need, you can ask me. I really mean it."

She smiled sincerely at her friend. There was one thing. "I don't think anybody could possibly show up here, but if anyone asks after me..."

"I'll say I haven't seen Sean Marks in five years. I'll just date today's signature on the card for a week after you rented the box. I'm a banker, but I've always been terrible with numbers. Don't be a stranger, okay? We care about you."

"Thank you, Paul. You can't imagine how much your friendship means to me."

What was life without friends, family? Without those connections strengthened by shared experience, life became mere survival. She was abruptly conscious of the weight of the pistol in her jacket pocket, a heavy reminder of the fact that she would never again be the girl Paul Gillman once knew.

Wire Dog jerked awake when she opened the cab door. Sean had called him for a number of reasons. He was a perfect addition to her disguise, and she didn't want to have her face seen by other cabdrivers. Wire Dog didn't strike her as someone connected to illegal activities—a real consideration when it came to cabbies. Every dark enterprise inevitably had some connecting point to organized crime, to the network Sam Manelli manipulated from his nest in New Orleans.

When Wire Dog pulled up outside the Hotel Grand, Sean handed him the fare with a ten dollar tip added, despite his unconvincing protest that it was excessive.

"I'm glad you called," he told her. "You wouldn't want to go hear some music sometime, would you?"

"Too much work to do," she said.

"Work your fingers to the bone, and know what you get?" he asked.

"No."

"Bony fingers."

She laughed.

61 | New Orleans, Louisiana

Johnny Russo took a handful of quarters from his pocket and poured them onto the steel shelf inside one of the few remaining phone booths in America with a door, or so it seemed. At the curb, Spiro stood leaning against the Lincoln's grill, his massive arms crossed over his chest.

Reading from a business card he held against the closed wallet in his hand, Johnny dropped a quarter in the slot and punched in the penciled phone number. He was phoning the Kurtz of Kurtz, Walker, Koinberg, Rustin, Winklin & Associates, Sam Manelli's high-profile criminal attorney.

Johnny Russo deposited the number of coins required for the first three minutes. He hoped he could be done in two. He really hated lawyers, and Kurtz, famous or not, was a strutting fag—or would be, given half a chance.

The phone was answered immediately. "Kurtz," the lawyer said. The sound of dinnerware and conversations placed the attorney in a restaurant.

"It's Johnny."

"Johnny?"

"Sam's guy."

"Sam's guy?"

Johnny raised his voice slightly. "Sam from New Orleans." He wondered why the lawyer wanted to act as though he had fifty more important Sams to sort through before he arrived at Sam Manelli, a mobster who'd bought the fancy-ass meal the fag and his pals were eating.

"I'm in the middle of something," Kurtz said pompously. "Is this important?"

"Would I be calling you to see what you're eating for dinner? I got some important hypothetical questions."

"Shoot." Kurtz sounded a little impatient, a tone he would never use with Sam, Johnny knew.

"Suppose somebody's lawyer dropped dead—choked on a candy bar or something. Say that by some chance, in this hypothetical scenario, the lawyer had in his possession, at the time of his death, pictures that were proof that the witness against his client was killed in a plane crash with marshals and one prosecutor, say from a New Orleans federal district. Hypothetically speaking."

Kurtz was silent for a few seconds. Johnny was sure the lawyer had assumed the story was going to be a threat and was relieved it was another lawyer who was dead.

"There would be nothing to prove that this man's client ever saw them?"

"Not a shred."

"Then if nothing physically linked this evidence to the dead man's client—only to the lawyer—it would more than likely be worthless in court."

"With no witness left against his client, would that mean the case would be dropped or whatever?"

Johnny heard ice tinkle. "The case against this guy's client would be dropped and the defendant would be released as soon as the lawyers could get to the judge. With the right prodding from the right attorney, this theoretical defendant of yours would be released before the sun goes down tomorrow."

"That was gonna be my next question," Johnny said.

"What else could it be?" Kurtz said snottily.

The lawyer hung up, leaving Johnny Russo with a full minute still paid for.

"Ya puke. My next question coulda been 'How long would it take me to have your head in a bucket?'" Russo gathered the scattered quarters and dropped them back in his pocket. He would have great news for Sam when he called at two A.M.

62

Winter didn't like to carry the heavy SIG Sauer in the shoulder rig unless he was on the job. Standing before his gun safe, Winter removed a compact semiautomatic. Eleanor's father had given Winter the World War II vintage 7.65 Walther PP as a gift when he had graduated from Glynco. He had purchased it from a dealer who specialized in collectable weapons. It was lightweight, lethal, and accurate enough at combat distances. He only had one seven-shot magazine for it, but it was comfortable to carry in his pocket. He lifted out the box of ammunition and fed the magazine, reassured by the stiffness in the hidden spring. The flying eagle and swastika on the pristine piece identified it as a German officer's weapon, which had received light use during World War II.

Since he had left Rush, he'd been thinking about Greg and what Hank had told him. He had also found himself thinking about Sean Devlin. He suppressed a cloud of guilt for thinking of another woman while he was in the bedroom he had shared with his late wife, even though he knew Eleanor wouldn't mind. God, he would give anything for Sean to pop up to collect the meal she'd mentioned. Given the danger he feared she was in, he knew the possibility wasn't likely.

The other person who had recently mentioned having a drink with him someday—Fletcher Reed—reminded Winter of something he wanted to ask the lieutenant commander. He dialed information and called the shore patrol office at the Cherry Point base. A woman told Winter that Reed had returned to the Norfolk Naval Base, where he was stationed, and gave Winter the phone number. When he called it, a security officer asked for Winter's number and said he would notify Reed and have him return the call.

It took less than ten minutes for the phone to ring. Before the caller spoke, Winter clearly heard vehicles in the background.

"Got your message," Reed said flatly.

"You get shipped out, or what?"

"I was on temporary duty at Cherry Point evaluating the patrolmen. Now I'm ass deep in petty crap and paper. It's the Navy. What can I say?"

"I need your help with something."

"You need *my* help?" He laughed. "Unless you spotted a drunken sailor spoiling for a fight, I doubt I can offer much assistance."

"Hear me out?"

"I'm listening." Winter heard a lighter and imagined a cigar in Reed's mouth.

"What do you know about our flight that went in Thursday night at Ward Field?"

"I just heard it crashed," Reed said. "Catastrophic failure or something, botched emergency landing. You said Ward Field?"

"Abandoned military base inland. What I am going to tell you is classified."

Reed chortled. "Of course it is."

"It needs to stay strictly between us."

"Cross my heart."

"You know anything about two bodies found Thursday night at Cherry Point?"

"The FBI was already on it by the time I got back. I haven't heard any more about it."

Winter told Reed who the dead men were and gave him an overview of the FBI's evidence on Greg Nations. As Winter went over it, he was struck again by what little sense it made. "The only thing a WITSEC inspector like

Greg could furnish Manelli with on a continuing basis would be an occasional location of a witness he was baby-sitting, which just doesn't add up," he told Reed.

"Unless he'd been selling the intel to someone like an information broker who then sold it to people who wanted the witnesses not to testify."

"Then how come no other protected witnesses have been killed?" Winter countered.

"Maybe it was about people who had left the program. Those people get killed from time to time, don't they?"

"I'd have heard about that through the USMS grapevine." He told Reed that if Greg had an offshore account, the money had come from legitimate sources.

Reed pointed out how naive that sounded. "Basically you're not open to any evidence to the contrary to what you believe? I got nothing to offer, Massey," Reed said finally.

"Fingerprints."

Reed sighed. "I don't know what you're talking about."

"I think the FBI screwed with their fingerprints," Winter said. "Those killers sure as hell weren't Russian soldiers. If they were ours, the FBI knows it and for whatever reason aren't going to admit it."

"How do you know that?"

"Come on, Reed. I think the FBI's showing Shapiro what they had was a trial balloon. Get the lies past Shapiro and me, and who else would raise a flag?"

"The FBI can't afford another scandal," Reed agreed.

"For some people, fabricating evidence is no more difficult than you or me backdating a sales slip."

"You're talking about a conspiracy between the FBI, the Russian government, the Navy, and the CIA. Hell, maybe even the Marshals Service. It sounds like the two hundred people who were in on framing O.J.," Reed said.

Winter couldn't blame him for being skeptical. "They

wouldn't all have to be aware of the entire picture to be directly involved. Just a handful of people at the top would have to know why they were doing what they were doing. They'd just have to control who knows what. You know how some people will follow any order."

"Those four guys were definitely soldiers," Reed mused. "Why not Russians?"

"How many Russians speak with a cracker accent? How many Russians have tattoos removed that leave a scar in the shape of a SEAL trident? I couldn't help but notice that the naked corpse was circumcised. What was he, a Russian-Jewish shock trooper?"

There was a long silence. Then Reed asked, "So all you want from me is to run four sets of fingerprints, which I wasn't supposed to keep? If I did *accidentally* hold on to a dupe set, as soon as I run them, the FBI will know all about it. This conspiracy cabal of yours involves the FBI."

"Would it be possible to run them against military fingerprints, just within the Pentagon's database?"

"Maybe."

"I think those four killers were once members of our military. I think the FBI already knows that because they have all the soldiers in the active database. If they were ours, I need to know who they really were. I need anything you can scrape up. If you draw a blank, at least I'll know I've done everything I can."

"I'll see what I can do," Reed said.

"You believe me?"

"I only believe that the tale you're spinning is slightly more intriguing than what I spent the morning doing— plaster-casting motorcycle tread marks on the seventeenth green on the officers' golf course."

"Thanks," Winter said.

"This is probably a waste of time, but just for the sake of paranoia, take down my private cell number and give me yours."

63

Sean luxuriated in the tub for an hour. She didn't feel safe but, for the first time since she'd returned from Argentina, she felt relaxed. When she'd told Paul Gillman her abusive husband was a federal agent, she'd unconsciously cast Winter Massey in the role. But Winter was probably one of the least violent people she had ever met. He'd killed to save her life. It was a strange feeling to have such a strong emotional bond with a stranger. Winter was a complex individual who had gotten more interesting with every conversation. Why couldn't she have met Winter instead of Dylan? Would she, could she, have told him the truth?

Her skin was wrinkling so she got out, toweled off, and went into the bedroom, where her coat was hung over a chair. She reached into the pocket and removed the cash and the passport.

Sally McSorley's passport had a five-year-old picture of Sean Marks in it because it was the phony passport her mother had acquired for Sean's emergency kit. In the picture, Sean had auburn hair tucked behind her ears. Sean decided the picture made her look innocent. Had she ever been innocent? As a young girl in Catholic schools? As a college student? As the bride of a murdering son of a bitch masquerading as a human being? Had she ever had any choice? She wasn't going to waste time feeling like a victim—self-pity was a waste of energy.

She snapped open the revolver and looked at the shells in the cylinder. They might well come for her, but one thing was certain—she'd be one kill that somebody was going to have to work hard for.

After dressing, she picked up the backpack containing her computer, and slipped the pistol into her coat pocket. She considered dipping into the bundle of cash hidden inside a secret pocket in her duffel, a feature that Hoover had used to sell her the bag, but decided to leave it and her passport alone. After closing her door, Sean hooked the DO NOT DISTURB sign on the doorknob.

In the lobby, she got five dollars' worth of quarters from Max and walked to a pay phone down the street. She dialed information.

"United States Marshals Service. How may I direct your call?" The young woman's voice was pleasant and very Southern.

"I'd like to speak to Deputy Winter Massey."

"I'm sorry, he's not in the office. Would you care to speak to another deputy or leave a message on his voice mail?"

Sean listened to Winter's recorded voice and hung up before the tone sounded. She dialed information again and asked the operator for the listing in Charlotte for Winter Massey.

"Sorry, no Winter Massey in Charlotte."

Of course he wouldn't have the phone in his name. She had an idea how he might list it. "Do you have a listing for Lydia or a Rush Massey?"

After checking, the operator told her, "I show a Lydia Massey in Concord, North Carolina. Same area code."

Sean didn't have anything to write with and she fought to remember the number as she pulled out her computer and opened it. She repeated the number until the computer booted up, and she typed it under a folder icon on her desktop, changing the file's name from "Misc," to "7045529988."

Staring down at the number, Sean felt suddenly insecure. She wanted to decide exactly what she would say to him. Would she ask for his help? How could she do that without putting him in danger? How much could she tell him? How many lies would she need to tell? She just needed to talk to him; maybe then, she would feel anchored again.

Nervously, she dialed the number, then dropped in the required number of coins. The voice that answered brought a rush of relief to her. She realized she was holding her breath.

"Winter?"

"Sean? Is it you?"

64 | Concord, North Carolina

When the phone rang, Winter was in his bedroom with the door closed, going over his conversation with Reed in his mind.

"Hello?"

"Winter?"

The sound of Sean's voice filled him with relief. "Sean, is it you?"

"It's me."

"A lot of people are worried about you," he told Sean.

"I figured my sudden departure might raise some eyebrows."

"Are you all right?"

"I'm perfectly fine. After you left, I tired of the company."

"Do you have money?"

"Enough."

"Why are you running?"

"I'm moving around at the moment to make sure when I stop I'll be out of danger."

"I was afraid you might have been kidnapped."

"No, I wasn't kidnapped. I just wanted to let you know that so you wouldn't worry. You can tell your chief marshal I am fine, and even though he lied to me, I forgive him."

"Lied how?"

"I've been watching the news and I can't help but notice they are playing fast and loose with the facts."

"You don't know the half of it."

"It's nice hearing your voice, Massey. I mean that. I'd love to chat, but I have to make a plane."

"Will you stay in touch?" He suppressed the urge to add *please.*

"I can't call back for a while."

"Why not?"

"You're kidding, right? Ever heard of traces? The marshals can't protect me. Look, I'll get in touch from time to time, if you don't mind."

"I'd like that a lot. You just promise that if you ever need my help, you'll call me?"

"So long, Massey."

The line went dead. Winter's heart sank, wishing there had been some way to prolong their conversation. He knew he had to help her. He dialed Hank's cell phone.

"Yeah?"

"You aren't working late again, are you?" Winter asked him.

"Yeah," Hank answered. "Sun to sun, son."

"Sean Devlin just called. She wants Shapiro to know she's all right. She said she knows he lied to her, but she forgives him."

"Lied about what?"

"Didn't say. Can you handle that?"

"I'll tell him. He might want to talk to you. The attorney general has set a press conference for Thursday morning. It won't be a secret after that, and you can get on with your life."

"Thursday," Winter said.

"If you need to talk, I'm here. You know that, right?"

"Yeah, Hank. I do. Thanks."

Winter hung up. He felt sick and, except for once three years before, more helpless than ever.

65 | New York, New York

Herman Hoffman read the note that had been placed on the table beside his Wedgwood plate, "I'll let you know what my orders are in a little while," he said to the man who had delivered it.

"Yes, sir."

"I need those call transcripts ASAP."

The man vanished.

Herman cut a slice from the veal medallion and chewed it, keeping his eyes on the plate. He lifted the wineglass and sipped. He patted his lips with the edge of the linen napkin, then pushed the note to Ralph and watched as he read it.

"We have her located. What now?" Ralph asked, looking up.

"I'm considering what the appropriate response should be. Eat."

Ralph cut a chunk of sirloin.

"Mrs. Devlin was at a pay phone in Richmond, Virginia thirty-three minutes ago. Richmond is a very big town to cover without assistance. With a transcript of the call, it might be possible to know if she is in a car passing through and picked out the phone at random, or is staying nearby and had no other access to a telephone. Or maybe she has access but knows better than to use a phone within close proximity of her hide." Herman speared a red potato and, holding it up, examined it as though seeking some imperfection on its skin.

Ralph didn't interrupt, just listened and chewed.

"She escaped a marshal surveillance team," Herman mused. "The woman vanished into thin air with the authorities covering airports, train and bus terminals. She has no one to turn to and can't gain access to her trust accounts or use a credit card without us knowing it." Herman rubbed his chin. "Ralph, what would you do?"

"Wait until she uses up her cash and resorts to a credit card."

"She may have resources we aren't aware of. The question is where is she heading and how soon. My instincts tell me that she will be staying in Richmond for a time, not because of her limited resources but the natural instinct to hide, keep a low profile. She will use the credit cards only to misdirect, so I'll ignore that. She will eventually have to go for her trust account, but we can't afford to wait her out. Not with Fifteen making such a ruckus."

Ralph's fork was frozen in midair as he listened. He knew very well who Fifteen was, but he had no idea what sort of ruckus his boss was referring to.

"I'll send a pair to Richmond. That way at least we will be in the area when we get our next fix on her."

"Send me, sir. I won't miss her."

"I have just the pair in mind. I don't want to tell Mr. Russo yet that she is alive. With luck, I won't have to. He's such an excitable fellow. For the present, we'll just let that sleeping dog lie."

Ralph nodded absently. "I'd like to go."

"I feel much safer with you here."

"Lewis says that if we don't take Massey out, he could be trouble later on."

"I won't be prodded into sanctioning a man who got

lucky. And if Massey wasn't lucky, I don't want to risk another man. I'll just let Fifteen deal with the deputy and I'll concentrate on the woman."

"Lewis is different now. I can't put my finger on it, but he's changed."

"Time and circumstances can do that. How's the wine?"

"Needs sugar."

"I doubt the vintner would agree, but go ahead."

Herman watched Ralph put a half spoon of sugar in the vintage Bordeaux and stir.

Herman was fast approaching the end of the trail, but he had never felt more alive. This operation, perhaps the last he would ever oversee, had been complex from its very inception. It could have fallen apart at so many junctures, but it had proceeded perfectly until Massey got in the way. Herman had rarely come up against a single adversary he could admire. On many occasions, he had ordered sanctions that pitted one, or several, of his men against a target protected by a large security force. Any single man who could kill four of his boys, as Massey had, clearly deserved respect. He was a remarkable warrior, but the skills that made him that hardly translated into his becoming a threat now that he was off the field—the fighting near him was over.

Herman would not send men against Massey for merely having been a remarkable obstacle. This was just a game, and sportsmanship dictated that coaches didn't punish opposing players for scoring.

While Winter and Lydia were clearing the dinner dishes, his cell phone buzzed from the bedroom. He got to it on the third ring.

"Yeah?" Winter answered.

"I found them. Those four men *were* Special Forces. But they died long before you met them."

"That's crazy," Winter said. "I killed ghosts?"

"You're thinking inside the box. You know what a cutout is? Technically anybody who drops their real identity in favor•of a new one for security reasons is a cutout. A protected witness would be considered a cutout, as would a CIA or FBI agent who is going undercover."

"You're sure they're cutouts?"

"Yes. As for Ward Field, it started out as a training base for pilots during the second world war and continued operations through 1974 before it was classified as redundant by the Air Force and closed. But the land and the base, although decommissioned in 1974, remains restricted airspace. According to a series of reports in *The Washington Post,* Ward was listed as one of the CIA's launching pads for sensitive operations. Remember Iran-Contra, when the CIA flew guns south and, according to some, ferried cocaine on the return trips in order to sell it on the streets to purchase more guns? According to the articles, Ward Field was a secret base where cargo planes landed and took off. Isolated plus restricted equals perfect."

"You're saying the CIA is behind the assaults?"

"Involved up to their eyeballs. Maybe the FBI *doesn't* have their prints. It's possible they were purged after they were dead and buried. I know the CIA missed the fact that the real prints are still on file at the Pentagon. You'd figure they would have purged those fingerprint records to cover their tracks."

"Unless someone wants to know when one of them is fingerprinted," Winter speculated.

"I'm paranoid enough to imagine there might be a trip wire set to alert the CIA, NSC, or maybe even military intelligence. Maybe I'll have some questions to answer about how I came to have those prints."

"The UNSUBs' bodies will match your print cards," Winter said. "That's mighty strong corroboration."

"Don't count on it. Those guys will certainly erase their trail, if they haven't already. I checked for similar reports of deaths in the Special Forces over a ten-year period. Even figuring that most are legitimate accidental deaths, there could be a lot of dead men still serving their country."*

"Maybe you should take a vacation."

Reed chortled. "My bags have been packed all afternoon."

"Do you have hard copies?"

"I'm mailing a set to a friend who will know what to do with them."

"I need a set," Winter said.

"This is sensitive stuff. This might end up being the only record there is of this. I think I better send it to somebody they aren't watching. You don't want them to come to you looking for these, do you? They've demonstrated that they can play rough."

"Nobody's watching me," Winter protested.

"You sure?" Reed asked him. "This isn't amateur night at the Apollo."

Winter felt a stab of paranoia after Reed hung up.

If the men on Ward Field and Rook Island were CIA assassins and the FBI knew, it would be devastating. If Winter had the evidence, perhaps Shapiro could use it and, if nothing else, make sure Greg's name wasn't dragged through the mud. One thing was for sure—no one would ever believe the CIA was involved in this without the proof Reed had. Winter could believe the FBI was in on keeping the CIA's involvement covered up. The question was why the CIA would have gone to such unbelievable extremes to kill Devlin?

Was it possible that the CIA was working to help Sam Manelli? What in God's name was going on when the government murdered its own soldiers and agents for a mobster's benefit? Winter wondered if Manelli's history of invulnerability to arrest and conviction was due to something the CIA was afraid he could let out of the bag? Or was it something that Devlin knew?

What was obvious to Winter was that—if they would kill so many people to silence one witness against Sam Manelli—the CIA surely wouldn't hesitate to kill a few more.

67 | Norfolk, Virginia

Fletcher Reed closed his telephone and placed the heavy manila envelope that he had carried in his overcoat pocket into the mailbox's open slot.

United States Marshals Service

Richard Shapiro, Director

600 Army Navy Drive

Arlington, Virginia 22202

He pushed it in, hearing it land on earlier deposits.

Fletcher breathed in the cool evening air, like a man

without a care in the world. He looked up into the night sky to take in the stars. He was relieved he had spoken to Massey—that Massey now knew what he knew. There was safety in numbers, but two wasn't much of a number unless one was the publisher of *The Washington Post*. He took out a cigar and lit it, giving the smoke to the breeze. He didn't know how rapidly the cutouts could respond, but he had assumed he had a comfortable lead. He had decided he would accept the danger if this was brought to the attention of people who could do something to right it. Six sailors' deaths had to be avenged. If Massey was the man Reed thought he was, they might have a shot at dispensing justice.

Before he had left the shore patrol office, Fletcher made a stop on the other side of the building to help ensure he succeeded in his mission. He had climbed into his Taurus and drove, constantly checking traffic in his rearview. Shadows without form might just be paranoia. There was the old saying that just because you were paranoid didn't mean there weren't people after you. He had made several quick turns, then pulled up at the line of blue drop boxes across the street from the base's post office and took up a position in front of one of them. If he was lucky, he could hide out for a day or so, and he'd be safe.

Fletcher got back into his Taurus and drove off. At the light a block away, he looked in the mirror and saw a Jeep Cherokee pull over to the line of mailboxes. A man climbed out and walked briskly around behind them. So they *were* on to him.

Eyes on the man unlocking the box, Reed hadn't seen the second car coming, but now he felt it. He turned his head slowly and stared into the cold eyes of the man in the passenger seat of a silver Cadillac Catera, four feet distant. His heart raced when he saw the cutout's gun rise over the base of the open window like a periscope. Fletcher didn't hear the weapon go off, but he felt a sting in his neck like a mother's corrective pinch. He jammed the accelerator pedal down. The drug's effects were immediate—his face felt numb, his muscles started to lose touch with his brain and his eyes began to rapidly lose their focus. The Cadillac was behind him, following. The speedometer's needle climbed toward ninety.

Through the closing fog, Fletcher fought to keep remembering that he was running because they would torture the additional information out of him. It would mean failure, and he and Massey were dead men as soon as they had *all* of the evidence in their hands.

As darkness closed in on him, he managed to jerk the wheel, and felt the car take flight.

68 | Richmond, Virginia

Sean couldn't remember ever having slept in her clothes as an adult, but she was wearing them when she stretched out on the bed in her room at the Hotel Grand. Her backpack was propped against the wall, waiting for her to grab it and slip down the fire escape to the alley. She had wedged a chair under the doorknob. It wouldn't hold up long under a determined assault, but it should give her time to get the gun in her hand.

Her father had done her a service by teaching her how to shoot guns. This Smith & Wesson fit in her hand like it had been designed for her grip. The hammer's click sounded like a promise that would be kept. It seemed to be charged with energy; anxious to roll its cylinder and strut its stuff.

She wasn't well versed enough in handguns to know if the standard .38 rounds in the chambers would penetrate the heavy wood of the hotel room door, but she was certain it would pass through clothing, skin, muscles, and vital organs. The thought of firing the weapon at someone made her shiver. On Rook Island, she had witnessed first-hand the extreme damage a bullet could do to tissue and bone. History was filled with examples of how a single bullet had the power to change the world.

Winter had killed only to preserve life. Dylan had killed for greed. On the other hand, Sam Manelli's killing was merely maintenance required to keep his world functioning as he designed it. The rules, which he strictly adhered to, were like oil, critical to keeping his machine performing smoothly.

Running away was a temporary solution because as long as Sam wanted her, flight just prolonged the inevitable. The four men coming onto the island and chasing her down were testimony to how badly he wanted her dead, what extremes he would go to in order to achieve that end.

Sean hated feeling trapped and helpless waiting to see what someone else was going to do. She didn't like the idea of waiting to see if the killers could find a stationary target. She wondered if she was better off as a target in motion, constantly changing her skin to confuse her pursuers. The urge to run appealed to her on a gut level because it was action that she could control. Reason told her that the safest move was no move, allowing her trail to go cold. When she did move, Sean wanted to have a long-range plan worked out.

She lay in the dark, like a rabbit in tall grass, listening for the elevator, a step on the fire escape. She tilted her head and studied the light strip at the base of the door, knowing that any breaking shadows could be a fox's feet.

69

As Winter lay in the dark, sleepless, his mind swarmed with troubling questions he had few answers for. He wanted to do something, but he was helpless unless Reed's discovery would help Shapiro make a difference. He wanted to be able to put this horror behind him, not become obsessed with things he had no way of resolving.

The doorbell rang, jolting Winter out of his thoughts. *Twelve past ten.* He slipped from his bed, put on jeans, lifted the Walther, and went to the front door, passing a worried Lydia standing in the hallway.

"I'll see who it is," he said.

He turned on the porch light and saw the top of a man's head through the half circle of glass in the door. He held the pistol behind his back as he opened the door.

The man standing there had a crew cut. A dark jacket over a knit shirt and chinos gave him a casual air.

"Sorry to disturb you, Deputy Massey." The badge case in his hand identified him as an FBI agent.

"What can I do for you?"

"If you'll accompany me," the man said. "Agent Archer would like to have a word with you. If you'll come with us to the airport, you should be back in a couple of hours."

"What's this about?"

The agent smiled. "It's about new information on a case."

Winter relaxed. He welcomed a chance to talk to Archer, hopeful that the agent had new information on the investigation. "Come in. I'll get dressed."

The agent came inside and stood with his hands clasped behind him at parade rest. "We should hurry."

"Give me one minute."

Winter passed by Lydia, who was peering up the hall at the stranger standing inside the doorway.

"I'll be back in a couple of hours, Mama. Official business."

Winter put on a cotton shirt, his running shoes, and a zip-up leather jacket. He pocketed his wallet and badge case and slid the Walther into his jacket's right pocket, cell phone in the other. He kissed his mother on his way out.

A Chrysler waited at the curb, its driver a silhouette. The agent got into the rear, so Winter climbed into the passenger's seat.

"I know this is a bit unusual," the agent behind him said.

"Nothing is usual these days," Winter replied.

"Ain't that the truth," the driver said, nodding solemnly.

Winter felt the cold muzzle of a gun against the left side of his neck and the hand that came around the seat reached into his pocket for the Walther.

"Who are you?" Winter asked. He thought about Reed's concern about someone listening in on their conversations. Christ, how could he have been so stupid?

"Just stay calm and you'll be fine," the man behind him said. "If I intended to hurt you, I'd have popped you when you opened the door."

He supposed that was true enough. He also figured the odds of his staying alive to see the sun rise were slim.

Ten minutes later, the driver turned off onto the road to the airport. After going through the gate, the driver went down the alley formed by large hangars and pulled out to a parked Lear 35.

"We're all going to get out and walk to the plane," the driver said.

The man who had been seated behind him climbed out and opened Winter's door. He motioned Winter out with a silenced SIG Sauer.

Winter got out. "Can I call my mother and tell her I won't be home? She'll be worried."

"Later," the man holding the pistol said.

Winter slipped out of the car. The driver entered the Lear's cabin ahead of Winter, the other man behind him. The pilots were going through their checklist when Winter sat down in the seat the driver pointed to and fastened his seat belt.

While the man with the pistol kept Winter covered, the car's driver reached into his pocket and took out a syringe loaded with clear liquid. As Winter stared into the barrel of the handgun, the driver pressed the needle into the side of his neck. At first, nothing happened, then slowly Winter's eyelids drooped.

70 | Richmond, Virginia

Just before dawn, a gray van edged to the curb across the street from the pay phone that Sean had used to make a couple of calls four hours earlier. Until after those calls were made, the hunter in the van had never heard of Sean Devlin, and even now he had no idea what she had done to warrant his attention.

The hunter, known as Hawk, had taken a leased jet from Memphis, arriving an hour after his assigned partner, a man he had never met, who'd had the necessary vehicles waiting when he arrived.

He stared out at the stretch of street and studied the environment surrounding his prey. He opened the envelope, slipped out its contents, and flipped through the pictures, physical description, and background information he had downloaded before he left home.

He lifted his secure cell phone, keyed in a number,

waited for the line to be answered, and said, "Hawk. I'm in position."

"Hawk, I'm waiting for another voice intercept. As soon as I have it, I'll call."

After Hawk ended the call, he glanced at his own reflection in the window, noting the deep Y-shaped scar on the side of his chin, his dark eyes like dry flints in the dim light, the parting in his long hair sharp as a knife's edge. "If she's still here, I'll know soon enough," he said to himself.

He put the phone down beside the target's picture. She was attractive. He scanned the biographical information. Exceptional student. Financially independent. Self-starter. Nothing in the bio suggested why she would be in Richmond. But she had come here, most likely because she needed something—money, a secret lover, shelter. He liked the area. There were lots of vagrants, vacant buildings, not much traffic, an old hotel. If he was her, he'd be in there. Eight floors, lots of rooms.

The hunter's mind was racing. Maybe she was just passing through town, but even so, why pass through this neighborhood? The street was not that close to the main traffic arteries. On the phone she had told the deputy she was moving around, and mentioned a flight out. Would she ask a cabdriver to take her to a bleak neighborhood just so she could make a call? Not likely. She came *here*. Such an elegant woman would stick out, and either she had picked the phone in this neighborhood knowing people would notice and recognize her picture if it was shown around, or she was disguised so she wouldn't be noticed.

Hawk was expert in prey behavior and how a woman like his target might think—if she was a normal woman. According to her file she was not a professional, she had merely married one. But the hunter knew from experience that files could be falsified.

Nothing Sean had done of late seemed to point to her being a citizen. According to his information she had not panicked when she and the deputy had faced pros, so she was calm under fire, which belied what he had been told. And she had slipped a very competent team of deputy marshals.

Hawk was like a pilot in the fog who had to trust his instruments—his instincts. Even if she was pants-pissing terrified, a bullet fired by a scared woman was just as deadly as one fired by a professional.

The hunter was in his element, feeling the thrill of the hunt. He scanned the shadowy street and leaned the seat back, prepared for a long wait.

71 | Atlanta, Georgia
Tuesday

A pair of guards came to escort Sam Manelli from his cell to processing and, an hour later, he passed a trio of scowling FBI agents and strolled out through the prison gates toward where Johnny Russo stood waiting beside a limousine. A group of reporters gathered behind a fence shouted questions.

Sam embraced Johnny. "Man, let's get back down to New Orleans," Sam told him. "I need to get some real food in me." In a move that was totally out of character, he waved at the assembled reporters like a victorious politician.

"We got a jet waiting, boss. Compliments of some friends of ours," Johnny Russo informed him. "You'll be back home in a couple hours."

"Man," Sam said loudly, "I wish to God Bertran Stern was alive to see justice served." He took a cigar from his pocket and bit the tip off before putting it into his mouth. Once inside the limo, however, Sam instantly lost the festive facade.

As they pulled off, several cars filled with photographers and reporters fell into traffic behind the limo.

"Where'd you get this car from?" he asked Russo.

"From the Rizzo brothers. We checked it over good anyway."

Sam didn't want to talk any business in any car, but he needed to make an exception. "Let me hear some music."

Johnny called out to Spiro. "Let's have some music!" Spiro turned the music up loud and fiddled with the controls until the rear speakers were fully engaged.

"What you found out about Sean?" Sam asked, speaking into Johnny's ear.

"Nothing," Russo admitted. "Like she vanished off the face of the planet."

"You tellin' me you still don't know where she's at? What did Herman say?"

"I haven't been able to contact him. Maybe he's lying low."

Sam shook his head. "No reason to. Nobody can touch him."

"All I know is he ain't answering his phone."

Manelli chewed down hard on his cigar. "Do this," he hissed softly, his lips almost touching Johnny's ear. "I gotta get her. You find her and bring her to me. You put the word out to everybody with eyes in the country. Every airport, bus, train, car rentals, cabbies, Teamsters, whatever. A hundred grand, a quarter million, whatever it takes and no questions. You need special people, hire them. You just make it happen."

He sat back. "Tell me, how was Bertran's funeral?"

"I didn't go," Johnny said, swallowing hard. "I couldn't make it with everything that's going on. It was on Sunday."

"They put their folks in the ground fast," Sam agreed. "He was a good lawyer."

Finished talking, Sam removed the cigar and yelled at the driver, "Spiro, cut that noise! You killing my ears."

Sean had left the hotel using a group of youthful German tourists for camouflage. She ate a late lunch at the coffee shop two blocks up the street. On the way back to the hotel, she stopped into the convenience store to pick up a six-pack of Evian. The clerk had the television set on—the words CNN NEWS UPDATE filled the screen.

The announcement said that two of the eight passengers aboard the Justice Department's jet that crashed Thursday night in Virginia were protected witnesses in transit along with five United States marshals and Assistant United States Attorney Avery Whitehead from New Orleans. The reporter stated that Whitehead had been spearheading the prosecution of Sam Manelli for conspiracy to commit murder. The names of the six marshals were being withheld until the next of kin were all notified. The newscaster said that the director of the FBI and the attorney general had scheduled a press conference for Thursday, to make further announcements on the status of the investigation into the crashed jet. There was no mention of the four UNSUBs or that a deputy marshal was killed on Rook Island, and the news report didn't connect the deaths of the sailors to the crash in rural Virginia.

The newscaster announced that there was breaking news in Atlanta, and the screen changed to show a reporter holding a microphone. The camera panned to a door where a stocky man strode toward a waiting limousine. Sean felt so dizzy she feared she would throw up.

The CNN reporter tied Manelli's release to the downed jet and reported that the dead witness had been a "confessed" contract killer who had implicated Manelli as having hired him to commit a dozen murders. The reporter said that all of the charges against Sam Manelli, which had been based on the deceased killer's accusations, had been dropped.

On the screen, Sam, standing beside Johnny Russo, waved at the reporters, a frown on his face. Sean felt as though someone had winded her. It was as if he was waving at her, that he could see her, knew she was there, watching him, fearing him.

Sean turned for the door, but the clerk's frantic calls brought her back to the counter where she had abandoned the six-pack of water and her twenty dollar bill. Sean smiled, waited for her change, and carried the sack out.

As she turned and made her way down the street she became aware of twin shadows—hers and another closing in from behind. Her heart started to pound as she slipped her hand into her coat pocket, gripping the Smith & Wesson. The shadow man reached out—Sean spun and found herself facing Wire Dog.

"Sally!" The cabdriver's smile evaporated at the ferocity of her glare.

"You son of a bitch!" she hissed, leaving the gun in her coat pocket. "You scared me."

Sally," Wire Dog started. "I—"

"Are you crazy?" she snapped.

"I saw you go inside. I thought—"

Sean could see Wire Dog's cab parked in front of the hotel as she stormed up the street. "Don't you know better than to sneak up on people?" she demanded.

"I'm sorry."

Checking for traffic, Sean crossed the street, Wire Dog beside her. "I have to leave tonight," she said. "There's been a change in my deadline."

"I'll take you to the airport—what time?"

"Eight o'clock sharp." She had decided she would just grab the first flight to anywhere.

It looked like most of the residents of the hotel were in the lobby, socializing. Max was sorting through the mail at the counter. He set it aside when Sean approached.

"Miss McSorley," he said. "I hope you are finding our 'Wolfe' room inspirational."

"I've gotten a lot done. It turns out I have to leave tonight. I want to tell you how much I've enjoyed my stay."

"It has been a grand pleasure having you." Max bowed his head. "I do hope you will return." He peered at her over his half-glasses and winked. "Good luck."

As she walked toward the elevator she noticed a young woman seated on a couch beside an older woman, who was laughing at something the other had said. Seeing that the ancient elevator was gone, Sean decided to take the stairs. As she climbed the steps, she was thinking how nice it was to hear people laughing. The two women in the lobby reminded her of how much she missed her mother.

73

The hunter had spent the morning waiting in the van, watching the street. Hawk's partner had passed his position several times, haunting the streets in the district hoping to luck onto the target.

At ten A.M. Hawk had gone into the hotel. He told the manager that he intended to purchase and renovate a commercial building in the area and said he would be looking for a quiet place to live while the construction was going on. The elderly manager took the bait and assured him that the hotel was home to a large number of monthly residents. He had several suites with kitchenettes. The hunter praised the magnificent lobby, the detailed plaster-work, the marble floors.

The hunter had asked, since he would be bringing in craftsmen for the project, how many rooms were available for transient guests. The manager said that floors four and above were for temporary guests. A look at the keyboard on the wall behind the counter told the hunter that twenty-two keys were missing from the pegs that corresponded to the rooms on floors four through eight. He thanked the manager, promising to get in touch as things progressed on his project.

He returned to his van and rested for the next hour. He watched as a cab pulled up in front of the hotel and a well-tattooed young driver went inside for a minute, then came back out. Instead of getting back into the taxi, the driver stood by the cab and looked up and down the street. Suddenly he trotted off down the street. The hunter used the mirror to track the kid after he passed the van and crossed the street. It looked like the punk was lurking outside a convenience store a block up the street. The hunter saw a blond girl, one in a group of nine kids who had left the hotel earlier, stride out from the store and watched as the young driver ran to keep up with her.

The girl seemed upset, pissed off, had her arms locked across her chest, her head tilted down. The young driver hurried along after her, gesturing with his illustrated arms. She crossed the street and walked toward the hotel. As the pair drew closer to the van, their faces filled the side-view mirror and the hunter's heart skipped a beat. There was not a doubt in his mind—the girl was his target, Sean Devlin. Using his binoculars, he read her lips.

Hawk made a call to his partner.

"I have her," he said simply. "Take up a stationary position across the street from the hotel and keep your eyes open."

He leaned back and yawned. He couldn't risk grabbing her off the street in broad daylight. He didn't know which room she was staying in. But it didn't matter, because he knew that at eight o'clock she'd be walking back out that door and he'd be waiting with open arms.

74

Winter had no way to keep track of time but, for what seemed like several hours, he had been the captive of a drugged state unlike anything he had ever experienced. While he was shrouded completely in a blanket of catatonia—unable to move a single muscle or open his eyes—his heart was beating and he had no trouble breathing. He was completely aware of everything going on around him—could hear everything perfectly. He could smell, even feel changes in the air temperature. The men who had kidnapped him didn't speak to him or talk at all from the time the driver had given him the shot until the jet landed sometime later. Winter spent the entire flight thinking about his situation and decided that, if he faked the state after it had worn off, maybe he could somehow escape.

He knew that at some point his mother would call Hank looking for him. When Winter failed to show up at the time he had told her he would, she would begin to worry. The trouble was, he couldn't count the times he had told his mother that he would be back at a certain time, and later, when he became involved in something and forgot the time, was made a liar. Lydia knew that he didn't like to wake her unless it was necessary. He worried that she might decide this was one of those times and wait to call too late. *Hell, it was already too late the second he got into the Chrysler.*

During the time he was under, he had squirreled away

his impressions. After the plane landed, he had been carried from the Lear and laid on a gurney, which had been put into an ambulance. He knew it was an ambulance because the man with the syringe had lifted his right eyelid to check his pupil. As they went, Winter heard cars and trucks on either side of them and other sounds indicating they were in a large city.

When the ambulance finally stopped, his escorts rolled the gurney into a building and straight into an elevator. After a short ride up, the elevator door opened and Winter had smelled coffee and heard a television set. The men rolled him a short distance down a hallway, turned into a room, lifted him from the gurney, and dropped him onto a bed, causing the springs to squeak. All he could do was lie there and wait for what would happen next.

Winter kept time by listening to the television.

He heard people walking outside his door, caught hushed conversations that he knew were not voices on the television.

Somebody came into the room.

He felt someone give him another shot.

"Don't worry," a voice said. "That was just to counteract the effects of the drug. It impedes the ability to move but allows the heart to keep beating." The voice was peculiar and totally unfamiliar. Within seconds Winter could move his fingers and his feet.

"Let me stress that you are not to try anything stupid," the voice instructed. "You are inside a fortress with no way out, unless I release you. There are armed men on the floors below us and above us. I know you are familiar with the nature of the men I refer to. The elevator is the only way out and it is controlled by my people. There is no reason for you to try to escape, because no harm will come to you unless you do something idiotic."

What the man said had the ring of truth.

Winter felt the muscles in his face coming back under

his control, and he lifted his eyelids. Slowly, he turned his head to see the man who sat on the bed next to his. What he saw startled him. Deep burn scars covered the left side of the man's face and neck like they'd been applied by someone with a blowtorch and a plan. The crimson wig on his head could have been modeled by a child out of straw. He was dressed in what appeared to Winter to be a velour sweat suit.

The disfigured man stared at Winter through eyes so pale they looked as though they had never been fully colored in.

Using a gloved hand, the man carefully put a cigarette between his lips and lit it with a Zippo. He exhaled languorously. "You will be able to stand up in a minute and will suffer no adverse effects," he said companionably.

"I understand," Winter said.

"My name is Fifteen. I know everything about you. I know about your long-suffering mother, Lydia, your dead wife, your blind son, Hank Trammel, and just about everybody left on this earth you care for."

Winter had known truly lethal men. He knew their smell, the acid they stirred up in his stomach, and the foul taste of copper they put in his mouth. And he knew instinctively that this man was a creature of the pit. He was a man who told people to kill, liked doing it, might sometimes do it himself. Maybe this creature was an interrogator.

"This building belongs to a man named Herman Hoffman. I believe you would know him as the old general that the boy George Williams mentioned to you."

"Is he your boss?"

"No."

"Are you CIA?"

"No, not specifically. That shouldn't concern you. Let me say that we service specific needs they and other agencies have, and the relationship is mutually beneficial.

"I have examined your conversation with Fletcher Reed about Ward Field and the cutouts. I have acquired Reed's evidence. He mailed a copy to your director and had a duplicate cleverly hidden in his office. All record of his computer incursion has been obliterated. Reed's misguided efforts went for nothing."

"What did you do to him?" Winter asked, resigned to the inevitable now.

"He thought some of my men wished him harm and he hit a tree in his panicked attempt to evade them, shortly after you last spoke to him."

Fifteen ground his cigarette out in a metal box and snapped it shut. "All that remains is for the Bureau to release the preliminary findings from their investigation. You are familiar with some of it, I understand. The evidence in the hands of the FBI is fact—incontrovertible proof. Believe me, not even Greg Nations himself could prove his innocence now."

"The evidence is all lies."

"What difference does it make?"

"Why are you helping Manelli?"

"As far as Manelli's participation in this"—he shrugged—"that's between Hoffman and Mr. Manelli. Only what concerns me is of interest to me."

"Why did he bring me here?"

"He didn't. I brought you here to reason with you to accept the inevitable. I want you to understand that by pursuing this you are only a threat to yourself. Hoffman's operation with Manelli was a rogue carried out by his group, which you managed to cut in half. I had no advance warning before Ward Field and Rook Island, and I've had teams rushing all over the country just to stay even with the mess the old man made. I can't tell you the resources that have gone into cleaning this up in order to protect other interests that matter far more than this does. Herman used his power shamelessly, his men irresponsibly, and lost four extremely valuable individuals to your gun. This was very disturbing to me, to all of us."

"Think how disturbing it is to all the people they killed."

"Whoever runs the country does so because we make that possible by removing obstacles, keeping the path free of threats to our country's security. For fifty years a few of us have been fighting a very necessary war. Every instinct I have tells me to let my men bury you, but I believe enough innocent people are dead. I would rather persuade you how futile any attempt to oppose us is and let you go on with your life."

The man who had been at Winter's front door stood in the hallway, holding the silenced SIG Sauer casually at his side, its barrel down.

"I am going to tell you how Herman obtained the intelligence it took to pull off the assaults."

"To illustrate to me how powerless I actually am."

"Exactly," Fifteen said.

Winter sat slowly up and put his feet on the floor. He felt light-headed from being incapacitated for so long but no other ill effects from the drugging.

"If you make any heroic moves, you will be killed. If you grab me, my people will shoot through me to kill you. Even if you managed to get out, my people would visit your mother and son before you could hail a cab."

Winter felt a surge of rage. "Can you tell me where I am?"

"I'll show you."

75

"You are on the fifth floor," Fifteen told Winter as they stood near the elevator. "Herman Hoffman, our host, is known as the Dean of Shadow because he oversaw the CIA's post–World War Two dark operations. After the Bay of Pigs, he realized there would always be politicians around to muck things up, so there needed to be an independent organization that could operate under the radar, a constant force presence in an ever-changing world. He developed the psychological testing that insured a steady source of talent, drawn from the pool of civilians applying for admission to the armed forces. Mostly he wanted men and women who, but for a few minor flaws, might have been great additions to the Special Forces."

"Like psychopathic personality disorder?"

Fifteen frowned. "A cheap jab, Winter. He wanted intelligent, motivated individuals who would dedicate their lives to a larger picture—be loyal to their controllers knowing only that their jobs were necessary without being in the loop with the decision-makers. Every armed forces recruit takes a battery of tests, and those tests have questions embedded in them that set off triggers, draw our interest. Of every twenty thousand of those men and women, perhaps twenty are selected for more in-depth testing. Out of every hundred who make it through the process, one or two might make the grade. Sometimes none of them do. There are units scattered all over the world, ready to respond at a moment's notice."

"So when Herman says kill six sailors and six deputy marshals, they just do it?"

"Yes."

The room was furnished with a large TV, couches, tables, chairs, and a blank blackboard. A short wall separated the rec room from a kitchen, reminding Winter of a fire station.

"No windows," Winter noted.

"This light is a blend of fluorescent and incandescent to simulate daylight. Follow me," Fifteen said cheerfully. He led Winter back the way they had come after leaving the bedroom.

"This is the bathroom, and just here . . ." Fifteen opened the door beyond the bathroom. "Our ordnance room. Sorry I can't let you go in, but feel free to look."

The room played host to stacks of machine guns, rifles, shotguns, handguns, and crates of bullets and other weapons, including grenades. There was also an open case of Semtex, the Eastern Bloc's version of plastic explosive, with about half of it missing. It was as harmless as modeling clay unless it was detonated by a nearby blast or one of the detonators stacked in a small box beside the crate.

"Very impressive," Winter said.

"Just hardware. I'll show you what's impressive."

Winter stood next to a garbage chute, while Fifteen opened the door at the end of the hallway. Fifteen led Winter inside. Three computers, along with assorted electronic equipment, filled a U shape of counters. On one of the computer monitors, a screen saver performed a series of optical illusions. Fifteen moved its mouse and the screen changed to show a satellite overview of a section of the Eastern Seaboard with four yellow dots on the screen.

"These are connected to CIA, FBI, and NSA supercomputers, as well as to our spy satellites."

The man carrying the handgun came in and whispered something to Fifteen.

"I have to go upstairs for a moment. Please relax until I

return. Just so you know, the phone isn't live, and the computers will not allow you access."

"No problem," Winter replied, bewildered.

"My man will be outside until I return." Fifteen closed the door behind him, leaving Winter alone in the communications room.

Winter turned his attention to the computer screen. Even without names to identify the dots' locations, he knew pretty much what they signified. One of them was Washington, another Rook Island, a third was Richmond, and the fourth dot Ward Field in rural Virginia. He clicked on one and the screen went dark, the CPU turning itself off.

A stack of sixteen-by-twenty-inch photographs beside the computer caught his attention. The first one on the pile was of Rook Island. Winter's heartbeat quickened. He located the safe-house roof, tennis court, pool, beach, and trees—and the radar station beyond them. The picture had no date stamp, but the shadows told him that it was a morning shot. Obviously, these people not only could get the pictures from space, but they could get the CIA to task or aim spy satellites for them.

The next shot was of Ward Field and had been taken Friday morning, when he was there. He knew by the ruined hangar, the techs in the debris field, the FBI's tents, and because the Lear was parked in the field beside Shapiro's Gulfstream II.

The Arlington shot had been taken at night. He made out the roof and parking lots of a building he was sure he recognized as the U.S. Marshal headquarters. Winter didn't understand the significance.

The final shot in the stack was a grid of streets and the tops of buildings; he assumed, because of the river, it was probably downtown Richmond because the fourth dot had appeared on that city. He could make out cars and even a few people. The shadows and the orientation told him that it was a late-morning or late-afternoon shot.

Someone had taken a grease pencil and circled what appeared to be a pay phone.

Winter was so intrigued by the pictures Fifteen had wanted him to see that he almost forgot he was in enemy territory.

An eight-by-ten photograph alone on the counter next to a printer distracted him. This was not a satellite picture, but one taken on a city street from ground level. A woman with spiky blond hair, dressed in black and wearing glasses, had been snapped as she exited a doorway, the name HOTEL GRAND etched into the glass window over the door. Despite the difference in her appearance, Winter recognized Sean immediately. He remembered the phone call to him at home the day before, the traffic noise—these people must have gotten information from the NSA, who intercepted the call and located the phone which led them to her, in Richmond.

He had to find out why they still felt a need to track Sean and convince Fifteen to call the dogs off her—unless it was too late.

He opened the door expecting to find the guard, but the hallway was empty. "Hello?" Winter called out. Nothing.

His watch told him it was 4:15. He opened the bathroom door, hoping to find the guard in there. The room was occupied, but not by the guard. Two corpses sat on the tiled floor, their backs resting against the wall. He knelt down to inspect them. Both wore ballistic vests under their coats. The emaciated men looked like winos. The closest had greasy hair and a nappy beard. His hands were callused, the fingernails caked with filth. He was dressed in new clothes, and the corner of something stuck out of his vest. Winter pulled out a foreign passport and opened it. The picture wasn't that of the corpse but showed a younger man with long hair and angular features. The name on it was Alexis Philipoff, a Russian national.

Winter slid the passport back inside the dead man's vest and hurried to the elevator. He pressed the call button. Fifteen had said he was going upstairs, but the car was rising slowly from below. The door opened and Winter got into the empty car. Before he could press a button, the door closed and started up.

When the elevator stopped, Winter stepped out into a circular foyer with granite floors, a curved faux marble wall, and an ornately carved stone arch with twin maple doors whose tops followed the curve. The domed ceiling had been painted black so that hundreds of tiny white bulbs transformed it into a quasi planetarium.

The elevator closed and started down again. Winter entered into a palatial apartment, his footsteps muted by a thick oriental rug on a polished oak floor. Paintings—classic pastorals and portraits—filled the walls. The ornate furniture looked too valuable to sit on.

"Anybody home? Fifteen?"

Winter opened the door on the far side of the room and stepped into the main hallway. The first room he came to was an office. The few papers, letters, and receipts that were scattered on the desk's surface appeared to be written in Cyrillic.

He opened the door to a bedroom that, in stark contrast to the rest of the apartment, was Japanese modern. Two life-size forms, dressed in samurai battle regalia, stood at either side of the bed. They looked like fierce insect-men, patiently awaiting the opportunity to lay waste to some invading army.

When Winter pushed open the swinging door into the kitchen, he was suddenly face-to-face with a man seated at the table, who was staring straight at him—or more likely into the fires of hell. "Ah, just great," Winter groaned.

Based on George Williams's description, the white-blond crew cut and the wrist encircled by a barbed-wire tattoo indicated that the corpse at the table was the old man's helicopter pilot, Ralph. Someone had garroted him using a length of wire, some of which was still deeply embedded in the open slit in his throat.

A dinner plate between his forearms held in its center a single human eye with its malformed keyhole pupil positioned so it stared up at Winter.

Lying on a folded napkin beside the plate like a utensil was Winter's Walther PP. He lifted it and sniffed the barrel to discover it had been fired recently. Reflexively, he put the pistol into his jacket pocket. A fresh coating of blood mixed with what was surely brain tissue, bits of white hair, and bone decorated the wall behind one of the kitchen chairs like an abstract painting.

If Winter was found in the building, the FBI could easily draw the conclusion that he was involved with them through their scapegoat, Greg Nations. Anything he said would be meaningless, and Fifteen's threat against his family meant he couldn't defend himself with the truth without endangering them. The realization that he had been set up built a fire in the pit of Winter's stomach. It made sense—the Russian passport, the weapons, all pointed to a facility used by mercenaries. Even though the corpses in the bathroom obviously weren't the men listed in their passports, he knew the bodies would match them before he was hauled off to jail. But the corpses' Kevlar vests made no sense.

Winter peered out into the service hall, looking for the missing body that had left the wall splashed with gore. The reinforced door to a rear stairwell was dead-bolted, its key removed.

Back in the kitchen, Winter noticed blood smeared on the handle of the refrigerator, more on the floor in front of it. Winter opened the door and found Herman Hoffman's dead body again basing his assumption on George's knowledge. The old man had been crammed like a Peruvian mummy inside the commercial-size refrigerator, a small bullet hole in his forehead—undoubtedly fired from the Walther now in Winter's pocket. A printed note read, *Curiosity killed the cat.*

There would be no FBI arresting him. There were several pale blocks of Semtex in the old man's lap, and a red indicator light blinked on a detonator. He understood that opening the refrigerator door had armed the device.

In Winter's experience, real-life bombs set by professionals didn't have illuminated panels of numbers counting down to the explosion like in movies. There was enough explosive packed into the Sub-Zero, and on the floor below, to erase the building, to destroy all of the evidence except for things like torsos, passports placed inside body armor, guns, and badges like his own.

Fifteen intended to solve everybody's problems at once.

76 | Richmond, Virginia

At 7:50 P.M., Hawk's van sat with its rear bumper twenty feet from the hotel's front doors. He checked his Glock and the four magazines in two holders on his belt. His partner had been parked across the street from the hotel since seven-thirty, his shape visible through the windshield of his high-performance Taurus SHO, which had a steel plate in the trunk angled to deflect bullets away from the cabin.

When the cab pulled up in front of the Grand, right behind the van, Hawk tightened his vest and watched through the rearview. After the tattooed boy sprang from the cab and sprinted inside, Hawk opened the van's door. As he stepped into the street, his long coat was whipped by a sudden gust of wind. He pulled a dark ball cap from the pocket of his coat and put it on.

He put the closed badge case in his left hand so the first thing Sean Devlin would see would be the familiar glint of a gold star set in a circle.

He nodded to his partner, who then stepped from the SHO and leaned against the front fender holding a semi-automatic twelve-gauge shotgun underneath his trench coat. Through the glass doors he saw the marble-faced counter across the lobby and the old man standing behind it. After crossing the lobby, Sean Devlin would come into view from his right. He would grab her and bring her outside, where he and his partner would whisk her away.

77

At five minutes before eight, Sean placed the pistol in her backpack. She had made the choice between taking the train and keeping the gun, or dropping the pistol into a garbage can before she got near the metal detectors at the airport. She had decided that getting as far away, as fast as she could, was better than having the security of the gun. She put on her coat, grabbed her backpack and duffel, and looked around the room one last time to make sure she wasn't leaving anything behind. In a few hours she would be in Seattle. She credited Sam Manelli's image on television for her heightened anxiety level, and she couldn't rationalize her fear by telling herself that he couldn't possibly have a line on her.

The phone rang and she jumped, almost dropping the backpack.

"Ms. McSorley, your driver has arrived," Max announced.

"Thank you. I'll be right down."

She left the room, made her way to the elevator door,

and pressed the call button. Four floors below, the gate closed and there was a rumble as the motor engaged. When the cage opened she stepped into the elevator and took a deep breath to calm her racing heart.

"We're due for rain," the operator remarked as they descended. "We can sure use it."

"Rain would be nice," Sean agreed. She wondered how rain could affect the life of a man who lived in the hotel and spent his days going up and down in place like a piston.

At the lobby level, he opened the gate for her and, even though it was night, he said, "Have a nice day."

Wire Dog, waiting outside the elevator like an impatient date, took Sean's duffel from her.

The two women Sean had seen earlier were still sitting together on the leather couch in the center of the lobby.

As she and Wire Dog passed by, Sean exchanged smiles with the women. The women stood, and the younger one's dark ponytail fell halfway down her back. She was well tanned and looked as if she made an effort to stay in shape. She had changed clothes since Sean had seen her that afternoon. Now she wore khakis, running shoes, and a jacket. The leather purse under her right shoulder was almost as large as Sean's backpack. The older woman, wearing a loose-fitting dress, had wet dark hair combed straight back.

Sean handed Max her room key and said good-bye.

As Sean walked toward the glass doors, a man wearing a black trench coat started inside, straight-arming the door open. He had a wallet in his left hand, which he held up as he entered. Through his open coat Sean saw a gun and a bulletproof vest covering his shirt. He glanced into the lobby, to his right, then immediately drew his gun.

Looking for an escape, Sean turned and saw the young woman from the couch striding toward the man. The large silenced pistol in her rising hand rocked gently as she fired it at the man in the trench coat. He fell backward from the impact of the shots. Sean saw that the object, now open as it fell from the man's left hand, was a badge case. She decided her only chance was to get behind the counter.

After firing steadily, the young woman ejected the empty magazine, which clattered to the stone floor, and took another from her purse.

Wire Dog dropped Sean's duffel and ran behind her toward the counter.

The older woman, walking toward the counter, raised a silenced pistol and began firing just as Sean and Wire Dog sprang over the counter.

Max stepped back, straightened, and stumbled backward as a bullet passed through his throat and slammed him against the antique room-key board, skewing it so violently that dozens of keys rained to the floor.

Sean jerked her pack around and pulled out her gun. She aimed the Smith over the counter at the advancing younger woman and squeezed the trigger. The compact gun roared, bucking in her hand. Before Sean fired a second time at the running figure, the woman had scampered into the lobby, taking a dive behind the heavy couch.

A plastic donations box on the counter near Sean exploded, scattering coins on the carpeted floor. Without looking, Sean reached the gun over the counter and fired in the older woman's direction. Sean had only three shots left.

Wire Dog seemed perplexed as he stared down at the blood covering his fingers. As the red stain on the side of his T-shirt blossomed, he shuddered and his soiled hand fell to the floor.

Sean heard the elevator door clanging shut and the car slowly rising.

When the front door burst open, Sean chanced a quick peek over the counter. Another man, also in a trench coat and carrying a shotgun, had come into the lobby. As he ducked behind the wide marble column on his left, three shots from the older woman's gun chipped plaster from its face. The man behind the column fired back. Sean assumed that if the woman was firing at him, he might be on her side.

When the man brought the shotgun around the column and fired, the older woman yelled out and went down hard.

"United States marshal!" the man yelled. "Sean Devlin?"

"There's another one. I think she's behind the couch," Sean called out from her hiding place.

Wire Dog's key fob hung from his pocket. Instinctively, Sean pulled at the chain and palmed the keys. Gripping the .38 in her left hand, Sean shifted her weight, swung up over the counter, and ran for the door on a course that would take her between the man and the young woman in the lobby. She understood that if he wasn't really a marshal, he might be working for Sam, and he'd kill her. For all she knew the two groups were competitive mercenaries—winner take all.

Sean extended the pistol out and fired the remaining three shots as she ran for the door, where she would be sheltered from the woman killer by the column between them.

Her backpack swung violently to the side as the young woman fired at her. After Sean was past his column, the man fired out into the lobby—thankfully not at her. He dropped the empty shotgun to the floor, pulled out a dark automatic, and began firing again.

Since Sean's gun was empty, she pocketed it, picked up the dead marshal's Glock beside her boot, and crouched behind the column, her back to the man behind the other column ten feet away.

"Go now," he ordered. "Taurus is across the street—key's in the ignition. Get in it and drive away fast. Call

Shapiro from the cell phone in the console. It's secure. Only that phone. Got it?"

Sean nodded. Her hand holding the dead man's Glock trembled. As the marshal peered out and aimed at the lobby, the young woman fired and he fell. His violated skull smacked against the marble, making a sickening wet sound.

Sean ran through the door. She saw the Taurus parked across the wide street and Wire Dog's taxicab at the curb. Figuring she'd get shot if she crossed the street, she went for the taxi.

Sean opened the driver's door and got in. She pushed Wire Dog's key into the ignition and the engine sprang to life.

The killer broke from the building, her ponytail flying behind her. She had her gun in a two-handed combat grip, aiming across the street. Before the killer spotted her, Sean pointed the Glock out through the windshield and emptied it at her through the glass.

The killer dived for cover behind a planter.

As Sean jerked the shift lever and floored it, the woman fired, hitting the old, big-bodied Chevrolet's windshield and grill as Sean roared up the street in reverse.

The killer ejected her spent magazine as she ran after the taxi, then shoved in a new one and resumed firing.

Her ears ringing, Sean tossed the empty Glock onto the floor as the car flew away still in reverse. Once she had enough speed, she stomped the brakes, and jerked the wheel to the side forcefully, spinning the car 180 degrees. While the Chevrolet was swapping ends, Sean pulled the shift lever down into drive and, when the car was aimed up the street, she floored the accelerator. Sean had learned the maneuver from a "special" driving instructor she had had in her fifteenth summer. Until that moment she had never had occasion to use the maneuver, but she performed it perfectly.

The wind coming in through the ruined windshield buffeted her stiff hair. She wasn't safe, but she *was* free.

She took a few turns at random in case the assailant had come after her. Steam poured from under the hood. Dash warning lights blazed. Less than two miles from the hotel, the wounded radiator finished bleeding out through the .45-caliber holes and the motor seized. Sean put the car in neutral and coasted to a stop at a curb.

As sirens wailed in the distance, Sean grabbed her backpack and ran for her life.

78

From her seat in the corner booth Sean could turn her head to watch the rigs pulling in from the service road, see the activity at the gas pumps, or watch the southbound traffic up on Interstate 95. Although she forced herself to appear disinterested, Sean was very much aware of each of the customers who came and went through the restaurant's doors—the majority of whom were truck drivers.

Three miles from where she'd abandoned Wire Dog's cab, she had met a seventeen-year-old couple in a convenience store and had offered the boy twenty dollars to take her to a restaurant near the interstate, which turned out to be a truck stop. The good thing about kids that age was that they didn't ask a lot of questions and would forget her as soon as she stepped from the vehicle.

According to her name tag, Sean's waitress was Bernice. She was so emaciated that Sean was amazed she could carry the coffeepot without snapping her wrists, which were hardly thicker than spools of dime-store thread. Ruby, the other waitress, was a strapping blonde with breasts like honeydews. She looked as though she had been plucked from the helm of a Viking ship, her face still red from the bitter North Sea winds. She roared at the drivers and made comments that elicited howls of laughter from the male customers.

Sean looked down at the backpack on the seat beside her, and studied the small hole in it. As she had run from the counter to the hotel's front door, the younger woman missed her rib cage by inches but had hit her inch-thick titanium-shelled computer. Sean had tried to turn it on just after arriving at the restaurant, but the sleek machine was dead. She didn't care, except that the hard drive contained information she wanted. She had $242 in her pocket, three credit cards, a driver's license in the name Sean Devlin, no extra clothes, no bullets for her pistol, and, now, *no passport*.

She didn't want to think about Wire Dog and Max, but couldn't shake the images of them. She knew if she hadn't come into their lives, both would still be breathing. That was hard to deal with, but the blame wasn't hers—that she laid at Sam Manelli's feet. Sam was responsible for the deaths at Rook Island, Ward Field, and now at the Hotel Grand. She had to get as far from Richmond as she could, fast, and she needed to alter her appearance again as soon as possible. The marshals would be looking for her and she couldn't rule out that Sam's people were somehow getting their fixes on her through them. She wasn't going to call Shapiro—not yet.

A wide-shouldered trucker swaggered in and took a seat at a table to Sean's left. With a shock, she realized that the driver was a woman. Her black hair was combed straight back, except for one dark cable that hung down over her left brow like a rat's tail. The freckle-faced woman sat with her knees wide apart, her shoulders rolled forward, forearms on the table fencing in the cup. She wore leather chaps, a belt with an oval silver buckle, and black boots with engraved silver toe covers. Her two-inch-wide watchband was made of silver and turquoise.

"Where you headed to, Clancy?" another driver called over to her.

"Baton Rouge, J.T.," Clancy said. "Picking up paper bound for Frisco and bringing a load of knit shirts back to New Jersey."

Clancy looked around the room, and finally parked her raisin-colored eyes on Sean. When Sean smiled, the trucker looked away, picked up the piping-hot coffee, and took a swallow of it before lighting a cigarette.

Sean's waitress seemed to know Clancy, so when she came over to give Sean a refill, she asked her about the female driver.

"Clancy Ross out of Houston. She comes through several times a year."

Sean took her coffee and her backpack and walked over to Clancy's table, where the driver studied Sean suspiciously.

"I hate to bother you," Sean started. "My name's Sally. May I sit down and talk to you?"

Clancy nodded, keeping her hard eyes on Sean. "If you're looking for a soft touch, sister, you're climbing a shaky ladder," Clancy said.

"Oh, no," Sean said. "That isn't it at all." She smiled as disarmingly as possible.

Clancy was clearly expecting an angle, but nodded for Sean to sit. "I'm listening, little sister."

"I'm a freelance writer doing a magazine story on truck drivers."

"For what magazine?"

"Whoever will buy it."

"Is that so?" Clancy's expression was doubtful.

Sean knew that she looked like a wacko who was running on desperation. "I was looking for a driver who would let me ride along for a few hundred miles. Share what the road is like with me. I mean, we all see trucks on the highways, but few of us know what a driver's life is like—your hopes and dreams and the long hours. And I was thinking that a female driver in a man's world was a great hook for a story."

"You think riding with a woman teamster is safer than with a man?"

"I think I would be more comfortable with a woman."

Clancy's breakfast arrived. She began eating it, hunched over the plate proprietorially like a prisoner protecting it from other inmates. Smoke curled up from the cigarette in her left hand.

"It's important to me," Sean implored.

Clancy spoke without looking up. "Where you been published before?"

"All kinds of places."

"You're full of shit, Sally," Clancy said, chortling. "Husband or a lover after you? Want my help, level with me."

"Husband," Sean conceded, sensing this inadvertent change in tactic would seal the deal.

"Here in Richmond?"

Sean nodded. "He's a cop. His father's a judge."

"And you want to get away to where?"

"Are you going near Charlotte?"

"I can take ninety-five to eighty-five south. It runs right through Charlotte," Clancy said without looking up. "Leaving in ten minutes."

"I'll just freshen up," Sean said.

There was a bank of pay phones on the wall near the bathrooms. Sean dialed a number and slipped quarters she had gotten from the cashier into the slot. She trembled involuntarily as the phone rang. She was ready to hang up after two rings, when an impatient voice answered. "Yeah, what?"

As soon as Sean spoke, the silence on the other end

was deafening. Sean was overwhelmed with the feeling that she had just made a very big mistake.

Ten minutes later, Sean climbed up into the cab of a black Diamond Reo with a pair of dice painted on the door and strapped herself into the passenger seat.

Clancy selected a CD and slipped it into the player. As the truck headed up onto the interstate, rich cello music filled the cab.

"Yo-Yo Ma," Clancy called out over the music. "He's Asian."

79

As a rail-thin six-year-old, Winter Massey had clutched his mother's hand as a guide in khaki shorts led a long line of tourists deep into the earth. Bare bulbs lit the cavern walls. Their guide had explained that the cave was once solid rock and that dripping water had entered the cracks in it and had, over millions of years, cut out the tunnels they were walking through. Winter had been frightened by the stalactites, which looked like pointy teeth with saliva dripping from the tips. At some point during that tour, the guide had extinguished the lights.

Winter came around and found himself in a place that was as dark as the cave in his memory, but the air was thick with dust from a recent explosion. There was a slight ringing in his ears not unlike what happened when he stood too close to a gun being fired without wearing proper ear protection. Beyond that ringing and somewhere close by, water dripped. And by tuning his ears past the water falling, he made out a persistent rumbling sound punctuated by a sharp scraping.

Why is it so dark?

Stay calm.
Am I hurt?
Broken bones?
Torn ligaments?
Broken neck?

Winter fought to push back the worst imaginable thought, but it persisted and filled his entire mind like a noxious gas. He couldn't see! He fought to see something—anything. He was looking out at a totally blank slate—nothing but thoughts. *I can't be blind. Please God, don't let me be trapped in darkness.* A picture of Rush formed in his mind—a before-and-after image. This is what it was like to be blind. Suddenly, he knew that it was just dark. A sudden giddiness swept over him and pushed away the panic. He assumed that the bomb had dumped rubble over him. It was still night. He might be crushed to death if the floor above him didn't hold up, or smother or drown, but if there was light he would be able to see it.

As he lay there, he gathered his thoughts and breathed slowly to calm himself and concentrate on surviving. Although he had obviously lived through it, he didn't remember the explosion, so he must have been unconscious. When he had seen the explosives in the refrigerator, he had bolted, running out into the service hall and jumping into the garbage chute. As he fell, he had slowed his decent by pressing the edges of his running shoe soles against the smooth metal sides like brakes.

Winter had never carried a lighter or matches, because he had never been a smoker. He had grown up resenting the odor his father's cigarettes had left in the Massey home, his nicotine-stained fingers. The sight of that sullen stranger in his underwear at the kitchen table, bleary-eyed, drink in hand, and enveloped in a cloud of smoke was one that continued to haunt him.

"Winter, you son of a bitch, you're alive," he said, pleased by the sound of his own voice.

He was flat on his back on an uneven surface. He felt pain but couldn't tell what part of his head hurt. He moved his fingers first, raising then lowering them. His wrists were sore but not broken, and his elbows and shoulders seemed fine. He moved his toes, ankles, and knees. He was in the building's basement lying on rolls of carpet padding or soundproofing material, which probably cushioned his landing and saved his life.

Sitting up made his head swim. There was a bump on the back of his head, but it was dry, so he wasn't bleeding. The air was thick with dust, so he pulled the folded bandana from his back pocket, opened it, and held it to his nose as a filter. *It'll make you less sad,* he remembered Rush saying.

Unable to see his watch, he had no idea how long he had been unconscious. *This is what it is like to be blind.* Since he was stuck in absolute darkness, he would have to make do with his remaining four senses.

Since the garbage chute was in the right rear of the building, at the far end from the elevator, he assumed that he was a good eighty feet from a street in some unknown city.

The slight ringing in his ears diminished as he concentrated on the low rumbling and scraping sounds. Standing was impossible in the dark, so he turned over slowly to his hands and knees and prepared to crawl to find the closest wall and follow it toward the sounds. He folded the bandana into a triangle and tied it behind his head to make a dust mask.

The dozens of rolls rested tightly against each other. "Okay, Massey," he said, "don't run headlong into anything. All you need is a rusty nail in your head." He crept forward, stretching out his left hand and waving the air like a man painting horizontal and vertical strokes on a wall. He slipped off the rolls and onto the concrete floor beneath them. He moved chunks of brick and wood aside as he went. His fingers found a brick wall and, using both hands, he discovered the mouth of the garbage chute, now choked shut with rubble. With the wall as a guide, he could concentrate on making his way toward where he hoped the rescuers were working.

As he moved carefully, the noise indeed grew louder. He made slow progress, keeping his left shoulder next to the wall to maintain his equilibrium while feeling with his right hand for obstacles. He stopped when he found what felt like a four-inch cast-iron waste pipe before going on.

He had moved a few feet from the pipe, when the rumbling diminished in stages—telling him that more than one piece of heavy machinery was involved in clearing rubble. The machines stopped altogether, leaving only the sound of dripping water. *The emergency workers have stopped! Are they giving up?* They might hear him if he could make enough noise. He had no idea how long the lull would last. He had to make noise. With a sense of urgency growing inside him, he groped his way back to the vertical waste pipe. Now, before the machines started up again, he needed something to beat against the cast iron. Without an alternative, he pulled the antique Walther out of his coat pocket and began hammering the gun against the pipe. *"S" DOT-DOT-DOT / "O" DASH-DASH-DASH / "S" DOT-DOT-DOT . . . DOT-DOT-DOT / DASH-DASH-DASH / DOT-DOT-DOT.* He yelled out when he heard answering metallic bangs.

The rumbling began anew and the scraping grew louder. Winter slipped the compact gun back into his jacket pocket. Without being able to see and no way to know what was above him, he sat with his back against the brick wall to wait in the darkness.

The noise of dozer blades clearing the street grew steadily louder until the door to the sidewalk-level service elevator was peeled back. When Winter saw a vertical sliver of light, vague as a neon tube through a thick fog, he wanted to cry out in relief but was afraid that even the slightest sound from his lips would cause the entire structure to cave in. He followed the light bar to its origin—a crack between a pair of steel doors. After locating the lever, he pulled the heavy doors open. Light blasted him and more dust billowed into his basement tomb. Winter stepped into the lift's rubble-coated floor to the shouts of men that were just silhouettes above him. He reached up, hands grabbed his, and he was jerked up out of the lift pit straight into a tortured landscape.

The sun's first rays were illuminating the fronts of the buildings across the street, which stood open and exposed like the backs of dollhouses. Herman's building looked like a candle that had burned down to the third floor. In the way of charges and sudden pressure change, the adjoining buildings had shaped the force upward or outward through the thinner walls at the front and rear.

Soot-faced firemen strapped Winter on a stretcher and, while he protested that he was perfectly all right, they muscled him over the piles of rubble. They handed the litter to a crowd of EMS technicians and cops. He knew by the insignia tags on the uniforms that he was in New York City.

After the cot was lifted into an ambulance, a man in a suit climbed in and cuffed Winter's right wrist to the stretcher's rail. "FBI. Just until we straighten out who you are and what you were doing in there." The agent pulled the Walther out of Winter's jacket pocket, examined it, then dropped it into his own coat pocket.

"You have to call the United States Marshals office and get Chief Marshal Richard Shapiro. I have to talk to him now."

"Before I call anybody, you've got some questions to answer."

"It's a matter of life and death. I'm United States Deputy Marshal Winter Massey."

"Where's your badge?"

"I don't know." He assumed that it was inside the building, a bauble left by Fifteen to be found by the people clearing the wreckage of a building that had headquartered Russian mercenaries who had been careless with their explosives.

"I didn't realize the Marshals Service was issuing World War Two weapons to deputy marshals," the FBI agent said.

"If you don't believe I'm who I say, call Supervising Agent, Fred Archer."

Winter knew the agent would contact Fred Archer long before he did Richard Shapiro.

80 | Charlotte, North Carolina

With steady determination, a young man in a wheelchair rolled himself up the sandstone ramp, turning the wheels of the chair with his hands, that rose to the front doors of the Federal Building in Charlotte, North Carolina. Lint spotted the young man's watch cap; the left collar of his windbreaker pointed up. Dark jeans stopped well short of his new tennis shoes on the footrests, their toes pointing toward each other. Barely any of the people coming or going from the building noticed the struggling young man, aside from quick sidelong glances.

Four court security guards wearing navy-blue blazers manned the metal detectors. The closest COURTSEC guard guided the wheelchair and its occupant around the side so it wouldn't set off the alarm. Kneeling, she inspected the chair and searched its occupant as he rocked in his seat, pressing his tongue against his jaw and craning his neck trying to watch her.

"Sir, you don't have any weapons on you, do you?" the guard asked, pronouncing each word slowly.

"Nooooo, ma'aaaam," he said, with great effort. He blinked owlishly, the thick lenses enlarging his eyes grotesquely. He lifted his closed fist from the wheel, and it quivered as he wiped his nose.

"Okay," the guard said patiently. "Where are you headed?"

"Oooo . . . essss . . . marshooos's : . . offeeese?"

"United States Marshals' office, hon?"

He nodded.

"That's a restricted floor. I'll have to call up and then someone will come down."

The woman lifted a receiver. "Who do you want to see?" she asked.

"Winnnnnntah Maaaaas-sssey."

"Winter Massey?"

"Uh-huh."

"Your name?"

"Waaaa . . . Warrrrrrd F . . . F . . . Feeeeel . . . da." He shifted violently in the chair.

"A Mr. Ward Field is here to see Deputy Massey," the guard said, keeping her eyes on the visitor as she spoke. "I'll tell him that someone will be down to see him in a minute." She replaced the receiver, rolled the chair to the elevator door, and went back to the metal detectors.

When the door opened, a man in his fifties with a handlebar mustache stepped out from the cab and took the grips of the chair. "I'm Chief Deputy Hank Trammel, Mr. Field. I'll show you upstairs."

As soon as the chair cleared the doors, Trammel pushed the button. As the door closed he pulled his pistol and held it against his leg, aimed down. Above the second floor, he pressed the button and stopped the cab. "Okay, pal. Who the hell are you?"

The young man in the wheelchair kept his wrists on the

tires, but his twisted fists relaxed and the bent fingers straightened. "My name is Sean Devlin."

"The hell it is. Sean Devlin is a woman."

"I'm her."

He reached over with his free hand and placed it on her right breast, hidden under the loose-fitting jacket. He pulled his hand away like he'd touched a hot stove.

She reached up and removed her thick glasses and the watch cap, altering her appearance dramatically. Her slicked-back hair was black.

"I'm a friend of Winter's. He'll tell you."

"Put your hands behind your back," he ordered. "I'm going to cuff you until I can find out if you are who you say you are. There are people looking high and low for Sean Devlin. If you're lying to me, you're going to stay in a holding cell for a very long time."

Keeping the gun in his right hand, Trammel used the other to take out handcuffs and to cuff Sean's wrists behind her. He put his gun away, replaced the cap on her head, and released the cab, which rose to the third floor. When the elevator door opened, he spun the chair around, pushed it out, and rolled it down a wide hallway.

"Is this really necessary? I *am* Sean Devlin and I came in here under my own steam," she insisted.

"Disguised and using a false name, Ms. Devlin."

"I knew Winter would recognize the name Ward Field. The disguise is for my own protection. I'm not a criminal," Sean said, exasperated.

Trammel stopped at a steel door with a UNITED STATES MARSHALS SERVICE sign on it. He punched a code into a keypad, then opened the door and pushed her chair into a wide hallway. Sean caught flashes of curious faces as he whisked her past an open door. She was rolled through the corner of a large, open space, where a young deputy sat at one of the ten desks.

No sign of Winter anywhere.

Trammel pushed Sean through a door and closed it behind them. He maneuvered the chair around a small conference table on the left, past a couch on the right, and parked her in front of his desk. He sat on the edge and, with crossed arms, stared down at her.

"Will you please uncuff me now?"

"It's policy to cuff felons while they're in here. Did you come here to turn yourself in to Deputy Massey?"

"Turn myself in? For what?" Sean hadn't broken any laws, unless escaping a surveillance team was against the law.

"The FBI issued a felony warrant for your arrest for the murder of five people last night at the Hotel Grand in Richmond, Virginia."

Sean's mind froze with the sudden realization that the authorities were blaming her for the deaths in Richmond. The hired killers chasing her weren't her only problem—at that moment not even her worst problem. It had never occurred to her that the cops would blame her, the intended victim, for any of the deaths.

Realizing that Trammel was still speaking to her, she tuned him back in. "... interpret your actions as turning yourself in. Every little bit helps."

"But I didn't kill anyone," she protested. She knew she had missed hitting both of the women who had been firing at her.

"Killing two U.S. deputy fugitive recovery marshals is a federal crime, and the state of Virginia will charge you for the murders of the three civilians. There's also interstate flight to avoid prosecution." Trammel picked up a sheet of paper from his desk and held it out for her to see. There was an identikit sketch of her as she had appeared when she had been staying at the hotel. It said that she was being sought for questioning in five homicides and interstate flight to avoid prosecution, just like he'd said.

"Interstate flight to escape *execution*," Sean said crisply. *God, where is Winter?* "How can they accuse me of this?"

"This says you are armed and should be considered dangerous. You armed?"

"I was fully searched at the door. Don't you have faith in the abilities of your security guards? If I were you, I wouldn't, because I'm sitting on an empty gun," she said, lifting her buttock to expose the weapon.

Trammel put the flyer down and, using two fingers to pinch and lift the weapon by the checkered grips, walked around the desk holding the Smith & Wesson out like something poisonous. He opened the chamber and ejected the spent cartridges, then dropped the .38 onto a manila envelope. He sat down behind the desk and studied Sean from across the cluttered surface. "Did you use this gun in Richmond last night?"

"In self-defense. Look, Winter will understand. He'll believe me. Let me talk to him."

"You didn't think Deputy Massey wouldn't arrest you, did you? Because if he was here, he would have to."

"I came to see him because people are trying to kill me. That's why I'm here, dressed like this. *They* killed the two marshals and two others—not three." Her mind fought to make a count of the fatalities. Two deputies and two civilians.

"One of the victims was a female bystander killed by an errant shotgun blast. Since she would be alive if you hadn't been shooting it out with the deputies at the time, it's a legitimate charge."

"I know now that the deputy marshals were there to protect me, but I didn't know they were marshals until the second deputy said so." She was dangerously close to tears. "The first deputy was already dead by then."

"So you shot that first deputy thinking he was after you?"

"I didn't shoot anybody. The two killers shot everybody

that was shot—except a deputy shot one of the women, who was not a bystander."

"A female killer?"

"There *were* two killers. They shot Max and Wire Dog. Max was the hotel manager. Wire Dog—his nickname, I don't know his real name—was a kid who drove a cab. Max did call him Skipper or Skippy—one of them was an older woman who was killed by the marshal with the shotgun—she was shooting at him—he did it on purpose—the other—"

Trammel shook his head skeptically.

"—woman—the younger one who killed the first deputy, killed the second deputy after that—the older of the women shot Max and Wire Dog while we were running to get behind the counter so I don't know—"

"Whoa!" Trammel snapped. "Damn it! Slow down. I feel like I'm riding a bronco. Women killers, cabs, dogs, and who can tell what."

Sean stared at the frowning chief deputy. She knew she was rattling on like a madwoman.

"Let's do this. Take a deep breath and relax. You just answer my questions, and if I need clarification, I'll let you know."

"Okay." Sean had to fight to clear her mind of confusion over the alarming turn of events.

"There were two killers in that hotel who were trying to kill you? And one was a woman. Is that what you're saying?"

"Both of them were women."

"And the deputies came in when?"

"One deputy came in, and one of the women shot him."

She replayed the scene in her mind. "I was headed for the door with Wire Dog, leaving town. He had my bag. A deputy, whom I didn't know was a deputy at that point, started in through the door and I thought he was trying to kill me."

"Why?"

"He drew his gun. Then the younger woman, who was coming toward us, shot him. Wait, the first deputy must have seen her gun and that's why he drew his. I thought he intended to shoot me, but when I looked around, I saw her gun was out and then she shot him. I shot at her after I was behind the counter, but I missed. The older woman shot at Wire Dog and me while we were running. She hit Max and Wire Dog. I fired once at the older one without aiming and missed her."

"You missed her with this .38?"

She nodded. "Then the second deputy came in and got behind a column and fired a shotgun at the older woman and killed her. I emptied the .38 when I ran to the door and got behind the other column. I picked up the dead deputy's pistol, which was lying on the floor. She killed the second deputy when he came around the column. I ran out and I shot the first deputy's gun at her when she came outside. Then I escaped in the cab, where I left the empty automatic."

"What did the younger woman look like?"

"Dark skin and long hair in a ponytail. I saw them earlier in the afternoon in the lobby and I assumed they were guests at the hotel."

"And this dog boy and Max were the only civilians killed?"

"Wire Dog."

"So these professional female killers killed four people but missed you, their primary target, completely?"

"Not completely. The younger one hit me."

"Hit you where?"

"In my computer. I had it in my backpack. She was shooting at me while I was running out and the bullet hit my laptop. There's a hole in it."

"Weren't there any witnesses?"

"The elevator operator might have seen some of it. I

know he went up when the shooting started, but he must have seen the woman shoot the first deputy and maybe the older woman shooting at us."

"Don't you think the elevator operator would have cleared it up with the cops, if he saw it?"

She remembered the operator and her hopes sank. "He's pretty old and the lobby is big and gloomy. I don't know what he actually saw."

"What kinds of guns did the women killers have?"

"Silenced ones."

"Automatics or revolvers?"

"Automatics. Why would the FBI assume I was responsible, if there were no witnesses?"

"You ran, and the FBI believes you and your late husband were a team. Those two dead marshals were specialists. The FBI believes you couldn't have killed them unless you were a professional. I would tend to think you killing those men was highly unlikely unless you were a pro."

"I couldn't kill anybody. Well, not unless it was to stay alive, and I certainly wouldn't shoot at people who were trying to help me."

"What about the money?" he asked. "Where did you get the fake passport and the five thousand dollars the FBI found with your things?"

She had known the cops would find her duffel, and that this question could come up. She decided to tell him the truth. "It was my mother's idea. She had me put that money and the passport in a safe place in case I ever needed it." She didn't tell him where she had left it, not wanting to make trouble for her banker friend. Trammel's eyes were unreadable, but they both knew that normal mothers didn't hide money and falsified passports in far-off cities in case their children had reason to flee for their lives.

"Why did you run away from the hotel in Arlington?"

"I was just freaked out after Rook Island. Out of the

seven deputies protecting us, they killed all but one. Shapiro said he wouldn't keep watching me, but he lied. I didn't trust that someone inside the Marshals Service wasn't involved. I don't trust *anybody* except Winter."

"If it isn't true about you and your husband being a team, why, now that he's dead, do those people still want to kill you?"

"I don't have the slightest idea. Maybe they think I know something. I also don't know how those fugitive deputies and those people found me."

"I know how those deputies located you," Trammel said. "Shapiro recorded your voice during a conversation. He got the NSA to add your voice pattern to an audio net covering electronic transmissions. The machines intercepted your voice, traced it. The two deputies went to Richmond and searched until they found you."

"What about those women? I doubt they followed my scent from D.C."

"That I don't know," he conceded.

"You've already decided I'm guilty."

He sat back and contemplated her for a moment. "I didn't say I thought you were guilty."

Her nose began to itch. "Can you *please* uncuff me or at least come around here and scratch my nose?" She felt a tear roll down her cheek.

Trammel shot up, came briskly around the desk, and removed her handcuffs.

Sean rubbed her nose, snatched a tissue from a box on his desk, and wiped her cheek.

"If you were guilty, you wouldn't have left your duffel in that lobby. A trained professional would have had her running money and fake passport on her person. I believe your story because it makes the most sense. I don't know how two professional killers missed you, but gunfights are confusing affairs."

"What's next?"

"I'm going to tell Director Shapiro what you've told me. What happens after that is up to him."

"Where's Winter?"

Trammel winced involuntarily. "I wish I knew." Hank lifted the telephone. "You still have that damaged computer?"

"In my motel room along with my leather jacket."

"You think there's a bullet still in it?"

"Yes."

"Are you sure that one of those women killers fired that round? Could either of the marshals have fired it?"

"I'm positive the younger woman did, because I remember feeling it get hit. Why?"

"Might support your story. I'm going to send somebody to your motel. In the meanwhile, you just relax."

Relax? Sean almost laughed out loud.

81 | Charlotte, North Carolina

While a deputy went to the downtown motel to retrieve Sean's leather jacket and her backpack containing the damaged laptop computer, Trammel e-mailed Director Shapiro. Sean sat on the couch, at first watching him but soon relaxed enough to nod off.

After the runner returned from the motel, Hank sent Sean's computer to his technician, Eddie Morgan, so he could retrieve the bullet from inside it. Trammel planned to send that along with Sean's Smith & Wesson for ballistic comparison purposes.

Trammel sat on the couch next to Sean. "Tell you what," he started after she had woken, "you call me Hank and I'll call you Sean. That okay?"

"It's fine."

"Sean, Rook Island and Ward Field are on a need-to-know-only deal. I have a good overview on the incidents, but I'm curious about what happened on Rook. I'd like for you to tell me what Winter did there when those men attacked."

"He saved my life."

"I know that. I'd like to know what you saw—how he did what he did."

Sean studied Winter's boss, unsure of what she should say. Trammel reminded her of a proud parent wanting to hear about his child's football game. "I'll tell you, if you're sure it's all right."

"The reports won't give it justice and Winter won't blow his own horn. So I want you to tell me everything."

Sean had gotten to the part in the radar shack where Winter was taking the UNSUB's suit off when the receptionist interrupted by tapping on the door, then opening it. She entered carrying a FedEx package. "Sir, I think you might want to see this. It's addressed to Winter and the return is a cafeteria on the Norfolk Naval Base. I know you said if we heard anything from Winter to let you know, and while this isn't *from* him—"

"A cafeteria at Norfolk?" Trammel queried, reaching out for the package.

"Reed is the only name in the return box."

As the receptionist closed the door behind her, Trammel opened the package and extracted a manila envelope as well as a number-ten envelope with the Navy's seal on it. Trammel unfolded the enclosed letter and displayed a worried expression as he read. "Fletcher Reed?" He stood and carried the package to his desk. "Sorry, Sean, this is important. I gotta check out this fellow."

"Fletcher Reed is a lieutenant commander with the shore patrol. He was on Rook Island before the FBI arrived."

Hank tore open the larger envelope and flipped through

the contents; a stack of eight-and-a-half-by-eleven sheets of paper. From the few Sean could see, each of the pages had pictures and type on them. He swiveled his chair to his computer and typed an e-mail using two fingers. Two minutes later, as he studied the pages from the envelope, a bell alerted him that he had received a response. Seconds after reading the short message, Hank stacked as many of the pages in his fax machine as could fit and sent them.

Sean watched from the couch. After Hank had finished faxing the pages, he left the room carrying them and returned two minutes later with a duplicate set. He carefully put the originals back into the FedEx envelope and slipped that into a larger envelope, which he sealed. Hank put the photocopies into a manila envelope. That done, he buzzed his secretary. When she came in, he handed her the originals. "Put this in the vault for now. This'll go out to the chief marshal with a couple of things Eddie is working on," he told her.

"If the bullets they removed from those bodies in Richmond don't match your gun or the dead deputy's Glock, that's solid reasonable doubt. FBI technicians don't miss much by way of evidence. It's doubtful that you shot your backpack with the same gun that killed those deputies. If you were a professional, and there was nobody chasing you off, you sure as hell wouldn't have left your bag containing your money and a passport behind. There should be evidence from all six of the weapons you mentioned. They can't believe you fired three guns from so many directions."

"They can interpret the evidence they *don't* miss however they like."

"You shouldn't worry about that. Director Shapiro has a seat in the big game. He'll do everything he can to help you, but you have to help us by not running off again. I want your word of honor on it."

"You have it. There's no place to run to and nobody who can help me."

"Okay, so you guys were in the radar shack," Hank said suddenly. "Winter dropped from the rafters on that sumbitch and snapped his neck."

New Orleans, Louisiana

The slipstream caught the cigarette that Johnny Russo flicked out of the Lincoln. He lit another before he closed the window.

A mile after leaving the interstate, Spiro turned right at the crossroads. He drove another fifty yards, then steered the Lincoln onto Sam's property. The gatekeeper opened the front gate while a guard gazed out of the window of the small building. Russo watched the gatekeeper pull the lever on the wall. Even though he had seen the guard disarm the device designed to protect Sam from unwelcome guests, he reminded Spiro to slow as he approached the bridge erected over the man-made gully a hundred yards beyond the gate.

As the Lincoln passed between the hills that guarded Sam's privacy from both sight-seers and surveillance teams, Russo saw two of Sam's bodyguards sitting in a golf cart parked beside the driveway. The pair returned Johnny's wave as Spiro drove past. Sam's guard consisted of serious-minded professionals, who in the way of well-trained attack dogs, were expected to respond only to their master's commands. Sam had recently imported seven young Sicilians—all blood relatives of his bodyguards—which put the number of men he had protecting him at fourteen—by far the largest number ever. He had always been satisfied before with a driver and two others who trailed him in a second car. His caution was indicative of the change in Sam since Dylan Devlin prompted his arrest.

Johnny's mission was tricky because the old man could always sniff out deceit. Sam based life-and-death decisions on a man's facial tic, a shifting eye, or the moisture of a hand he was shaking.

Spiro parked in front of the house beside Sam's Cadillac. Three of the new guards stared at the newcomers as though they had never seen them before.

"Damn Zips," Spiro said distastefully.

"Wait with the car," Johnny told him. "Make nice with the boys. It's important you develop a relationship with them, since you're going to be working with them from now on."

"How, with sign language? They shouldn't come here if they can't talk English."

"Whose fault is it you never learned to speak Italian? Maybe I'll get you some foreign language tapes for Christmas."

Inside the house, Johnny found Sam standing at his expensive gas range overcooking sausages in a big cast-iron skillet. Two of his recently imported young guards sat on stools at the counter waiting like patient hounds.

"Johnny!" Sam said. "You hungry? Grab a plate."

"Nah, Sam," Johnny said. "I passed by my house and ate with the kids a little while ago." The idea of putting anything Sam cooked into his stomach was only slightly less frightening than having a crackhead holding a cocked pistol to his temple. "I wanted to get a shower and change."

"It's nice to keep close with your kids. Where's Spiro?"

"With the car." Understanding why Sam had asked, he added, "He ate already, too."

Sam reached over and turned the radio up before he spoke to Johnny in a low voice. "They don't understand

English," he said, meaning the young men seated at the counter. "So, what you got up your sleeve?"

Be calm, Johnny. "Sean called me."

Sam burned Johnny with his gaze. Smoke was seconds from billowing from the black skins of the sizzling meat. He pulled the skillet off the flame. "So when was it she called you?"

"This morning." He spoke with a nonchalance he didn't feel. In his mind he pictured morning as actually being late at night. "She wouldn't say where she was, just said she saw you on TV, and that it wasn't her fault about—"

"Where is she?"

"She wouldn't tell me. I asked her and said I'd send somebody to get her. I even offered to go myself. She wasn't interested."

"You came straight here?" Sam asked.

"Sure."

Sam smiled at him warmly. "After you passed by your house to eat a little bite with the family and wash up?"

"It was one thing after the other all night, last night. I stank. I had to shower so I wouldn't draw flies," Johnny said, trying to lighten Sam's mood.

Sam's now-clouded eyes were impossible to read; the smile had turned into a sneer. "You wanted to shower and eat before you brought me this word I been crazy out of my head to get?"

Johnny tried to picture Sam as an old man more dead than alive. With Sam standing there, the image wouldn't take shape because Sam looked as invincible as he had when Johnny was a child. That cancer sure had its work cut out for it.

"You get in touch with Herman yet?" Sam asked, changing the subject.

"His number is disconnected," Johnny said, bracing himself for a storm. Herman Hoffman's contact number did indeed have a message saying it was no longer in service. Only the last time Johnny had called it, one of Herman's men had called him back within seconds. The cutout's message had been that despite appearances, everything was under control. Johnny had no choice but to believe him.

"We need to talk," Sam said. "Go on downstairs and wait for me. I'll be right there soon's I feed the boys."

The guards were eager as Sam speared the sausages and put them on their plates beside the nests of linguini, which looked seriously undercooked. Johnny suspected that as soon as Sam left, the men would dump the inedible feast down the garbage disposal.

Downstairs, outside the steam room, Russo changed out of his clothes and wrapped a towel around his waist. He was pissed that Sam thought he had nothing better to do than look for that bitch, but he had no choice—for the time being.

He comforted himself with something he had read in a book of World War II battles. *The greatest generals in history had the ability to turn their weaknesses into strengths.*

Johnny Russo saw himself as a general who had proved time after time that he could improvise with the best of them.

 **Javits Federal Building
New York, New York**

Because of what he had learned since the Rook Island massacre, Winter wasn't about to trust the FBI. He had sat at an interrogation table in a room at FBI headquarters since being rescued three hours earlier. Two agents had taken turns sitting with him, asking him the same questions over and over. He was a veteran of interrogations from the other side of the table, and he couldn't answer any of their questions without opening up more lines of questioning that he couldn't afford.

He couldn't say how he came to be in the basement of the destroyed building without telling them that he had been kidnapped by cutouts posing as FBI agents. He couldn't tell them any of what Fifteen had told him. Nor could he tell them what he had witnessed on the upper floors of the bombed building. He couldn't tell them the killers on Rook Island and at Ward Field were more cutouts controlled by a CIA-connected man named Herman Hoffman, who was hooked directly to CIA satellite feeds. And, equally important, there was nothing he could say to these people that would help Sean Devlin, if she was still alive, which seemed doubtful based on the fact that they had located her. His best chance to accomplish anything was to tell Richard Shapiro everything he knew and let the director decide how to proceed.

When Fred Archer entered the room, the agent sitting across the table from Winter stood up and left, closing the door behind him.

"Hello, Fred," Winter said.

"Every time I turn around, I run into you, and its always under unpleasant circumstances."

"I want to talk to my director," Winter said.

"You think I care what you want?" he carped.

"It's a matter of life and death."

"What isn't with you?"

"Sean Devlin is in danger."

"First tell me how you came to be in a bomb factory—a building used to house killers working for the Russian Mafia."

"I'm not sure that's the case."

"Don't try and tell me you didn't know that. We know you were in on this with Gregory Nations."

"I wasn't."

"Why were you meeting with them, then? How are you

the sole survivor? Don't tell me you were their captive, because you had a gun on you when you were found. Were
you trying to destroy the evidence linking you and Nations
to them and got caught by the bomb you set? How is it you
ended up in the basement? Did you come down after setting the charges, to find the door locked?"

Winter's temper flared as he realized that Fred was try-
ing to counter any possible explanation he might have.
"Sean Devlin's life depends on me talking to Richard
Shapiro. Is that good enough?"

"Mrs. Devlin's stock isn't worth much with the United
States Marshals Service these days."

"How's that?"

"In Richmond last night, your 'damsel in distress' killed
two of your fugitive recovery deputies. She also killed the
witnesses; an old clerk, a cabdriver who'd been carrying
her around on errands since she arrived there, and an innocent woman who was caught in the crossfire. Every cop
in America is searching for her. Her life is in danger only if
she resists arrest."

"Meaning?"

"She's about as good at killing as her husband was.
Despite her innocent act, she was in up to her eyeballs
with Dylan Devlin."

Archer took a piece of paper from his pocket, unfolded
it, and tossed it on the table. It was an FBI flyer showing a
sketch that resembled Sean as she had appeared in the
surveillance picture Winter saw in Hoffman's building.
Winter wondered how Archer would respond to a little bit
of the truth.

"Looks like a photograph of her I found in that building, which was taken of her in Richmond coming out of
the Hotel Grand."

Winter saw Archer's eyes shift their focus.

"Does the Hotel Grand mean anything to you?" Winter
asked.

"What would that picture prove?"

"It would prove that people located her in Richmond and sent a photograph of her here to the people who were in that building. If somebody was killed in Richmond, whoever took that picture was responsible, not Sean Devlin."

"But you don't have the picture, do you?"

"No."

"Then there's no proof of what you say, is there? You're grasping at straws, Massey. We've got you by the balls, and no fantasy can save you."

"Something's been bothering me, Archer. At first I figured you just wanted to close this investigation down fast and that was why you were framing Greg Nations."

"Framing?" Archer laughed.

"But it's more than that. They got to you, didn't they?"

"Who's *they*?" Despite his protest, Archer's face reddened.

"We both know who *they* are."

Archer leaned in close. His breath was stale, his eyes angry. "You should have stayed out of this. I have more than enough evidence to hang you. You're going to be spending your twilight years looking through steel bars, you murdering prick."

Archer's cell phone buzzed and he put it to his ear. "Archer." He straightened. "Yes, sir? I'm with him now." He sat on the edge of the interrogation table and stared down at Winter as he listened. "When?" He frowned. "Yes, sir. Absolutely."

His expression soured as he pocketed the cell phone. "We're leaving here in a few minutes," he told Winter.

"Am I under arrest?"

"Not yet."

"So can I make a phone call?"

Archer set his phone down in front of Winter and left the room. Winter looked over at the mirror set in the opposite wall, imagining Archer behind it, glaring in at him. Winter dialed USMS headquarters, gave his name to the operator, and asked to be connected to Chief Marshal Shapiro.

"I'm glad you're okay," Shapiro told him.

"Sir, it's urgent that I talk to you ASAP," Winter said. "Sean Devlin is in imminent danger. I—"

Shapiro interrupted, "She's safe, under our care. Chief Deputy Trammel will meet you in New Orleans this afternoon and explain everything. We'll talk as soon after that as possible."

Archer returned as soon as the conversation was over. Winter handed the phone back to him. "If you have the pull, I could use a shower, and some clean clothes would be great."

Archer left the room again, and Winter stretched his aching arms. He had no idea what was going on, but short of being skinned alive, it would be preferable to what he had been through over the past two days. He looked at himself in the wall mirror and smiled at the stranger whose dust-white hair made him look like a much older version of himself.

He was sorely relieved that Sean was okay and wished he knew the story on Richmond. The very idea that she could kill two fugitive recovery professionals and innocent people was ridiculous. How he was so sure of this, he didn't understand. He only knew that what he had seen in her eyes, made him believe, unequivocally, in her innocence.

When his phone rang, Fred Archer was in a borrowed office just down the hall from where Massey was taking a shower. He was poring over the reports coming in from the search of the ruins of the bombed building. "Archer," Fred answered.

"Fred, there's a hot dog stand downstairs out front. Go there now."

The hot dog stand was where Fifteen said it would be. As Fred approached it, the smell of cooking sausages made his stomach churn. As he stood there he was aware of someone standing beside him and turned to find Fifteen wearing a trench coat, a wide-brimmed fedora, and sunglasses.

"I'd like one fully loaded," Fifteen told the vendor, who had the good taste not to stare at his mutilated customer.

Fred couldn't think of anything to say. He had never been out in public with Fifteen before.

Fifteen took the hot dog, piled so high with chili and onions it looked to Fred as though it would be impossible even for a man whose mouth opened fully to eat without making a mess.

"Aren't you eating?" he asked Archer.

"Not at all."

Fifteen made no move to pay for his meal, so Archer reached into his pocket, pulled out a ten, and gave it to the vendor.

"Keep the change," Fifteen said.

Archer followed his benefactor to the stone steps where Fifteen sat, perching the hot dog on his lap. Archer sat down beside him, aware that people were staring at the odd couple.

"Did he tell you how he came to be inside that building?"

"No."

"Did he tell you anything he saw while he was there?"

"Not a word."

"I didn't think he would say anything. You'll let me know if he does?"

"Yeah, sure. But he told me that he knew somebody had gotten to me. The director wants me to—"

"I know what your director told you, Fred. Shapiro put

the brakes on the interrogation with an offer your director's boss couldn't turn down."

"Yeah."

"Here you are, headed to New Orleans to do battle with
that old crocodile Sam Manelli. Remember our deal?"

Archer remembered the favor Fifteen had asked in return for the Rook Island evidence that had all but solved
the most important case of his career. The Russian connection, evidence on Nations, the search warrant leading
to the instant picture of Dylan dead. This should have been
over—but for Massey's interference, it would have been.

"This is divine providence, Fred. Sean Devlin can get
you to him, so this deal is a very opportune one for you.
You are about to get credit for solving the most important
case of the decade and avenging all of those unfortunate
deaths. This is where you take your step into the national
spotlight, Fred. I so envy you."

Archer's brain formed an image of him standing at the
FBI podium staring out at an ocean of correspondents and
knowing that untold millions would be hanging on his
every word, memorizing his face as he spoke. He smothered a shit-eating grin with his hand.

"Two or three years here in New York, as assistant FBI
director, heading the largest FBI office. Solving one high-
profile case after the other until everybody in America is
chatting you up. Book deals, movies based on your tri-
umphs, *Meet the Press...*" He broke a piece of the wiener
off and chewed it thoughtfully. "And then, when the time
is right, FBI Director Fred T. Archer. That's *our* goal for
you, Fred. That's going to be your future—if you do this
right."

Archer nodded.

Fifteen said, "I'll tell how you should proceed from
here."

Archer listened, taking the information in and filing it
neatly in his mind.

"Once your team gets to New Orleans, things will be fluid and you'll be using an encrypted tactical radio channel. We'll be able to monitor your operation and advise you of minute-by-minute developments if we are to make sure this comes off without complications."

Fifteen wiped chili from his scarred lips. "You will get full credit for taking Manelli down, and nobody will ever know you had help. You'll look brilliant."

"I can't begin to tell you how much this means to me."

"Don't bother trying, then."

When a Lincoln Towncar pulled up to the curb, Fifteen stood. He turned to Archer and touched his hat's brim before climbing into the car and disappearing into morning traffic.

84 | Charlotte, North Carolina

Hank hated using the computer instead of the encrypted phone because his typing was so slow, but Chief Marshal Shapiro was understandably wary about telephones now. The e-mail system they were using was routed through personal accounts on Yahoo! Shapiro told Hank it was the safest method there was, because unlike electronic transmissions, the NSA wasn't able to spot-check the millions of personal e-mails for matches.

> Hank—Just spoke to W.M.—he's alive and well. Bring S.
> to Express Aviation Charlotte 1200 hours today—You
> will be escorting her to New Orleans for a day or two.
> Full explanation/written orders on plane. Take W.M. the
> copied set of the pages you faxed to me. Courier me
> the originals.

Hank was elated Winter was safe. He had made a copy of the pages Lieutenant Commander Reed sent Winter in order to preserve fingerprints on the originals so they could be matched later to a specific copier or printer. He kept an overnight bag in his car so he and Sean could make the noon flight easily. Now he needed to put Lydia at ease.

She answered on the first ring.

"Lydia, your boy is fine," he told her. "It was like I thought. He got sidetracked and couldn't call."

"Thank God. I've been going crazy. I can't believe he would act so irresponsibly. Actually I can." Her tone was sharp. "Where is my son?"

"New Orleans."

"New Orleans?"

"Lydia, is my wife still there?"

"Yes, she is."

"Can you ask her to bring me a change of clothes for Winter and his gun rig?" Hank's wife, Millie, had been waiting with her for word on Winter since seven that morning.

"What was he thinking?" she said, her anger rising to the surface. "He had me worried to death. I don't know how much more of this I can take."

"I'm sure he'll explain everything to you as soon as he can. Lydia, I need those things pronto."

"I'll collect them."

Hank's secretary buzzed him.

"I've got to go," Hank said. He pressed the button, switching lines.

"Sir, Eddie says he's got your bullet."

Hank strode through the bullpen, down the corridor past the booking room and the holding cell to the door marked EVIDENCE LAB.

Eddie Morgan ran the lab where evidence collected by the deputy marshals was packaged and shipped. He also ran the fingerprint table and the mug shot camera, and maintained their electronic equipment. He was short and overweight, balding, and had nervous, darting eyes. Sean's computer was open, and the technician was studying the electronic guts that he had spread out under a lighted magnifying glass on an adjustable armature.

"Get my bullet?"

Eddie held up a small plastic bag with a mushroomed bullet zip-locked inside it. "Stopped against the battery."

"Forty-five?"

"Two-hundred-twenty grain, .45-caliber hollow point. The motherboard and the power supply are toast."

"Ed, I want you to carry the gun and this bullet to the D.C. lab. I want the chain of this evidence unbroken, so you are to personally hand it over to the lab boys."

"This is worth looking at." With the eraser of his pencil, Eddie pointed to an object. "This little guy sure isn't a factory part. It was connected to the power supply."

Eddie stood back to allow Hank to look through the glass. The small apparatus consisted of a gray plastic box the size of a folded matchbook and a disc no larger than a half dollar. There was nothing at all printed on the shell.

"What is it?"

"I've never seen anything like it."

"Well, box it up, too, and then I want you to get on a plane. If there is no flight immediately, tell Eloise I said she's to lease you a fast one. I'll alert HQ you're on the way."

"If you say so, Chief."

"I just did." Hank patted Eddie on the shoulder.

Sean showered in Hank's private bathroom. After drying off, she removed the store tags from the outfit she had selected to wear. Hank had sent a female deputy to shop for clothes from a list Sean had furnished covering the items she needed. At Hank's request Sean had made a list of styles, colors, and sizes. After she put on a gray turtleneck and khaki slacks, she turned her attention to the mirror. Her hair looked to her like a baby chicken's that had been rolled in oil-well mud and dried by a high-speed fan. She took the brush from the CVS bag and did her best to straighten it out. After being in spikes since she'd left Hoover's urban nonsense shop, it wasn't going to lie down without a fight.

Her mother's face, so like her own, floated into her thoughts. She missed Olivia. The soft side of Sean, the good parts, had come from her mother's genes and the safe environment she had fought so hard to create for her daughter. From her father, Sean had inherited an ability to see solutions logically, to separate herself from emotion, and to think clearly in stressful situations. She had never once panicked, never been frozen by fear, and that was why she was still alive. She had never been so aware of how fortunate she was in the evolutionary lottery—the Lucky Sperm Club.

She was concerned about Winter and knew that she wasn't alone in that. What she felt for her lost protector was complex, but there was a great deal of affection in the mix.

She was comfortable with Hank Trammel. His initial gruffness had melted away to reveal a rough gentleness. In her mind, his sending someone out for her toiletries and new clothes had been an act of thoughtful generosity.

When she came out of his bathroom, Hank was sitting behind his desk looking over some papers. "We're leaving in an hour," he said, looking up and smiling at her improved appearance. "To meet Winter."

"Where is he?" she asked. She felt like jumping in the air.

"New Orleans."

The two words hit Sean like a blast of arctic air, filling her with dread. "New Orleans?" Her mind fought to understand what this sudden development meant. She fought to mask her feelings.

So, Winter was alive and well. She tried to concentrate on that one fact and not to think about who else was in New Orleans.

She couldn't let on that she was certain that once she got to New Orleans, she wouldn't be leaving again.

 | ### Charlotte Douglas International Airport

A stainless-steel briefcase waited for Hank Trammel on the table separating two of the facing leather seats in the Cessna Citation III's cabin. Hank sat with his back to the crew, giving Sean the seat facing forward. From across the table, she watched him dial a combination, open the case, and lift out an envelope, leaving a laptop computer and its components inside. Before he broke the foil seal and slipped out a stack of several sheets of paper, Hank put on his reading glasses. While the plane taxied, lifted off, and for the first five minutes of the flight, he studied the documents in silence, idly twisting the tip of his mustache. After finishing, he removed his glasses. The playful light that had been in his eyes before he read the papers Shapiro had sent was out. Clearly Hank was seething, but she couldn't imagine what he had just read that had darkened his mood.

"Is it bad news?" she asked.

"It's sure not good. You know, it's a bit odd that you haven't asked me once why I'm escorting you to New Orleans."

"You said to meet Winter."

Hank frowned. "That was as much as I knew until I read this," he said, putting his hand on the stack of pages. "Remember when I told you Shapiro tracked you to Richmond by setting a net to catch your voice pattern?"

Sean nodded, uncertain where this was going and increasingly unsettled by Hank's chilled manner.

"The NSA generates transcripts of intercepted calls."

Even before he handed two stapled-together sheets of paper to Sean, panic bloomed inside her.

Verbatim transcription. Call initiated Tuesday 10/22/02 at 22:31:21 hours EST. Phone of origination: Bernhard's Exxon, 221 N. Service Road, Richmond, Va. Number called is a mobile listed to Palma Hamamagian, 221 Norway Street, Chalmette, La. Voice tag positive for subject Sean Marks Devlin. Second subject positive for suspected organized crime figure John Michael Russo known associate of Sam Manelli. Due to continuing request for any call containing individuals listed with Organized Crime tags additional copy forwarded to FBI-OC task force. Call duration 1:21.

Russo: What?

Devlin: You tell Sam I didn't know anything about it.

Russo: Hey, kid, you okay? We were worried you might of got hurt in that mixup. It's cool, I mean, but you need to tell him face-to-face. He knows it wasn't your fault. We're cool, you and me, right?

Devlin: Mixup? I understand he had to stop him. But they came for me, too. They've tried to tag me twice now. Two were after me tonight. They left a mess.

Russo: What are you saying? That's crazy talk. You know, this ain't no conversation for a telephone. Face-to-face only, you know that. I'll meet you. Where you at?

Devlin: You think I'm stupid, Johnny?

Russo: Nah, kiddo, you sure ain't. It's cool. I swear. There is no trouble from us. We don't know what's happening. Let me help you.

Devlin: Help by calling them off.

Russo: Hey, kid, I don't know what you're talking about. Listen, nobody sent nobody to see you. We have to talk this out.

Devlin: I will talk only to Sam from now on. Where is he?

Russo: I'll send somebody for you. I'll come personal. We can't ask him to . . . you know . . .

Devlin: I'm not crazy enough to walk in there to see him or meet you.

Russo: Give me a number and I'll have him get back to you.

Devlin: I'll call you back. You have him near your phone tomorrow afternoon. Anybody takes another run at me, all bets are off, Johnny. I haven't done or said anything, so don't make that change.

Russo: This is all crazy. We'll fix it if we know what's going on. We would never let nobody—

Devlin: (interrupting) You sounded really surprised to hear my voice. If what you say is true, why is that?

(called disconnect 22:32:42 hours EST)

Russo: Aw, flying Christ.

(call terminated 22:32:46 EST)

She handed the transcript back to Hank. Her mind felt like it had been deadened with Novocain.

Hank's glare was icy, his facial muscles tense. "See where the FBI's Organized Crime section was copied on this? Both Director Shapiro and the FBI are naturally curious about this call. I have to admit I'm wondering about it myself." He slammed the transcript facedown on the table.

Strangely, somewhere beneath the fear, she felt relieved that he finally knew. But it didn't alter anything except perhaps to reinforce his opinion that she hadn't been honest with him in his office. She had been as truthful as she could afford to be. "You want to know what, exactly?" she said calmly.

"We are going to New Orleans because the FBI is going to swap Winter for you." His tone was suffused with disgust.

Being delivered to the FBI was an unpleasant surprise.

"As part of the deal between Shapiro and the FBI, he has expressly ordered me *not* to interrogate you. I suppose the FBI wants to do that themselves. I reckon they don't want us to know what you are going to tell them, which I doubt you would tell me anyway."

"Okay, so you can't interrogate me. What would you want to know if you could?"

"I'd start by asking how you, someone I honestly believed was as innocent as the driven snow, would know to call a phone number that's listed to whoever this Palma

Hamajama is, to speak to this thug Russo about Sam Manelli and what are obviously the attempts on your life. How do I know you aren't lying about what happened in Richmond?"

"That's all true. Everything I've told you is true."

"Why didn't you level with me? That means you have lied, if only by omission. You are a threat to Manelli, aren't you?"

"The truth is I'm not a threat to him—he's a threat to me."

"Obviously Manelli thinks you are. And, had I just been interrogating you, you would not have answered my question truthfully."

"I'm not responsible for what Sam Manelli believes. I *do* want you to believe me, because I am a total innocent in this. I swear to you—that's the truth."

Hank glanced down at the papers, then back up. "I don't want you to be blindsided by what is going on. Monday morning I showed Winter evidence the FBI had compiled on the assaults. They had proof that Greg Nations sold Manelli the location of the safe house and the time Dylan was being moved."

"You think that Greg could have done that?"

"Somebody inside WITSEC gave the operation up to Manelli. Shapiro says the FBI was planning to make the case that Winter was in on it with Greg—still can if they want to."

"I don't understand. How can they say that?" she asked, genuinely confused.

Hank reached into his bag and took out a bottle of water. He offered it to Sean and, when she declined, opened it and drank half of it. "Shapiro's letter says that Winter's home phone records show that he called Cherry Point and then Norfolk Navy Base yesterday. There's no way to know what he discussed. Those calls were followed by an incoming call from a cell phone registered to the shore pa-

trol at Norfolk. Last night, after seven P.M., there was
a call from that same cell phone to Winter's cellular.
Shapiro thinks that one was Reed giving him the information that we got by FedEx this morning. Worse still, Reed
was shot last night while he was driving his car, a few minutes after his call to Winter. He crashed. Military cops
found a dart from a gun in his neck. Witness saw a car
chasing his.

"Around ten last night, a man showed up at Winter's
house and took him away in a car. Winter told his mother
it was official business and that he'd be back in two hours.
Lydia called me at six this morning because he hadn't returned, so I called Shapiro."

"Was that man working for Manelli? Did he take
Winter to New Orleans?"

"The FBI found Winter in the basement of a building
that blew up in New York early this morning. They took
Winter to New Orleans because that's where your friend
Mr. Manelli is. The FBI has a large-scale operation in motion, built around you."

"Around me?"

"The FBI assumes you can get them Manelli, so that is
why Shapiro could make a deal to exchange you for
Winter. They intended to hang Winter for being in a
building filled with explosives and weapons and who
knows what. They say the place was being used by the
Russian bunch that assaulted Rook Island and wiped out
your husband's detail."

She let that sink in. "I'll do anything I can for Winter.
But I can't tell the FBI anything about Sam that will help
them."

"That's between the two of you. This transcript makes
it clear to them that you can get close to Manelli, and
that's what they're going to insist you do. The A.G. has to
make sure Manelli pays for all those dead people. You help
him and your problems can vanish."

She laughed, feeling trapped and desperate. "If I get anywhere near Sam Manelli, or Johnny Russo, I'm dead."

"I doubt the FBI can afford to let anything happen to you."

"Do you honestly believe the FBI can protect me from Sam Manelli—in New Orleans? Look at the protection Dylan had."

Hank shrugged. "Nobody can force you to do anything, but if you help the FBI get Manelli, the attorney general will clear you of the federal and state charges. He gave Shapiro his word on it. If you don't, I expect you'll be prosecuted for Richmond at the very least."

"Won't the ballistic evidence clear me?"

"Ballistic evidence is open to interpretation and the FBI's experts can testify pretty convincingly. They control the investigation, the media spin, witnesses, the evidence. If Winter is right about fabricated evidence on Greg, there's no telling what they can pin on you. Looks like you're going to have to select from a shortlist of nightmares."

"They're liars," she said, feeling overwhelmed and lost.

"World's full of liars." Hank winked at her. "But I don't entirely believe you're one of them. I figure you're as honest as your circumstances allow you to be."

All in all, Sean thought that was a fair assessment.

87 | New Orleans, Louisiana

The Windsor Court on Gravier Street sat within rock-throwing distance from the city's new downtown casino. The hotel was built in the 1980s, intended to be the finest in America. Fred Archer was probably the first person to encamp an FBI army in the 3,000-square-foot, four-thousand-dollar-a-night penthouse suite, but the staff could easily assume the group was the entourage and security for a reclusive movie or rock star.

While the FBI agents went about checking their equipment cases and making telephone calls on encryption units, Winter sat on a couch below a pastoral oil painting of a sleeping child nestled in the curve of the body of a furry dog, which was keeping vigil. The painting was a perfect metaphor for WITSEC. He wore a fresh T-shirt in contrast to his filthy jeans.

At two-thirty P.M. Special Agent Finch led Hank and Sean into the living room. Trammel seized Winter's hand and slapped him hard on the shoulder. "Hey, Hoss," Hank said.

"Hank. It's good to see you." A few hours earlier he had been sure that his life was over.

Sean smiled when Winter turned his eyes to her. "Like my hair? I did it with a sand wedge."

"It looks fine, Sean," he said, meaning it.

"Let's get this show on the road," Archer's voice interrupted as he strode into the room. "Take him and go," Archer ordered Hank. "We have a lot of work to do."

"Let's get going. I'll buy you both lunch at Galatoire's."

Archer folded his arms. "Sean Devlin, you're under arrest for the murders of two United States marshals and interstate flight to avoid prosecution."

Winter bristled. "You know that's total bullshit, Archer. She didn't kill anybody."

Archer turned to Trammel. "Get him out of my sight."

"My Walther?" Winter asked Archer.

Archer nodded at Finch, who disappeared for a few seconds and returned with the antique Walther PP, which he handed to Winter.

"*Now* get him out," Archer said.

"What the hell is your hurry?" Hank asked through

clenched teeth. "You think giving these people a couple of minutes to talk will jeopardize your record as the world's biggest prick?"

Archer frowned, but seemed to decide that Hank's was not a wholly unreasonable request. "Two minutes." He left the room with Finch following like a dog expecting a treat.

"I'll be at the door," Hank said.

"Exactly what's the deal here?" Winter asked Sean when they were alone.

"They want me to do something for them in exchange for making something that happened in Richmond last night go away."

"What do they think you can do for them?"

"Help them get Sam Manelli."

"That's crazy. What makes them think you can do that?"

Sean looked down. "Because I know him."

"How?"

"It's a long story—I didn't know Dylan knew him, much less worked for him. But Sam doesn't know that, and he won't believe it no matter what I say. He thinks I betrayed him, even though I didn't. I have to do this, because unless the FBI gets him, I'll never be safe."

"So on Rook, those four *were* sent by Manelli to kill you. That's why they were still after you?"

"As far as Sam is concerned, I'm unfinished business. After those women tried to kill me in Richmond, I thought maybe I could explain to him that I didn't have anything to do with Dylan betraying him. I made a call to one of his people hoping to buy some time, and the FBI found out. I decided to find you so we could try to figure out a way to get this mess sorted out. You have to believe that I was going to come clean with you."

Tears filled her eyes. "I'm sorry, Winter. All I've ever wanted is to live a normal life, and this is the only way that's ever going to happen."

"Archer can't make you do anything that puts you in danger."

"The FBI does what it wants."

She was right. Winter had witnessed Archer's sleight of hand. He knew that Archer wasn't interested in the truth unless it fit where he needed it to.

"I know who the killers were and I think I can prove Greg wasn't involved. After I talk to Chief Marshal Shapiro, I believe he can put a stop to all this."

"Time's up." Finch was standing in the doorway.

Winter kept his eyes on Sean's. Finch turned his back.

"You watch yourself," he told her. "I'll do everything I can as fast as possible."

"Winter, can I hug you? For luck?"

He squeezed her to him and held her there, then kissed her on the forehead. "I'm going to do whatever it takes to make sure nobody hurts you."

She looked into his eyes. "No. You go home to your family. I'll call you when this is over. I'll be fine."

Winter released her. "After this is over, nobody will have to order me to watch over you."

She smiled and hugged him again, squeezing very hard. "I'd like that. Now, go."

He walked out, leaving Sean in an expensively appointed den of wolves.

88

The Delacroix Hotel had been constructed in New Orleans's pre-World's Fair building frenzy in the 1980s with profits from the importation of cocaine. It had been seized by the DEA and, although it was managed by a private company, it remained property of the United States of

America. As it was a seizure, every penny above direct operating costs was profit. The fact of government ownership was not publicized, but when upper echelon officials of the Department of Justice stayed there, it was at a reduced rate.

Winter and Hank talked en route to the hotel, located a few blocks away from the Windsor Court. As soon as they got into their room on the fourth floor, Hank unpacked the laptop Shapiro had sent. He reached into his bag and took out a FedEx envelope. "This is the package Reed sent you from Norfolk."

"Great." Winter read Fletcher Reed's note:

Massey,

    If I spoke to you, I didn't want to mention over the telephone that this package containing my originals was coming to you because if I am right, some of the people mentioned on these pages will do whatever it takes to stop it. They may not come after you immediately if they think they have all the copies I made of these. I sent one to your director and left another set in my office for them to find. I sent yours from another department so it might slip through. If they are smart enough to find this, then they're too smart to be stopped by us anyhow. I hope I'll be around to see you nail these animals. If not, we sure gave it the old college try. Enclosed are the original print cards I pocketed on Rook Island as well as the matching print cards from their military records and their first death certificates, all dated well before that night. The thing they all have in common is that in each case the corpse's identification had to be made using dental records or DNA. Also included are all of the suspicious deaths of Special Forces guys (back to 1980) who are likely candidates for membership in the black-bag club.

I have no idea how you can use this, but you seem the industrious type and I hope you'll figure something out.

I still owe you that drink.

Fletcher Reed

"Fifteen didn't tell me that a dart had anything to do with Reed's accident."

"Sounds to me this Fifteen character didn't expect you to live long enough to check out the details."

After reading the note, Winter flipped through the files, studying the faces of the young men. Some of them had become killers, while the others had suffered actual fatal accidents during or just after their Special Forces training. There were whites, blacks, Latinos, and Asians on the pages, but no women at all, because Special Forces were supposedly boys' clubs. But, according to what Sean had told Hank, there had been at least two women, certainly cutouts.

"Fifteen told me that Herman Hoffman developed the test to single the murderers out from the herd. I don't have any proof of it, but Hoffman and Manelli had a long-running relationship and I bet Hoffman sold Manelli intelligence, or maybe Manelli gave Hoffman wet work for a price. He told me that Hoffman was with the CIA until the Bay of Pigs. I heard while I was living here that Dominick Manelli was involved with other mobsters in plots to kill Castro, and the CIA trained some of the Cuban liberation soldiers on land owned by the Manellis. Maybe their relationship started with that."

Hank finished connecting his cell phone to the USMS computer and turned it on. Winter watched Hank type in the commands to make the connection before he looked back at the papers on the table in front of him.

"Just because Sean knows Sam Manelli," Winter said, "it doesn't mean anything."

"She's holding out, Winter. There's a lot more to her and those gangsters than she's admitted to."

"I trust her."

"You're too involved to be objective."

"You like her, too," Winter said.

"Oh, she's easy to like. There's something about her you can't help but admire.""

"She agreed to swap herself for me, Hank."

"She's definitely fond of you. But I missed the part where she had a choice."

"I'm not going to let anything happen to her," Winter told him.

"The FBI will protect her," Hank said. "They can't afford—"

"I'm not about to leave her safety up to Archer," Winter said. "He's tied into Fifteen as sure as I'm sitting here."

"Beg pardon?"

"Archer'll set her up as bait for Manelli. The last thing in this life Sam Manelli is going to do is admit killing anyone, especially to her. I'd venture to say, after the FBI's been trying for forty years to get him on anything, Archer knows that, too. Say Sam's brain-dead enough, or wants to kill her bad enough, to actually meet with her. The question is what is better for the FBI? A recording of Manelli admitting to being behind the killings? Sam threatening to kill her? Him making an attempt on her life? Or the FBI catching the old bastard in the room with her still-warm body?"

"No contest," Hank admitted, without looking from the computer's screen.

"The only thing better for everybody concerned is if a desperate Sam Manelli, who has just killed this woman, is then killed in a gunfight with Archer's adrenaline-revved SWAT team. Even if I wanted to turn my back on her, and

I don't, Fifteen isn't going to sit still as long as there's a chance I'll help people find him."

"You never did know when to quit a thing," Hank said. "I expect if anybody can do something about this Fifteen character, it'll be Shapiro, not you."

"You can walk away from this, Hank."

"I was never good at knowing when to quit a thing, either. Let's see what Shapiro thinks," Hank said. "He's online."

Hank pecked at the keyboard using his index fingers.

Winter's here.

"You best do this, Winter."

Trammel put the laptop on the coffee table in front of Winter. Shapiro had answered,

I want everything Winter has.

He typed for ten minutes, relaying what he had learned that was relevant, even describing Fifteen and his threats against his family. He told Shapiro that he believed it was possible Archer got his fabricated evidence from the CIA, which was protecting Fifteen's dark operatives. He told his director that, although he had no proof, he believed the FBI was still working with the CIA.

Shapiro typed:

Good work, Winter. I'll figure out how I can best use your information. You've earned yourself a rest. Take the plane and go home.

Winter wasn't finished. He typed:

Sir, after all we've lost trying to protect Sean, I don't see how we can throw away our investment now.

Winter—obviously we have no authority to interfere in
the operation of another agency. At this juncture I don't
know how to get around that.

Winter had already worked out his response:

Maybe I could stage a training exercise for a few of the
local deputy marshals to study surveillance methods of
other law enforcement agencies, with a possible
recovery of a hostage from a hostile environment
thrown in.

Shapiro's answer was:

Practice makes perfect. Chet Long will supply whatever
you require.

Five minutes later, Chet Long, the chief deputy U.S. marshal for the New Orleans district, called to say he'd be
there in ten minutes for a pow-wow and that he had
pulled all of his available deputies off what they were
working on and had them collecting to await Winter's
orders.

Winter used Hank's cell phone to call Lydia.

"Sorry for scaring you, Mama."

"Hank's there with you?"

"I'm looking right at him."

"Winter, is everything all right?"

"Never better, Mama. I expect I'll see you guys tomorrow or the next day."

"Take your time," she said, as cheerfully as she could.

89

Fred Archer punched Johnny Russo's telephone number into a pad on the portable panel's keyboard. Sean wore a set of earphones outfitted with a microphone. A city-traffic sound track played in the background. Archer sat across the panel from her, wearing the second set of earphones.

Russo answered immediately. "Yeah?"

"Where's Sam?" Sean said.

Sam's voice came on the line, causing Sean to jerk involuntarily. "Why didn't you come to see me instead of this telephone thing?"

Overwhelmed for a second, she didn't know what to say.

"I hear that somebody's been messin' around with you," Sam said.

"That's a surprise?" Sean retorted, feeling genuine anger. "They came to an island, then they followed me to another city, and you're telling me you don't know anything about that?"

There was a long silence, during which Sean could hear Sam's raspy breathing. She knew he wouldn't say anything that could be played back to him in court.

"I don't know nothing about any of that. Sounds like one of them shoot-'em-up movies or something else crazy. You can tell me all about whatever this is when I see you."

"When I see you? Aren't you listening? My marriage ended suddenly and those aren't suitors chasing me all over. The cops are blaming me for that big mess at the hotel in Richmond last night. If they get me or you do, it's all the same."

"You afraid of me?" There was something that sounded like concern in his tone, Sean wasn't that easily fooled. *Snakes seem perfectly harmless until they bare their fangs.*

"I have nothing to lose. I have no place to go and no means to get there. If we don't get this straightened out—"

"I said I'd fix it," Sam told her impatiently.

Archer motioned for her to set a time for the meeting.

"Tell me where you at now and I'll have someone come pick you up."

Archer nodded vigorously at her. Sean had done as he said and let Sam insist that she come see him, not have him believe she was the one who desired a meeting.

"I'll meet you at the old Maison Blanche garage. I'll be in a purple Chrysler convertible."

"Herb will pick you up in an hour on the fourth level. He'll bring you to the house and we can talk about what's up and I'll take care of everything."

An hour? Before Sean could ask for more time, Archer ended the call by flipping a switch on the board.

"We got work to do," he told her.

"One hour?" Sean snapped, jerking the headset off. "Are you nuts? You can have all of those safeguards you been jabbering about in place in an hour? You said it would take time to make sure everything was ready. You're as crazy as Manelli is."

"He's always been suspicious," Archer said calmly. "If we give him more time he'll start working his channels; he might find out we're here and queer the deal. We can be ready in one hour. Right, Agent Finch?"

"What if his people shoot me in the garage?"

"He'd never do that."

"How can you be so sure?" she demanded.

"It's not his style, that's why. I know everything there is to know about Manelli. He'll have his driver pick you up because he can't risk doing that himself and because he'll figure the chances are good we've put you up to this. The driver will try to shake a tail, but we'll be right there. No matter what he does, we'll be on you. Isn't that right, Finch?"

"Absolutely, sir," Finch agreed. "We have the latest electronic tracker. It's a fail-safe operation."

"This is messed up," Sean said. She threw the headset onto the couch in disgust.

"Do you really think we'd let Sam Manelli hurt you?"

"I don't know if you would or not. Do I think you could stop him from doing it? Absolutely not. And if you truly think you can, you're a bigger putz than I already thought you were."

"You're going to be wired. First admission or threat, we roll in and pop him."

"As soon as his driver finds the wire or spots your people, he drives away. Then you can go home, because Manelli won't come within ten miles of me. If he thinks you're behind this, they'll search me before I meet with him."

"Think we aren't way ahead of that?" Archer left the room and came back carrying an Atlanta Braves baseball cap, which he handed to her. He pointed at the cloth-covered button in the top. "This contains a new generation position and communication bug. The transmission is not detectable by normal bug catchers. It will tell us where you are, and we can hear conversations at an unlimited distance, thanks to our nice satellite. And we'll make sure we know who goes into the lot."

She tried the cap on and looked in the mirror. "Lucky me. I'm on a winning team."

90

Sam Manelli handed the cell phone to Russo and stared out through the grimy office window into a warehouse filled with vending machines.

"It's a setup," Sam announced.

"You think so?" Russo asked, seeing a faint light at the end of a long tunnel. "That would sure explain a few things."

Sam's hooded eyes studied his protégé, then he nodded slowly. "Feds using her to get me. If she thinks I've been trying to kill her she's too smart to show up here all of a sudden. No telling what they told her. FBI birds probably got her backed in a corner on this Richmond thing she told you about."

"There was a big shoot-out in a hotel there. They could have staged that themselves to fool you."

"Well, that's possible. We don't have time to check it out, do we?"

"What she told me is just what I told you. Word for word. Forget the meeting, then," Russo said, seeing an opportunity to appear like he was acting out of concern for the older man. "Sam, what they got at this point? Nothing. Keep it that way. You stay away from her a few days or whatever. There'll be time when this is all cooled down to get her." Russo knew Sam wasn't about to start taking his advice now. When it came to that bitch, he was beyond reason.

Sam shook his head. "I'm gonna handle this right. This is one of those loose ends that could get all unraveled if I don't knot it up quick. I'm not gonna sit back and wait and see what's gonna happen. Something about this whole mess is all wrong. You can't get in touch with Herman, and I don't like that one bit. I go back a long time with Herman. I've given him a lot of money over the years, and maybe he's up to something—gone squirrely from plugged-up brain vessels or something. Maybe somebody killed him."

"Let me take some of the guys and handle it, Sam. I'll get her for you. Don't risk yourself this way. Far as they can prove, you're clean."

"I already decided." Russo saw a new level of coldness behind Sam's eyes. "I want you out at the place in an hour and a half. We gonna have a long talk with her so you and me can get all this figured out."

Johnny shrugged. "You know what's best."

Manelli locked his hands behind his thick neck and studied Russo. "I'm puzzled about why that bird Dylan pulled this crap in the first place. It never did make sense. It's like that thing about an iceberg being mostly where you can't see it, but you still know it's down there."

"What can I say I haven't said a million times? Devlin fooled everybody. He totally checked out. I should know."

"Yeah," Sam started, seemingly puzzled, "you checked him out personal and you gave him a clean bill. And always before that, you was so good at sniffin' out rats."

"I knew how important it was that he was the real deal, Sam. I want this straightened out as much as you do."

Under his shirt, sweat streamed down Russo's back. This was the suspicious Sam before him. Until he acted, it was impossible to know what was on his mind. Usually, the people that Sam decided were betraying him first learned of his suspicion in their last moments. Sometimes, depending on his mood, those last moments had been known to be hours. Age had only hardened the brickbat that served as his heart.

"Well, at least take the radio Herman gave you with the fed frequencies on it."

Sam rose suddenly and Russo winced, thinking Sam was going to grab a steel pinball machine leg from a stack near the desk and pulverize him with it. Johnny had seen Sam do just that in this very room. Sam left without saying anything. Johnny's smile withered. He figured that, unless Herman's cutouts did this thing right, crabs could be dining on his eyes before dawn.

A figure blocked the doorway and Russo flinched, afraid for a second that it was Sam back to finish him off. "Boss?" Spiro said.

Relief filled Russo. "Spiro, Sam's gone?"

"Yeah. They all gone. Everything cool?"

"Close the door a minute." Johnny lifted his cell phone and pressed the digits. There was a strange clicking sound which was the encrypting device on the other end, which scrambled the signal on both ends.

"Johnny," the familiar cutout's voice said. "Is everything clipping along?"

"You were right, Lewis. She's here now," Russo said, fighting the panic he felt. "He's picking her up in an hour."

"Good. Sam has the radio?"

"Yeah. What should I do?"

"Do exactly what you'd normally do. We're on top of this, like I told you."

"Sam figured the FBI is using her to get him. It's like he's psychic. I don't like it."

"Of course he did. Sam's a genius, Johnny. He'll get her and we'll get him and the FBI will clean it all up. That's all settled."

"If your guys had done what they were supposed to do, she would be history and we'd all be winners already."

"What's Sam's plan?"

"All I know is he wants me at his lodge in like ninety minutes. You know where it is, right?"

"We'll be there. Don't worry about it."

"You just make sure this time."

"Trust me on this."

" 'Trust me' is what Herman said. I still don't know why he didn't tell me Sean was alive. I found that out when she called me out of the blue. So if we're going to work together in the future, I got a bone to pick with him. Because there's not going to be anybody but me for you people to work with. Right?"

"Herman has been retired because this didn't go as he'd planned. He messed up, not me."

Russo wanted to scream. Just as he was starting to relax, the world tilts off its axis. "Who's taking his place?" Russo was already thinking about an alliance with Herman's replacement, hoping for somebody younger, sharper. "I think him and me should meet after this is over."

"You'll love his replacement, Johnny."

"Just remember, Lewis. If you don't get this right, I'm dead. If the men think I might fail, they see any weakness, they'll turn on me like jackals."

"I'll see you in a little while. By the way, you might want to keep your head down when we come in. You make sure your guys don't start shooting at us, or we'll respond and you'll be recruiting their replacements for the next six months."

"Remember, none of my guys get whacked accidentally."

"We'll be completely surgical. It's what we do."

Johnny felt better. Lewis was an amazing individual, and Johnny had no choice but to trust him as he had before. What Sam didn't know was that his bodyguards understood that their futures lay with Johnny—that Sam's rule was done. Sam was dying but, as strong as Sam was, that could take another couple of years, and Johnny wasn't nearly as patient a man as Sam was.

91

A chilled, steady rain kept pedestrians on both sides of Decatur Street moving rapidly and the vehicles rolling slowly. Jax had been a long-closed brewery complex when it was turned into a fanciful tourist mall—reminiscent of a medieval castle with flags flying from its sheltered parapets—with views of the Mississippi River and the French Quarter.

Three FBI vehicles were parked facing the levee at the rear of the vast lot beside the complex. Archer's assault-suited FBI SWAT team sat in the step van waiting patiently, while the surveillance techs sat at portable consoles, anxious to field test their equipment.

Archer, occupying the passenger seat of the black Crown Victoria, strummed his fingers nervously on the armrest. He had good reason to be nervous. Special Agent Finch sat stiffly behind the wheel. Every seven seconds the wipers would cycle, clearing their view of a concrete wall three feet from the grill. Like a sullen teenager, Sean Devlin sat slumped in the backseat with her arms locked across her chest. An unoccupied purple Dodge convertible waited next to the Ford. Finch jumped when Archer's radio squawked to life.

"Big Chief, this is Eyes One. The covered wagon has left the barn, headed toward the lower forty. ETA is fifteen minutes."

"Roger that," Archer said. "Okay, all teams, prepare to roll when the covered wagon starts back to the barn."

In a low voice, Finch translated the radio lingo for Sean. "The team watching Manelli's estate just told us that Manelli's car is on the way from there."

"Okay, Mrs. Devlin. Get ready. I have a team covering the garage. Manelli's driver is on his way, alone. Soon as you get in, make sure you keep noise coming so we always know. Remember that we are running tape." Archer tilted the ball cap toward his mouth and whispered, "Ears, you getting this?"

"That's a roger," a voice said. *"The signal is ten-ten."*

Archer handed the cap to Sean. "Remember, you just get Manelli to admit being behind the hit on your husband. We need him to admit he ordered it—financed it. Conspired with others. That is all we need."

"I hope he's thoughtful enough to incriminate himself *before* he kills me."

"We will never be more than seconds away. Just get in your car and go. We'll be with you the whole time."

Finch said, "This will be over before you know it."

"I just hope it isn't over before *you* know it." Sean straightened, and when she did she felt suddenly queasy.

"I can't do it," she said. "Not now."

"What the hell do you mean?" Archer growled.

"I'm getting a headache," she said, alarmed.

"Don't you dare try and pull anything," Archer threatened. "We're not changing the plan. I have people on you and if you try to make a run for it, they'll shoot you as a fleeing felon."

"Seriously, I'm getting a migraine," she said. "Would that surprise you?"

"Finch," Archer snapped, "go into the van and get some aspirin over here, now!"

"Aspirin?" Sean said. "I need something a lot stronger than that."

Archer snapped at her, "You'll take the aspirin and you will *not* get a headache! Do you understand me?"

Sean took four tablets, praying they could stave off a migraine. Keeping her head perfectly level, she slipped the ball cap on gently, and climbed gingerly out of the

Crown Vic. Oblivious to the rain, she slid carefully behind the wheel of the convertible. She eased the door closed, not daring slam it for fear of promoting the headache.

Take two bullets in the head and call me in the morning.

Inside the USMS ordnance room, United States Chief Deputy Marshal Chet Long handed Hank and Winter a pair of vests to put on under their coats. He pointed to a box on the table. "There's two pairs of binoculars, a tactical radio with earphones. Your FBI pals have been using the encrypted tactical channel it's set on. We'll communicate with cell phones. What else?"

"Manpower?" Winter asked as he inventoried the box.

"Best I could do out of my office on this short notice is the pair I have watching the Windsor Court, and five others I've called back in. I have three more coming in off leave. Shapiro has a high-test, four-man team en route—be here in three hours. If we're lucky, this won't get under way until after they get in, and you'll have the specialists."

"That would be nice," Winter said absently. He wasn't going to put his faith in what might make it, but in what he had.

"There are a few locals, men with integrity I can trust in a pinch—damn few around not on Manelli's payroll one way or another. My brother-in-law's a highway patrol captain. He's agreed to put some of his men at our disposal, and he has started moving some additional units into the area. To make sure this doesn't leak out, the patrolmen won't know what exactly we're up to until the operation is well under way."

"I think this will go down soon," Winter said. "Archer doesn't strike me as a patient man."

"We're looking at only another hour of daylight," Chet said. "Guys, I'm not set up for major assaults at the moment. No heavy weapons—my MP-fives and most of my chest armor is in Lafayette with a Fugitive Recovery detail. I have a half a dozen ARs, and a few Mossy twelves." He lifted two long guns from his cabinet and handed them to Hank. "Take an AR and a Mossberg. Two twenty-round mags for the carbine and thirty double-ought shells for the scattergun should be plenty. Oh, I put rounds for your Walther in there."

"Appreciate it," Winter said.

"I put the Manelli file material in the box. Afraid there's not much in there except for the layout of his house and office and a list of property he owns."

Chet's cell phone rang and he answered it, listened, and hung up. "Damn if you weren't right. My deputies say they're moving out of the Windsor Court."

"Let's go, Hank," Winter said.

"Nice to have time for planning," Hank quipped.

"The covered wagon has left the barn for the lower forty?" Hank Trammel said, snickering. "Sounds like that old boy got his code inspiration from watching John Wayne movies."

"Whatever works."

Winter watched the FBI vehicles parked across the Jax lot from them through binoculars. According to one of Chet's deputies there were two agents in a white Taurus sitting outside a parking garage one block off Canal Street—the city's main traffic artery and one of the four streets that enclosed the French Quarter.

Winter was no stranger to the city, but as he was sitting

in the Jeep, rain peppering the roof, he wasn't waxing nostalgic, or thinking about the city in any terms other than it being where Sean Devlin was located. The restaurants and shops, and every other place he knew and loved, were like so many cardboard boxes, facing streets he might need to navigate to keep her alive.

"I wish we knew what the grand plan is," Hank said. "Think Manelli's meeting her in the parking lot that team is watching? It seems too public a place for such a private man."

Winter punched in the speed dial number for Chet, who was monitoring the deputy watching the agents who were watching the parking garage. "Is there just one way into the garage?" Winter asked.

"Yes," Chet answered.

"Sounds like Archer's people are watching Manelli's house or office. So 'lower forty' should be the parking garage."

Chet said, *"I can tell from how long it takes Manelli to get to the garage whether he's coming from his house. His office is six minutes away tops. House is at least fifteen minutes from there."*

Winter rang off. He knew that the SWAT team and the techs were in the step van and Archer, Finch, and Sean in the Crown Vic. "We'll stick with Sean," he told Hank.

"Nothing is going to happen without her," Hank agreed.

"Car door's opening." Winter watched Finch climb out and enter the motor home. Seconds later he returned to the car and got behind the wheel. Winter put his binoculars on the female deputy marshal sitting in a minivan across the lot from the FBI vehicles. If the vehicles split up, she was supposed to stick with the van and Winter with whatever vehicle had Sean in it.

Winter figured that the last thing the FBI was worried about was anyone trailing them. He'd decided that he wanted to remain in the best position he could manage to extricate her from any potentially disastrous situation.

Winter had read through Chet's files on Sam Manelli to get to know Manelli better. They were of very little help, since they held only information the marshals would need to serve a federal warrant on the gangster. Manelli's bodyguards were private investigators licensed by the state to carry concealed firearms. Sam owned the security firm and had a sweet deal that allowed the firm to own twenty-five John Doe licenses and give them out without having to clear the guards through local law enforcement for a year. That arrangement alone showed how much political power Manelli had.

"There's Sean," Winter said, watching as she climbed from the Ford and slipped into the convertible parked beside Archer's Crown Victoria. She pulled off, leaving the step van and Archer sitting there. "She's heading for the garage."

"*Covered wagon is entering the lower forty,*" a new voice on the radio announced. Winter assumed it was one of the agents watching the parking garage.

"*Let me know when it pulls out with the cowgirl,*" Archer's voice answered.

"Keep her in sight, Hank."

Hank followed the convertible, allowing other vehicles to get between them.

"He's meeting her in the lot, Winter," Hank said. "I can beat her there and wait. We could even slip into the lot if you want to."

"No." Winter was trying to keep his head clear, to keep his emotional attachment to Sean out of the equation. He wanted to do what Hank suggested and maybe get into the lot so he could watch her with his own eyes, but that might further endanger her. He wanted more men. He wanted better ways to keep up with her. He wanted to know exactly what Archer's intentions were, what Manelli was thinking. He was terrified that Manelli had someone waiting in the lot to ambush and kill her. He wanted to head her off, take her out of the convertible, and run away with her and keep her safe, which he could not do.

The telephone buzzed and Winter put it to his ear. *"Guys, there's a black Caddy that pulled inside the lot, must be the covered wagon,"* Chet said. *"The driver is alone. He's too tall to be your guy."*

"His driver is picking her up," Winter said. "Chet, let me know if your guy can see her in the car when the Caddy leaves the garage. She's wearing a red and white ball cap and black leather jacket."

Hank kept going straight toward Canal Street after she turned and entered the lot.

Chet added, *"The van and Archer's sedan are rolling."*

"What do you want to do?" Hank asked, slowing.

"Pull over and wait for her to come out. What the hell else can we do?"

"There's no place to pull over," Hank told him. "Should I make the block?"

"I'm thinking!" Winter snapped. He spotted the feds seated in a white Taurus that was parked at the curb. Winter, having flown from New York with the agents, recognized them. The driver was yawning.

93

Winter had decided to run ahead of the Cadillac carrying Sean. While he had kept it in view, Hank drove to Manelli's country home on Lake Pontchartrain, north of the Mississippi River. Hank pulled off the road and parked on a driveway that wound through a wooded lot across the road from Manelli's place.

Gazing between the trees through the binoculars, Winter had a view of the gatehouse and the driveway up to where it passed behind the hills. The deputy following the van had told them that the FBI caravan, now including the second Bucar, the Taurus, was parked just off the Interstate behind a Texaco station a mile away. Winter didn't think they were close enough to protect Sean.

Manelli's Cadillac came flying up the road, turned right at the intersection, and pulled up to the gate, which opened to allow the car to enter, then closed behind it. Winter, studying the lone gatekeeper, saw him reach up by the gate shack door and flip a lever before the Cadillac pulled away. The operator didn't move but watched the car. The vehicle slowed to a crawl to cross a low bridge, then the Cadillac sped off. Winter swung the binoculars back to watch the gatehouse and saw the keeper flip the lever back in the original position, then go back inside.

Winter had nothing but respect for Sean's bravery, her calmness under fire and her intelligence. He didn't want to interfere unless he was sure she was going to be harmed.

What was eating at him now was the fact that Sam Manelli had a well-earned reputation for staying one step ahead of everybody, so reckless or suicidal behavior—like bringing Sean Devlin to his home and killing her there—simply didn't make sense. Once Sean was inside his compound, Sam would be cornered, and if he killed her, he'd be stuck with the corpse of a person the agents knew was alive when she'd arrived.

Both Hank and Winter had binoculars up to their eyes.

"She's in the car, all right," Hank said. "I can see her cap."

"The guard at the gate flipped that lever again after the car passed the bridge," Winter said.

"Some sort of signal, maybe? An alarm?"

"I don't know. Something about the bridge."

The FBI radios fell silent after Archer learned that the

Cadillac was back on Manelli's property. So far, according to the reports from "ears" to Archer, Sean had remained silent and only music had come over the air. After five minutes, Archer's calm voice came over the radio and asked for an update on the "cowgirl" and asked if the "range boss" was with her yet.

The voice filled the police radio. *"She's in there, sir. I heard the car doors and the barn door closing. No voices at all. Just kitchen sounds and singing."*

"She's singing?"

"No, a man."

"We wait for the words from the range boss," Archer said calmly. *"And then everybody will sit tight until I give the order to go in."*

"Something's wrong. I'm going in." Winter could no longer force himself to believe everything was all right. He took a pair of earplugs Hank had brought him and inserted them into his ear canals. The plugs were fitted with a valve designed to close at any sudden loud noise while allowing normal sounds to enter.

"Sam's guys'll shoot you for trespassing."

Winter's mind was suddenly filled with questions he needed answered. *Where are all those bodyguards? Why hasn't Sean said anything? How do I know they knew that Sam was in there before this started?*

"Cover me, Hank." Winter sprang from the Jeep, ran across the road, scaled the fence, and sprinted across the lawn toward the house. Trammel opened the window and aimed the AR-15 at the gatehouse as Winter ran. Hank watched Winter through the gray curtain of rain.

The guard, visible through a window, had his back to Winter and didn't see him, but a well-hidden FBI watcher did. The voice that had first announced the covered wagon leaving the barn came over the radio once again. *"Sir, Massey is over the fence, running toward the barn."*

Archer's curses filled the airwaves.

Hank pulled down the Velcro flaps exposing the large gold letters—U.S. MARSHAL—so the FBI didn't take him for an armed guard. Taking up the carbine, he climbed from the Jeep.

Hank was dropping down on the other side of the wrought-iron wall, when the caravan came roaring up the road from the interstate. Archer's Crown Victoria led, the Taurus third after the van. Archer's tires screamed as Finch made a sliding turn onto the road, then slammed to a stop at the gate. Archer held his badge out the window so the gatekeeper could see it.

As the gate opened, the step van arrived. A SWAT team member sprang out and wrestled the gatekeeper down, cuffing him. Archer blasted off down the driveway with the van trailing right behind him. The white sedan with FBI agents stopped to block the gate.

Hank crossed the wet grass heading for the driveway where it entered the hillocks surrounding the house. He was almost there when he heard an earsplitting explosion. He turned around to see Archer's Crown Victoria stopped and enveloped in a cloud of steam. Archer's head had made a six-quart-bowl-size impression in the passenger's side of the windshield.

The step van's driver swerved to avoid Archer's car, and went headlong into the gully. Its rear end rose dramatically as the grill slammed into the bank.

Hank stopped dead in his tracks, staring in disbelief.

The SWAT team members and FBI techs, who poured out the side door of the van and into the ditch, moved like they were injured, in shock, or both. As the steam faded, Hank saw that the front end of the Crown Victoria was mushroomed against the end of the bridge, which had risen into the air. There was little help he could offer them, but he lifted the phone and dialed Chet.

"You best order up a mess of ambulances to Manelli's

house, Chet," he said. "Damn near Archer's whole bunch is in need of medical attention."

Sure his efforts were best put elsewhere, Hank turned and ran up the driveway, following Winter.

Winter held his SIG out in a two-handed grip as he approached the Cadillac parked in front of Manelli's house. He peered in at the rear seat, where a lifelike dummy was secured by a lap belt. Sean had never been in the car at all. Sam had somehow gotten her; no matter what Winter had to do, he was going to find out where she was.

He was at the front door of the house when he heard two crashes behind him, but he ignored them. He went inside, moving rapidly down the wide hallway, following the sound of a man singing. He swung his gun, aiming from the hallway into every room as he moved toward the rear of the house. Winter shouldered the kitchen door aside and, stepping into the kitchen, aimed the SIG at the Cadillac's driver, who was wearing the Braves cap Sean had on when he had last seen her. The man sat at the counter over an open sandwich, with a cigarette hanging from his lips and a mayonnaise-smeared kitchen knife in his hand.

"U.S. marshal! Where's Manelli?" Winter demanded.

"It wasn't my turn to watch him," the man quipped. He set the knife down on a dish beside his dinner plate. Winter reached to the driver's shoulder holster and took out a heavy Colt Python revolver.

"I got a permit for that in my wallet."

Winter placed his gun in his own shoulder rig, cocked the revolver's hammer, and aimed the magnum at its owner's forehead. "Where is she? Where did Manelli take the woman?"

"Where's your warrant?" the man asked, unfazed. "Mr. Deputy, that pistol ain't a search warrant."

Winter shifted the magnum slightly and fired. The explosion was a muted *whomp* to Winter, thanks to the earplugs, but deafening for the driver. First vaporizing the lobe of the man's left ear, the bullet punched a black circle into the refrigerator door. The muzzle blast also blew the Braves cap off and left a comet-shaped powder burn the width of a silver dollar on his cheek. Blood trickled down the man's neck, staining his collar bright red.

The shocked driver reached slowly up to cover his ruined ear with his hand. "You *shot* me?"

"Wrong!" Winter yelled. "You shot yourself with your own gun and I couldn't stop you." Winter spoke loudly so the driver could hear him over the ringing in his ears. Immediately Winter swung the barrel to the left, aiming at the other ear. "And you are going to keep shooting pieces off yourself until you tell me where they are."

"You're a cop!" he shrieked.

"Not today."

"I don't knooow!" the man hollered, his terrorized eyes now the size of quarters.

Trammel exploded into the room aiming the AR-15 before him. He was red-faced, wet from the rain, and breathless, but obviously relieved to find Winter was all right.

"*He shot me!*" the driver wailed.

"He'll do that," Hank said. "I'll see you kids aren't interrupted." Hank pushed the door open and took up position behind the doorjamb so he could see down the hall to the front door and have cover.

"I swear ta God! I don't know! They took her off in the green van. That's all I know," he pleaded.

"*Who* took her?"

"I don't know!"

"Blow his dick off!" Trammel called out. "That's an order."

Winter dropped his aim accordingly and the man collapsed into a fetal position on the floor tiles. "What make van?" Winter yelled.

"I don't know where or why. An eyeless Ford! Mr. Sam and some of his guys."

"What do you mean, *eyeless?*"

Three ambulatory members of the SWAT team came in through the open front door and scattered through the house, yelling, "FBI! FBI!" Special Agent Finch hobbled in behind them.

"United States marshals!" Hank hollered.

The Crown Victoria's airbag had skinned Finch's forehead and nose, and he was walking like a hunchback in an old Frankenstein film. The knees of his trousers were open and bloody flesh was visible through the holes. He stared down at the driver and then up at Winter holding the driver's pistol. "Where are Manelli and Mrs. Devlin?" he asked. Finch managed to bow and lift the Braves cap by the bill from the floor. "This is our bug," he said. "Where is she now?"

"Manelli outsmarted you," Winter said acidly. "Did you people even make sure that he was here to begin with?"

"We didn't have enough time," Finch protested.

"She was never in his car! This putz put your cap on a dummy so you would think it was her. There's nobody else here—not so much as a guard. They are somewhere else, you idiot. Where's Archer?"

"There was some kind of a booby trap in the road. I never saw it. Archer's dead," Finch said solemnly.

"Know how you said that lever the guard threw before the Caddy rolled in might have something to do with that bridge? Winter, the end of that damn bridge shot straight up in the air and Finch here drove right slam into it—

Archer's head did its best to go through the windshield, but I guess it broke his fool neck," Hank said.

"He didn't have his belt on," Finch said defensively.

"House and basement are clear!" a voice yelled from the hallway, bringing Finch around a little.

"Maybe there's hidden doors, false walls...a secret cave," Finch said.

"Secret cave?" The driver, still lying on the floor, laughed.

"He knows where they are," Winter said, pointing down at the driver. "Leave us alone and I'll get it out of him."

"He's FBI," the driver said. "He ain't gonna let you shoot me no more. You crazy ass-bite. I'm suing all you bastards!"

Finch shook his head and stared at Winter. "You interfered with an FBI operation, Massey. The attorney general is going to—"

"The only thing I interfered with was that bastard making a sandwich, you moron," Winter snapped. He wanted to scream with rage and beat the truth out of the driver. The FBI had screwed up and he had followed right along with them. Finch sat down on a stool and stared at the half-made sandwich. The SWAT team leader came in. "The houth is keer, thir," he said. The words sounded wet and soft because he was missing his front teeth and his lips were like torn pillows filled with meat.

"Check all the walls for—" Finch started.

"Secret caves," Hank offered.

"We're done here," Winter said. "Let's go, Hank."

"You're both under arrest," Finch said.

"I got a permit," the driver said. "I wasn't doing nothing wrong and he shot me!"

"Massey, put that gun down," Finch said. "It's obvious that she informed the driver about the cap. No telling where she is."

"No way she did that," Winter snapped. He put the

driver's gun on the sandwich. "You think this is gonna stay a secret, Finch? I know Archer wanted Sam to kill Sean and that he planned to have your SWAT team kill Manelli. I know it and so does Director Shapiro, and soon the world will, too. You're finished and Archer is going to be glad he's dead. And if anything happens to her you'd better hide where I can't find you." Winter started from the room with Hank behind him.

"Hawt!" The jar-headed SWAT team leader aimed his MP5 at Winter's back.

"You planning to stop me, Finch, you tell him to kill me."

"Let them go," Finch said, resigned.

Winter stopped at the open door to Sam's den. On his way up the hall earlier, he had looked in. Now he was drawn into the room by the multiple cabinets packed with guns.

95

Sean clenched the wheel as she steered through the French Quarter. Two blocks from the parking garage, light bloomed in her periphery and, seconds later, again. She could only pray the aspirin tablets could stop the migraine, or slow it. She cursed herself for having left her pills behind at the hotel in Arlington. *Dear God, not now.* Archer either hadn't believed she was getting sick or didn't care. She fought back the urge to panic.

Squinting now just to see, Sean drove up to the fourth floor of the garage, where the Cadillac's driver, facing her from the far ramp, flashed his headlights at her. The brilliant lights brought the headache whipping into her brain like a tornado. Sean pulled into the first open space, her left tire rolling up over the concrete stop. In her pocket she carried a note that she had written in her hotel room: *FBI following me. I'll call after I shake them.* All she had to do was somehow get Archer's stupid baseball cap inside the Cadillac while the driver was reading the note. If the FBI would just follow the Caddy a few blocks—long enough for her to get away. She had made no plans beyond surviving the day.

The plan. She fought to keep her thoughts ordered despite the pain in her head. She wanted nothing but to curl up in the backseat.

She forced herself to climb from her car, steadying herself by putting her left hand on the roof. The driver slid the window down. She was looking at him as though through a dimly lit tunnel. She had the note clenched in her fist, but before she could pass it on, she was aware of the sounds of someone approaching fast. Before she could turn, a hand covered her mouth. Another set of hands felt her roughly all over. Someone snatched off her cap and she caught sight of a man opening the Cadillac's back door and slipping the hat on a figure seated in the rear. While the men wrestled her inside a van parked nearby, the Cadillac pulled off, tires chirping. She was trying to fight, to escape. *This is all wrong! Not yet! Please, God!* The men pressed her into the bench seat between them and one of them belted her in.

"Calm down before you hurt yourself," Sam Manelli said from the seat just behind Sean. He leaned forward, his warm breath on her neck. "We jus' give the feds a little time to get after the car."

Through the pain and darkness, she managed to say, "Migraine."

She was aware that the guard beside her handed Sam the note she had failed to pass to the driver. As he read it, he squeezed her shoulder with his free hand. Behind her, a radio came to life. *"Covered wagon is headed to the barn. Cowgirl is in the back. Signal track is ten-ten."*

"The FBI is all idiots," Sam said with total conviction as he crushed the note into a ball.

Through the curtain of pain in her skull, Sean was aware of these things: that her neck was surrounded by Sam's thick arm, that if he chose he could crush the life out of her, and that she was helpless to do anything about it.

"Go by Merle's place," Sam instructed the driver. The driver crossed Canal and parked in an alley off Baronne Street. Sam stepped out of the van and the man in the front passenger seat accompanied him to a door. Sean closed her eyes. After what seemed like a couple of minutes, Sam and his bodyguard returned. As he climbed in, Sam handed a paper bag to the man seated beside Sean. Sean had to squint to see what was happening. The man reached into the sack to remove a syringe already filled with a few CCs of liquid.

"Please," Sean pleaded in a whisper.

"Doc said this will fix a migraine headache," Sam said.

The man slipped the covering from the needle and held her arm stiffly in place. Sean resisted until she felt the sting of the needle.

Sam placed his hands on either side of her head and rubbed gently. "How's your headache now?"

"Don't hurt me, Sam. I didn't know...."

She was fully expecting Sam to increase the pressure until it hurt worse than the headache. "You sleep a little now, and when you wake up you're going to tell me what I need to know. Then you won't have nothing to worry about."

One thought rang out in her clouded mind. *Winter will come.*

As the van headed away from New Orleans, she closed her eyes and slept.

When Sean awakened, the headache was a dull shadow of its former self. She was in a dimly lit room, lying on a wide bed. She sat up and looked around. When she realized exactly where she was, fear seized her. This was a room she had been in before. It was Sam Manelli's bedroom.

Winter concentrated. The photographs in Sam's den depicted the gangster with various other men in hunting outfits over the years. One man with prematurely silver hair appeared in several of the pictures—Winter figured it was Manelli's underboss, Johnny Russo. In one picture there was a green Ford van behind the men. An elderly black worker standing by the van wore a coat with INTERNATIONAL LIQUID STORAGE emblazoned on the back.

"Might be smart to get the hell out of here, Winter."

"And go where, Hank?"

"Get with Chet. Run down Manelli's possible hideouts listed in the files. Warehouses, offices, those kind of—"

"No time. He'll find out about this soon or he'll finish his business with her and have an airtight alibi. We have to get to him fast."

Winter was studying the items in the room like a tourist in a museum. He noted a lodge in the background of several pictures and a boathouse in others. "I'd bet when Sam got his hands on Sean he took her where he feels secure."

Winter was thinking and trying to decompress, to ditch the frustration and anger he felt. He had to distance himself emotionally, to depersonalize Sean, but he kept seeing her in his mind—at the mercy of butchers and knowing that nobody was in any better position to help her than he was. If he was going to help her, he had to forget that this was anything but a riddle to solve.

"Manelli is a sadist. He went to a great deal of expense and effort to kill her and Dylan. He believes that Dylan and Sean were responsible for putting him in jail, and almost taking down his empire. Manelli will take his time with her. He'll need to find out what she told and to who. He'll want to show off his power over her, his reach, his cunning, his winning out in the end like he always has. I suspect he'll want to do everything to her he wasn't able to do to Dylan. Fact is, our only chance to save her is if he keeps her alive as long as he can to torture her. We need time and a lucky break."

Hank crossed the room and joined Winter to stare at a large satellite picture in a heavy cypress frame. It was a remarkably crisp aerial photograph of rural, industrial acreage. The photo was centered around a storage tank farm.

"You used to be able to call NASA and order one of these on a whole city, or just your neighborhood. I saw a picture just like this in the offices of an oil exploration company of an operation in Alaska. You could see elk grazing in it, not a quarter mile from the derricks." Hank touched the glass. "That's a towboat pushing a double line of barges. Mississippi River."

Winter studied a tanker moored at a dock from which three large white pipes ran up and through the levee, then over the road before they dropped down on the other side of a fence and entered a building. Smaller pipes exited the control house and channeled liquids out to each of the thirty storage tanks, each capable of holding maybe millions of gallons. A black lid on a tank had the company's initials painted on it in white letters. When he spotted something at the edge of the marsh, outside and south of the farm's fences, he took the picture down from the wall. "I know where she is, Hank." He twisted it—the glass breaking as the frame snapped apart. He pulled the picture out, folded it and slipped it into his jacket.

A SWAT team member standing in the hall ignored them as they passed. As soon as they reached asphalt, they ran back up the driveway and across the grass, toward the Jeep. As they crossed the road they saw the red lights of approaching ambulances.

Injured SWAT team members and dazed technicians were huddled near Archer's corpse. Through the drizzle, they looked like wet birds on a line, waiting for the sun.

97

The plane was parked on the tarmac east of the sixty-foot-tall Quonset-shaped hangar. The four cutouts in dark all-weather coats disembarked carrying equipment cases, which they loaded into the rear of an ebony Chevrolet Suburban 4x4 before driving off. The rain obscured their view of Lake Pontchartrain and the twin bridges that stretched twenty-five miles to the north shore, but they weren't on a sight-seeing mission.

Thirty minutes after leaving Lakefront Airport, Lewis turned off River Road onto the road marked only by a NO TRESPASSING sign. He was only a quarter-mile short of the tank farm but couldn't see the tanks through the wall of gray. The road he turned off on had been built to give access to the property when the owners had wanted to turn it into a business park. The oil bust in the late '80s had ended the developer's dream.

During the half-mile drive down the narrow road, the quartet passed two more signs warning illegal dumpers to void their truck beds elsewhere and one promising prosecution to the fullest extent for depositing waste.

Lewis glanced in the rearview at Apache, his eyes drinking in her features. She was beautiful and no more than five-five. She had sharply defined muscles, long flowing black hair, narrow lips, and high cheekbones. Her professional name was Apache because she was half Apache and half African-American, raised by a whiskey-blind grandfather. She had been discovered by talent scouts who spotted her in an FBI arrest report. She had been arrested for taking on four large white men who were imposing their will on her when she took a folding knife from one of them. She had sent three of them to the hospital and one to the morgue. Later, she had taken on three reservation cops—two of whom she disarmed and handcuffed together before the third clubbed her unconscious with a weighted nightstick.

The paved road ended at a cul-de-sac surrounded by what appeared to be a good start on a mountain range constructed entirely of rubbish.

Tomeo sat in the backseat next to Apache. He was Chinese-American and wore his thick black hair combed straight back. He was almost six feet tall and had been a Navy SEAL. His easy smile and sense of humor gave people the impression that he was the opposite of what he actually was.

Mickey, the team's fourth member was in the front passenger seat. "We've got company," he said.

"I see him," Lewis said evenly.

A battered Ford pickup truck of indeterminable color was backed into a tall horseshoe of garbage. A short, bandy-legged man wearing a yellow plastic rain poncho stood beside the open tailgate trying to look innocent of violating warning signs against dumping refuse. Lewis parked the big Suburban broadside to the truck, blocking it in, and lowered his window. Trapped, the man took tentative steps toward the invading vehicle, peering out from under the poncho's plastic hood.

Lewis lowered the window and studied the man. He could have been in his fifties or seventies—the lack of teeth made guessing his age difficult. Beneath a crop of wild white hair, his face was crisscrossed with crevasses and he peered at Lewis through eyes whose muddy irises appeared to have been laid in ancient ivory.

"How y'all do nah?" he inquired, grinning uncertainly.

"You taking that trash out for me," Lewis said, "or dumping?"

"I was taking," the dumper replied, nodding suddenly as though the motion was necessary to power his next breath. "Lots a good stuff in here people trow away, you know." He opened his arms like a welcoming store owner.

"No signs threatening anyone for taking the shit away," Tomeo said.

"This heah you place?" the man asked, his voice cracking. "I don't mean no trespass atall."

"You out here alone in this nasty weather?" Lewis asked him.

"Yeah, was jus' bout to leave out wit' my little load here."

A broad-faced pit bull with chewed-up pyramid-shaped ears leaped down from the truck's open window and approached the strangers in the Chevrolet. He stopped beside his master and measured the Suburban's occupants by sniffing the air with his upraised nose. Not liking what he discerned, he growled and the hair on his neck rose.

"He don't bite, though," the man said. "Get on back in the truck, Badger," he said. "We be going now, if you let us pass on by."

"I never cared for dogs," Lewis told the man.

"He all right, though, this one," the man said defensively.

"They're plain stupid. Don't know when to growl and when not to."

"Don't we have work to do?" Apache sounded annoyed.

Lewis looked in the rearview at Apache in the seat directly behind him. His hand rose to the window's ledge. He squeezed the trigger before the man standing in the rain saw the pistol. The SOCOM's silenced bark was not much louder than the sound of the dog falling over on its side. Its stiff legs quivered. The dumper was speechless, his now-open mouth a hole ringed in pink gums.

"What you wan' do dat for?" the old man asked.

"I like your clothes," Lewis said. "Take 'em off."

The dumper slowly removed his coat and handed it to Lewis through the window. He pulled off the flannel shirt, his boots, and his overalls, and Lewis took each with his free hand while maintaining his aim.

The old man stood bent and shivering in the rain beside his dog. He looked down at the animal and crossed himself. Before he looked back up, Lewis squeezed the trigger twice again, making holes in the old man's throat and in the silver triangle of hair between his breasts. The dumper took two steps back and collapsed.

"Aw, Lewis, that was fucking cold, man," Tomeo said. "You should have done the old guy first."

"Why?" Lewis asked.

Apache shifted in her seat. "Because, Lewis, that old man just watched you clip his best friend. He died knowing that his dog was dead," Apache said. "For Christ's sake, it's like shooting a child in front of its mother."

"I did it to spare the dog's feelings," Lewis said. "That noble beast died thinking he was protecting his master."

"What's wrong with shooting a kid in front of its mother?" Mickey said jokingly. "I mean, if shooting a kid was necessary."

Lewis said, "Guys, go give our dearly departed the burial they so richly deserve."

The men opened their doors, jumped out and carried the man's body off into the garbage, where they covered him over with a wet piece of carpet and piled that over with a tire and black trash bags. Tomeo grabbed the dog by its back legs and, like an Olympic hammer thrower, swung him in a circle before releasing the thick carcass to sail off into the refuse.

Mickey and Tomeo returned to the Suburban, which drove across the field to the tree line some one hundred yards north of the dump site. They parked deep enough inside the woods so there was little chance of the vehicle being spotted.

Lewis killed his headlights and, with the rear doors open, the four changed into their assault suits, impervious to the cold rain and the thick smell of rotting vegetation drifting in from the open marsh.

"Time to sell some death," Lewis said.

98

Hank drove the Jeep as fast as it could go and still remain on the wet asphalt. Winter trusted Hank's skills, which allowed him to concentrate on the purloined satellite photo. Chet had stayed on the telephone so he and they could plan the best way to accomplish the rescue of Sean Devlin with a minimum of casualties.

What Winter had seen in the satellite picture was five flat rectangles of uniform size out in the flooded marshland behind the tank farm. He instantly recognized them as duck-hunting blinds. He then spotted the roofs of two buildings set in a one-hundred-yard-wide strip of trees running alongside a drainage canal. The canal was open to the marsh through a series of channels. The smaller roof looked like a boathouse with a dock extended out from it near the mouth of a channel, which would allow the hunters to take boats directly from there out to the blinds. The larger roof had a chimney on the end facing the marsh and was farther back from the water. Winter's only hope was that the lodge and boat shed he had seen in the pictures of hunters posing with dead ducks on Sam's den wall were the same buildings represented by the flat roofs in the satellite photo.

Winter had been talking to Chet about needing to find the tank farm where the letters ILS were painted on the top of one of the larger storage tanks. Chet said, "Sure I know exactly where ILS is. It's out River Road about fifteen miles." That was when Winter realized that the driver had already told him where Manelli was heading. When Winter had asked Manelli's driver what the make of the green van carrying Sam was, the man had said, "Ford," and he had then said what Winter thought was "eyeless." *Eyeless* was how the locals pronounced the initials ILS. The lodge was just behind the tank farm.

Chet procured a helicopter. The assault force was waiting for it to come in from Callender Field naval air station to pick them up and deliver them to Manelli's duck lodge. The sky was overcast and it was raining, but Chet had been assured that the ceiling was ample for the helicopter to stay below the cloud cover and above obstructions. After the assault was under way, more of Chet's deputies would come in by way of the tank farm's front gate.

The tank farm was a several-hundred-acre rectangle of land that had been cleared so nothing obstructed the views of the giant white containers from the company's offices. A line of oak trees stretching along the highway was probably there to make the facility look less threatening—less like a collection of circular bombs waiting for a spark. The fence, an unbroken silver line in the picture, backed up to a wooded area where the lodge and boathouse were located.

"Chet," Winter said into the cell phone. "According to this picture, the fences on both sides of the tank farm run all the way back across the drainage canal and stop in the marsh. The farm's back fence connects the sides and puts

Manelli's place smack in a shallow U of fence. The main way in is through the tank farm, down the paved access road to the back where it turns into dirt and goes through a gate onto Sam's place. We can't go in that way, but when you guys come in you can land just outside that gate. We'll try and get behind them and help you from inside after we make sure *they're* in there."

Winter hung up. "Okay, Hank. The parcel just before you get to the terminal was cleared almost back to the canal. There's a paved road on that property that dead-ends in a cul-de-sac. Looks like they were dumping trash there when this was taken. We can drive back to the trees and go in that way." Winter looked up. "We should be coming up on it any second. That's the turnoff up there."

"Forget it," Hank said.

"Son of a bitch." Winter felt like hitting something.

Through the gray rain, a black Suburban 4x4 with tinted windows was turning onto the access road. "Keep going. Could be some of Manelli's people patrolling. We'll have to go in from the other side."

As Hank drove past the INTERNATIONAL LIQUID STORAGE sign, Winter surveyed the main buildings. "There are uniformed guards in the gatehouse window, and those gates could stop a bulldozer."

"This is it," Hank said as they passed the corner of the ILS fence where dense woods ran up to within ten feet of the road. Hank pulled onto the shoulder. "Good news is there's an access road of sorts. The bad news is, I can see the road because somebody recently smashed the grass down."

"Stay in their ruts."

Hank cut the Jeep's lights before he turned off River Road and, holding the Jeep in previously formed tracks in the tall grass, entered the woods.

"Take it slow, Hank. Let's don't run up on anybody."

"I been sneaking up on shitheads for forty years, two of

those long-range recon in 'Nam. Except for Millie, I ain't been caught yet."

"Wives don't count." Winter managed to laugh, but his stomach was lurching.

"It's going to be dark as eight inches up a bull's ass in a few minutes." Hank wound the Jeep through the trees. Where foliage was thin, the massive white storage tanks offered Winter the opportunity to figure their position using the picture for reference. He could only see by using a map light.

"More than one vehicle went in," Hank said. "Grass is pressed down in this direction so they didn't come back out this way. At least three cars, maybe four."

"Was one a green van?" Winter joked.

"Be nice to have some backup about now. This place is flat spooky. You know, it's been a long time since I was in a scrape and this has the potential to get very ugly. I just hope I can still give a decent account of myself."

"You're fifth-generation Texas border-ranching scrappers. What the hell else could you possibly do but give a decent account of yourself?"

"I meant comparatively speaking. We've never faced anything like this together."

"Then it's about time."

"Just try not to make me look bad in front of anybody."

Winter laughed. Hank turned left off the logging road, threaded the Jeep fifty feet through the trees, and cut the engine. Walking was a lot safer because the wet grass muted the sound of their footsteps on the dead leaves.

"If Sam was listening in on Archer's tactical channel like we were, I hope Finch hasn't been talking about us on it. I heard them mention your name when they saw you jumping that fence."

"Finch doesn't know about the lodge—unless he's a psychic."

Hank dialed Chet while Winter folded the satellite picture and pushed it between the console and seat.

After Hank listened to Chet, he ended the call. "Chet's highway patrol captain has set up 'license check' roadblocks east and west of us to seal River Road. He has EMS standing by and he's less than an hour away depending on how long it takes the chopper to gas up and get there."

"They don't keep them fueled?"

"The first chopper had a problem. The alternative is for them to drive in, and they'd be at least that long coming by road."

"Chopper's crucial for surprise," Winter said. "Let's go."

Winter and Hank got out. They opened the rear end for the shotgun and Winter's quilt-lined, water-resistant jacket. Both men wore dark baseball caps for the limited rain protection they offered. They closed the rear and vacated the Jeep, carrying their long guns like hunters.

They walked on the tire depressions to avoid the undergrowth, moving at a brisk clip. The intensity of light grew as they approached the edge of the woods where the marshland was open beyond the drainage canal. They paused where the woods stopped some fifty feet from the water. Out beyond the algae-covered canal lay the marsh—a tortured, nightmarish wasteland where solitary trees stood on islands, blackened and decaying.

"Bingo," Hank whispered.

Fresh tire impressions led up to, and beyond, a double gate in the ten-foot-tall hurricane fence. There was a small sign wired to links that read, NO TRESPASSING.

The gate was closed, but the heavy chain and padlock meant that they would have to climb the fence or get into the canal to get to Manelli's place.

Winter saw no evidence of guards. "I'll lead over the gate while you cover me," Winter whispered. "Hand signals only from now on."

Hank nodded his agreement.

As Winter approached the gate, he heard a snap and turned to find himself looking down the barrel of a shotgun held by a young bald man wearing a camouflage suit that had allowed him to blend with the foliage. The fellow couldn't have been more than nineteen or twenty years old. At the sound of a whistle behind him, Winter turned his head slowly to see another man aiming his shotgun at Hank's head. The men's pump guns were painted in olive-and-gray camouflage to match the hunting outfits.

The bald man jerked up his gun's barrel, obviously telling them to put their hands up.

"You boys out duck hunting?" Hank asked. "You know, son, you could be Rudolph Valentino's greatest grandson. Your buddy over there looks kind of like a young Yul Brynner. Actor from *The King and I?*" He mumbled, "Before your time, I suppose."

Yul was oblivious to the raindrops splashing against his head. His eyes were like cherry pits. His mud-slathered loafers looked ridiculous with his hunting outfit.

The young man Hank had called Valentino looked older than his partner. His coat's hood was up but pushed back so his peripheral vision wasn't hampered. He barked a phrase in Italian and, using his gun, also motioned for them to raise their hands.

"Want my hands up?" Hank raised his hands slowly. "Up?"

"*Sì,* make all hand op. You op hand, *bastardo!*"

Valentino pressed his shotgun's barrel under Hank's chin while he took the AR-15 carbine from Hank and slung it over his shoulder. As deftly as a pickpocket, he unzipped and reached into Hank's coat, and one by one, extracted the .45 Colt auto, handcuffs, the cell phone, and Hank's badge case, putting each object into his own coat's pocket. After Valentino patted Hank down to his cowboy boots, Yul relieved Winter of his shotgun, his SIG, his cuffs and the Walther PP. While Yul was kneeling to check Winter's pant legs for weapons, Winter looked down through the open V of the bulky camouflage coat and spotted the grip of a semiautomatic handgun tucked inside Yul's belt.

As the guards marched them toward the gate, Valentino put two fingers against his teeth and emitted an earsplitting whistle. A third man, holding a high-powered semiautomatic deer rifle, strode through the tall grass from the direction of Sam's lodge. He was well over six feet tall and his black hair, glistening with raindrops, hung to his wide shoulders. Winter thought maybe it was his long narrow nose that made the big man's eyes seem too close together.

"Big boy," Hank said.

"*Silenzio!*" Valentino snapped. He poked the barrel of his shotgun so hard into Winter's back that only the vest kept the jab from drawing blood.

"Spiro," Valentino said, announcing the giant.

Spiro swung open the gate and stood glaring as the guards directed their captives through.

"This is all private property," Spiro said. He pulled the heavy chain around to join the center poles, then closed the large padlock.

"Finally somebody speaks English," Hank said. "Where I come from, it's rude to hold people at gunpoint."

"Where these guys come from, it's just like a handshake."

"*Polizia,*" Yul said.

"Of course they're cops," Spiro said sarcastically. "Who the fuck else would be stupid enough to come back here?"

The guards handed Spiro the badge cases and he inspected them in turn. "Deputy United States Marshal Trammel . . . and Deputy Winter Jay Massey." Spiro pocketed the badges, pulled a red cell phone from his pocket, and dialed. All he said was "Just two marshals."

Winter figured Valentino had been posted back alongside the logging road and followed them on foot to where Yul was waiting. Winter didn't miss the irony that he and Hank, like Archer's FBI earlier, hadn't bothered to watch behind them.

Winter had decided to let Hank do the talking because it would serve to keep their attention focused more on his partner, leaving Winter to look for an opportunity to turn the tables. Worst case, Chet would have to come in blind and rescue them along with Sean Devlin. Winter was thinking that when Chet's men hit the ground, maybe he and Hank could still help them from inside. It was nice to know that if Manelli or his people tried to leave the lodge, the Highway Patrol would be there waiting.

"You let us walk back through that gate and we'll forget the scatterguns in our faces. You can still stop this short of kidnapping federal law enforcement officers."

"Where's their bracelets?" Spiro asked. When the guards didn't respond, Spiro said, "Handcuffs."

Valentino said, "Handcuffs! *Sì*, handcuffs!" Valentino and then Yul handed the cuffs to the giant, reluctantly. Winter knew that with the three-foot width between Spiro's shoulders, it would have taken both pairs connected together to join Spiro's overlarge wrists behind his back.

"Hands behind your backs." Spiro cuffed the deputies with their own equipment. He unslung his rifle and placed it in the crook of his left arm. "These boys'll shoot you in the heads if you try *anything*. I'm probably not as good a shot as them, but this thirty-ought-six will go straight through both sides of those puny vests you're wearing."

Winter walked along the road toward the lodge, wondering how much worse things could get before Chet showed up—hoping he wouldn't find out.

99

The majority of Manelli's boathouse had been constructed on piles so it extended out over the canal. Although rain battered the boat shed's tin roof, once the door closed behind them, there was no sound from outside. A sudden chill filled Winter's hollow stomach.

"You sit down here, old man," Spiro told Hank. Pointing his finger in Winter's face then at the floor, he told him, "You there." Hank and Winter sat on the plywood floor six feet from each other. Winter kept his head down, but he had seen what he needed.

The boat shed's interior was one open space, thirty feet deep by twenty wide. A steel rack on the wall to Winter's right held four flat-bottom, one-man pirogues—stable marsh boats that, when loaded, needed only three or four inches of water to float. He and Hank faced an empty table and a workbench standing against the west wall. A propane torch, extra bottles of gas, a chain saw, a large wooden vise, pliers, an ice pick, a thin-bladed filet knife, a pair of limb-pruning loppers, a rubber mallet, and an old meat cleaver were neatly placed on its surface like surgical instruments in an operating room.

Behind them, a hinged four-by-eight-foot section of floor near the eastern wall had been opened. A steel cable from a motorized hoist attached to a ceiling beam disappeared into the rectangle of dark water. The guards took turns putting all of Hank and Winter's equipment on the sturdy table standing against the wall alongside the workbench. The young guards stared silently at their captives, guns ready, fingers on the triggers.

"Hey, Fabio!" Hank said.

Spiro frowned at the name. "Save it. Mr. Russo will be here in a minute." He slipped off his camouflage coat and laid it on the workbench.

"*Silenzio!*" Valentino commanded.

The door opened and Johnny Russo entered, water dripping from his trench coat. He merely glanced down at the deputies as he crossed to the table. He lifted Hank's cell phone, pressed a button, read the number from the display, and turned it off. He looked at the weapons, using the flat of his index fingernail, he flipped open one of the badge cases.

Russo said, "What you fellows up to, besides trespassing?"

"We were checking out the place next door," Hank said.

"The last number you called—who was it to?"

"I ordered pizza," Hank said. "They should be delivering it shortly and we can all share it."

"Next smart-ass shit to come out your face is gonna cost you some teeth, old man."

"What's this old man crap. I'm only fifty-seven."

Russo's eyes flashed his impatience and he snapped his fingers loudly in warning.

"Local deputy," Hank said. "For directions."

"How'd you know about this place?"

"An assistant attorney general just said that some judge was overheard talking about this place and how Manelli hunts ducks here. We're scouting because the attorney general is thinking about planting some listening gear in those blinds in time for duck season. He was thinking that Manelli—"

"*Mr.* Manelli to you," Russo snarled, his face reddening.

"That *Mr.* Manelli might talk business while he was in a duck blind."

"The FBI didn't send you?"

"Why would the FBI tell us anything? We're glorified errand boys doing whatever the judges can dream up or nobody else wants to do; like come out in shit like this and be bullied by people like you. Look, Mr. Rosco, we didn't know anybody was back here today."

"Mr. Manelli is retired from anything any prosecutor would be interested in," Russo replied, oblivious to the slight.

"I must have missed the announcement in the *Mafia Gazette*. I don't give a bird fart about *Mr.* Manelli, you, or your gun boys."

Russo turned to Winter. "The old guy telling the truth, fellow?"

Winter nodded. He didn't believe Russo would do anything to them given the fact that he didn't know who else was around. The duck blind story seemed reasonable enough.

"Let us go and we'll get off Mr. Manelli's land," Hank told Russo.

Russo laughed expansively. "I just bet you would."

"Let me talk to *him*," Hank said.

"Tell you what I will do. I'll tell you a story. Once upon a time," Russo started, obviously enjoying himself, "there were two dumb-ass deputies who, just after they called their local deputy pal, drove right off into the canal. The older man was driving—bad eyes, no headlights, and the rain and all—and he panicked when the water rose so they both drowned in their car, screaming like women."

Hank said, "We swim real good."

"If you can swim out of this, you're way past good."

"Listen, you can't be so stupid you think you can just kill federal officers," Hank said. "You, *Mr.* Manelli, and these other freaks will be on death row before you can kiss a cat's ass."

"It's been a rotten week for you marshals," he said smiling maliciously. "I doubt two more dead feds will make much difference."

"Mr. Manelli is not going to like it when he takes a fall for your knee-jerk decision," Hank said.

Russo replied, "I doubt he'll give it any thought. Nobody is ever going to know I was here today."

Winter turned his head to watch Russo cross to the winch and grab the dangling command bar. When he pressed the up button, the spool turned and a large moss-encrusted steel cage emerged from the water. Dark brown crabs fell through the grid and rained back into the water, leaving behind an enormous bone with quills of shredded tissue standing from it.

We are not going to die here. We will find Sean alive, and this sadistic bastard and Manelli will pay for everything they have done, Winter told himself.

Russo unlatched and threw open the top of the cage, wiping his hands together to dry them. "Give them ten minutes each, Spiro. Then get these young men to help you put them in their car and drive it into the canal on the other side of the fence. Then you come back to the lodge."

"Sure," Spiro said. "It'll take a while to lug them back to their car."

Russo stared at the cage, thinking.

"After you drown them, go get their fucking car and bring it to the canal. Then put them in and submarine it." Russo inclined his head toward the two guards. "On second thought, just drown the fuckers and throw 'em off into the canal. I mean, who gives a shit."

"Sure, okay," Spiro said, nodding slowly. "I get it."

"Do it, then!" Russo snapped. "Then come back to the lodge."

Russo started for the door. "Gotta run." Waving his hands and snapping his fingers, he said something to Yul in Italian. The guards listened intently, waited for him to finish and nodded. "*Sì,*" Yul told him.

"*Addio,*" Russo said, saluting the young guard like a soldier.

After he left, Yul turned to Valentino and said *"La testa della scimmia."* Valentino snickered.

Winter watched over his shoulder as Spiro leaned his high-powered rifle against the wall near the winch.

Hank winked at Winter before he shifted so he was facing Spiro.

Spiro stared at Hank, then raised his hands high over his head, made fists, and brought his arms, like bird's wings, down slowly until his fists were knuckle to knuckle. His red T-shirt looked like it was painted on his torso. As he repeated the motion with his arms, his muscles seemed to inflate and the tendons in his neck stood out like steel wires. His face trembled and his eyes looked as though they might fly from their sockets. The guards exchanged looks, fighting back laughter.

Valentino told Yul something else in Italian and they both snickered.

"Let's get this over with," Spiro said, crossing to Winter.

"You don't speak Italian? Kind of like Spanish, especially the insults," Hank told Spiro as the giant moved to where Winter sat with his shoulders hunched.

"Come on, boy. Time to swim." Spiro knocked Winter's cap off and grabbed him by the shoulders.

"That bald boy called you a queer."

"I don't give a happy shit what that gibberish means." But the giant's tight lips showed he did very much care.

"Don't have to get your panties in a twist. They say steroids shrink up your dick to where it looks like a newborn's."

Winter kept his head down, fighting the urge to look directly into Spiro's eyes.

"Technically speaking, it isn't an insult if it's true," Hank told Spiro. "Oh, they don't have to speak English to know you'd suck a dick. That squaw-looking hair. I bet you got sphincter muscles that'd pinch the head off a catfish."

"Watch out, old man!" Spiro warned.

"A hundred dollars says when you smell Old Spice you get a hard-on."

"Shut up, he's going to kill us!" Winter exploded. "This is all your fault."

"He's a faggot and it's my fault?"

Spiro released Winter's shoulders and turned to Hank. Winter lowered his head and started rocking in place. The handcuff key in his shirt pocket might have been in the marsh for all the good it would do him.

Spiro wagged his finger at Hank. "You're trying to get me to lose my shit and break you up so people could know it wasn't no car accident. You're wasting your time. I ain't stupid."

"Even that moron *Rosco* knows you're stupid. I just wanted one last blow job and I know you'll give it to me."

"It's Russo, you . . ." Spiro dropped down on one knee and punched Hank hard in his stomach.

Hank fought to catch his breath. "Foreplay . . . be damned, then."

"Please don't kill me," Winter pleaded. The young guards laughed at him.

"Jesus Christ," Hank said. "This muscle woman isn't smart enough to work that cage. You're more likely to die of old age while we're waiting for this idiot to figure out the controls. Duh, boss, it'll take a really long time to carry them back to their car," Hank mocked.

Spiro grabbed the collar of Hank's coat, dragged him over the floor to the cage, and lifted him. Hank kicked him in the shin, but Spiro didn't seem to feel it. He shoved Hank into the space, then latched the door while Hank kicked against it. Spiro grabbed the winch's control wand, flipped the toggle to raise the cage up, and let it swing over the water.

"The crabs got your blow job, old man."

Hank started yelling in Spanish. *"Oh no, no aspira mi pene!"* Oh, no, Kill me, kill me! I'd rather be dead! The guards may not have understood Hank's Spanish or the English exactly, but they were laughing. *"Sta dicendo che è gonna fuck lui!"* Hank howled.

Yul stood facing the cage with his left shoulder to Winter. He was aiming his shotgun in Winter's general direction, but his attention was focused on Hank and Spiro. Valentino was between Yul and the cage, with his back to Winter. His shotgun rested in the crook of his arm, barrel pointing at the floor.

As Winter had hoped, the guards didn't perceive him as a threat—Hank was doing a perfect job holding their attention. Spiro, too consumed with anger to think of anything but making Hank suffer the only way he could, started to lower the cage slowly into the water, stopping the winch and then starting it again.

Winter slipped his cuffed hands under his buttocks and feet and sprang behind Yul. Before the bald young man could react, Winter looped his handcuffed arms over the young man's head and shoulders and gripped the shotgun. Covering Yul's trigger finger with his own, Winter had his left hand flat against the receiver for leverage.

Powered with a burst of adrenaline born of fear and anger, Winter overcame Yul's resistance and swung the gun's barrel to bear on Valentino.

As Winter sprang, Valentino turned, reflexively raising his own gun. Without any choice, he fired at his partner just as Winter pressed Yul's finger against the trigger.

Ba-boom! The shotguns' reports overlapped.

The blast from Valentino's Wingmaster punched a fist-size hole through Yul's chest, and the buckshot hit Winter's vest with the force of a mule's kick. He landed on his back with Yul's dead weight on top of him.

Winter's blast hit Valentino wide of his chest. He pivoted hard and fell backward, landing against the wall, six feet from the opening in the floor. The blast had blown the guard's right arm clean off below his shoulder. The naked arm lay on the floor, its hand still gripping the gun's stock.

Spiro released the control wand and turned to the carnage like a bear in the ring. The cage continued to descend and Hank, who was fast disappearing into the murky water, hollered, "Go, boy!" before the cage vanished in a stew of bubbles.

Winter found himself beneath Yul with no chance of pumping the shotgun to rearm the chamber. He released the weapon and pulled his cuffed hands back over the dead guard's head.

Valentino seemed to be staring at his appendage lying just beyond his boots. Blood sprayed out through the open sleeve to the rhythm of his beating heart.

Spiro jerked Yul's shotgun away by the barrel and slung it across the room. He grabbed the corpse by a foot and pulled Yul off Winter. Winter drew his feet back and, when Spiro lunged at him, he kicked out hard, splitting open the big man's chin like he'd used a knife.

Winter rolled away, made it to his feet, and went for his SIG on the table. Spiro caught him from behind before he got there. The enraged giant locked his massive arms around Winter's chest and, when Spiro squeezed him, Winter thought his ribs would cave in.

"You like that, you fuck?" Spiro raged.

Winter drove the back of his skull against Spiro's nose crushing the cartilage and simultaneously stomped his heels down on Spiro's toes.

Most men would have let go. Spiro merely loosened his grip for a fraction of a second, but just long enough so Winter—his arms pinned and useless—could twist around to face his captor. Spiro's nose and chin were bleeding. Face-to-face, Spiro met Winter's eyes, smiled, and squeezed harder.

Winter sank his teeth into Spiro's narrow nose and shook his head violently. He felt the tip of Spiro's nose separate, then spit the grape-size nugget out and bit down on Spiro's chin. Spiro released Winter and grabbed his damaged nose, howling.

You . . . like that . . . you fuck? With his hands outstretched, Winter stumbled toward the table again after his gun. He had seconds to get Hank up, and he'd have to put Spiro to sleep to accomplish that. He made it to the table and grabbed his SIG by the barrel.

Spiro caught him by the neck of his coat and slung him away from the table.

The handgun flew away toward the workbench.

Winter landed beside Yul's body and managed to reach inside the dead man's coat to grab the gun from his belt.

Spiro went for his high-powered rifle still leaning against the wall next to Valentino. He jerked the weapon up to his shoulder and whirled to aim down at Winter. "Now, you fuck!" he howled, tears streaming down his cheeks. "You fucking, fucking . . . fuck . . . FUUUCK!"

"Wait!" Winter yelled. "Russo said to drown me!"

Spiro hesitated.

Bringing the Browning Hi-Power up from behind Yul's prone body, Winter gave the giant a triple tap. Spiro fell sideways into the water, leaving most of his brains behind.

Winter set aside the Hi-Power, scurried over, grabbed the control wand, and flipped the toggle from down to up. The wheel pulled the cage up out of the water, pushing Spiro's floating corpse aside.

"What took you so long?" Hank sputtered. "My damn boots are ruined."

Winter reversed the winch and guided the descending cage to the floor. He helped Hank out. The older marshal looked around the room, surveying the carnage. "Son . . . you have made . . . one hell of a mess."

Winter reached into his pocket to get his handcuff key to unlock his cuffs.

"You tired?" Hank said, after Winter had unlocked his cuffs.

"I'm getting my second wind."

"What happened to your mouth?" he asked Winter after seeing Spiro's blood on him.

"Nosebleed." Using his coat sleeve, Winter wiped the blood off.

Winter lifted his SIG from the floor and pushed it into his holster, snapping the thumb break closed. Water dripping from his clothes, Hank took up his Colt from the table and holstered it.

"My boots are so full of water they're gonna hear us coming a mile off. Best I—"

Boom! A sharp report filled the room and Hank collapsed.

Winter turned and saw the barrel of the Ruger KP-90 drop to Valentino's leg, and Valentino's head fall forward—his chin against his chest.

At some point, while Winter was busy, the guard had freed his semiautomatic and, using the last of his energy, managed to squeeze the trigger.

"I'm okay. I'm fine," Hank said, sitting up.

Winter kept the Walther pointed at Valentino's head as he crossed to him, put his thumb between the hammer and firing pin, and twisted the gun away. He cursed himself for not checking on the man as soon as he had gotten Hank safely up. In the excitement he had lost a vital thread that could have cost both their lives.

Winter removed Hank's wet coat and, using the bullet hole in the shirt's sleeve for a starting place, he pushed his finger through and ripped the material wide open. The bullet had hit Hank's left arm above his elbow. Winter saw shattered bone inside the exit wound, and the blood flow was steady, so the artery wasn't cut. The bullet was lodged in the side of Hank's vest. Using his belt, Winter made a tourniquet just below Hank's shoulder.

"Scratch," he told Hank. "You can hardly even see it."

"Ruined my best shirt."

"Maybe Millie can turn it into a short sleeve."

"Based on our movie stars here"—Hank winced—"I'd say I got off pretty light. I still got my gun hand and I can walk."

"Hank, you're going to sit here. If anybody comes here looking for them, you shoot the bastards. In the meantime, loosen this every once in a while so you don't explode. I'm sorry, I didn't think..."

"It ain't your fault," Hank offered. "I could have checked him out myself."

Winter got the cell phone, dialed Chet, and told him that Hank was wounded, in the boathouse, and would be fine until they arrived. Chet told him that their helicopter was there to pick them up and he wouldn't be able to use the phone because of the chopper's noisy engines. Winter turned the phone off and handed it to Hank.

"You keep it," Hank said.

Winter put Spiro's coat over Hank's shoulders. "I know it stinks, but it'll keep you warm. Winter reached into the pocket and removed Spiro's red phone. "I'll use this if I need to make a call. You wait here for Chet," Winter told Hank sternly. "He'll be here in twenty minutes."

"You keep your narrow ass out of that lodge, Winter. *You* wait for Chet. That's an order. I am your superior officer."

"You think I'm crazy, Hank?"

"What I *think* is none of your business. I know for a damn fact you're crazy."

100

Winter approached the lodge as stealthily as possible, finding it remarkable that there were no guards posted between the two buildings. The fact that there had been a gunfight and no one heard anything was testimony to the quality of the soundproofing Manelli had installed.

Almost every window inside the building was lit. A green van and three SUVs were parked across from the lodge in a small clearing. In the photo taken from space, which had reduced everything to the shape of its surface, Winter hadn't been able to see that there was a covered porch entirely wrapping the second floor. The lodge was built so the ground floor was half as large as the second. Steel beams supported the end closest to the canal. The only way up to the porch from the ground floor was by means of a staircase located beside the front door. Just before he made it, someone sitting on the steps in shadow lit a cigarette. If the man hadn't been a smoker, Winter would certainly have walked right into him.

Winter crouched and made for the back of the lodge. Looking up as he approached the building, Winter clearly saw the old gangster pass by an upstairs window. He made his way around the far side and came up toward the front, looking for a way inside.

Winter heard conversation and the sounds of dining, so he passed a sliding glass door and peered into the lit kitchen from the cover of night. He counted four guards, all wearing handguns. A pair of shotguns leaned like umbrellas against the wall by the door. He figured perhaps there might be more men upstairs and probably more watching the road.

Winter carried three full ten-round magazines for his .40-caliber SIG Sauer. He had loaded Yul's second magazine into the man's Browning Hi-Power giving him fifteen 9-mm rounds, which in addition to the partially used magazine gave him another eleven. He had eight rounds in the old Walther PP, giving him a grand total of sixty-five bullets, each one a potential death sentence. Winter doubted that Sam would have more men than he had bullets for.

He had not considered taking up any of the long guns, because he knew before he left the boat shed that he was going inside the lodge and any shooting would be at close range. If Sean was alive, she was going to stay that way—not be killed by Sam in response to Chet's assault team arriving or by an errant shot from a long gun. Inside the building, a rifle bullet could go through a man and still travel through walls to hit something. Indoors, a shotgun blast could spread .30-caliber lead balls until something solid stopped them. That something solid was not going to be Sean. And, the fact was, he was a far better shot with a handgun.

Without backup, he couldn't walk straight in through the front door with a gun in each hand—there was no way he could control so many men at once and be free to do anything but guard them. He closed his eyes, took a deep breath, and allowed himself a mental picture of finding Sean alive and well, of taking Sam Manelli hostage and using the threat of killing the old bastard to hold off his guards until Chet's assault force arrived.

Winter went back to the door leading into the darkened room next to the kitchen and slid it open silently. He had the SIG in his right hand already, so after he closed the door, he pulled Yul's Hi-Power from inside his belt. Illumination coming into the bunk room from a slightly open hallway door allowed Winter to make out the line of bunk beds and the shape of a man lying asleep in one of them.

After crossing the room, Winter stood at the hallway

door, listening. A split second before he moved out into the hall, he heard the hard-soled shoes of someone entering the hall from the kitchen.

He moved quickly aside, flattening himself against the wall beside the door.

The man pushed open the bedroom door a few inches and called in, "Angelo, get your ass up!" before he returned to the kitchen. Angelo got up and ambled into the bathroom, closing the door behind him.

Winter slipped out from the bunk room, crossed the hall, and started carefully up the staircase that led up to a central hallway. At the top of the stairs he peered to his left around the corner. The opposing walls rose to the vaulted ceiling that peaked twenty feet above. There were two doors on each side of the hall. Beyond the hallway's throat, edged with vertical rough-hewn cypress beams to support an arch of the same material, was a great room. What Winter could see of the living room included the back of a couch and overstuffed leather armchairs arranged before a massive fieldstone fireplace centered in a wall of window glass. Winter decided to find a door that would allow him to get out onto the porch so he could see into the great room. The acoustics were such that Sam's loud voice filled the hallway as if he was using a public address system.

"Where's Spiro? I thought you went to get him," Sam growled.

"He's with two of the new guys watching the back gate. He'll be back soon."

"I think the boy should have paid more attention to his school and less to that weight-lifting rigmarole."

Winter was almost at the closest door to the stairwell when Manelli crossed the room and stopped, framed in the archway. In person, Sam Manelli was a living illustration of dynamite coming in small packages.

All the aging gangster had to do was turn and he would

be staring at a stranger thirty feet away holding a pair of pistols. Winter didn't want to do anything until he had located Sean, but if Manelli turned, he would take the man hostage. If there were more people in the great room sitting silently, or if Sam was to yell out for the downstairs guards, it could get bad. If Sam yelled, Winter would run into the room and perhaps shoot everybody there. Sam walked away without turning. Relieved that he didn't have to shoot Manelli yet, Winter put the Hi-Power in the small of his back and slipped through the nearest door.

He entered a dimly lit bedroom, stopping beside a partly opened closet door. Ahead, he saw a bed with the covers disturbed. What must have been a bathroom door was closed, but light leaked out from under it and he could hear water running in the sink.

He heard footsteps moving down the hallway and someone tapping at the door before opening it. Winter slipped into the closet, eased the sliding door almost closed so he could peer out through the crack and ready himself. As the door closed, Winter saw Sam Manelli's profile, less than two feet away.

101

Shadows among shadows, the quartet of cutouts moved west through the narrow line of trees along the drainage canal. They cut a hole in the eastern ILS fence and slipped through. Their starlight goggles painted the world a Saint Elmo's fire green. They wore sensitive, sound-activated headsets and could talk to each other in an emergency.

Nearing the gate separating the tank farm from the lodge property, they slowed and crept to the edge of the road, where it exited the tank farm and entered Manelli's property. A clot of four guards, who couldn't have been more visible to the cutouts if they had been on fire, stood just inside the gate. As one of the men waved his hand in the darkness, his lit cigarette looked like an acrobatic firefly.

Lewis took up his position not fifteen feet away from the four guards.

Tomeo, Mickey, and Apache kept going toward the lodge.

Normally they would have taken out the four guards and moved on, but Lewis was not going to put a single team member at unnecessary risk. He wanted a lightning strike whereby all of the exterior guards were neutralized at once. He didn't want any of the guards to have an opportunity to resist—or for a shout or a gunshot to alert anyone inside the lodge. The body armoring all but removed that risk for Tomeo and Apache, but his and Mickey's lighter suits offered superior maneuverability with full protection of only their torsos. Even if the inserts were missed, the latest version of Kevlar would take multiple rounds in the same spot without failure.

According to Russo, there could be as many as fourteen guards there, all of them aware that they were not to fire at anyone without Russo's orders. Russo thought the cutouts were going to erase only Sam and Sean.

Despite what Lewis had told Russo, Fifteen's orders had been clear. "Erase everybody there and leave no witnesses." As Lewis had put it to his people, "If they didn't come here with us, they're staying after us."

Figuring his team was in position up the road, Lewis raised his MP5 SD and fired at the men standing like cows in the curve of a nameless dirt road.

102

Sam Manelli stood at the foot of the bed staring at the bathroom door. If the aging gangster had ever smiled, there was no evidence in the famous mask, which seemed to have been carved from a lifetime of suspicion and displeasure. The water stopped running.

The old man sat on the edge of the bed, his knees facing the closet. The bathroom door opened and Sean Devlin climbed up onto the bed and sat cross-legged, facing Manelli. Stunned, Winter watched Sam lean over and kiss her gently on the cheek.

Winter stepped out of the closet, aiming the SIG at Sam Manelli, his finger on the trigger, already knowing that the first bullet would strike his square head in the center.

Manelli reacted by standing up to face Winter.

When Sean saw Winter, she slid quickly off the mattress and stood between Winter and Sam for a split second before Sam shoved her behind him.

"Go ahead an' do me," Sam growled. "Just leave her alone!"

"Winter, no!" Sean cried out. "Don't."

"What the hell is this, Sean?" Winter demanded. He couldn't accept what he was seeing before him.

"It's okay, Winter. Sam, he's the deputy that saved my life on that island."

"Okay? This old reptile's been trying to kill you," Winter told Sean. "He sent the people who killed Martinez and Greg! His people just tried to kill Hank and me." Winter's hand was trembling from anger, shock. "I'm not dead, you old bastard, your three in the boathouse are."

Manelli's blue eyes were suddenly curious. "When was you in *my* boathouse?"

"Russo told your clowns to drown us." Winter kept the SIG aimed at Sam's head, wanting to squeeze the trigger.

"I don't believe that," Sam growled. "Why would he do a thing like that and not tell me? When?"

"Fifteen minutes ago. A creep named Spiro and two guys grabbed us. Russo came to the boathouse and said for them to drown us in your crab cage. One of them shot my partner."

"Is Hank all right?" Sean asked, genuinely concerned.

"Will be soon as the assault team gets here." Winter took the handcuffs from his jacket pocket and tossed them onto the bed. "Put those on him, Sean."

"That's not necessary," Sean said.

"You're a crazy man," Sam barked. "How does Johnny know you? What reason would he have to kill you?"

"Shut up, Manelli. Cuff him, Sean, or I swear to God, I'll drop this psychopath right here."

"Winter, he didn't know they tried to kill me on Rook or in Richmond. It was a mistake."

"Who the hell else would want you dead? He got Hoffman to send those men after Dylan, didn't he?"

"You can't prove that," Sam protested.

"He didn't send them after *me*."

"So it's all right because they only killed everybody else?"

"I didn't mean it that way. Of course it isn't okay."

"For Christ's sake, Sean! Why the hell would you believe *him*?"

"Winter, Sam's my father." Winter saw a framed picture on the bedside table. In it a smiling child of ten or eleven held a shotgun in one hand and a dead duck in the other.

Winter let that sink in as he studied her eyes. His confusion melted away, leaving him feeling every scrape and bruise on his body ... and completely out of patience.

"Then cuff Daddy or I *will* kill him," he said with a certainty that he knew left no room for doubt.

103

Winter found Johnny Russo standing in front of the wet bar with his back to the archway, holding his cell phone up to his ear. The L-shaped bar, on Winter's left was eight feet long, four deep, and its closed end faced the archway wall. The front was made of stacked cypress beams, identical to those used in the archway, and topped with a two-inch-thick slab of granite.

To Winter's right was a wide gun cabinet filled with shotguns. In front of him, living room furniture faced the stone fireplace, which was centered in a wall of glass.

"Spiro, you bonehead prick. Turn on your damned phone," Russo muttered.

"He can't get a signal in hell," Winter said.

Russo spun around to the sight of Winter, standing in the archway aiming two guns at him.

Winter was primed with anger. Russo was responsible for what had happened to Hank and him in the boat shed. He wouldn't hesitate to make this strutting silver-haired prick doornail dead.

"Just a minute!" Russo put his phone on the bar, keeping his hand there.

"Step away from the bar," Winter commanded. He already knew that Russo wasn't armed. Sam had told Winter that Johnny's .357 was behind the bar, where he'd set it down when he came in earlier that afternoon.

Slowly Russo smiled. "You're no deputy marshal. Why

didn't you just say you was with Lewis? Sam and Sean are in that first bedroom, and you can clip 'em easy—Sam's not packing."

Who is Lewis? What others? Winter couldn't imagine who he was talking about. He didn't get a chance to ask.

"You're dead!" Sam's voice boomed from the hallway behind Winter.

Johnny Russo's face seemed to sag as Sam Manelli passed Winter and stepped into the room. The fact that his wrists were handcuffed in front of him didn't seem to make Russo feel any safer.

Sean stood at Winter's right side.

"Stop right there, Manelli!" Winter ordered.

"You ain't getting away with this," Manelli growled at Russo. "You been trying to get Sean clipped! You just told this bird to kill us. I don't know how you got Herman to double-cross me and try to kill my kid, but I am gonna find out. You better talk quick or I'm gonna kill you."

"It was Herman's idea. He set it all up for the three million." Russo's face was pale and sweat glistened on his forehead.

"And you knew about it? Why was he going to kill Sean?"

"Sam . . . you . . . you were gonna leave her everything legit and I wouldn't have any way to hide my street money. It was just business." Russo stepped back, hands outstretched in supplication. "We're talking millions of dollars. You'd have done the same thing."

"She's *my* kid! I decide what to do with what's mine. You supposed to make your own legitimate businesses—"

"I don't need any more of your money," Sean told Sam.

"You gonna get it, though," Sam snapped at Sean. "And that's that."

"Johnny, I gave you and Rose the cab company as a wedding present, for Christ's sakes, and it's a solid business. My legits was always supposed be Sean's. I never gave you reason to think my niece was gonna get any more of what's mine. I gave you the whole *other* side of the business."

"If Herman's men had done it right, there wouldn't be any question about that." Russo was regaining his composure, knowing that Winter wouldn't let Sam touch him. "You're finished Sam. It's all mine now."

"I'm gon' kill you, Johnny. By God . . ."

"Why don't you call your men, Sam? You'll see they won't come unless *I* call them."

Sam moved forward. "I'll show you who's done—"

"Not one more step, Sam!" Winter warned. "Who is Lewis?" Winter demanded.

Winter was alerted to activity downstairs by sounds rising up from the stairwell behind him—something shattered, and there were sounds like kitchen furniture being moved. Thinking the downstairs guards were on their way up, he aimed the Hi-Power back at the stairwell behind him while keeping the SIG on Russo and Manelli. "I don't give a damn who they answer to. If those men come up, I'll kill them," Winter reminded Sam. He didn't trust Sam any more than he did Russo. He didn't believe, as Sean did, that Sam was interested only in protecting her. He had allowed Sean to overhear Sam confronting Russo, but that was the only concession he was willing to make—and that was because *he* wanted her to hear the truth.

"Who is Lewis?" Winter repeated.

"You can ask him yourself."

Winter turned just as a pair of armor-clad figures stepped out from the stairwell. He fired the Hi-Power at them before they could bring their machine guns to bear, and he shouldered Sean toward the wall where the gun cabinet stood. He took cover behind the left vertical beam.

Even without their yelling out "police," Winter knew their weapons and the full-body armor marked them as the enemy. Had he hesitated a fraction of a second before firing on the figures, the cutouts would certainly have killed him and Sean.

While Winter fired down the hall, Sam scrambled after Sean.

Russo took cover behind the bar. "Come get these sons of bitches!" he shouted gleefully. As he got his magnum from behind the bar, Winter knew the wet bar was as bulletproof as the beam he was depending on to keep him alive, which meant he was going to be fighting a war on two fronts. Unless Chet's men arrived soon, it would be a short skirmish.

The cutouts recovered and fired up the hallway into the great room. The sounds of the bullets striking objects was louder than the MP5 muzzle blasts. The fusillade filled the air. The thick glass windows beside the fireplace exploded and sheets of heavy glass crashed to the floor.

Sam kicked the glass out of the gun cabinet and pulled out a long-barreled, side-by-side ten-gauge L.C. Smith goose gun. Sean, understanding that her father couldn't use the shotgun with his hands cuffed, took it from him as he opened the drawer for shells.

Winter set down Yul's handgun long enough to reach into his pocket and toss his handcuff keys to Sean. He knew that a shotgun in Sam's hands would at least keep Russo from shooting him in the back.

Winter picked up Hi-Power again, leaning out just far enough to keep his exposed flesh to a minimum, and fired both weapons, the bullets hitting the figures like sledgehammer blows knocking them back against the wall, but the killers defiantly remained on their feet. The butts of Winter's bullets, embedded in their Kevlar armor, looked like copper buttons. Between the ceramic plates inside the thick seamless armor and helmets with Lexan face shields, the pair would be almost impossible to kill with just handguns. Before they again opened fire with the

MP5s, Winter was safely back behind the beam. The Hi-Power was dry and Winter reloaded using the magazine with the eleven bullets left in it after he had tagged Spiro. That done, he ejected the SIG's empty magazine and slammed in a new one. *A dragon is vulnerable to an arrow fired under her scales.*

Sean pressed the breech lever aside and broke open the shotgun.

Russo came up from behind the bar and aimed the revolver at Sean, who was waiting for Sam to hand her shells.

Seeing Russo with the magnum, Sam lunged in front of his daughter, took the bullet, and, as he fell to his knees, a half dozen shells poured from the box in his hand and scattered on the floor. He slumped heavily between Sean and Russo's gun.

Winter turned at the sound of the magnum, but Russo was already back down.

Shell casings rained in the hall as the MP5s chewed up the front of the beam Winter was using for cover. When the pair stopped to reload, Winter placed both guns' barrels on the vertical flat of the beam so only his forehead was exposed to the cutouts' guns. Holding the SIG in his left hand, six inches higher up the beam than the Browning in his right, Winter fired rhythmically.

The pair was advancing slowly. The smaller figure had a long dark tail of hair dangling below the back of the assault helmet. *A woman?* He hit her helmet with a Hi-Power round, knocking her off balance, then put a round from the SIG in her pelvis, seating her on the floor. His next two rounds pierced the upturned soles of the woman's boots. She screamed out as the bullets hit their marks. Winter was back behind the beam before rounds from the man's freshly reloaded machine gun chewed mercilessly at it.

Russo fired again, that bullet slamming into the beam

inches from Winter's face. Before Winter could turn and get a shot off, Russo had ducked again. He yelled, "I got Sam in the gut!"

Blood seeped out from under Sam. His skin had turned cigarette-ash gray.

Kneeling beside him, Sean took up two of the ten-gauge shells, pressed them into the chambers, snapped the breech closed, and aimed it at the bar.

Seated on the floor, Sam picked up the handcuff key and opened the lock on his left wrist, letting the open cuff dangle from his right.

"You can't shoot for shit, Johnny," Sam called hoarsely.

Woman or not, the seated figure in the hallway was just a target. Five seconds after he had shot through her boots while her partner was trying to help her up, Winter fell to the floor. When he leaned out, aiming down the hallway, he was four feet lower than the man had anticipated. Winter shot at the woman's helmet, just above the visor. The impact levered her head back so his second shot drilled in under her exposed chin. She flew straight back, dead. When Winter turned his attention to her partner, he took immediate cover in the stairwell. *Less confident in that armor now?*

Winter ejected the empty magazine and sat up fast, reaching into his jacket to get the last full SIG magazine from his holder. He heard, behind him, the crunching and snapping of someone putting weight on broken window glass and the *phit-phit-phit*, of a silenced three-shot-burst. Like blows from a baseball bat, two of the rounds hit him in his armored lower back and one his thigh. A full magazine in one hand and the SIG in the other, Winter looked back in time to see a third figure outside on the porch, aiming into the room at him through the window.

A blast from Sean's shotgun made vapor of the left half of the man's neck and the gun's enormous recoil rocked her back. The cutout was dead on his feet, but with his gun's barrel rising as he fell back, the bullets harmlessly peppered the cypress ceiling.

Winter fought to catch his breath. He felt the warm blood, the dull ache, and knew that the third bullet had done serious damage to his thigh. He didn't have time to check on it.

"You're hit!" Sean cried out.

When the assailant in the stairwell fired again, Johnny pointed his gun over the bar and fired blind at Sam and Sean. He missed. Sam reached for the shotgun, but Sean wouldn't give it to him.

Winter popped the cutout as soon as he stepped back into the hallway and reached for his dead partner, perhaps to recover her unused magazines. Winter hit him in the side of his knee and in his left glove as he leaned over. Judging by the way he twisted out of sight, Winter knew he'd made an impression on the man.

Winter pantomimed the motion of tipping up a bottle to Sean, pointed to the bar, and opened his hand to imitate an explosion. Sean fired at the liquor bottles behind the bar, raining liquor and glass down on Johnny. "Stand up, Johnny!" she called out. "I got a bone to pick with you."

"Woo-wee," Sam said, coughing. "I believe she 'bout to shoot you good."

The cutout in the hallway fired three-shot bursts to keep Winter pinned, and when he paused, Winter leaned out and emptied the SIG's last magazine. He was out of time, but he was going to try and sneak a round from his Walther PP under this cutout's visor when he came. The air was thick with cordite as Winter lay there with the gun aimed up, waiting. But the cutout didn't pass through the arch and appear above him. Winter heard the cutout's boots on the stairs, going down them fast, making no effort to be quiet.

Winter looked at Sean, aimed at the bar, and called out, "Sean, slide me your shotgun!"

Winter slid the empty Hi-Power across the floor.

Primed, now thinking the sound was the shotgun on its way across the floor to Winter, Russo stood anticipating a shot at an unarmed and wounded deputy. When Russo went down, it was because Winter's bullet had struck his shoulder. Winter could have killed him, but he only shattered his shoulder so he couldn't shoot at them. Winter wanted to ask him some questions.

Sean fired after Russo was down, breaking more of the bottles. When the alcohol hit the wound, Russo cried out in pain.

"Hooray, you, Dep'ty. You a bright one, boy, you!" Sam howled. "You a damn idiot, Johnny!" He laughed, then began coughing.

Russo screamed. "You fucking shot me! You're all gonna die!"

"I think your friend, Lewis, went home, Russo," Winter said.

"Bullshit!" Russo croaked. "He wouldn't do that."

Sean called out, "Hey, Johnny?"

"What?"

"Crybaby."

It was remarkably quiet for a long second—air coming in from the broken windows caused the hanging cordite cloud to swirl and ebb.

Winter knew why the man had run when he heard a familiar thumping sound and the Blackhawk's brilliant halogen spotlight lit up the windows.

"Looks like the war's over," Winter called to Russo. "Why don't you resist when they come in? They'd like nothing better than to blow your head off."

"I give up." Russo tossed his revolver over the bar. It smacked the floor and slid under the couch. He stood up slowly with his right hand holding a bar towel against his shoulder wound.

Sean laid the shotgun down and hurried over to check on Winter's leg. Winter held the Walther on Russo, who stood inside the bar looking down at Sean, a sour expression on his face. "Think I'm done? This is no biggie. I'll turn state's evidence and walk away from this. The feds want Sam, not me. I can put him away for keeps and they'll give me anything I want to do it. Sam gave me the money I passed to Herman Hoff—"

The sound of the ten-gauge's blast caught Winter off guard.

Russo still stood there. His eyes were still fixed on Winter and Sean but were now bulging, froglike, from their sockets. His jaw and his tongue were gone, and the cypress wall beside him looked like someone had hurled a bowl of spaghetti against it.

Winter swung the Walther's barrel toward Sam, who dropped the shotgun down by his side. He had reached down, lifted up the weapon and fired at his criminal protégé's mouth.

"Tell 'em about me now, you rat bastard!" Sam yelled.

Russo tried to talk, but all he could manage was a series of gurgling noises.

Sean grimaced and turned away.

Despite the coughing fit it brought on, Sam laughed.

104

Through the downpour, Lewis and Tomeo fled east in defeat, moving through the woods as fast as they could without sounding like hunting dogs charging through the undergrowth, hot-trailing a deer. They stopped long enough to allow a six-man assault team, which was running in from the gate, to pass within ten feet of their position. The helicopter that had dropped off the team was circling the lodge.

No more than three minutes had passed from the time Lewis' three cutouts had entered the lodge until Lewis had ordered the withdrawal of his sole remaining team member.

"That guy with the handguns," Tomeo said. "I've never seen anything like that shitter. I've got bruises all over my body." He held up his padded left hand. "He broke my fucking knuckles. He knocked Apache down and put one in under her chin. All the time I was firing—every time I drew a bead, he knocked the cold shit out of me. He was like a machine. I never had a clean shot at him."

"Massey," Lewis said. "Let's get out of here while they're still busy."

"I think Mickey hit him. Sean yelled out he was hit, right after she took Mickey out."

Lewis said. "Sam must have shot Mickey. She doesn't have the balls. If Massey was hit, they'll take him to a hospital," Lewis said. "Or the morgue, if we're lucky. If he's dead, we can go home."

105

The sound of boots thundering up the stairs brought Winter a surge of relief. *"Police!"* Chet Long yelled out from the stairwell. "Police officers—Massey?"

"It's all clear, Chet!" Winter called out.

"We need a doctor," Sean said as the men in black stormed into the room, weapons raised. U.S. MARSHALS was stenciled on their chests and across their backs, and they carried riot guns and AR-15s.

Chet knelt beside Winter and asked, "How bad?"

"Through and through," Winter replied, wincing as a sharp pain from the leg wound hit him. "One of them got away before the helicopter arrived. Five-foot-ten, fully armored like his partner there."

"As soon as we can get a dog in here we'll search the woods and try and round him up. The Highway Patrol has River Road closed tight, so he ain't driving out."

"Please," Sean pleaded, indicating Sam Manelli, whom she was kneeling beside. "He's badly hurt."

"Radio EMS we have four for immediate transport," Chet ordered. "Tell the coroner he might want to bring a big truck because there's bodies scattered all over the place."

Sean slipped a bullet-ruptured throw pillow under Sam's head.

Winter told Chet, "You get Hank from the boat shed?"

"He's probably on his way to the hospital by now," Chet said as he pressed a towel against Winter's thigh to stop the bleeding. "Clue me in, Winter. At first blush it looks like the guy out on the deck and gal in the hall killed Sam's men with those H and Ks, then came up after . . . who— Sam and Russo?"

"Far as I know."

"Who the hell do you think sent them?"

Sirens announced the arrival of patrol cars. Blue strobe lights reflected in the outside windows.

"I'm not sure," Winter lied easily. There was no way he was going to repay Chet for saving his and Sean's lives by involving him in the other side of this mess. Winter figured that the woman cutout he'd killed might be the hitter from Richmond that missed Sean there. "Do me a favor and bag her SOCOM for ballistics."

Chet glanced at Sean, who was holding Sam's hand. "Weren't we supposed to be rescuing her from him?"

An EMS crew arrived, and as Sam was being lifted onto the cot, he looked down at Winter and winked.

A pair of EMT techs rolled a gurney containing Russo from the room.

Winter nodded.

"Who shot the man out on the porch?" Chet asked.

"I did," Sam said. "I went down kicking ass. If you don't remember anything else, you remember that." He grimaced in pain. "Somebody, get this gal away from me." He released Sean's hand and closed his eyes.

"Let's move him to the wagon," the EMS tech said.

Sean's eyes filled with tears as she stood and watched her father being rushed down the hall. She knelt beside Winter and took his hand.

"Are you all right?" Winter asked her.

She shook her head slowly. "I'm not sure what all right is."

"Let's get you out of here," an EMS who had been wrapping Winter's leg said. Two men lifted him onto a stretcher and carried him out. Sean followed. As the crew took Winter from the house toward an ambulance, they passed by another. Inside, one technician was writing something down while another gave Sam Manelli CPR. Despite the chest-pumping charade, it was obvious there was no longer any reason to rush the gangster anywhere.

Chet stuck his head into the ambulance Winter and Sean had just entered. "Hey, Winter, the other guy's making a run for it. He fired on the helicopter. I doubt his armor is going to be very effective against the M-60."

"He in a black Suburban?"

"How'd you know that?"

"Lucky guess."

"Hold up," Chet told the ambulance crew. He had his phone to his ear, listening. "He's on River Road heading west," Chet told Winter. "The units east of here are joining the pursuit. Okay, he's heading for the roadblock. Wait . . . he left River Road and he's heading up the levee."

"He gets in the river, you'll lose him, Chet," Winter said. "Tell them to stop him."

"Okay, Bird One," Chet said into the microphone. "You are authorized to use lethal force to stop that Suburban."

Seconds later, the cloudbase in the western sky suddenly took on a muted orange tint. "That's all, folks," Chet said.

106

Looking out over the tank farm, Lewis watched the fireball climb. Lewis knew how cops thought, how they acted. Figuring that all of the highway patrol prowlers available had chased after Tomeo, he pulled out from among the piles of garbage. Lewis had figured the authorities would have no idea of the exact size of the force they were opposing. In the pandemonium, while the cops were focused on Tomeo in the fleeing Suburban and the bloody meat they had left in and around the lodge, Lewis could have led a herd of elephants out onto River Road. It was possible that Tomeo had bailed out of the vehicle before it exploded. It didn't matter to Lewis because it wouldn't change anything. Tomeo was on his own.

Lewis kept the windows rolled up even though his nose was assaulted by the lingering stench of cigarettes, dog, and the old man's fetid body odor. He drove to River Road and aimed the Ford truck toward New Orleans before turning on the headlights. He hoped that the mattress and other trash didn't tumble out of the truck's bed and draw unwanted attention.

107

Sean had held Winter's hand from the time they got into the ambulance until they had wheeled him into the emergency room at Charity Hospital.

At the hospital Winter heard from one of Chet's deputies that the cutout had been ambushed by the chopper at the top of the levee. His armor hadn't been any help, especially considering that the Suburban's overlarge gasoline tanks had gone up, incinerating him after he had been riddled by most of the 7.62-mm rounds the M60 fired directly into his windshield from rock-throwing range.

The nurse gave Winter a shot of something that felt icy cold. He was unable to concentrate on anything at all—the crisp pain in his leg evolved into a dull pressure as the overlapping voices faded to whispers and trailed away. Winter was aware of the gentle lapping of water against the raft he found himself floating on—lying out in the warm sunshine, someplace far, far away. . . .

Winter was alone in a corridor that seemed to stretch for miles in either direction. The door he had come through had vanished, Winter watched as a small speck grew into a person. As the figure drew closer, he could see that that it was a young man, seventeen or eighteen, wearing fatigues and a green beret.

Before he could clearly see the soldier's features, Winter knew the young man was familiar to him. Even the uniform didn't mask the cocky stride, the set of his friend's shoulders. Greg Nations was not merely younger than he had been when Winter first met him at Glynco—he was altogether different. Only the eyes were the same. The jaw was rounder, the nose wider, the cheeks fuller, and even the ears angled at nearly ninety degrees from his skull.

"Greg?" Winter said. "I thought you were dead. They told me you were dead."

Greg skirted him and kept going.

"Greg!" Winter yelled. "Greg, wait! Where you going?" His heart was breaking. Grief and a sense of overwhelming loss filled him. "Don't go! Talk to me! Please!"

Winter caught up to him in a few strides. He grabbed Greg's shoulder and turned him so they were face-to-face.

The soldier was no longer Greg Nations. The soldier was now Lieutenant Commander Fletcher Reed, but where his eyes should have been, there was smooth skin, eyes crudely drawn on with a dark marker pen.

Winter woke with a start in a real hospital bed. Sean was curled up in a chair beside him, watching him.

"Bad dream," he said.

"Do you feel like listening?" she asked him.

"Of course," he said truthfully. He wanted to hear everything she had to tell him.

108

"I would have told you about Sam," Sean began, "but from the time I was old enough to understand, my mother drummed into me that I should never tell anybody he was my father. It was my first and best-kept secret."

Sean studied Winter's face for a reaction, but he just nodded and smiled weakly. "I can understand why you might keep a thing like that to yourself."

"It was because my mother was afraid that Sam's

enemies might kidnap me to hurt him. He had a lot of enemies always looking for an edge. My mother met Sam while she was at Newcomb studying painting. She was in a club one night and he saw her. He pursued her and she thought he was exciting. One thing led to another and she got pregnant. She told me that Sam was her first experience and she didn't take the necessary precautions."

"Good thing she didn't," Winter said.

"Sam wanted her to marry him, but she knew it was impossible. She was a free spirit and knew he would have smothered her, plus there was the danger angle. She ran away and lived with her aunt in Boston and had me. Sam showed up at their doorstep and my mother said that he picked me up and cried from joy.

"My mother refused to return to New Orleans, but she agreed to let him support us and to form a trust for me, which he gladly did. It's grown over the years and it allowed me to have a nice life, paid for my education, and supports me still. Because Sam loved me, my mother agreed to let him be involved in my life.

"Sam spent Christmas and my birthdays in Boston with us, and I used to spend summers here in New Orleans with my mother. Sam's men all thought she was his mistress. That way we could stay in his house or at the lodge, and except for having to use different last names and lie about where we lived, it was fine. Bertran Stern, his lawyer, knew who we were, and we communicated through him."

"I remember that on the porch that night, you told Angela and me your father taught you how to shoot guns."

"That picture of me with the duck was taken one winter when my mother and I came down and he took me hunting the first time. I didn't like killing birds, but I did it for him. He made sure I was skilled in defending myself in every possible way."

"I got a taste of that on the beach."

Sean laughed. "You sure did. He made sure I learned karate, defensive-driving techniques, and a lot of other survival skills normal girls don't need to know."

"If he was so protective, how could you have believed he was trying to kill you?"

"I never knew him that well, and it's sad that I didn't. My mother, a beautiful and vibrant woman, never dated another man. A few years ago she confessed to me that it was because she didn't want Sam to think for a moment that she would betray him in any way. She told me that the one unpardonable sin in Sam's eyes was betrayal. She said that he would kill anyone who betrayed him, and I knew she was totally serious. I knew from a hundred sources that Sam had killed friends and members of his own family who had crossed him. I didn't think about it until after those men came to Rook and you said Dylan was working for Sam. Then I assumed he thought I had betrayed him with Dylan. But I never told Dylan that Sam was my father. I planned to eventually, but the time never felt right."

"Russo knew you were Sam's daughter."

Sean nodded. "When I met Johnny, he was working at Sam's vending company and he was nice to me. At some point, Sam told Johnny that I was his daughter. I had Johnny's private number because in the last few years Sam used Johnny to communicate with my mother and me. Sam trusted Johnny, but he never should have trusted anybody from his own world."

"You didn't ever mention Sam to Dylan?"

"The only way Dylan could have known about my connection to Sam was if someone who knew told him."

"He worked for Sam. Maybe Sam told him."

"Sam told me Dylan didn't work for him. He said he'd never met him and that he couldn't believe Dylan was bringing him down with lies. Sam assumed I had told Dylan about him and that Dylan lied about killing those people for Sam so he could get a deal with the government.

"If Dylan was killing Sam's enemies for someone, it could have been Johnny, because they would have had the same enemies. Sam was effectively out of the crime business, had no reason to kill anybody, but Johnny did. Maybe Johnny set it up so Dylan knew enough about me to get close to me."

"I'm sure it was something like that," Winter said.

"I knew what Sam was. One night when I was ten, I looked out a window at Sam's house and saw him knock a man to the ground and kick him until he was unconscious, while two of Sam's men watched. Sam was smiling like a lunatic the whole time he was beating that poor man."

"That's terrible. I don't blame you for keeping your relationship secret."

"I just want what I've always wanted—to live a normal life without ever again having to lie about anything to anyone."

"You deserve that," Winter told her.

109 | McLean, Virginia

Ten o'clock in the morning found Fifteen in the basement of his house sitting on his sleek Italian leather couch, his feet on a matching ottoman. The cigarette smoke swarming around him caught the flickering light cast by his television set, which was showing a nine-ball championship between two female opponents. He knew that the Asian champion, his favorite, would win, because he had watched the tape at least a dozen times. Now, like never before, knowing the outcome of the contest was comforting.

His frown deepened as his eyes moved from the champion-to-be leaning over the pool table to make a shot on the three ball to the coffee table where an ashtray, piled high with butts and ash, kept company with a vase filled with an explosion of silk flowers. The table was also littered with newspapers detailing the explosion in Manhattan and the intelligence reports on the New Orleans fiasco.

Herman Hoffman had passed on to all of his people the belief that they were untouchable, because the organization had been designed to be both too valuable an asset to the government and too dangerous to screw with. Now that invulnerability was ancient history—a blood-splattered myth.

Since he had met with his liaison at the CIA two hours earlier, Fifteen had been sitting alone in his basement weighing his options, smoldering over the mistake he had made. He cringed at the memory of the smug, sawed-off CIA lackey who had passed on the CIA director's threats, knowing that Fifteen didn't dare do more than sit silently and take the man's insults, one by one, nodding all the while like a shell-shocked imbecile. A month ago no one would have dared confront him, much less dictate to him.

Blame it on ego. Herman's and his.

Herman had set the failure in motion, but Fifteen had blown it all with the deputy in New York by playing games instead of just taking care of the business. All he'd had to do was leave Massey there paralyzed and set the explosives for ten or twenty minutes, instead of toying with him. He had put the deputy into a sealed building with no way out, knowing that he would eventually open that refrigerator if only to scrounge some food. Fifteen had someone stay in the neighborhood until after the bomb went off, to ensure it did. The detonator was set for twenty seconds, not even enough time for Massey to piss his pants. How could he have escaped and ended up in the basement? It wasn't possible, but obviously it had been too possible. It was so damned unnecessary. He had known better, but he had given in to his own stupid arrogance.

Fifteen still couldn't believe that of the eight heavily armed cutouts who had tried to kill Massey on two occasions, he had killed six of them. In total, of the hundreds of rounds they had fired at him, the best killers on earth had managed to put a grand total of one bullet into the deputy's leg. And Fred Archer was dead—all that grooming wasted.

He had honestly believed that it couldn't get any worse, that he had fixed everything Herman had screwed up— had total control of the situation at every turn. Massey's death in that building would have sealed the blame, divided it between Greg Nations and Massey. Manelli's and Russo's deaths and the retrieval of the GPS from that computer would have insured that everything was settled, that the cutouts were out of peril. But that was not to be. Every time he thought he had everything back on track, there was Massey tossing another crowbar into the gears and him running to put it right.

Using information Massey and Fletcher Reed had collected, the director of the USMS, Richard Shapiro, had effectively derailed their dark ops train. Shapiro had the CIA by the nuts, and the agency had reacted by threatening to cancel Fifteen's organization's operating license, cut his ties to intelligence, and even throw Fifteen to a congressional oversight committee. The last threat was a bluff. There was no way the CIA could afford to have the cutout cells made public. But there could be a private reckoning—a bullet in the ear, a knife in the jugular, a heart attack, or perhaps a *sans*-parachute halo jump into the Atlantic.

Shapiro had somehow gotten his hands on the Global Fifty GPS from Sean Devlin's computer, and unbelievably, knew what it was, how it was used, and that the CIA owned the technology. He said he could prove that Archer's evidence against Greg Nations was fraudulent. Massey had told Shapiro everything he'd learned about Herman Hoffman and Fifteen, and about the existence of the cutout cells.

Fletcher Reed's computer printouts were a map to the members of the cells. And there was the matter of the fingerprint cards from Rook, which matched those of four long-dead soldiers whom Reed identified. Fifteen was still sure he could have gotten all of Shapiro's evidence back if the CIA would have let him—an action they had expressly forbidden.

Fifteen looked back up to the tournament on television. The Asian player had a beautiful, lithe body and coldly calculating eyes.

Shapiro had offered a compromise the CIA had accepted. In return for holding back his evidence, Shapiro had wanted very little. He asked for WITSEC to be cleared, Gregory Nations to be exonerated, and the cutouts to refrain from any further hostilities against Winter Massey and Sean Devlin. He suggested that the FBI might arrest a Russian Mafia leader—they had one named Dobrensky they decided was perfect—who would be linked to the dead cutouts, men who would still be identified as Russian mercenaries. Dobrensky would be tried for conspiring with Manelli to furnish the talent to kill the protected witness. Attorney General Katlin would get a nice show trial and everything would be tied up with a big red bow for the American public. To explain how the mercenaries found Rook Island and the WITSEC airplane, it had been decided that Avery Whitehead, a bachelor nobody was particularly attached to, was to play the money-corrupted villain who had sold the intelligence on the WITSEC locations to Manelli.

Fifteen knew that the compromise would work to

everyone's satisfaction. The organization would stay in business, with Fifteen overseeing the cells, although the CIA would have tighter controls on the organization—the inevitable consequence of Rook Island and Ward Field. Fifteen suspected that Herman had done everything he had done, knowing that it would alter, if not destroy, the organization he had fathered, the thing he had owned and couldn't stand to see survive him.

The catch in this all—the thing that had Fifteen worried—was the realization that if Lewis completed his assignment, the deal was off and Shapiro's revelations would create apocalyptic repercussions. The fact was that Fifteen couldn't contact Lewis, his last cutout in the field. Before the CIA had informed him of the developments, Fifteen had already ordered Lewis to complete his assignment at any and all costs.

He remembered something his father had once told him: "You learn from your mistakes only if you survive them." Herman hadn't, but maybe *he* still would.

His only hope was to dispatch a team to New Orleans and pray they would find Lewis and stop him before his success made them both dead men. He lifted the telephone receiver and dialed.

110

When Winter got out of bed, his leg throbbed against the bandage, his back hurt, his head felt like his sinuses were filled with BBs, and every joint and muscle in his body ached. Sean helped him, standing firm while he leaned on her and eased into the wheelchair. He hated having to sit in the thing because the idea of having someone push him through the hospital like an exhibit was abhorrent to him. Winter was buttoning his shirt when an orderly wheeled Hank Trammel into the room. A cast held Hank's left arm out even with his shoulder, bent at the elbow.

"I wanted to say good-bye."

"We're about ready to check out," Sean said.

"Wish you'd join us at the hotel," Winter said. "I think we earned a couple days off on an expense account."

"Place would look like a convalescent ward, and truth be told, I'd like to sleep in my own bed, since last night I was damned sure I'd never see it again. Sean, can I get a couple of minutes with Winter to discuss some marshal business?"

"Sure, Hank." Sean waited for the orderly to leave and then closed the door on her way out.

"Got a message from Shapiro." Hank handed Winter an envelope, which he'd opened.

Hank,

Greg Nations and WITSEC are fully exonerated. Winter Massey and Sean Devlin cleared.

The item you sent was a (CIA only) GPS device that transmitted its location over satellite to a designated receiver. It went active when the laptop computer was turned on. With those coordinates, satellites could capture photo images, like the ones Winter saw in New York. The way it was set up, it could also send text messages typed into the computer's word processing program.

Special deputies will keep you, Winter, and Sean under guard until "certain" people are called off for good. Terms are for all concerned parties to develop full memory loss on this entire episode, which, all things considered, should be agreeable.

So it is all over. Destroy this.

"What's the computer deal?" Winter asked.

"The thing Eddie found in Sean's laptop when we got that bullet out. I told you yesterday."

"You didn't."

"I thought I did. Can you tear this note up for me?"

"Sure." Winter ripped the note into small bits and Hank took them in his good hand, walked into the bathroom, and flushed them down the toilet.

"Some dang deal, when it takes both of us to destroy one damn piece of paper. If we had a book to get rid of, it could take us a week."

"So that GPS thing explains how they tracked Sean and how the cutouts located us and compiled all their satellite intelligence. It explains how those women hitters found her in Richmond."

"It doesn't explain who planted it," Hank said. "Who could have smuggled the gizmo into the safe house and put it into that computer? You think those killers were after her computer and not her at all?"

"The cutouts were after Dylan for Sam, but they were after Sean for Russo. It was Russo who wanted her dead and got Hoffman to do it for him. Maybe those killers on Rook intended to take the computer out too, before they were interrupted."

"Chet said Sean was fussing over Manelli at the lodge like they were old friends and Sam had to tell them to get her away from him. He says there was a picture of a kid that looked a lot like her in Sam's bedroom. She get around to telling you what the deal was with her and those guys?"

"Sam was her father."

"No way!"

"The whole time Sam was trying to get to Sean to protect her, Russo was trying to get her killed. If she and Sam had talked things through, Russo would have been cooked, because Sam didn't know Sean was ever a target.

When you and I arrived, Russo was waiting for the cutouts to show up and wipe out Sean and Sam. He was going to kill us in the boathouse because, without our word to buck the setup, Sam would have gotten the blame for us and Sean. I'm sure Archer's bunch was set to get the credit for taking out Manelli. I think the cutouts would have clued Archer as to where Sam was after they were finished. I wonder if Archer knew Sean wasn't in that car. Maybe he'd have just sat there at that service station off the interstate until he got a call from his contact telling him to go out to the lodge. As far as Fifteen knew, nobody would have been around to contradict whatever Archer and his men said about what happened out there."

"I knew Sean was hiding something, but *that* would never have occurred to me. Why exactly did Russo want her dead?"

"Sean was Sam's heir. Johnny is married to Sam's next-closest living relative. Hank, I'd like to keep Sean's secret between the two of us. She doesn't deserve any more pain due to an accident of birth. Protecting her was why Sam told those guys at the lodge to get her away from him. She doesn't need the notoriety of being Manelli's daughter. Might be other people who would benefit—from her death."

"Guess that explains the passport and five grand she had," Hank said thoughtfully. "Who on Rook Island could have sent Herman's guys a message? Obviously Sean didn't know that thingie was in her computer, because she handed it over knowing I was going to open it up to get the bullet out. You were there—who else used it? It's obvious, even to me, that one of the deputies had to have done it."

Winter's mind moved to put together a picture, to concentrate on the computer. "She typed poems into it. Just a minute! Dylan typed her a threatening letter Thursday." Winter tried to visualize the text. "He said something like he was leaving and she was staying behind. And he had my name in the note, which would explain how the cutout on that boat knew my name. Christ, it told them when the crew was taking Devlin out. But he sure wouldn't commit suicide by tipping Herman's killers off."

"You see him type that note?"

"No."

"Gregory only *told you* Dylan typed it?"

"I didn't actually see Devlin with the computer, but I know Dylan typed it."

"How?"

Winter had a clear image of the message on the screen. He could picture Greg's hands holding the computer so he could read Dylan's note. "Greg told me he did," Winter said.

"Greg only *told* you Dylan Devlin typed it. Jesus, Winter."

"Greg didn't hide that GPS in the computer," Winter said with absolute conviction.

"How do you know that's the case though?"

"Greg was so electronically challenged he couldn't change a lightbulb without help, so I doubt he'd be able to hook anything up inside a computer even if he could have opened it up. And most important, he wouldn't have sold out a witness or put his people in danger any more than you would. The last reason is the only one that matters. It was in there before Sean came to Rook."

111

At Shapiro's request, the Justice Department made the penthouse suite at the Delacroix Hotel available for Winter, Sean, and a team of WITSEC specialists for security. Originally designed for a drug importer with reason to be paranoid, the top floor, number eleven, was a secure space. The regular elevators stopped on the tenth floor, and access on up to eleven required a key. The fire door on eleven could be opened only with a six-digit code, and both landings were covered by surveillance cameras.

Deputy marshals brought Winter's overnight bag upstairs from the room he and Hank had shared for an hour the day before. Sean's suitcases had arrived from USMS headquarters overnight. The two main bedrooms, each containing five hundred square feet of space and covered balconies, had bathrooms done entirely in exotic stone with gold-plated fixtures. While it wasn't to Winter's taste, it was comfortable enough.

Sean had spent the afternoon with Winter in his bedroom, both fully clothed and on top of the California king bed, propped up against a wall of pillows. They talked and watched the news and ordered from room service. Winter's leg pain was a constant dull ache, but he refused to take anything stronger than aspirin.

Sean had never met a man like Winter. She had thought often since Rook about the first time she had seen him, climbing aboard that helicopter, and how her feelings had evolved from that day.

She stood on the balcony, aware that Winter was watching her from the bed. She liked having his eyes on her. He had saved her life twice, each time placing himself in mortal danger. And it was more than the fact that she felt safe when she was with him. She knew now that she'd never felt this way about anyone before.

Sam's death dominated the local media. There were mob experts and reporters from all over the country who told the stories of Sam's "alleged" brutality. There were interviews with people who had remained silent about the gangster and now, true or false, they were ready to talk. "I was ten years old," one older man said. "Me and my pals were playing on the Magazine Street wharf and we saw

Sam Manelli and another guy shoot this third guy and throw him into the river. As they were driving past us, the car stops and Sam hands us each a five-dollar bill. I went home and told my old man what I saw, and my daddy said, 'You didn't see nothing.' I never told this in forty years."

There was footage showing him at various ages, all of it taken outside, in public. The interviews with him consisted of a shouted question from a journalist and, in answer, the same dismissive wave. The media had openly called him a gangster and he had made it easy because he had never once opened his mouth to deny or confirm it.

"Hey, Sean, come here," Winter called from the bed. "You'll want to see this."

Charles Hunt, the stoic director of the FBI, stood at a podium. He opened a piece of paper, looked down, and said, "Ladies and gentlemen, I would like to read a short statement.

"Last evening, as part of a complex international criminal conspiracy, specialized teams of agents from the FBI and the United States Marshals Service set out to serve arrest warrants on Sam Manelli in New Orleans and Vladimir Dobrensky of New York. Dobrensky was taken into custody without incident and will be arraigned this afternoon in federal court. The serving of Sam Manelli was unfortunately not without incident. One FBI supervising agent was killed, and two US deputy marshals were wounded. In addition to three Russian mercenaries, twelve of Mr. Manelli's bodyguards were killed along with Mr. Manelli. John Michael Russo, Manelli's crime captain, was seriously wounded and taken into custody. He died an hour ago after slipping into a coma early this morning, but after furnishing evidence of the link between Manelli and Vladimir Dobrensky. While we regret the loss of life during the operation, our agents were merely reacting to being fired upon."

Without shifting his stance or moving anything except his hand, Charles Hunt turned the page over.

"There will be a joint press conference tomorrow morning at noon to fully explain the connections between the arrest last night and the loss of life on Rook Island, North Carolina, and Ward Field, Virginia. Due to last-minute developments in the investigation, I will not be taking any questions at this time. At the news conference tomorrow the attorney general will give a full explanation and your questions will be answered."

The reporters all raised their hands regardless, and when Hunt didn't respond immediately, started yelling out questions. The FBI director folded the piece of paper. He answered the shouted questions in the way Sam Manelli always had—with a single dismissive wave as he stepped down from the stage and strode away.

"I guess they need more time to work up an official story," Winter said.

"They've got their work *cut out* for them," Sean retorted. She took the remote and turned off the set.

After dinner, while Sean showered in her bathroom, Winter lay in bed, unable to stop thinking about Greg. It was over, but even so, something was gnawing at him. If not Greg, who could have planted the GPS? How could he be so wrong about a man he was so close to? He had to figure out an alternative, or admit to himself the unthinkable.

When Sean returned to his bedroom wearing a robe, she didn't knock; which seemed perfectly natural to Winter. Her hair was still wet, brushed back. She closed the door, pulled the drapes, and came to his bed without saying a word. As Winter watched, she dropped the robe to the floor and stood beside the bed, naked. He didn't think the angry bruise on her shoulder, a gift from the ten-gauge goose gun's recoil, detracted from her perfection in the least. She came to him and their first kiss went on and on and swept Winter away. That kiss made everything they had been through seem like some vague memory. After making love, they lay together, side by side for long minutes, caressing each other, kissing.

"Winter, what are you thinking about?" she asked.

"You."

"Besides me," she laughed.

"The thing I still don't understand," Winter said, "is how that GPS device got into your computer."

"I don't know."

"Try to remember. When was the laptop out of your sight?"

"Well," she said, thinking as she rubbed his stomach, "Dylan gave it to me a few days before I went to Argentina as a first anniversary gift. It was pretty much always with me in South America. The marshals in New York turned it on to check it out after we were in the first safe house. Greg brought it and my suitcases to me after he searched everything. Greg took it back to Dylan so he could type me a nasty message."

"I read it."

"From there, I had it with me until Hank took it."

Winter's dream, where Greg turned into Fletcher Reed, suddenly played in his mind. A change from one into the other. Why? Metamorphosis is a change of identity.

"Sean," he said, leaning up on an elbow. "Can you look in my bag and see if the material Reed sent me is in there?"

She went to the dresser, opened the bag, and brought Winter the envelope. Winter emptied it and flipped rapidly through the pages, finally stopping on one and pushing the others away.

"What is it?" Sean asked.

He took two of the sheets and used them to cover the lower faces of one of the young soldiers Reed had identified as a cutout possibility. He stared at the young soldier with the American flag in the background. He was eighteen, ears sticking straight out from the shaved scalp, the features soft. Suddenly, he knew what the dream he'd had about Greg meant—what his subconscious was trying to tell him. Everything made sense.

"What is it?" Sean asked again.

"Nothing." Winter stacked the sheets and fed them back into the envelope, dropping it onto the floor beside the bed.

"You sure? It didn't seem like nothing."

"Just a thought I had that didn't pan out."

"I'm sorry."

"It doesn't matter. Everything's fine. The criminals are all dead and everybody is satisfied." Winter looked into Sean's eyes and smiled reassuringly. "Only one thing to do now," he said, pulling her to him for a long kiss.

"Aren't you afraid you'll injure that hip?"

"No pain, no gain."

Winter hated to lie to Sean, but telling her what he knew would serve no purpose. If he was right, he would tell her later, when all of this was far behind them.

113

Winter lay in bed with his eyes closed. As the hours had slowly passed, and sunrise approached, he'd allowed his mind to wander. There was such a subtle change in the room's atmosphere that he almost missed it. A slight breeze came in from the direction of the sliding glass doors onto the balcony.

He had left his SIG in the shoulder rig hanging on the chair near the bed. He didn't have to look to know his gun was no longer there. Now he was fully alert, aware even of the breathing pattern of the intruder. Winter felt his heartbeat quickening. The cutout stood silently at the foot of Winter's bed dressed in black, like a dark ghost—the grim reaper in a nylon mask.

Winter felt the muzzle of his own gun's barrel pressed against his big toe.

"I didn't know how long it would take you to show up."

"You knew I was coming? You're full of shit, Massey."

"I knew the helicopter didn't kill you. The last guy inside the lodge ran out just before the helicopter landed. If I couldn't hear a Blackhawk with the windows blown out, he sure couldn't have heard it from where he was in the hallway. I figure you radioed him that the helicopter was coming and he was the guy the helicopter took out."

"His name was Tomeo."

"And yours was David Lewis Harper, then Dylan Devlin. What's it now?"

"Now it's just Lewis," the killer said, surprised. "Russo told you."

"No, he didn't. In a way, Greg Nations did. I knew you'd have to come for me."

"This isn't personal."

"It's as personal as it gets. You killed my friends. You're what you've been your whole life; a soulless, pathetic, arrogant prick."

The hammer made a dry click as Lewis cocked the SIG that he was aiming at Winter's head. "You just know too much."

"I'm no threat to Fifteen, because everybody already knows about him and Herman Hoffman. They know about the CIA's GPS inside Sean's computer. They even know you're still alive. You're doing this because you know I'm your superior and you just can't allow me to live."

"You're right about one thing. You are dead, Massey."

"You're dead wrong. You've made a fatal mistake. Killing me with my own gun was a totally predictable move."

Winter couldn't see the expression on the assailant's face, but he knew there would be no fear in his cold green eyes. If the man he'd known as Dylan Devlin had possessed normal human feelings and emotions, Herman Hoffman would never have selected him to seduce a woman and frame Sam Manelli so his, and Russo's, plan would work.

"Checkmate, loser," Winter said.

The cutout reacted the way Winter had known he would. Unable to accept he'd been outmaneuvered by a deputy marshal, he failed to raise his own gun, which he held in his left hand pointing at the floor. Dylan Devlin squeezed the SIG's trigger.

There was an earsplitting report. The sheet at Winter's right side was burned black by the blast, shattered open where the bullet had passed from the World War II vintage Walther PP in Winter's right hand.

The SIG's hammer had snapped on an empty chamber. Dylan Devlin, a man who had been declared dead, was indeed dead when he hit the floor. Winter's SIG Sauer was still locked in the cutout's right hand; the silenced SO-COM .45 rested on the floor beside him.

Two of the deputies that Shapiro had sent stormed into the bedroom, guns at the ready. The light came on, blinding Winter for a second. He set the Walther down on the bedside table.

"All clear!" one of them shouted.

The deputy in charge came in holding a shotgun, and Sean came around him a second later, jumping up onto the bed and putting her hands on Winter's chest. Her eyes were wide with fear and concern. She looked at the masked shape on the floor and back at Winter. "Are you all right?"

"I'm fine."

"Who is that?" she asked.

"It *was* Russo's pal, Lewis."

"I thought the helicopter got him on the levee? You said it was over," she said. "It wasn't, was it?"

"It's over now. He was the last one."

"You knew he was coming," she said accusingly. She lowered her voice. "That's why you sent me to my own room last night."

"I thought he might and I figured you'd been through enough already. Go back to your room while they deal with this. I'll be there in five."

She nodded. "Okay, if you're sure." She kissed his cheek and left the room.

The deputy in charge knelt beside the body, checking the neck for a pulse. "He's all done." He lifted up the nylon mask and inspected the bullet hole that was centered in the cutout's throat. The round had punched through, exiting at the base of his skull, exploding the medulla and severing the spinal cord.

Winter hadn't really paid any attention to the deputies on the detail, because they didn't come into his room and he hadn't been outside it. When he looked at them he spotted an unpleasantly familiar face. Winter had last seen the man, now wearing a USMS khaki assault suit, when he had been standing in the hallway in Herman's building holding a silenced SIG Sauer—the same man who had beckoned Fifteen from the communications room—the same man who had first appeared as an FBI agent on Winter's porch. Winter glanced at the gun in the cutout's hand, which he was putting into his side holster.

"We'll clean this up," the cutout said. His eyes remained locked on Winter's. There was no malice in them, but there was also no warmth there, either. "You need help, Deputy?"

"I can manage," Winter said as he slid over to the side of the bed where the crutches waited.

"I believe you can," the cutout said, smiling wryly. "Good luck."

114

"It's *really* all over?" Sean asked Winter once he was in her bedroom.

"Word of honor, ma'am."

"Where do *we* go from here?" she asked, studying him with serious eyes.

"Far as I'm concerned, that totally depends on you."

"Yesterday you told me that nobody would ever have to order you to keep me safe again."

"I stand by that offer."

"Are you sure? I mean after all this, do you really want to be reminded of the time since we met, the losses you've suffered, the pain this has brought you?"

"I don't understand."

"Won't I be a reminder of the terrible things you..."

"Do I remind you of the terrible times we've been through?"

"Oh, no. Of course not. I want to know if you're sure, that's all."

"I've never been as sure of anything in my whole life, Sean. I was hoping we could get to know each other better, under calmer circumstances."

"Quality time. Calm circumstances. That sounds wonderful."

"I've got some people back in North Carolina I want

you to meet. I think you'll like them and I know they'll like you. Why don't we just take it as it comes?"

"I'd like that, Winter. I'd like that a lot."

Sean was suddenly overcome, so Winter pulled her to him and held her tightly as she wept.

Now she was finally free to shed tears for Angela Martinez, for Wire Dog and Max, and for all of the others she had cared about but couldn't grieve for before. And she cried because a man she loved—a man who loved her—was comforting her.

Now she was truly safe.

They stretched out on the bed. Sean put her head on Winter's shoulder, her arm across his stomach and hugged him.

Winter put his hand on her shoulder and massaged it gently.

For a very long time, they stayed just like that.

about the author

Inside Out is John Ramsey Miller's second novel.

His career has included stints as a visual artist, commercial photographer, advertising copy writer, and photojournalist. A native son of Mississippi, he has lived in Nashville, New Orleans, and Miami, and now resides in North Carolina, where he writes fiction full-time.

Visit him on the web at www.johnramseymiller.com

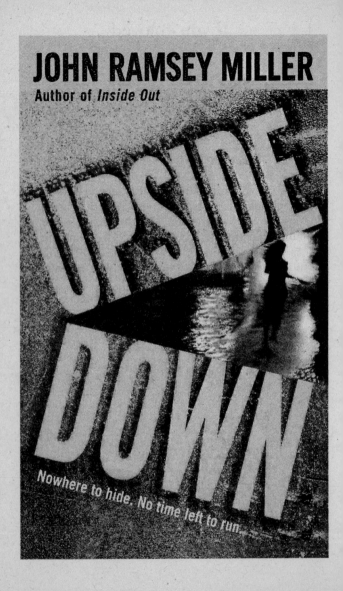

JOHN RAMSEY MILLER
Author of *Inside Out*

UPSIDE
DOWN

Nowhere to hide. No time left to run...

If you enjoyed
John Ramsey Miller's
INSIDE OUT, you won't want
to miss his electrifying thriller
debut, **THE LAST FAMILY**.
Look for it at your favorite
bookseller's.

And read on for an exciting excerpt
from the second white-hot thriller
featuring U.S. Marshal
Winter Massey:

UPSIDE DOWN

by

John Ramsey Miller

on sale in July 2005 from
Dell Books

UPSIDE DOWN

On sale July 2005

Baton Rouge, Louisiana
Friday / 4:01 A.M.

From ground level, the automobile graveyard looked boundless. The moon was like an open eye that, when it peered through holes in the clouds, was reflected in thousands of bits of chrome and glass. After the four figures passed under a buzzing quartz-halogen lamp set on a pole, long shadows ran out from them, reaching across the oil-stained earth like the fingers of a glove.

The quartet entered a valley where rusting wrecks, stagger-stacked like bricks, formed walls twenty feet tall. One of the three men carried a lantern that squeaked as it swung back and forth.

The woman's tight leather pants showed the precise curve of her buttocks, the rock-hard thighs, and the sharply cut calf muscles. A dark woolen V-neck under her windbreaker kept the chill at a comfortable distance. The visor on her leather ball cap put her face in deeper shadow.

They stopped. When the man fired up his lantern, hard-edged white light illuminated the four as mercilessly as a flashbulb.

Marta Ruiz's hair fell down the center of her back like a horse's tail. In an evening gown she could become an exotic, breathtaking creature that made otherwise staid men stammer like idiots. "How far now?" she asked. Her accent had a slight Latin ring to it.

"Not too far," Cecil Mahoney said, looking down at the much shorter woman. An extremely large and powerfully built man, Mahoney looked like a crazed Viking. His thick bloodred facial hair so completely covered his mouth that his words might have been supplied by a ventriloquist. He wore a black leather vest over a black Harley-Davidson T-shirt, filthy jeans with pregnant knees, and engineer boots. His thick arms carried so many tattoos that it looked like he was wearing a brilliantly colored long-sleeved shirt. Silver rings adorned his fingers, the nails of which were dead ringers for walnut hulls.

The other two men were dull-eyed muscle without conscience or independent thought. Cecil Mahoney was the biggest crystal methamphetamine wholesaler in the South and the leader of the Rolling Thunder Motorcycle Club. Stone-cold killers pissed their pants when a thought of Cecil Mahoney invaded their minds. Few people could muster the kind of rage required to use their bare hands like claws and literally rip people into pieces like Cecil could.

The three men didn't see Marta as a physical threat. How could such a small woman harm them—kick them in the shins, bite and scratch? They had seen that she was unarmed when she stepped out of the car and put on a nylon jacket so lightweight that any one of them could have wadded up the garment, stuffed it into his mouth, and swallowed it like a tissue.

They turned a corner, moved deeper into the yard.

"Over there," Cecil said.

They stopped at the sharply angled rear of a Cadillac Seville with its front end smashed into a mushroom of rusted steel. Marta's sensitive nose picked up the sickly sweet odor, folded somewhere in the oily stench of petroleum and mildewed fabric, of something else in decay. One of the henchmen lifted the trunk lid while the other held up the lantern so Marta could see inside.

"Careful you don't puke all over yourself, little girl," Cecil warned.

Marta leaned in, took the corpse's head in her bare hands, and twisted the face up into the light. The way the skin moved under her fingers told her a great deal. There were two bands of duct tape surrounding the head; one covering the mouth and nose and another over the eyes and both ears. It made the features impossible to read, which was now irrelevant. Other than hair color, this corpse was not even close to the woman she had come to identify and to kill.

"Where's the reward?" Cecil grunted.

"The money is in my car's trunk, but whether or not it belongs to you is a question I can't yet answer," Marta told him.

"That's her, and I'm getting that reward."

"Perhaps, perhaps not."

"Okay, gal, you've seen her enough."

The low position of the lantern made Cecil look even more menacing—his small water-blue eyes glittering. He used a lot of what he sold. From the start he had made it abundantly clear to Marta that dealing with a woman was beneath him. His first words to her had been that he didn't know why anybody would send a "split tail" to do important business. He had referred to her as a "juicy little thang." If she played this wrong, she would be raped and murdered in some unspeakable manner. She knew the piece of trunk cheese was no more Amber Lee than Cecil Mahoney was the Son of God. The needle marks on the dead woman's arm alone were enough to tell her this girl was some overdosed waif. It followed that the envelope Amber had in her possession would not be there. Marta hoped Arturo was having luck tracking the woman in New Orleans.

"You failed to mention that she was dead. Why is that?"

Cecil's patience was thinning. "Bitch choked on her own vomit. Look, honeypot, a hundred thousand clams was the deal. So stop with the questions. Let's go get my money."

"It wasn't a dead-or-alive offer, Mr. Mahoney. There were questions that we needed to ask her, and can't now. My boss expects accuracy in the information he receives from me. You said that she was alive. When did she die?"

"It's damn unfortunate. Boomer found her dead yesterday evening choked on puke. Ain't that right, Boomer?"

The man holding the lantern nodded. "I found her dead yesterday. Choked on her puke."

"I wonder how she gained so much weight in so few days."

"Well, she's just bloating up 'cause it's hot in a car trunk."

"Hot in there," Boomer agreed.

The temperature had not risen above fifty-five degrees in the past two days. "Take *it* out," Marta told the men.

"What the hell for?"

"It will be abundantly clear to you, Mr. Mahoney, when they take *it* out."

"Get old Amber out, then," Cecil ordered. Boomer put the lantern on the ground and both he and the third man reached in, wrestled the body from the trunk, and dropped it to the oil-crusted black dirt like a bag of trash. In the lantern light the men looked like depraved giants. As Marta squatted beside the corpse, she pinched her cap's brim as if pulling it down and withdrew from it a wide matte-black double-edged ceramic blade that fit inside the bill. She palmed it, holding the blade flat against her forearm. She knew what was going to happen in the coming few seconds just as surely as if they had all been rehearsing it for days. "You are right, Cecil, it doesn't smell so good. Like it's been dead longer than one day."

"Bodies," Cecil said. "Who can account for spoil rates?"

She shrugged. "You have a knife?" She held out her right hand, palm up.

"Knife for what?" he asked.

"A knife, yes or no?"

She didn't know how much longer Cecil would allow this charade to run. Still entertained, he reached into his vest pocket and placed a stag-handled folding knife in her hand. She opened it using her teeth and tested the edge for sharpness with the side of her thumb. Much better than she would have hoped. *A man and his tools.*

"You could shave your little pussy with it," Cecil muttered.

Nervous snickers—six fiery, obscene pig eyes.

She reached out suddenly and sliced through the duct tape, laying the corpse's cheek open from the jaw to the teeth twice to form parentheses that crossed at the top and bottom. She jabbed the blade into the flesh and lifted out the plug in the same way one might remove a piece of pumpkin to make a jack-o'-lantern's eye. The dark purple tissue was crawling with what looked like animated kernels of rice.

"Aw, man!" Boomer exclaimed.

"You're trying to pull one over on me," she chastised.

"Hell, honey," Cecil said, "I never was too good with times and days and all. I'm better with arithmetic like adding up you and this corpse and getting a hundred thousand in cash money." Cecil and the other two men had her boxed in, the open trunk at her back. That was fine, she wasn't going anywhere.

Marta remained on her haunches, tightened her leg muscles, and bounced up and down gently so maybe they believed that she was nervous. She would have preferred to be barefoot, because she had gone without shoes for most of her life and felt more secure that way. The sharp clutter in the junkyard made that impractical. "You think you are getting a dime for this fraud, you're even a bigger moron than people say you are."

"How about I dump you and the maggoty little whore in the trunk and take the cash?"

"What will you tell my boss's men when they come to find me?"

Cecil slipped a revolver from behind his back and held it by his side, barrel down. He cocked the hammer, probably imagining the sound intimidated her. "That you never showed up. Must a run off with his cash. Or I'll say, 'Just kiss my ass.' Boys, I think it's gonna be plan two."

"What is plan two?" she asked. She was aware that the man on her left had pulled a pistol from his coat pocket. The man called Boomer had something in his right hand.

She didn't care what it was, because unless they all had grenades with the pins already pulled, they might as well be holding tulips. She turned Cecil's Puma knife in her hand so the blade was aimed up.

"Plan two is the old 'snuff-the-Beaner-cunt' plan."

"You aren't man enough to snuff this Beaner, Cecilia Baloney." Her next words were hard as Arkansas stone, certain as taxes. "And as a woman I resent the C-word coming from the rotten-tooth stink-hole mouth of a stupid, syphilitic, dog-fucking redneck puke." Keeping her left fist in shadow, she twisted the flat blade she had taken from her cap into position.

The other two men sniggered at her insult, which infuriated Cecil. "Watch it happen . . . you stinking wetback blow job." As he raised the gun up, she launched her light body into the air, slicing the Puma up through Cecil's right bicep like an oar's edge through still water. Before his handgun hit the ground, Cecil had spun and fled for the front gate, howling and holding his useless arm.

Marta spun a full revolution, a whirling dervish with her arms extended so that one blade was much higher than the other. After the spin, she squatted between the confused men. Balanced on her haunches, she looked like a jockey on the home stretch—her elbows out like wings, her hands in front of her face level with her chin like she was pulling back hard on reins. Instead of leather leads, the wetly lacquered blades radiated out from her fists. Knowing the men were no longer a threat, she focused straight ahead, her eyes following Cecil as he ran through the valley of wrecks.

The nameless third man pulled his hands up to his neck, perhaps to see what the sudden blast of cold against his throat meant. His scream gargled out from a new mouth below his jawline. He stamped his boots a couple of times like he was marching in place to music and collapsed. His feet quivered as though he was being electrocuted.

Boomer dropped to his knees and stared at the bloody pile growing on the ground below him. When he turned his eyes to her in disbelief, she smiled at him.

She said, "That was the Beaner cunt's plan number one." She stood and, laughing melodiously, loped out into the dark after Cecil.

By the eerie lantern light, the kneeling man worked to gather up the steaming mess that had slid out of him and put it all back.

New Orleans, Louisiana

Faith Ann Porter yawned and looked over at the venetian blinds for any sign that the sun was rising. Her watch's display read 6:13.

The small reception area always smelled like a place where somebody really old lived. The space was strictly a prop, because there was no receptionist. Usually Faith Ann's mother could hardly afford to pay the office rent, much less hire someone to sit there at the desk to greet the few people who ever came there. Not a single one of her clients had ever been to visit her, and the fact was that the vast majority of her mother's calls were outgoing. Even so, it was absolutely necessary to maintain a professional office.

The upper part of the front door to the five-room suite,

which was at the end of the hallway, had a frosted glass panel in it where each tenant's name had been hand-painted backward on the inside since 1927, the year the building had been constructed. At that moment, Faith Ann was lying prone, peering through the brass mail slot, watching the fifty feet of hallway between herself and the elevator lobby. Not that she believed the mysterious woman was going to show up this time either. Most likely she'd been awakened and dragged all the way down here before dawn for nothing.

"Watching won't make her get here one second sooner. If she sees your eyes looking out at her from down there, she'll think we have rats. You shouldn't snoop," Kimberly Porter said from the door.

"You just told Mrs. Washington that you liked my in-quisitive nature. You said my curiosity shows intelli-gence."

"You were listening in on the extension while I was talking to your teacher!"

Time to change the subject. "I bet you got me up early for nothing. I'll be sleep-deprived when I get to school . . . for nothing. I'll bet you a dollar she won't even show up. I'll bet you another dollar if she does she's just some lu-natic trying to get money for some old letters she proba-bly scribbled up herself, knowing you'd do anything to save Harry Pond."

"Horace," Kimberly corrected automatically. "If she's right, he's really not guilty."

"You think everybody you represent is innocent."

"I don't think any such thing. There are lots of other lawyers with investigators who try to prove innocence. When that fails, they call me."

"To do legal mumbo jumbo. Hocus-pocus high jinks.

Pick a card, Your Honor." Faith Ann plopped onto her back and clapped her hand to her chest. "No sir, that isn't really an ace of hearts, I say it's a two of clubs, your honor. So, since it isn't the ace at all, like you thought, my client is *not* guilty."

"You little monkey!" Kimberly said. She leaned down and tickled her daughter's ribs.

"Child abuse!" Faith Ann said, laughing, squirming, and trying to push her mother's hands away.

Kimberly straightened. "What I do is not trickery. Horace Pond might be one in a hundred. This is exactly why there shouldn't be a death penalty. It is preferable to—"

"'Free a hundred guilty people than punish one innocent one,'" Faith Ann interrupted. "Like freeing a hundred criminals to go out running around doing crimes is going to happen. You know most people don't agree with whatever old jerk it was said that. Uncle Hank, for one."

"For your information, Miss Know-It-All—that 'whatever old jerk' was Supreme Court Chief Justice Earl Warren of *Brown v. the Board of Education*. And I know Hank Trammel does too agree."

"Then why does Uncle Hank have a sign on his office wall that says LET NO GUILTY MAN ESCAPE? You know who said that?"

"I somehow doubt it was Earl Warren."

"Old Hanging Judge Parker. He hanged men as quick as his marshals could round them up."

"I believe that sort of behavior is precisely why Earl Warren said what he did." Kimberly walked from the reception area.

Just as Faith Ann was about to get up and follow her mother, she heard the elevator door open, so she looked out through the mail slot. Sure enough a woman stepped out. It had to be *her* because her mother's office was the only one on the fourth floor except for an eyeglass repair shop run by a frowning man who just came to work when he felt like it. People didn't bring their eyeglasses, either. The glasses came by UPS and the mail, from optometrists all over the city. Lots of times, boxes and mailing envelopes containing broken glasses sat in the hall outside his door, waiting for him to show up. Faith Ann made it her business to know what was going on around her at all times.

Faith Ann called out over her shoulder urgently, "Mama!"

"I'm coming," her mother called back from her office.

The woman, who was rapidly approaching the office on high heels, reminded Faith Ann of a movie star, probably because of the scarf that seemed to be there to keep the balloon of blond hair from rising right off of her scalp. Her cinched-up trench coat accented a narrow waist and substantial breasts. Faith Ann's eyes locked on the rolled-up manila envelope protruding from her shoulder bag, which the woman was gripping like she expected someone to run up and try to snatch it. She removed her sunglasses and shoved them into the pocket of her coat.

Faith Ann stood and pulled open the door for the woman just before she reached for the knob, which startled her. Faith Ann was instantly assaulted by a wave of sickeningly sweet perfume.

"You look rather young to be a lawyer," the woman said, trying to make a joke. Her brown eyes hardly rested on Faith Ann at all as they darted around the room.

"My mother is the attorney."

"You're what, sixteen, seventeen?"

"Twelve." Faith Ann didn't let on that she knew the woman was being all hokey with her, trying to make friends or something. "You can hang your coat up," Faith Ann offered, pointing to the standing coatrack.

"I'll just keep it on." Faith Ann was disappointed that she wouldn't get to see what kind of outfit was under it. The woman's eyelashes looked like spider legs, and her brows were arched lines that had been carefully drawn on her forehead, maybe with a sharp-pointed laundry marker. Faith Ann just couldn't help but stare at her.

The woman looked relieved when Kimberly appeared in the doorway. "I'm Kimberly Porter, Ms. Lee. I see you've met my daughter, Faith Ann."

"She's just cute as a bug. I'm sorry," Ms. Lee said, "could you lock the door?"

"Nobody ever comes here this early," Faith Ann said.

"Of course I can," Kimberly answered.

Faith Ann turned the deadbolt herself. She was amazed at how calm and professional her mother was acting. Faith Ann knew that what her mother really wanted was to jerk that rolled-up envelope out of Ms. Lee's purse and rip it open to see if it really was "explosive eleventh-hour evidence."

"Call me Amber," the woman said and put her hand on the envelope like she'd caught Faith Ann thinking about it. "I'm sorry I've been so vague about things, but you'll see I have good reason. Do you have the *thing* we discussed?"

She means money, Faith Ann thought.

Kimberly nodded. "Come into my office," she said, leading the woman into the hall and into the first door on the right. Faith Ann started to follow, but her mother's raised brow stopped her. "Faith Ann, you go do your homework in the *kitchen* while I meet with Ms. Lee."

"I already did it all."

"Well, then paint me a picture I can frame."

"I don't have my art stuff here."

"Well, then draw something with a pencil." She raised her brow and through clenched teeth said, "*Please*, Faith Ann."

As soon as Kimberly closed the door, leaving Faith Ann in the hallway, she scooted down the hall and turned into the next doorway, which opened into the conference room. She stopped in her tracks when she saw that her mother was closing the other door in her office, which connected the two rooms. The conference room held a large table with eight wooden office chairs around it that the building's owner had robbed from other vacant offices as an added incentive to get her mother to move into his building. The shelves were loaded with her mother's law books, most of which were full of cases you couldn't be a lawyer without knowing. Stealthily, Faith Ann slithered down on the floor, placing her ear as close to the crack at the bottom of the adjoining door as possible. It was a heavy wooden one and might as well have been a vault door for the sound it allowed through—or so her mother believed. Being an adult, Kimberly had never bothered to lie down and put her ear to the crack to make sure nobody could listen in.

"I'd like to record this," Kimberly's professional voice said, "if you have no objections. It'll help me later, and it will simplify things down the road when I am in front of the Governor."

"If you want to, but I wouldn't trust the Governor," Amber's voice said. "I mean, I've personally seen him in the club. Jerry owns half the cops—all the ones that run things. He could never have pulled off doing what he did to Judge and Mrs. Williams and framing your client without the police being involved. Nobody in this state can be trusted—especially not in law enforcement. After he found out I had this, the police put out a warrant for my arrest, for embezzling of all things. Jerry did that easy as snapping his fingers. If the cops get me, I'll be fish food."

"Don't worry, my uncle is a U.S. marshal. He'll be in town late this afternoon. He is on a first-name basis with the Attorney General of the United States. I doubt your Jerry owns *him*."

"I guess he'd be all right . . ."

"Let's start by having a look at your evidence."

Faith Ann heard the contents being removed from the envelope, followed by the familiar muttering that signaled her mother was giving her undivided attention to something that she believed was very important.

"Who is this Jerry?" Kimberly asked, sounding like she did after a long run.

"You're obviously not from around here. Anybody around here would know who he is."

"Is he a gangster of some sort?"

"Well, yes, but not so's you'd know it by the papers . . ."

"Dear God!" Kimberly blurted out. "Is this *him* in the picture? This is sick."

Faith Ann realized that she was holding her breath and exhaled slowly. This was great! Of all the neat conversations she'd ever spied on, this one was better that all the others put together.

"This *isn't* a hoax," Kimberly stammered, sounding confused. "Forgive me for ever doubting your claims, but in cases like this people often say they have evidence exonerating a death row inmate—especially at the eleventh hour. They almost always turn out to be . . . less than helpful. No, I've seen the crime scene pictures and this is the same room and those are the same people. But they are both alive in all but two of these."

"The negatives are in there. I don't know much about photography, but I don't think you can fake those. So, is it worth a grand so I can get out of town until he's in prison?"

"Why did he make these? Why did he keep them? This is insanity."

"You're right. No person in their right mind would have." Amber continued, "I can't hardly sleep a wink without seeing those pictures in my head."

"And he knows you have these?"

"Yes, he does. It's a long story."

"I've got time."

Faith Ann was so fascinated by everything she heard during the next couple of minutes that she was still lying on the hardwood floor absorbing the information when Kimberly suddenly opened the door. After having to step over her daughter, she pulled the door closed and lifted Faith Ann up off the floor with the hand that wasn't holding the fat envelope full of evidence. "I guess you heard all that, Miss Nosey-Britches?" she said in a low voice.

"I dropped something."

"It's a clear violation of professional etiquette to eavesdrop."

"Why did you tell her that fib— Uncle Hank was coming tonight?" Faith Ann asked accusatorily.

"Because it's true."

"No, it isn't. Today is Friday. They're going to be here tomorrow—Saturday."

"They're coming in tonight. They're staying at a guesthouse and having dinner with some old friend of Hank's. Then they're coming to see us tomorrow."

"Can I see the pictures she brought?" She knew asking was a waste of breath. Her mother had already commented on how horrific they were. Faith Ann had heard tales of mayhem and murder since she was old enough to understand the adult conversations going on around her. Every capital case her mother took on came with lots of boxes, most of them containing crime scene pictures taken by the cops. Faith Ann looked through those whenever she got a chance, despite her mother's best efforts to hide the graphic files. "Pretty please?"

"Absolutely not!" Kimberly went over to the copier and, one after the other, put each of the eight original photographs facedown on the glass, then pressed the button to make copies of the pictures. Faith Ann couldn't see any of the images, which was infuriating. No dead judge and his wife, no rich killer named Jerry doing something truly horrible to anybody. Of course Faith Ann didn't *want* to see anything like that, but as a lawyer in training, she needed to study all of the legal evidence she could.

Kimberly gathered the photocopies from the bin. At the table, she slid the copies into an envelope, added a glassine sleeve containing dark strips of negatives, and sealed it by licking the glue strip and pressing it closed. Faith Ann's heart sank. Kimberly put the curved original photographs back in their envelope. She swung away the corkboard adorned with pictures of her clients to expose a wall safe that some doctor had used once upon a time to store his drugs. Kimberly opened the safe and took out a stack of bills, which she put in her pocket.

"I want your word of honor that you will not to attempt to open that envelope," she scolded. "I want your absolute word of honor."

"I give you my mile-high word of honor," Faith Ann said, knowing that the envelope was sealed, which placed snooping inside it outside her tampering abilities. She made the appropriate X motion with her trigger finger. "I cross my heart and hope to die and stick a needle in my eye. I will never look at those pictures unless you tell me to."

"There are times to be curious and times, like now, to refrain from snooping. Tell you what. I'll fill you in on all of this after Horace Pond is free. Word of honor. And, Faith Ann, I *am* so very proud of your intelligence and..."

The two distinctive voices originating from the office changed Kimberly's expression to a look of terror. The voices weren't coming under the door into Kimberly's office, so they had to be carrying down the hallway, meaning that Kimberly's office door was open like the conference room door.

"Hide!" Kimberly whispered, pushing her down under the table.